THE SANCTUARY SERIES
BOOK 2

An Unholy Fellowship

tom r. mcconnell

Wednesday Ink

Published by Wednesday Inc, LLC Portland, OR, 97266

Cover art by Roslyn MacFarland

ISBN: 978-1-950879-21-2 (paperback)

ISBN: 978-1-950879-19-9 (mobi)

ISBN: 978-1-950879-20-5 (epub)

✾ Created with Vellum

*This book is dedicated to queer people who were abandoned and rejected by their
birth families to find themselves in loving families of choice.*

ACKNOWLEDGMENTS

It goes without saying that my writer's group is the best there is. They have, once again, gone through this manuscript chapter-by-chapter to help me make it what you see here. They are an amazing group of writers. Thanks Jadzia De Forest, Sean Gallagher, Tawnya Baer, Janis Williams, and Jenny Fryer. A shout out to my beta readers as well: Janis and Tawnya (doing double duty), and R. Roderick Rowe. To Roslyn McFarland for her amazing cover artistry. And the Northwest Independent Writer's Association for their generosity and patience in helping me learn all the things an independent writer needs to know these days.

CYMRU

Môn

Rhos
Tegeingl

Arllech-
wedd
Rhufoniog
Arfon Nant Cymeirch
Conway Dyffryn Clwyd Maelor
GWYNEDD Dinmael Maelor
Efionydd Edeyrnion Saesneg
Lleyn
POWYS FADOG
Ardudwy Penllyn Mochnant
Mawddwy Mechain
Meirionydd Ystrad
Cyfeiliog Mar Caereinion chell Cydewain
Arwistli
Geneu POWYS
Glyn WENWYNWYN

Pennardd GWY A
CEREDIGION RHWNG FREN
Mabwnion Maelienydd
Iscoed Gwnionydd Elfael
Buellt Hereford
Teifi
Cantref
Mawr Ewias
Cemais Emlyn Lacy
DYFED
Rhos Arberth Wydigada BRYCHEINIOG
Penfro Velfry Ystrwyf Cydweli Cantref Bychan GWENT
Carnwyllion Gwentlwg
Gower MORGANNWG
Tir
yr Glyn
Iarll Ogwr
Coety

Miles
0   10   20   30   40

ONE

The old woman knew the Angel of Death was nigh.

She had no idea how long they had been walking. A dozen furlongs back, she heard a bell toll Matins. It must be nearly Lauds by now. She would not yield to the lad's pleadings to rest, but kept them moving, trying to generate enough heat to keep them from freezing. After much whining and protest, he would not advance another step. It was then she fashioned the sling and hoisted him onto her back to carry him, pudgy arms encircling her neck, tiny hands clasped under her chin.

Her shoes wrapped with rags for extra warmth, the old woman trudged along the deserted road. Keeping to the side, she skirted cottages and farms and used any trees or copses close to the track to avoid being seen. Bent into a stiff wind, she squinted her eyes against the stinging snow. Stiff with ice, tufts of straggly gray hair stuck out from her hood.

"Hush, little one," she said. "No more tears."

The child whimpered softly in her ear.

"Soon, Ernulf," she said, her voice silky, attempting to soothe the fussing lad. "Ye have three summers and must be brave. Hush, now. We find warm soon."

The sky was a starless gray and devoid of moonlight. A bridge appeared out of the darkness in front of them, the river flowing silently underneath. Ice encroached from both shores leaving a narrow open run and slowing the water's lazy progress to the sea. The only sound was the lonely voice of the wind as it whistled over the ground, around the low-slung stone walls bordering the fields, and through the trees lining the road. It carried the smell of wood smoke from hearth fires kept going long into the night against the cold.

A tightness in the old woman's chest increased with every step.

The smell of smoke grew as she neared the lane that would pass though the center of the next village. Guessing the church was still at least a furlong ahead, she stopped briefly to catch her breath, gently shifting her precious cargo to a more secure position. The pain subsided a little. She tried to take a deep breath. Her lungs were too weak and would not fill. Slowly, she stepped forward again, a prayer on her lips.

She passed shadowy shapes of villein huts, peeking out of the drifted snow flanking the lane. They must be close. The village forge loomed to the side, the ever-present odor of burning charcoal from its furnace fire, banked until morning, wafting over the night air. The usual clang of the smith's hammer and the whoosh of the bellows were still, the windows dark, and large doors, closed for the night, covered the gaping maw in the front.

Soon, the monks would rouse themselves from sleep for prayer, and she expected to hear the bell toll any moment. It was essential to get the boy there before they began without being seen. She tried to quicken her pace. Agonizing pain, beginning in her chest, shot through her shoulder and down her left arm. The severity of it caused her to stumble. She stopped, clutched her breast and grit her teeth. She let out a groan that sounded like the wind. Head swirling, she tried again to take a deep breath, but could only manage a wheeze.

Peering through the driving snow, she saw the ghostly shape of a wall ahead. She trudged forward, scanning for a gate that she hoped would lead to the small church.

"Almost there," she whispered.

"Where?" the boy asked.

"A safe place," she reassured. "A holy place."

Shuffling through the powdery snow, her feet felt as though they were encased in lead. Still, she put one foot in front of the other, praying each step brought them closer to safety. The pain came again. She stopped and stood, rooted in place, stooping from her burden, hands resting on bent knees. Try as she would, she could not stifle the groan she felt coming.

"Myfanwy?" The boy's voice was full of fear as he gripped tighter around her neck.

"It be fine, child," she said, her breath raspy. She plodded ahead another few yards. She spied a gate through the white haze and warily looked around. The likelihood of anyone being out at this hour in this cold was slim but, still, she was cautious.

About to grasp the latch to the gate, the pain came again, so intense it crippled her. "You hold too tight," she said, loosing the child's grip around her neck. Her knees buckled, and she flung herself against the wall to keep from falling. Sinking to her knees, she reached out her hand for the cord attached to the small brass bell that hung next to the gate. Her freezing fingers clutched at it, but the rope slipped through them as she continued downward. The bell gave off one barely audible clang, and fell silent.

The child on her back pitched to one side and nearly fell off. Resting on her hands and knees, she fought to gain control of her breathing.

"Ddim eto. Mwy o amser," she said, her hoarse voice entreating the old gods for more time.

The peal of the church bell broke through the silence and the fog tolling the hour, a ghostly sound seeming to emanate from nowhere.

Head spinning, her whole body trembled. She coughed, moisture spraying her lips. She ran her tongue across them and tasted the blood. There may not be much time and she must hurry. Summoning what meager strength she could, the crone threw back her cloak and fought to untie the sling across her shoulder with one hand, the other planted firmly on the ground for balance. Her fingers would not work. Abandoning the knot, she tried to maneuver the sling over her head to ease the boy to the ground. Eventually, he tumbled out of the sling and struggled to stand.

"The latch," she said in a voice that was barely a whisper. "Ernulf, pull the latch."

Only the child's eyes showed from a break in the cloth wrappings. He stood and stared at her, clearly confused and frightened. She waved her hand toward the gate, but the boy did not move.

Though it took some time and effort, she climbed to her feet, and after waiting for her head to clear, she stepped up to the gate, drew the latch and pushed it open. Putting her two hands gently on the boy's shoulders, she guided him through the gate and into the courtyard of the church. Then, without a word she turned, and grabbed the bell cord and pulled it several times. The high peal pierced the air, its urgency quickly swallowed up by the night. She rang it again.

She was about to close the gate when she heard his voice. "Myfanwy?"

The plaintiveness in his cry made her stop and have second thoughts. But only for a moment. She shook her head with determination and as tears streamed down her face; she turned away. If they followed her, they would only see one set of prints going to and from the gate, and not those of a child. She had taken but a few steps when the pain came, more forcefully this time. Waves of searing agony wracked her whole being as her heart seemed to explode in her chest. The child's tiny voice drifted on the wind as the crone's old, worn body crumpled to the ground. She gasped and the sound of her breath rattled in her throat.

"Myfanwy?" Ernulf cried as he ran toward her "Myfanwy, get up."

She would deny him nothing, but could not get up as he had

asked. She lay there clutching her breast, blood-laced spittle flying out from between clenched teeth as the sound of her pain roared past her lips.

"Go inside!" she hissed, motioning toward the gate. Another wave of pain assaulted her. The boy stood, transfixed, and started to cry. Suddenly, he threw himself on the old woman, clawing at her and weeping out of control. When she did not move or respond, he drew back and could only stare.

"Nani?" he whispered.

Ernulf began to shake the old woman's body, pulling at the rags and repeating her name as he tried to crawl back into the sling still tied over her shoulder. She was his only refuge, and she knew he was frightened. As he continued pulling at her, she felt herself roll over. He fell backwards, his legs pinned as she rolled on top of him.

Then, in an instant her world went white as the snow around her. The old woman's struggle ceased. She became still, her lifeless eyes open to the sky, no longer squinting against the stinging snow. The last thing she heard was his sobs drifting away on the wind.

✝   ✝   ✝

BROTHER RHONWELLT SHUFFLED TO THE WASHBASIN, BROKE through the thin layer of ice and splashed his face to wash away the sleep. The bitter chill of the water nearly took his breath away. His rest had been fitful, and it was especially hard to rouse himself from his warm bed for Lauds. Though away from the priory and ministering to his own parishioners for over fifteen full moons, he and his young assistant, Brother Ciaran still faithfully observed all prayer times, even those in the middle of the night. For Rhonwellt, the habits of a score-and-ten summers would not die easily. Yet, on cold nights such as this, the temptation to stay abed was strong.

"Come, lad. God awaits."

As Rhonwellt stepped to the corner of the room to relieve himself in the chamber pot, Ciaran peered out from his hood wrapped in his bedclothes.

"Oh, Brother Rhonwellt," he groaned, "it is so cold my breath hangs on the air. God will hear me just as well if I pray from here. Will He not?"

Finishing at the pot, then lighting a candle, Rhonwellt cast an indulgent smile toward the cot where Ciaran lay. "If you pray from your bed," teased Rhonwellt, "you would be wise to add a prayer to strengthen your resolve toward obedience. We are instructed to pray eight times a day, in Ecclesia...,"

"...in the church. I know, Brother Rhonwellt."

"And, so we shall. Just because we are away from the Priory, does not mean we relax the Rule. Now, up with you."

The young monk threw back his covers with a groan and quickly pulled on a pair of thick woolen socks and pushed his large feet into his shoes. Hauling his tall, rail-thin frame upright, Ciaran let loose a loud yawn and attempted to stretch the sleepiness away. He then crossed the rush-covered floor and took his turn at the chamber pot.

"I do not think I shall ever get accustomed to rising in the middle of the night to pray," he said to the wall. Ciaran emitted another hearty yawn and the dark brown curls of his tonsure bounced as he shook his head to stave off the drowsiness.

"You have managed since you were twelve," Rhonwellt said. "Five summers should be more than enough time to reconcile yourself to the hours we keep."

"A lifetime would not be enough. But I am resolved." Ciaran walked to the basin and splashed his face with the frigid water. Rhonwellt handed him a linen for drying and offered a warm smile. The young monk blushed and buried his face in the cloth.

"I shall uncover the coals and put on some peat before we go into the church. It should catch and lift some of the chill for when we return."

"But, the church will be bitter as well," the young monk protested. "How do you propose to remedy that?"

"I do not propose remedy at all. It will test your devotion. After you," said Rhonwellt, opening the door.

The two monks filed out of the small cottage and walked the two dozen steps to the back door of the church. The dry snow made crunching sounds under their feet. A small drift, blown up against the bottom, fell inward as Rhonwellt opened the heavy door and the monks entered.

By most standards, the Church of Saint Tysilio was small, not much more than a chapel. A single room with no crossing, the whole of it would fit into one the of transepts at Saint Cattwg's. However, splendid craftsmanship made up for any lack in size. The roof trusses were sturdy, gracefully arched and amply adorned with Celtic knotwork. A local artist had started painting the walls with scenes telling stories from scripture. The pictures served to bring the sacred stories to life. Sir Tristan Cunniff, lord of the manor and Rhonwellt's beloved since boyhood, had commissioned a new oaken altar carved with a likeness of its namesake, Saint Tysilio, seventh century Welsh Bishop and scholar and son of a Powys king. A rather large crucifix and two candlesticks made of gold sat proudly on a fine linen cloth covering the top. The smaller size of the room cut down on any echo and eliminated the need for Brother Rhonwellt to shout when performing Mass.

Walking to the front, both brothers knelt and signed the cross. Rhonwellt rose and went to a cresset lamp left burning in a side wall, put flame to a taper and lighted the candles on the altar. Ciaran yawned as he tugged on the bellpull, the clear peal of the bronze bell calling out the hour and the call to prayer. In this weather, the faithful seldom came to pray in the middle of the night.

Candles lit and the bell rung, the two monks knelt side-by-side and made the sign of the cross. They sang out the first few notes of the introduction to the first Psalm when Ciaran snapped his head around, eyes wide open and alert.

"What was that?"

"What was what?" replied Rhonwellt.

"It sounded like the bell at the front gate."

"I heard nothing."

Ciaran addressed his attention to the stillness. "I swear it rang, but only once."

"Well, I did not hear it," said Rhonwellt. He turned to look at Ciaran, but saw no mischief in the young monk's eyes as he had expected, only concern. After a moment, he said, "Shall we proceed?"

They finished the verse and were starting to sing the Psalm when Ciaran stopped short. Rhonwellt turned toward him.

Ciaran answered the question in Rhonwellt's gaze. "I am sure I heard something,"

Rhonwellt and Ciaran looked at each other. Without warning, the high peal of the bell invaded their devotions. Ciaran bolted for the large double doors at the front of the church. Looking behind him, just as Rhonwellt crossed himself, Ciaran quickly stopped, turned back to the altar, genuflected, signed the cross, and sped on his way.

Joining Ciaran at the entry, they opened one door a crack and peered out into the darkness. Visibility was less than a few paces. They strained to see. The great heavy door creaked as Rhonwellt pulled it open and they stepped outside onto the porch and stared around the courtyard.

"Listen," said Ciaran. "Did you hear it?"

They stood motionless, training their ears into the night.

"It sounds like someone is crying," said Rhonwellt, straining to see through the swirling snow.

"There, by the gate," said Ciaran, pointing.

"I see it!" said Rhonwellt. "What is that?" Rhonwellt called over his shoulder, already running toward the gate. "Ciaran, bring light!"

Torch in hand, Ciaran caught up to him a moment later.

Rhonwellt stood looking down. On the ground lay the body of an old woman, snow piling up around her as though the wind knew she had died and had begun her burial. Her face was deeply lined and careworn, her lifeless eyes still black as night.

"Dear God, there is a child," said Rhonwellt, "trapped beneath her."

While Ciaran pulled the whimpering boy from under the body, Rhonwellt knelt down, pushed her stringy gray hair aside and laid his fingers on the large artery in her wrinkled neck.

"Is she dead, Brother Rhonwellt?" asked Ciaran, dread on his face and in his voice.

"I fear so," said Rhonwellt, signing the cross. "I can feel no pulse and her face is cold." He put his fingers to her wet lips and brought them to his nose. "Blood," he said. He then placed his hand inside the neck of her ragged garment. "But where her body remains covered, it is yet warm. She is not long dead. But, it must have been she who rang the bell. The child is not tall enough to reach the cord."

Ciaran crossed himself and holding the child in his arms knelt beside Rhonwellt. They both began to recite the Prayer for the Dead.

"Myfanwy?" whimpered the boy.

Ciaran abandoned his prayer.

The boy broke away from Ciaran's embrace, knelt down, and touched the old woman's face.

"Oh no child, you must not..." said Rhonwellt.

When she did not move or respond, the boy drew back and simply stared. "Nani?" he whispered. Then, he began to shake her, repeating the word over and over.

Reaching out, Rhonwellt took the small hands in his, drew the child away and leaned in to look at him.

"It is too late, child," he said. "She is with God now."

The child remained motionless in the cold and the snow while the monks resumed their prayer, his crying gradually subsiding.

"Come now," Rhonwellt said at last, liftiong the child into his arms. "We must get you in where it is warm."

"What about...her?" Ciaran asked hesitantly.

"We shall move her onto that bench," Rhonwellt said motioning toward the church porch. "The cold will keep her until we can deal with her come morn. However," he said close to Ciaran's ear, "we must cover her to keep birds from taking her eyes."

"I shall retrieve a shroud from the church," said Ciaran, "while you take him inside. Then I shall wake Sir Tristan."

"She will be no more dead come the morn."

"He is the law and must be told."

"He drank heavily yestereve and will likely be in foul humor. It can wait until he has had his rest. Come little one," said Rhonwellt, "let us find you something to eat." Seeming reluctant to leave the old woman, the boy looked from Rhonwellt toward the old woman's body and back several times before his gaze finally settled on the monk. The child held out his arms, allowing Rhonwellt to pick him up.

Once in the cottage, Rhonwellt sat the boy in front of the hearth and lit a second candle. As the peat caught flame, Rhonwellt added twigs and worked the fire to life, while the boy sat quietly following his movements, occasional sniffling and sighing the only sound in the otherwise quiet.

The boy turned at the squeak of the hinges as Ciaran opened the door and entered, stomping the snow from his shoes.

"It is done," said Ciaran.

Rhonwellt gave a brief nod. "Pour the lad a cup of cider. Water it well. I will cut some bread."

The child had resumed his weeping, though less woefully. He ate between his sobs. Rhonwellt knelt in front of him.

"Have no fear, child. You are safe here. I am Brother Rhonwellt and this lad is Brother Ciaran," Rhonwellt said, gesturing behind him. The child only stared, his eyes wide and unblinking, slowly chewing the bread, his body shaking with the staccato breaths from his weeping.

"Myfanwy?" the boy called again, his panicked gaze redirected toward the door.

That name was Welsh. "Do you speak our tongue?" Rhonwellt asked him.

Facing back toward Rhonwellt, the lad gave a hesitant nod.

"Fine," the monk said, smiling reassuringly. "What is your name, child?"

The boy's eyes tracked from Rhonwellt to Ciaran and back several times. "Ernulf," he said in a quavering voice. Then, regarding to the door, he asked, "Where is Myfanwy?"

"Who is Myfanwy, child?" asked Rhonwellt.

Ernulf shrugged his shoulders. "Nani," he said.

"Ah," said Rhonwellt. "Your nani is in the church. Do not worry for her. Remember? She is with God now." Rhonwellt tousled Ernulf's hair and smiled at him. "Now, be a good lad and eat your bread and drink your cider."

Ciaran moved nearer to the fire, rubbing his hands together over the flames.

"What do we do now, Brother Rhonwellt?"

"There is nothing to be done until the morrow. Then we shall see her body prepared for burial."

"Surely, we cannot prepare the body of a woman, Brother," protested Ciaran.

"No, we cannot," agreed Rhonwellt. "At first light, you shall go fetch Esyllt and I shall set her to the task."

"The old witch?" said Ciaran, horror spreading across his face. "Certainly not for a Christian woman."

"What makes you so certain that Myfanwy was a Christian?"

"Well, we know Esyllt is not Christian."

"You are right," said Rhonwellt, "she is not. But, Esyllt is wise and well respected in these parts. The fact she clings to the old ways does not make her a witch."

"But, brother, the Church says anyone like her who is not Christian is a witch."

"The church teaches many things, lad, but not exactly that. And, my heart tells me Esyllt is a good woman, Christian or not."

"Brother Rhonwellt, why do you always challenge the ways of the Church?"

"The state of the world says it needs challenging."

"Prior Alwyn says the state of the world is the result of it being challenged," replied Ciaran.

"Perhaps. However, the Church is far too powerful to worry about any provocation from a lowly priest like me."

"If that were true, Brother," replied Ciaran, "why are they burning so many heretics?"

Rhonwellt was silent for a moment. "We have other matters to worry on at present, such as, who is Ernulf and why did Myfanwy bring him here. Esyllt and Myfanwy have a similar look. It would be worth the asking whether Myfanwy is known to her."

Turning their attention to Ernulf, they found the boy curled up on the bench, lulled into sleep by the warmth of the fire, the half-eaten bread still clutched in his hand.

"Assist me, lad, and let us see what is underneath these rags," said Rhonwellt. "They are wet and they smell." The monks proceeded to unwrap the child from his tattered coverings and cast them aside.

"God's teeth! What have we here?" said Rhonwellt, startled.

Ciaran silently formed his mouth into a large oval.

Ernulf was dressed in a murrey tunic of linen and dark green hose. On his feet were well-made calf slippers. His blonde hair was oily, and his face was dirty. However, not the accumulated grime of weeks without washing, but surface grime recently applied.

"Someone has gone to great lengths to disguise our Ernulf," Ciaran observed.

"Indeed."

"Why would anyone do that, Brother Rhonwellt?"

"I do not know." Why, indeed?

Ciaran took the bread from Ernulf's hand. Reaching for a cloth, he cleaned the sleeping child's face. "Do you think we shall find Myfanwy is finely dressed underneath her rags as well?"

"I do not," replied Rhonwellt, putting more peat on the fire. "A woman of means, unused to work, could not have carried him far, especially if she were dying. And her hands are not those of an idle woman. Myfanwy was clearly in service."

"Why do you say she carried him, brother?"

"Did you not see the sling wrapped around her? Ernulf was in it when you pulled him from beneath her body. That is how he became trapped there. I think we shall find that Myfanwy was used to hard work and was of a more common lineage."

"Then she stole the child?" said Ciaran. Turning to Rhonwellt he scrunched his face in thought. "She stole Ernulf and when she saw she was dying, dumped him here?"

"No, lad. He called her nurse. There was a bond between them. She used the last of her failing strength to see him to safety."

"How can you be so sure, Brother?" Ciaran asked. "How did she die?"

"I do not know for sure, but will be able to tell more when I can see her body in full light."

TWO

Little stirred in the early hours during midwinter. The heavy winds that blew through the night had finally subsided and a light snow fell in lazy swirls to the frozen ground. Smoke from resurrected hearth fires said people were up and about, but remained indoors, busy with midwinter chores; spinning and sewing, repairing plows and tools and caring for the livestock sharing their shelter. On clear days, there were fences to mend and firewood to gather or cut. Though the shorter days brought with them a slower pace, there was still plenty to do.

As first light turned the morning sky to a paler shade of gray, Sir Tristan followed Ciaran down the hill and out the gate, past the tithing barn to the church next door, his servant, Hewrey, at his heels. He found Rhonwellt waiting for him in the courtyard next to the body.

"Christ's teeth!" the knight said, staring down at the canvas-covered form, his brow knit. "Will death never cease to stalk me?"

"I wished to keep this out of local whisperings until after you could come and see her," said Rhonwellt pointing at the corpse.

Tristan gently pulled the covering away from the old woman's head. Her face was ashen, her eyes frozen open. Though the cold helped slow corruption of the body, when Tristan bent close, he could smell the stench of death.

"Who is she?" Tristan asked, dropping the canvas. "And close her bloody eyes!"

"It is too late for that," said Rhonwellt. "They will have to be weighted with coins."

"Do not waste coins on a villein."

"What has you so nettled?"

Tristan did not answer, only made grumbling noises and spat on the ground. The morning air was freezing. He was in no mood for complications, and death always resulted in complications.

"We do not know who she is," Rhonwellt continued. "We were at prayer when Ciaran heard the bell and the sound of weeping coming from outside. Considering the cold and the hour, we were surprised to hear any sound at all."

"She was already dead when you found her?"

"Yes, though she was still warm, so it had not been long."

"Then she is dead three or four hours."

"About that," said Rhonwellt.

"Why did you not summon me when you found her?"

"I can see your humors are out of sorts now," replied Rhonwellt. "I would hate to see their state had I disturbed your sleep."

Tristan was looking closely at her again when Hewrey asked, "How did her die?"

"Her heart failed her, Hewrey" replied Rhonwellt, drawing on his training by Brother Anselm to be a medicus. "Notice the blue gray coloring here." As Rhonwellt pointed at her nostrils, they all bent in to look. "And, see the swelling of the large artery in her neck. Her face was very flushed when first I saw her, though it has paled since. These are all signs that her heart gave out. But there was also blood from her mouth, a sign of injury within her body. Heavy exertion while being mortally wounded could easily kill her."

"Then, her death was natural?" Tristan asked.

"It would depend on how Myfanwy received her injuries," said Rhonwellt. Ciaran crossed himself. "But it was her exertions coupled with injury," Rhonwellt went on, "that killed her."

Tristan looked puzzled. "What do you mean? If you do not know her, how have you learned her name?" He frowned. This was not how he wanted to start his day. He wished he were back at the hall, seated in front of his hearth, a cup of wine held firmly in his hand.

"I think you had better come with me," said Rhonwellt. They went through the chapel to the cottage. Rhonwellt opened the door, holding a shushing finger to his lips. They found Ernulf fast asleep under a brychan on the bench near the fire.

"This is how we know her name," said Rhonwellt, holding out his hand toward the child.

"It be a babe," said Hewrey in an excited whisper.

"Bloody Christ," Tristan said under his breath.

"His name is Ernulf," whispered Rhonwellt, "and he told us Myfanwy was her nurse. That is the extent of our knowledge at this time."

"Peasants do not have nurses," exclaimed Tristan.

"As you can see," said Ciaran, pulling back the brychan, "the child is no peasant."

"He be high-born?" said Hewrey, his voice straying from a whisper.

Tristan groaned and closed his eyes. The morning grew worse with each passing moment.

"Maybe not high-born, Hewrey," replied Ciaran, covering Ernulf again, "but, he is no peasant,"

Tristan turned his attention back to the child. "We have a well-bred lad and his nurse appear from out of nowhere in the middle of the night. Who are they? And, why were they out at such an hour? Then, the nurse drops dead on the door step to the church. If we are amerced, it will cost us much coin."

There was a moment of silence and then Ciaran spoke up. "I

think the old woman stole the child. But, Brother Rhonwellt disagrees."

"Stole him? From where?" said Tristan, raising, then lowering his hands in frustration. "And from whom?" he asked, dropping onto a bench. He looked around but there were no replies. "They do not live on the estate. We would know them if they did."

"I am not of the opinion she stole the child," replied Rhonwellt, "as much as stole away with him."

"What the bloody hell is the difference?" Tristan asked.

"The difference is the intent," Rhonwellt retorted as the others simply stared with blank faces. "Why would someone steal a wealthy child? Especially a boy."

No one answered.

"Would a high-born child be worth money for its return?" Ciaran asked.

"If he is not the heir," replied Tristan, "he would likely be worth nothing."

"What if he is the heir?" posed Rhonwellt.

"Then he be worth money," said Hewrey, squatting next to the bench and staring at Ernulf.

Ciaran thought a moment. "But, Myfanwy was an old woman. How could she hope to accomplish such a scheme by herself?"

"I say she could not," replied Rhonwellt. He took a couple of circular paces in the small space.

"She would need accomplices," said Ciaran.

"Exactly. And why would she not go to them?" said Rhonwellt. Without waiting for an answer, he went on, "She came here. She struggled through the night, injured, to bring the boy here."

"That would ruin any such plan for ransom," replied Tristan, half aloud.

"If she knowed she were about to die, though..." said Hewrey.

"If ransom were the motive, she would not risk coming here," said Rhonwellt, folding his arms and cupping his chin with his hand. "No,

I think she came here with a purpose." He stopped pacing and directed his gaze toward the fire.

"What purpose?" Tristan asked.

"What if the child was in danger and her only thought was to get him to safety? If that were the case, nearly any place would be safer than where they were, especially a church."

"Then you thinks they was headed here," said Hewrey.

"I do," answered Rhonwellt.

"It is a wild theory," said Tristan, unconvinced. He extended his hands over the warm hearth.

"It is at least a possibility," replied Rhonwellt. "Ernulf kept calling her nurse."

"It is," Tristan said, though he begrudged the admission. "But, that still does not give us the slightest clue as to who they are."

"You are right," replied Rhonwellt. "It does not."

Rhonwellt poured a cup of cider from a jug left sitting on the hearth near the fire. He handed it to Tristan.

"No mulled wine?" the knight complained, staring at Ernulf.

"The sun is barely up," retorted Ciaran, one brow raised. "I think not."

"Then I will get it at the hall," said Tristan.

"Yes, but you shall have to earn it by walking from here to there," the young monk replied, raising his brow a bit further. "And once there, you shall have to deal with Hewrey."

"Clucking old beldames, the lot of you," Tristan replied, shaking his head. "Here," he said to Hewrey, handing him the cup, "you drink this. I shall wait for the wine."

Hewrey took a healthy gulp. "Master," he said, choking, his voice breathy. "Are you sure yer not be wantin' this?" he asked. "Whoo! Very fine."

Tristan looked up to see Hewrey winking at Ciaran who winked back.

Hewrey drained the cup and licked his lips.

Tristan glanced from Hewrey to Ciaran. He grabbed the jug and passed the opening under his nose. "What...it has turned," he said, tossing his head and squinting his eyes. He relieved Hewrey of the cup, filled it and drank heavily. He waited for the cider to go down.

"Can we please get back to the problem at hand?" said Rhonwellt. He turned to Ciaran and Hewrey. "You two, set up trestles in the back of the church and put the body there. Then, go Ciaran, fetch Esyllt. We shall need her to come and prepare the body for burial."

"Brother Rhonwellt," whined Ciaran, "must I?"

"Hewrey can go," said Tristan.

"No, Ciaran will go."

The young monk looked stricken as he made for the door. Hewrey clapped an arm around his shoulder as they exited. "Not to worry, old Esyllt be harmless enough," he said as they closed the door.

Rhonwellt waited for a few moments. "What has you so out of sorts today?" he asked Tristan.

The knight looked up, reached over and took the monk's hand in his.

"This unexplained death has reminded me of the events at the priory last year. I do not have a good feeling about it."

"It cannot be the same," replied Rhonwellt.

"Let us hope it is not."

☩   ☩   ☩

Brother Ciaran moved quickly, though mindful of slippery ice hidden beneath the surface of the sparse snow. Arms crossed in front of him and buried deep in the sleeves of his heavy woolen robe, face nearly hidden in its large hood, he shivered against the biting cold. Esyllt's cottage lay another six furlongs ahead.

He wished Sir Tristan had insisted Hewrey come to fetch the old woman. Why had Brother Rhonwellt been so adamant that it be he that go instead? "Sometimes, he is mystifying," Ciaran mumbled.

Each step that brought him closer caused his gut to churn and made him queasy. He attempted to distract himself, but everywhere his mind went, it encountered troubling thoughts. The church labelled Esyllt a witch. If the church said it, it must be so, even if Brother Rhonwellt said she was not. Ciaran loved his friend and wanted to believe what he said. His fear of the church, however, gave him doubts. Rhonwellt must be mistaken.

Even after a lifetime at the priory, faith did not come that easily. One still could not be sure what to believe.

Why had God allowed another soul to die with so little care? It was a question that plagued Ciaran often. If the old woman had truly perished in a valiant attempt to save a small, defenseless child, as Brother Rhonwellt believed, why had He not saved her? This time, Ciaran had to agree with Brother Rhonwellt. It was tremendously unfair that a loving God could be so capricious.

Ciaran side-stepped a puddle.

Seeing the old woman's corpse, reminded him of Brother Mark's brutal murder the year before at Saint Cattwg's. Ravaged by one of his brothers and ultimately murdered by another, it was the first time in Ciaran's sixteen summers he had watched someone die who had not departed this life from the peace and comfort of his own bed or one in the infirmarium.

Brother Rhonwellt had asked him to help prepare the monk's body. He found he was both repulsed and fascinated by the task. Though it was a corpse, Ciaran had never seen nor touched another naked body but his own, and his curiosity about the sensation was compelling. It terrified him then. It troubled him still.

Passing a rough cottage off to the side of the lane, Ciaran inhaled the odor of fresh-baked bread. A woman in the yard tossed grain out to a flock of chickens clustered about her feet.

"Good day, brother," she called out.

"Good day, mistress," Ciaran replied, sketching the sign of the cross. "God keep you."

Brother Rhonwellt said the crimes against Brother Mark had been committed in the name of love. Through his own experience, Ciaran learned Brother Mark was not what he seemed. The comely young monk was by no means an innocent. When secrets of Brother Mark's many sins came into the light, God's retribution had been swift and harsh. That had scared Ciaran the most. Then, the murderer paid the price for his own sins with his life as well. They banished the defiler to another priory. God had revealed another face during those events and Ciaran struggled to reconcile himself to the memories.

Ciaran often longed for the placid summers of his boyhood and his early days at the priory, sheltered from the harshness of the outside world. Maturing from a child to a youth, he only gradually became aware of the struggles and longings other young men his age faced, though he had not experienced them first-hand and did not fully understand them.

It was about then Sir Tristan Cunniff arrived, a scruffy knight, sullen, mysterious, and much too fond of wine and ale. He learned Sir Tristan was the source of a painful wound that had rent Brother Rhonwellt's heart as a lad no older than himself. Their reunion was awkward, fraught with anxiety yet, Brother Rhonwellt had tried to find joy in it as they struggled to make their way forward after so long a separation.

Here, to his surprise, Ciaran learned that the intense bonding between men he had witnessed at the priory could also happen outside the cloister. It did not exist merely due to the lack of women. He knew brothers who formed very deep and lasting friendships, according to the custom of Anam Cara practiced by the gaels on the big island to the West. These bonds did not always lead to carnal pleasures of the flesh, but he had seen pairs of monks steal away in the night to spend time in the belfry or cellarium, or other places of darkness. Though the prior preached against such things, Ciaran also noticed he largely ignored it.

But, to Ciaran, the bond between Sir Tristan and Brother Rhonwellt seemed different; more than the platonic couplings among the monks and purer than the furtive encounters that abided in shadow and secrecy, a tale was one neither man was eager to tell. Since leaving the priory, Ciaran had gleaned their story by bits and pieces, either on the walk home following supper at the Hall, when Brother Rhonwellt would become reflective after a second cup of wine, or in late-night conversations after Compline. The details gave rise to conflicts within himself. Long ago, as boys on the verge of manhood, Rhonwellt and Tristan had pledged their love to each other. Tristan was first-born of a respected knight; Rhonwellt, a local Welsh farmer's son.

Their affections declared a sin, both of the lovers were savagely beaten, then separated—squiring Tristan out to a knight and sent to war, Rhonwellt left beside a river to die. Tristan spent nearly the whole time, up to the threshold of the sunset of his life, in the Holy Land, fighting for God and Church. Rhonwellt was rescued by a young monk, Brother Anselm, and spent his life at the priory in Cydweli serving that same God and Church.

Brother Rhonwellt was Ciaran's dearest friend. As long as Ciaran could remember, however, his friend often exuded a bone-deep sadness. Now, Ciaran knew whence it came. Often he watched Rhonwellt struggle with what he saw as the vagaries and inconsistencies of the church. It made Ciaran wonder that a man who looked the perfect servant of God would have such doubts. Yet, his devotion to his mentor knew no limit, and it pleased him to see some of that unhappiness lifted with Sir Tristan's return.

Sir Tristan was the darker of the two in both temperament and physicality. Battle weary, with an angry scar running the length of one side of his handsome face, the knight wore his wounds like armor, a thick crust of protection to keep the world at bay. Plagued with a deep melancholy that found him at the bottom of many a barrel of wine, he kept his own counsel when the black bile held sway. At first Sir Tristan intimidated him, but Ciaran slowly became accustomed to the knight's darker moods and feared him less as time went by.

Ciaran topped a small rise in the road. He did not see a patch of ice under the snow and nearly fell. Arms flailing, he was trying to steady himself as Esyllt's cottage appeared in the distance, smoke drifting upward through the roof thatch. At the sight of it, the knot in his stomach returned and his spirits plummeted once again.

The young monk had little knowledge of people outside the faith and they frightened him. To his astonishment, Ciaran found Esyllt well liked and respected, and since Ryd Lliw did not have a real medicus, she served as physician and healer to the village and surrounding farms, her vast knowledge of herbs and cures rivaling that of Brother Anselm. Still, Ciaran did not understand her and feared her. Most disconcerting were the stories about how she sang when she tended the sick or the dying and prepared the dead for burial. Her songs were not the chants he knew from the church. Rather, they were songs sung in unfamiliar tongues, and Ciaran could not help but wonder if they were really songs of the Devil. But, Brother Rhonwellt insisted she was not a witch, and he was usually right about such things.

Ciaran approached the cottage door, hand poised to knock. He hesitated, put his hand down, raised it again and put it down a second time. He noticed a small bundle of herbs hanging over the door. He recognized some sprigs as fennel. He did not know the others. Fennel was used to ward off evil spirits, he was certain of that. There should have been a lot more hanging there than this little sprig to keep this place safe. He shuddered, raised his hand once more to knock when he heard footsteps from within. The door flew open. A grizzled old woman, short and bent, stood boldly gazing out at him.

"Well? I cannot be waitin' all day for ye to knock."

Ciaran stared at her, silent, unable to speak.

She stared back, apparently waiting for something. Moments passed as they held one another's gaze, each sizing up the other. Gradually, her wrinkled face broke into a sly grin. "Be ye afeared of me, monk?" Esyllt said at last, eyeing Ciaran in the doorway.

"A little, I think," he replied.

"Good," she cackled through a toothless grin.

Glancing around the interior of the simple abode, it was not the squalid place Ciaran envisioned. Rather, it was warm and tidy. The room contained only what the old woman would need; a bed, a large table and a bench next to the hearth. There was only one place to sit. Obviously, she received few visitors.

The rest of the space was taken up with shelves, laden with sacks, jugs, jars, vials and bowls. Whether it was the unfamiliar scents or his fear of the old woman he was not certain, but he felt uneasy. The small room smelled strongly of herbs, some familiar to him, others not. Some scents reminded him of the infirmary at the priory, others made him shudder.

Again he wished Brother Rhonwellt had sent Hewrey in his place. Hewrey would not be afraid. He doubted Hewrey feared anything.

"Come monk, shut the door," she said, scolding him. "Keep the warm in."

Ciaran hesitated. Esyllt took him by the arm, dragged him inside and pushed the door shut. Unable to stop himself, the young monk recoiled at her touch. He quickly sketched the sign of the cross.

Her gaze grew suddenly intense. She looked him straight in the eye.

He was seized with fear. Was she trying to do magic on him? Groaning and shaking uncontrollably, he put his hands in front of his face, palms out to ward off her spell and closed his eyes to shut her powerful gaze out.

"Calm ye'self, monk. Ye tremble like a rabbit in a snare," she said, cackling again and shaking her head. She turned away toward her fire. "Brother Rhonwellt sent ye?"

"Yes, mistress," replied Ciaran, a quaver in his voice.

"I be no one's mistress and none be mine," she snapped. "Esyllt will do."

Ciaran froze a moment, recovered himself, then continued. "There is a body at the church that awaits preparing for burial."

"If ye come for Esyllt, it be a woman."

Ciaran nodded without speaking and pretended to look around the room, avoiding her eyes while stealing sidelong glances at her.

A woman of indeterminate age, Esyllt was short and wiry. A lion's mane of coarse, dingy white hair stuck out from under a round kerchief of linen gauze held in place by a slim head band of intertwined grass. Her bent frame caused the frayed hem of her heavy, brown wool dress to drag the ground in front. Her dingy shift, gathered at the throat and wrists, showed above the low neck of her dress and at the end of its sleeves. A long apron covered the front. Her tiny eyes twinkled with mischief. "Whose body it be?" Esyllt asked. She began to collect certain jars and vials and a sack or two from the shelves and set them on the table.

Ciaran started at the sound of her voice. "We do not know."

"How could ye not know?" she snapped, turning to look at him. "Ye should be knowin' everyone from the village and the farms about."

"She is not from here," replied Ciaran, shrinking from her tone.

"Oh?" the old woman replied, a look of surprise creeping across her face. "Hmmm. How did she die?"

Ciaran did not answer.

"Was it the sickness?" Her voice hissed like a snake, making some movement with her hands that Ciaran thought must be a hex.

"She is just an old woman, much like you." He could barely get the words out.

"Like me? Ye mean wicked, do ye not?" she said with a wink, her tongue darting out from between her gums to lick thin lips. "Do ye think old Esyllt be a witch, monk?" she asked cackling again.

Ciaran swallowed hard, his mouth pasty and dry. He desperately wanted to cross himself, but his hand would not move. He struggled to make his voice work. It only croaked when he spoke. "Brother Rhonwellt says that you are not," he replied, eyes closed as if repeating a prayer. His heart was beating like the hooves of a runaway horse. He scolded himself. She was only a harmless old woman. "I only meant that she was old like you," he stammered aloud.

"I be more than old," said the crone. "I be ancient! Why, nearly as old as the dirt under your feet." She laughed loudly and winked.

He forced a credible smile. He did not know why the old woman made him so uncomfortable, but the feeling was visceral. Ciaran wanted to believe what Brother Rhonwellt said about her, that she was good, but something inside him filled with doubt. Where was his faith? Suddenly, Ciaran was filled with shame and wanted desperately to leave.

Esyllt picked up a large basket and handed it to him. "Hold this," she commanded.

She quickly put the items she had collected into it, added a bowl and a stone pestle, then grabbed two bundles of herbs from the low hanging rafters overhead, and put each of them carefully on top. "Brother Rhonwellt has chrism?" she asked, starting to reach for a small vial from one of the shelves.

Ciaran looked startled and nodded. How did she know about chrism?

"Esyllt knows ye ways," she replied through a gummy smirk. "This be not the first Christian old Esyllt has prepared."

"We do not know if she is Christian," he said. He sounded defensive.

"Brother Rhonwellt will use it anyway," she said. Ciaran suspected she was right.

After banking the ashes in the hearth, Esyllt wordlessly wrapped herself in her heavy woolen cloak, flipped up the hood and opened the door. "Spill nothing," the old woman ordered as she pushed him out into the cold and snow, pulling the door closed behind her.

"Yes, mistress," he said, breathing a sigh of relief.

THREE

A white handkerchief, snagged on a low tree branch, waved in forlorn surrender at three men on horseback, all dressed in heavy woolens, leather jerkins, tall boots and cloaks. Each had a sword hanging from his belt. Seething, a thickset, muscular Saxon, long yellow hair to his shoulders, scowled at the carnage. Atop a chestnut courser, he gripped the front of his saddle, his lips pressed into a tight, thin line. An overturned cart lay on its side at the edge of the small copse of silver-birch about three furlongs off the road from Neath, an elderly man, his throat slashed, dead next to it. The man's scabbard was empty, his sword gone. The signs showed that, despite his age, he had tried to fight. The bodies of two armored guards lay some distance off, the arrows of a skilled bowman protruding from their bodies, one through the side of his neck, the other his throat. A third lay near the cart where he had fallen, run through by a sword. The smell of death hung on the air. Their eyes were already gone. Blood seeping from the corpses had turned the surrounding snow a reddish black.

Clothing chests lay open and empty, their contents strewn for thirty paces in every direction. The cart pony and the guard's horses were nowhere around. A shivering, tricolor harrier crawled from between the thick layers of a pile of clothing. Eyeing them with a forlorn look, it raised its head and barked once, then whined as it lay back down next to the cart.

Where were the rest of them? And, why was the dog still here?

Dry, powdery snow, blown up against the windward side of the corpses and cart, had obscured any tracks that might have offered clues.

"What you make of it, master Wulfric?" asked a tall, scrawny man with a pock-marked face and greasy hair.

"Looks like brigands, Osgar," answered the Saxon, "most likely on horseback. Footpads would not be this far off the track, and would be no match for three armed men on mounts. They appear to have been dead for about two days, although the cold weather makes it hard to tell for certain."

Wulfric dismounted and walked over to the cart, the snow flattened all around it from the fight. Since it was on the leeward side, the wind had not obscured the marks on the ground there. Wulfric studied a small wedge-shaped space formed beneath the cart where the end of the axle held the rear of the box off the ground. The compacted snow made an indentation the size of an adult and that of a child a few inches away.

The form of the adult was small, probably that of the nurse.

That crafty old hag! It appeared she and the child were pinned under the cart. There was no blood. What of the mother?

"I do not see Merewyn, Ernulf or his nurse." said Wulfric. "Osgar, you go that way," he said, pointing East.

"Aye," said Osgar.

"Leo, you go West. See if they are nearby."

"They may have tried to run," replied Leo, a fellow so average in appearance that he could easily go unnoticed.

"They cannot have gone far," said the yellow-haired man as he spun his horse around and headed through the trees. "Find them."

The men fanned out in opposite directions, searching the copse for more bodies. After carefully combing the area, they met back at the cart.

Agitated, Wulfric sat with his hands crossed on the pommel of his saddle, his eyes dark with worry. "You found nothing?"

"No, my lord," his men answered.

"No sign of nobody," said Osgar.

"This will put Selwyn in a lather, for certain." Wulfric scanned the scene again, hoping to spot any detail he might have missed. Anything. "There are no weapons lying around," he said. "The swords and knives were decent steel, and would fetch a price."

"There be no money chest," said Leo.

"They took it," Osgar replied. "It were heavy, would slow them down. They took all the food, too." He paused, licking his lips. "You think they done the young mistress a'fore they killed 'er?"

Wulfric worked the muscles in his face at the comment, but let it slide. "We found no bodies so we cannot be certain they are dead," he said, fighting for control.

"Osgar, that all you think on?" said Leo, spitting off to the side.

"Mostly," Osgar replied, chuckling. "At least I would a done 'er afore she died. You, on the other hand... ."

Leo swung and missed Osgar's head.

Sidling his horse nearby Osgar's, Wulfric grabbed the man by the throat and threw him to the ground. Dismounting, he shot Leo a look of disapproval. "Speak like that again about your mistress," he barked at Osgar, "and I will cut out your tongue and feed it to you."

Leo chuckled as the scrawny one glared, wide-eyed, at Wulfric. Rubbing his throat, Osgar struggled to his feet and backed away.

Leo slowly looked around. "Snow has covered the tracks. No tellin' how many they was."

"I say at least four to get the best of three men trained to arms. The bowman most likely picked off two of the guards from a distance, then the rest moved in. Outnumbered, the old man and the last guard were easy kills." Wulfric climbed back into the saddle. "I think the three of them survived. We just need to find out where they went and if they are together."

"Do you think they was took?" asked Leo.

"I think the old woman fooled their attackers into thinking she and Ernulf were dead. It is likely they appeared dead when the cart rolled over. They lay under it for a time, packing the snow. It partially melted from the heat of the bodies." Wulfric scowled. "Only two lay there. I fear they took the other."

Leo sniffed the air. "Strong smell of hearth smoke. Not far to the next village, I wager."

"This an estate or Welsh land?" asked Osgar.

"This part of Wales is nearly all held by Normans. There will be a castle or hall close by. And a church."

☩   ☩   ☩

Rhonwellt and Ciaran sat quietly in the cottage breaking their fast. Esyllt's chanting and occasional mutterings could be heard next door preparing Myfawny's body for burial.

"She was talking to the corpse, Brother Rhonwellt," said Ciaran, forcing the words out through a mouthful of gruel. His voice was unsure.

Rhonwellt said nothing as he spooned porridge into his own mouth.

"She was casting spells, Brother Rhonwellt."

Leaning in over his bowl, Rhonwellt chewed his mouthful of grain and legumes, looking up through his eyebrows at the young monk across the table.

"I heard her, Brother."

"You heard her voice," said Rhonwellt, "but, were you listening to her words?"

"I dared not, Brother."

"So, you were frightened because you heard her talking to someone you know to be dead?"

Ciaran nodded.

Rhonwellt put his spoon down on the table, and clasped his hands under his chin. "I heard her, also," he said. "But, I listened to what she was saying. She was talking to Myfanwy as she would to an old friend, someone she might have loved. She said she could see by her hands she had worked hard her whole life. That, even in death, her face showed she had been kind. And, though not perfect, Esyllt was sure she had been a good woman. She praised her for her valiant effort to save Ernulf at her own peril—that the Master would be glad. She sought only to acknowledge her goodness, not to berate her for her sins and shortcomings. In death they do not matter."

"They do matter," said Ciaran. "She may yet find herself in the fires of Hell."

"You are right," said Rhonwellt. "She may. But, she is gone. Her fate is sealed. The most anyone can do now is pray for her soul."

"Is that not what Mistress Esyllt should have done?"

"Perhaps mistress Esyllt believes Myfanwy has found her place in Heaven by her good works, rather than through any lack of sin."

"We are taught the only way to Heaven is through repentance, Brother Rhonwellt."

"We are," Rhonwellt replied. "But, somehow I feel that if the only people in heaven were repentant and free of sin, Heaven would be a remarkably empty place."

"Do you not want to go to heaven, Brother Rhonwellt?"

"We are monks, lad, called into service to God. I am not sure heaven is a mere choice for us, considering the alternative." Rhonwellt picked up his spoon and shoveled the rest of his porridge into his mouth. It had gotten cold and had started to congeal. He swallowed hard, imagined a prayer of thanks for the nourishment, and rose from his seat. "Esyllt will be nearly finished by now. I must go and anoint the body." Rhonwellt felt around the inside of the pouch hanging from his waist for his vial of chrism. He turned to Ciaran. "When making an assessment of a person, you must look at the whole person, not just the things that you are comfortable with or the things that trouble you. The traits that are most obvious do not always present the truest picture of their character." Rhonwellt closed the door.

For the rest of the day and all that night, Rhonwellt took his turns sitting vigil over Myfawny's remains with Ciaran, Ronan, and Edward the stable boy. Convinced her efforts to save Ernulf were an act of Christian charity, he had given Myfanwy absolution so she could be buried in a consecrated grave. However, when the diggers tried to pierce the ground, they found the soil frozen, so Rhonwellt asked Tristan to order a fire built on the grave site. When it was time to inter the body, the fire was allowed to burn down and the ashes were scraped off. Only then did the ground prove soft enough for digging.

On a cold but sunny morning, Rhonwellt offered prayers as Myfanwy was laid to rest in a common grave at the edge of the churchyard. Since Myfanwy was not known locally, six villagers were paid a quarter-penny each to stand as mourners. Still fearing Ernulf may be in danger, Rhonwellt had Hewrey stay with the child at the hall, insisting his existence be kept secret a while longer.

Rhonwellt and Tristan walked at an easy pace, silence their companion, as they climbed the low rise to the hall. Rhonwellt, arms folded in the sleeves of his robe, hood up, head down, seemed solemn; Tristan, hand resting on the hilt of his sword, typically sullen. Though Myfanwy had died naturally, Rhonwellt had tried in vain to convince Tristan something sinister was afoot. And yet, Tristan had said the affair reminded him of the three murders at the priory the year before and owned he had seen enough death in Outremer, and was the reason he had returned home. A contradiction to be sure. Rhonwellt silently prayed that, though it was no murder, this would be the end to the deaths.

Passing through the gatehouse, Tristan broke the silence. "All is well with Ciaran?" he asked.

"Well enough," replied Rhonwellt. "He is young and still discomfited by death. Some time in solitude with God will do him well. He will be fine. Right now, he is more concerned with Esyllt. He is quite in terror of her."

Tristan pushed open the heavy door. The sweet, dry scent of fresh floor rushes mingled with the smell of smoke from the hearth hung on the air. Hewrey and Ernulf sat warming by the fire.

"Master," said Hewrey, jumping to his feet. "Brother Rhonwellt. Come by the fire and keep master Ernulf company whilst I fetch you drinks."

The child sat quietly holding a cup of cider, staring into the flames, his feet swinging forward and back from the high bench. He looked up briefly, made no acknowledgment, and lowered his head to again stare into the fire.

"Well, master Ernulf," said Tristan. "What are we to make of you, lad?"

Ernulf looked up at Tristan and held his gaze. Rhonwellt watched the two of them stare at each other; Tristan offered a weak smile, Ernulf's face showed no emotion at all.

"Can you tell us nothing of who you are or whence you came?" said Tristan, not actually expecting an answer.

The boy stared a moment more, then turned away.

"We know he can speak," said Tristan, exasperation creeping into his voice, "and we know he can understand us. Yet, he will tell us nothing."

Hewrey returned with drinks. "No reason to be afeared, lad," he said to Ernulf. "Master asked you a question."

"Has he said nothing to you?" Tristan asked Hewrey.

"No, master. Nothin'. Just quiet, he is."

The iron hinges groaned as the large door to the hall swung open. The hostler from the stables stepped inside, but remained at the edge of the screens. Hewrey crossed the floor to see what Ronan wanted. Ernulf slid down from his bench and padded after. After a few moments, Hewrey was returning to the fire when Ernulf ran past the screens, headed for the stairs.

"Beg pardon, master," said Hewrey, looking over his shoulder toward the sound of the child's footsteps ascending to the solar, "three men at the gate. Old Ronan says they be strangers."

Tristan rose and in ten quick strides was peering out the arrow slit next to the door. Rhonwellt stood at his shoulder as they watched the approaching riders.

"Who can they be?" asked Tristan.

"I do not know," said Rhonwellt, "and I am not encouraged by their looks."

"Nor am I," said Tristan. "The big one looks Saxon, the other two, just shifty. We must be hospitable, but careful. They are armed."

"I will see to Ernulf," said Rhonwellt. "Say nothing of the child, at least for the time being. I still fear for his safety."

"You have no proof he is in danger," Tristan argued, looking back toward the monk.

"I have grown wary of men since leaving the priory. We do not know their purpose, so please, say nothing of Ernulf."

"Do you take me for a fool?" Tristan asked, admonishing him. "As a soldier, I am wary simply *because* they are strangers. Of course I will tell them nothing. Go see to him and I will greet our travelers."

Tristan waited for Rhonwellt to disappear up the stairs and then opened the door and stepped outside. He stood, hand posing loosely on the hilt of his sword, legs spread wide, head high, an open smile on his face. He did not try to hide any wariness in his eyes.

The men rode up the incline to the hall door and came to a halt. The yellow-haired Saxon stared openly at Tristan.

"My lord," he said.

"Sir Tristan Cunniff. Welcome to Ryd Lliw and Narrow-ford Hall."

"Wulfric atte Halyfax," said the Saxon. His speech was the guttural and clipped tongue of the North.

"May I offer you some ale?" Tristan could easily see the bulk of the man's body beneath his jerkin. Any deficiency in his skill with a sword could easily be made up for by sheer size.

"Thank you, my lord," said Wulfric. "A bit of time by a fire would be most welcome."

"These days are bitter, indeed. Ronan will see to your horses," said Tristan.

"No need, my lord," said the man quickly. "Our stay will be brief."

"Very well, come inside and warm yourselves and take refreshment," said Tristan. He stood aside and let the visitors pass. Closing the door, he looked after them, uneasy, scrutinizing their movement. Years on the battlefield had taught him to size up a potential enemy in mere moments. That he was still alive was testament to his skill.

The big Saxon moved easily, sure of himself. That one would hold his own. The scrawny one, on the other hand, was hesitant and oafish. The way he kept glancing at the big blonde said he got his bravery from the strength of his leader; he would fight, but would pose no real threat. The stocky, third man was guarded and belied his appearance. He bore watching. It was probably best not to lose sight of him in a fight.

Following them to the fire, Tristan saw Hewrey return from the buttery, carrying drinking pots and jug of ale, his dagger strapped to his waist. When the men had seated themselves, Hewrey poured them drinks.

The big Saxon looked at the cup warily, smelled it and took a sip. He swallowed, smacking his lips. "The ale is fine, not bitter. I thank you."

"The village alewife's drink is favored in the area." Tristan took a sip from his cup, eyeing them over the rim.

"Then your mistress does not make her own?" asked the Saxon. Tristan did not reply. After a gulp from his pot, Wulfric spoke again. "I see there was a funeral this morning as we came riding into town."

The hairs on Tristan's neck stood on end. How had he not noticed them? "Alas," he said, struggling for composure, "death is ever with us, even in midwinter when it can be most inconvenient."

Tristan felt the Saxon waiting for him to say more. After an awkward silence, Wulfric said, "I just thought it might have something to do with my business here."

"And, how is that, sir?" asked Tristan, making sure to keep all expression from his face.

"I regret, I am here to inform my lord that highwaymen have been at work near here. Perhaps even on your demesne."

Tristan lowered his cup in surprise. "Highwaymen? Why do you think that?"

"We came across the scene of an attack," said Wulfric. "Four dead bodies, three man-at-arms and an old man. An over turned cart, its contents spread about. Money, weapons...anything of value is gone. Cart pony and horses taken, too."

New threads seemed to be appearing in this mysterious tapestry. Could the Saxon be the weaver? "Where was this?" Tristan asked.

"Over twenty furlongs south of the village, a ways off the side of the road near a small beechwood. The pasture wall there is in need of repair."

"I knows this place, Master," said Hewrey.

"They cannot be from this village," said Tristan, after a moment, "or we would have heard."

"Then, they would be strangers to you," said Wulfric. "Travelers who met misfortune on the road passing through your demesne."

"It would appear to be the case." Tristan bristled at the Saxon's mention of the crime occurring on his land, but gave no outward indication. There was that question of amercement, again. Any fine would be expensive. "How long ago, would you say?" he asked.

"One day, two at most."

"No hue and cry was put forward so there were likely no witnesses to the crime," said Tristan. "We would not be sure who we are looking for." Tristan relaxed a little. No witnesses said no fine.

Tristan caught a narrowing of Wulfric's eyes. "However, I will get to the bottom of it," said Tristan. "I shall send men to collect the bodies straight away. Hewrey claims to know the place. He can lead them there. Our priest will see to burying them. Although, in this weather, four graves would be difficult to manage. Epiphany is not long past. We may have to be content to shroud them and cover them with stones until spring thaw."

Tristan's back stiffened and his hands tightened on his knees as he watched the big Saxon take stock of the hall. Wulfric looked around the room, his eyes settling on the screens passage leading to the kitchen, buttery and solar. While Tristan concentrated on the Saxon, he trusted Hewrey to keep an attentive eye on Osgar and Leo.

"Your hall is well built," said Wulfric. "It should afford you much protection."

"Thank you, sir. It is old, built just before I was born. I knew the place as a child and much admired it. Fallen into disrepair, the hall has been much improved since it came to me."

Wulfric continued to look around.

"In surveying the scene of the attack," said Wulfric, employing a sudden change of subject that surprised Tristan, "it appeared that there may have been two or three others, one small, perhaps a child, whose bodies were nowhere to be found near the wreckage. We pray they may yet be alive."

It seemed to Tristan that the man had chosen his words carefully. Was he fishing? Perhaps Rhonwellt was right in his fear for Ernulf.

"If this is so," said Tristan, choosing his own words just as carefully, "they would seek refuge in the village. I shall keep an ear to the ground."

When Tristan offered no more, Wulfric rose and gave a slight bow.

"Well, I have done my Christian duty and kept the law." He motioned to Osgar and Leo who had risen with him. "We thank you for the fire and refreshment. We shall be on our way. Good day to you, my lord, and God's peace to you."

"To you as well," said Tristan. "The village has an inn, with a good room and passable food if you desire lodging for the night."

"We are there already," said Wulfric. The Saxon bowed again

and with a flourish of his cloak, turned to leave. As he opened the door, he took a final look around the hall and the three exited.

✝   ✝   ✝

"Did ye see 'em?" said Leo as they climbed into the saddle.

"Shut up, you idiot!" hissed Wulfric.

The three turned their mounts and headed down the hill toward the gate. When they were safely out of earshot from the hall, Wulfric stopped, unsheathed his dagger and pointed it at Leo.

"You should learn to hold your tongue."

Leo, eyes wide, leaned away from the point of the weapon. "Sorry, my lord," he whispered. "But, did ye see 'em."

"See what," asked Osgar, clueless.

"The child," said Leo. "They have the child."

"There was a small lad," said Wulfric, "well hidden behind the servant as he spoke to the old man who went to announce our arrival. I could not be certain it was Ernulf. He was nowhere present when we entered the hall. And, no woman presented herself as mistress while we were there. He appears to have no wife, yet there is a child. I think we shall stop at the inn a while longer. The knight was evasive. It is why I did not acknowledge who we are."

"If he has Ernulf, why did he not say when you says there might be a child?"

"The knight is clever. I would not say so, either, if it were me. How could he be sure we were not the ones who attacked the caravan?"

"We be no highwaymen," said Osgar.

"No, but we are strangers. Considering the circumstances, that alone would make the knight suspicious of us."

"If it be Master Ernulf, how we goin' to get him?" Osgar asked. "I have me doubts the knight will just hand him over. Elst why hide him?"

"I do not know," Wulfric replied, "but, we shall be stopping a day or two and can ask about the village. Someone will know of him."

"I seen you sizin' up the hall," said Osgar.

"It is strong and will be easy to defend," Leo said.

"It is. But, we shall find a way. Now, let us make for the inn and get out of this cursed, bloody cold."

"I hopes that servin' wench be there," said Osgar.

Leo rolled his eyes. "That all you think of?"

FOUR

Holding Ernulf's hand, Rhonwellt descended the solar stairs and found Tristan looking out the arrow slit in the wall by the door.

"He was under the bed in your chambers," said Rhonwellt.

Tristan made an incoherent sound, indifferent, as though he had not been paying attention.

When they reached the hall floor, Ernulf ran to Hewrey who knelt by the hearth tending the fire. Rhonwellt joined Tristan, peered over the knight's shoulder, and watched Wulfric and his lackeys wend their way down the hill and out the gate. "He was very frightened," continued Rhonwellt.

"Of what?"

"Surely, you are not that dull of wit," said Rhonwellt, wondering if Tristan was being purposefully obtuse. "Did you not see how he fled when he spied the men riding up the hill?"

"I just put it down to shyness. After all that he has endured..." Tristan's voice trailed off as he continued to stare out the small opening, stroking his chin with his thumb and forefinger. When he turned to face Rhonwellt, the worry lines creasing Tristan's face smoothed to a smile.

Tristan slipped an arm across Rhonwellt's shoulder and started leading him toward the hearth. The monk felt a shiver pass through him. Doubtless, Tristan sensed his body tighten, but did not let go. Rhonwellt tried to relax. It was still so hard to give in, not to Tristan, rather to himself. He still could not forget the time he had almost died as a result.

Rhonwellt steeled himself against the memory, drew a breath to cleanse images of the past. "Once I pulled him from under the bed," he said, a slight tremble in his voice, "I could see the terror in his eyes. I asked him if he was afraid of the men visiting the Hall. He said only hewthyr."

"Uncle? The Saxon?"

"I do not know," said Rhonwellt, glancing at Ernulf. "That is all he said."

"Then the lad knows him. And Wulfric knew who the murder victims were, yet he feigned ignorance and made pretense to keeping the law."

Rhonwellt felt Tristan's hand move to the spot between his shoulder blades.

"Do you think he committed the murders?" Rhonwellt asked, his face growing hot.

"That is the question that begs answering, now. Is it not? You may be right about Ernulf being in danger." Tristan shook his head. "One day I will learn to have more faith in your intuition."

"Who are they and what do they want with the child?" Rhonwellt asked.

"I do not know. But I feel we may find out before too long."

"You think they will not leave the area right away?"

Tristan gave a brief nod. "Hewrey, have Ronan ready Sag for me and harness a team to the large wagon. Then take the wagon to the village and round up three or four men to help us collect the bodies. I shall come for you shortly."

"Yes, Master," said Hewrey, his voice dripping resentment, "but it is so cold."

"Then be sure you wrap warm," said Tristan. "Now, go!"

With a grumble, Hewrey disappeared behind the screens, then reappeared, wrapped in his thickest wool cloak, and made for the door. When Ernulf padded across the floor to follow him, Hewrey put his hand up. "No, little one," he said, "you must stay here with Brother Rhonwellt. I be back soon. Not to worry."

Ernulf hesitated.

"Go," Hewrey commanded, turning the child around and gently but firmly pushing him away.

Ernulf slowly retreated.

Tristan released his hold on Rhonwellt. "I must go," he said. "Stay by the fire and keep the lad company until we return."

"What will you do with the bodies?" asked Rhonwellt, seating himself on the bench. "There are too many for the church."

"For now, we shall put them in the tithe barn," said Tristan, retrieving his sword leaning against the wall by the cupboard. "We can decide what to do on the morrow," he said. He strapped his weapon about his waist.

"Thankfully," said Rhonwellt, "we shall not need Esyllt again since there are no women."

"That should make Ciaran happy," replied Tristan with a laugh.

Rhonwellt watched Tristan leave, but the sense of the knight's touch lingered. The monk was still uncomfortable showing affection in the presence of others. Even simple gestures left him struggling to find the proper response. Not the least troubling was his continued surprise at its profound effect on him. Each occurrence flooded his being with memories, not just in his mind, but remembrances that dwelled dormant in his flesh but became immediately active and recognizable when experienced anew.

If he were ever to give in to his longings, it must be a conscious decision, not the result of pressure. It must never be an act he would regret. The thought of it was seldom far from his mind, but the reality was no closer now than it was a year ago. He was glad for Tristan's patience. All the same, he could not help but wonder how long the knight's forbearance could last.

There were other memories stored in his body too—ones filled with pain. Though the blows were a thing of the past, the emotional bruises had never faded. Those impressions filled him with panic. The accompanying voices, always there in the background, soft and insidious, awaiting moments of insecurity, kept hissing that what he felt was a sin. He could not quiet them. Ultimately, he did not doubt his love for Tristan, only his ability to get past his fear to show it.

Rhonwellt felt something touch his face. For a moment, he thought it another memory. Reaching up, he felt a tiny hand. Ernulf was standing on the bench next to him, tracing the path of a tear as it rolled down Rhonwellt's cheek. The monk turned to see the child's eyes full of questions as he gazed at the monk.

"Sad?" Ernulf asked.

"Sometimes, yes," replied Rhonwellt, conjuring up a smile for the boy. They regarded each other for a few moments. Rhonwellt raised his hand to tousle the child's long straw-colored hair. Ernulf abruptly turned around and sat on his lap and leaned against him. Rhonwellt wrapped his arms around the boy and moments passed in silence as they sat, lost in the flames.

"Hewrey has gone with his master, so I must feed the fire," said Rhonwellt, at last. Ernulf turned to look over his shoulder at the sound of the monk's voice. Then, sliding off his lap and down to the floor, the lad padded to the pile of wood stacked against the wall. He loosed a piece from the top and stood clear as it tumbled to the floor. Rolling it end over end, the wood was soon lying next to the hearth. As Rhonwellt lifted it onto the fire, Ernulf hurried back to the pile for another piece.

Soon the fire was ablaze once again, and the two stood and watched with satisfaction.

"Well done, child," said Rhonwellt.

"I am Ernulf," he replied, without hesitation while looking up at the monk in earnest.

"Of course you are," said Rhonwellt, comprehending the meaning. "Well done, master Ernulf."

"Where is Myfanwy?" Ernulf said, turning his attention to the fire.

"I told you. She is with God."

"Will she come back?"

"No, my son."

"Why?"

"She cannot, is all. When souls go to be with God, they must stay with Him. They cannot come back."

Ernulf leaned into Rhonwellt as they stood side by side, gazing into the fire, silently soaking in its warmth.

☦   ☦   ☦

A SMALL DOG DARTED FORWARD AS TRISTAN APPROACHED, nipping at the legs of his horse. It barked, then retreated to the cluster of bodies lying on the ground.

"Easy, boy," Tristan said, to soothe the horse. "Away with you!"

The dog skulked off, but remained nearby.

Hewrey had recruited five men from the warmth of the Saint George to collect the corpses. Though rigor had since subsided, the bodies were stiff from the cold, which made them easy to carry. Since the corpses were clustered together, the knight had the men retrace their steps each time they retrieved one to keep the site whole. However, Tristan soon realized the effort would be for naught. The men tramped carelessly around the area leaving behind a profusion of new prints to confuse the evidence even further.

While Hewrey and the men busied themselves loading the wagon, Tristan skirted around the scene of the slaughter, scrutinizing it from every angle. Everything was as Wulfric had said, even to the flattened snow under the cart. If the big Saxon was right, it could explain how Myfanwy and Ernulf survived. Yet, the Saxon had hinted at a third missing person.

Accumulated snow, blown by the wind, had obscured any old sign, however, fresh tracks showed Wulfric and his men had scoured the site, using little care during their investigation. Local farmers were predicting the weather would soon warm enough for a melt. If they were right, Tristan intended to come back for another look after the snow and ice had gone in the hope that there may be something there, now covered and unseen. He would issue orders throughout the estate that no one enter the copse until further notice.

Satisfied there was nothing to see from a distance, he dismounted and walked carefully among the bodies and around the overturned cart. "I doubt this place has any more to tell us of the happenings here," said Tristan. He had decided preserving the scene was not possible. "The cart does not appear damaged. Remount the wheel and tie it to the back of the wagon. Then, refill the chests with their belongings and load them on, as well. I want all traces of this horror removed."

"You heard Master," said Hewrey. "Get a move on lads so you can get back to your ale pots at the tavern. It be bloody cold. And have a care where you walks, like Master says."

Tristan and Hewrey watched the men load the last chest onto the wagon. They groused at the prospect of riding back to the village with the corpses, but at Hewrey's urging, agreed it was better than walking over twenty furlongs in the cold. Hewrey climbed into the driver's place, snapped the reins and clucked to the team of mules.

"So this be where the old crone come from, Master?" asked Hewrey from his seat.

"Yes. She must have traveled with this lot. It is the only explanation for her presence. The big Saxon said as much and yet did not."

"He were lyin' sure, Master. Why?"

"Men lie for many reasons. If Wulfric and his men did not ride with Myfanwy and her fellow travelers, then were they following them? And did they only follow them or were they in pursuit? Why are people from the far North in southern Wales in the dead of winter, so far from home?"

"How do you know that be where they from, Master?"

"I was there for a short time as a lad. People from that region have a distinct way of speaking and style of dress. Braies instead of hose and wraps, shorter tunics. Remnants of the old Saxon tongue."

"He looked and sounded queer. That be a fact."

"I must bring the culprits to justice, or it may fall on me to pay."

"Pay for what, Master?"

"Amercement, a fine. If a crime is committed on my land and there are witnesses, the family of the victim can claim payment from me if the culprits are not brought to justice."

Hewrey just shook his head from side to side. "No sense to that."

"Well," said Tristan with a scowl, "it is the law. I must find who is responsible. We can only hope this accursed weather will slow them down and make their escape from the area more difficult."

"Three to four rogues draggin' extra horses and a cart pony should be easy to find." Hewrey spat off the side of the wagon into the snow.

"True enough. But I do not think they will keep them for long. The horses from the men-at-arms may fetch more than a few coins. They will rather have money than extra mouths to feed. I will spread word to local stables to be alert for any strangers trying to sell them well-bred stock."

The main street of the village lay nearly deserted, as few were foolish enough to endure the cold unless they must. Those that did, stared openly as the wagon full of bodies rolled through, the small dog following at a safe distance. Many sketched the sign of the cross and bowed their heads. Two young children, whose fathers rode the wagon with the corpses, ran along side, pestering the men with questions. Faces appeared in doorways and windows, following the solemn procession with their eyes. One face stood out, standing in the doorway of the Saint George, Wulfric atte Halyfax. Rather than eyeing the bodies, he concentrated his gaze on Tristan, who nodded as he passed. Wulfric returned the acknowledgment with a hard, narrow-eyed glare.

The train turned into the yard of the tithe barn, a large timber structure built on a low stone foundation with a thatched roof. Larger than necessary to accommodate the tithes collected for Saint Tysilio's, the village used it more as a communal barn for all the farmers on the estate. Rhonwellt was waiting for them there.

The men unloaded the remains and carried them inside and laid them on wood slabs set on a row of trestles. The monk covered them with shrouds. Heads turned at the sight of the body with the nearly severed head. While two men carried his torso, a third held his head to keep it from tearing loose. After laying the body down, the man who carried the head went to retch in a corner.

"What will you do with their belongings?" Rhonwellt asked.

"Pull any clothing you find that is for Ernulf," Tristan replied, "and take it to the hall. Store the rest in the loft and I shall deal with it later."

When they had finished, Tristan gave Hewrey several coins with instructions to take the men to the tavern and buy them ale and leave them a quarter-penny each.

"I saw the Saxon lurking about as we passed. Buy him and his men a drink. But have it sent. Do not speak to them. See if you can determine what he and his men are about. Do not let him know you are interested. Understood?"

"Yes, Master." His enthusiasm was clear.

"I did not give you enough to get drunk. See that you do not."

"Yes, Master." Hewrey's second reply was far less enthusiastic.

"And get rid of that bloody dog!" Tristan said, pointing at the harrier who sat warily by the barn door.

☥   ☥   ☥

THE SAINT GEORGE BUSTLED WITH THIRSTY PATRONS. IT WAS only just past quarter Nones but darkness had nearly settled in.

Unable to work the fields in this weather, the men needed to pass the time, and over a dozen had been there most of the day, out of the cold, away from wives nagging them to fix a fence or mend a broken plow. Word of the attack must have spread quickly. As soon as Hewrey and the men walked through the door, patrons deluged them with questions about the wagon full of corpses and what they had encountered at the scene of the murders.

Wulfric glowered from a table in the far corner at the back of the room. As soon as Hewrey had secured pots of ale for the helpers, he sent a round of drinks to Wulfric and his men with Sir Tristan's compliments.

"You know them men?" the serving girl asked. Alma, a pudgy lass of about twenty summers, had dull eyes and a generous mouth that showed glimpses of blackened teeth when she talked. Her large breasts jiggled when she laughed.

"They told Master about the murders and where the bodies was."

"I do not think I likes 'em," she said.

"Why, lass?"

"First off, they talks funny. Second, they been askin' all sort of questions. Bein' nosy like."

"They talk that way because they be from the North," said Hewrey, puffing himself up. "Way up the top of the land. What questions they askin'?"

"Funny stuff." Alma leaned into the table conspiratorially so Hewrey could hear her above the din without her raising her voice. "Did we know about the attacks or if anyone escaped? Queryin' 'bout your Master. Asked about his wife and how old was his child. Your Master got no wife, we say, no child neither. They look funny when we says that."

Could that mean they seen the babe? Aloud, he asked Alma, "Did anyone mention the old woman we buried the other day?"

"I think Alfie says so. Maybe. Not sure. You want I should ask?"

"No. Forget it. They say anything else?"

"Nothing I can remember."

"Keep your ears perked," said Hewrey. "Let me know if they asks about the old woman."

"Anything for you, Hewrey," said Alma, winking as she swung away with a giggle.

"That's me girl," said Hewrey, as he swatted her rump and watched her walk away to make her rounds of the tables, talking jovially with various patrons. Slowly she found her way to the table where Wulfric and his men sat glaring from across the room.

Hewrey drew his attention back to the men seated with him, trying not to show any obvious interest in the Saxons. His companions teased him about his partiality to the serving girl.

"You best stop looking at young Alma's arse, lad," said Daffyd, the tanner. "You be makin' ole Meg green, if she hears. She will not stand you fancyin' another lass."

Hewrey sat blushing when Daffyd put a hand on his arm and nodded across the room toward Wulfric and his men. Eyes full of fury, the Saxon had gripped Alma's wrist tightly, and raised his hand as if to strike her. Watching her struggle to get away, Hewrey leapt from his seat, tipping his bench and sending it crashing to the floor. He took a couple of menacing steps toward the back of the room. At the sound, Wulfric placed one hand on the table and started to stand while reaching for his dagger with the other.

"Leave her be!" Hewrey shouted.

Hewrey's companions rose and quickly restrained him.

"Your master said stay clear," said the one closest, whispering in his ear. "That one be a swordsman, a trained fighter. He will kill you, sure."

"And who will stop me?" Wulfric called out. "You?"

"Me and the lads will, my lord," said the taverner, emerging from behind the counter, cudgel in hand.

About a dozen patrons slowly rose from their seats, the occasional staff or walking stick appearing discreetly from their midst and though menacing looks covered their faces, their air was confident and relaxed. There was strength in numbers.

"I do not make it a habit to argue with my betters, my lord. I welcome your trade," the taverner continued, "but, you will not rough-handle my lass. There be no need. She are but a young girl doin' what she is told. You want to play rough with a lass, find a doxie and pay for it. There is plenty be willing."

As Hewrey fought to free himself, the Saxon lowered his hand and released the girl. A smirk, full of contempt, slowly spread across his face, but stopped at his eyes, as he raised both hands in front of him, palms out in mock surrender. Then, with a flourish of his hand, he bent in a low bow and sent Alma on her way with a slap to her bottom.

Hewrey shrugged off his captors, his gaze never leaving Wulfric.

"Sit, lad. You be no match for the likes of him. Let it be and finish your ale."

Within moments, the fracas was forgotten and everyone was back to their own companions and conversations. Alma crossed to Hewrey's table, her face white as the snow outside.

"You all right, lass?" asked Hewrey, wrapping an arm around her waist and drawing her to him.

"Aye," Alma said, rubbing her wrist and looking back across the room for a brief instant.

"What did he want with ye?"

"To know what I says to you 'bout him. He were right mad."

"Nothin' else?"

Alma thought a moment. "Not him. But one of his men says, 'I thinks we oughtta just go get him.' He said it earlier."

"Go get who?" asked the tanner.

Alma shrugged.

Hewrey jumped up and laid a coin on the table. "Drink up, lads," he said in a whisper. "I best tell Master."

FIVE

H im," said the lad in a whisper, pointing to a man sitting across the room, "the one with the leather jerkin and green tunic. He look like he have a coin or two to spare."

The lass sitting across from him looked glum.

They sat in a dark corner, far to the back of the room, safely out of the lamplight. Traveling all day, they had made it as far as the castle town of Cydweli. The tavern hosted only a moderate crowded this late in the evening. A bone-thin serving girl with no lips and frizzy brown hair bantered easily with the few customers while the taverner wiped the counter with a greasy rag.

"Yes, you do." Noah ran his hand through his greasy hair. His dark eyes grew serious as he looked furtively about the room. "Joss, we gots no money, and I got a hunger so fierce my belly be tryin' to eat my backbone."

"How about I just lift his purse?"

"Do what it takes, pet."

"Do not call me that," she said flatly. "He called me that. I hate it and you know it. Call me Jocelyn."

"Just do it!" Noah spat in reply, pinching her leg under the table and making her wince. "It be late and he may leave. The landlord be lookin' like he wants to close up."

Jocelyn could not help but worry. What if there was a repeat of the incident in Oxford several fortnights before? Forced to flee in the middle of the night, since then she liked to take a little extra time in sizing up a mark. It was less dangerous that way and yielded fewer surprises.

She stared at the man in the green tunic. He looked harmless enough—would have been almost handsome but for a rather large nose and hideously crooked teeth save one missing in the front. He was of average height, muscular with auburn hair. He carried a knife but no sword and appeared fit enough to handle himself in a fight.

Jocelyn crossed the room, taking her time, keeping her eye on the mark. Jocelyn now noticed his eyes were brown. They had looked black from across the room. Would this one be good for a drink first, or would he want to go straight to a room? It was so cold; she hoped he would not choose the alley in back of the tavern amid the smells of piss and garbage and make her lean up against a wall.

Absorbed in a bread trencher of stew, the man appeared to not notice Jocelyn approach. She walked around to stand in front of him and leaned over, both hands resting on the table.

"How is the stew?" asked Jocelyn.

The man looked up. "It is good enough," he said, his eyes narrowing when he saw her. "What do you want?"

"I thought you might like some company," Jocelyn replied, a seductive purr in her alto voice.

"And how much will this company cost me?" His mouth twisted into a wry smile. After a moment he went back to eating.

"A pot of ale," said Jocelyn, "maybe a little stew. Couple of pennies."

"And what is in it for me?" he asked, without looking up from his meal.

"What would you like?"

"I think you know what I would like," he answered. "Can you

deliver that?"

The man was no unsophisticated peasant. Glancing toward the back of the room, where Noah's prickly stare met her gaze. She pushed cautiously forward.

"Well, I usually can bring a man to satisfaction," Jocelyn said, effecting a smile.

"Could be," the man replied.

Jocelyn pulled out the bench on her side of the table and sat down, putting her at eye level with the man. She ran her hands over the wool of the dress covering her thighs.

"A pot of ale?" she asked.

The man nodded without looking at her. Jocelyn motioned to the serving girl who brought one to the table. The man continued to shovel the thick stew into his mouth and when the trencher was empty, started tearing pieces off and shoving them in around the juice. Jocelyn's mouth watered and her stomach ached. After he had consumed half the bread, the man pushed the rest across the table to Jocelyn.

"How does..." he said, looking directly at Jocelyn as he dragged his sleeve across his mouth, "...a lass like you wind up in a nothing place like Cydweli? Cannot be many men here about with a taste for someone like you. You do better in a real town like Cardiff."

"Men with a taste for a lass like me are everywhere," Jocelyn replied, without pause.

"Probably so," he replied, snickering over the top of his ale pot.

Jocelyn felt his eyes bore into her and she looked down at the table.

"You on the run?" he asked.

Jocelyn tore off a hunk from the trencher and ate it slowly, trying not to appear too rattled by his question. "No," she replied, forcing confidence into her voice. She stole a glance toward the back corner. Noah was eyeing the bread greedily. Jocelyn suppressed a smile, knowing how hungry her brother was.

"I am Jocelyn."

"Good name," the man said into his ale pot.

"It is my own. The one my ma give me." Jocelyn said. She did not appreciate being baited. The man offered no name in return.

"No matter," said the man suddenly standing, "I'll not be payin' for talkin'. Let us be about it."

"Do you have a room?" Jocelyn asked.

"No room," he snarled. "Out the back with you."

✢   ✢   ✢

NOAH WATCHED AS JOCELYN AND THE MARK WENT OUT THE back of the tavern. As soon as the door closed, he bolted from his seat, dashed to the table and grabbed the last of the bread and the half full ale pot. His dinner secured, he retreated to his corner to wait in the dark for Jocelyn to return with the money. He chewed slowly, savoring the taste of the gravy. Sometimes he thought he could be a better brother, treat Jocelyn more kindly. Jocelyn had grown strong and self-reliant. Noah worried she did not need him anymore. But he wanted money. Noah's only concern was the money. Jocelyn did all the work, took all the risks, and he demanded all the money.

"Keep nothing from me," he told her, "or I make you pay. I be holding the money for us both."

He hit her once to get his point across. She surprised him when she picked up a stout club and hit him back. He did not regain consciousness for some time.

Life for the siblings had never been good, but they were doing reasonably well for themselves in Oxford. It was over four-hundred furlongs from the village where they had grown—far enough away that their father would never have found them even if he had looked. Noah very much doubted he had.

The young man took a long drink from the pot and let it go down slowly, relishing how it felt in his throat. There had been no other option but to run away. Back then, Joss needed protection from further violation at the hands of their father. Da had turned to Joss after their mother ran off with a tranter. She was only twelve. At first, Noah had tried to intervene, and received several beatings for his trouble. da's fists were the size of a draught horse's hooves and, though he could fight, Noah was no match for his old man's brutality. The last time they fought, da said he would kill Noah the next time. After that, the lad could only stand passively by until the ordeal was over, and try to comfort Joss after.

He chewed another wad of bread. Where was Joss and the mark, and what was taking so long? Noah glanced toward the back door.

As their father's drunken rages had grew steadily more dangerous, he feared for both their safety. When he reached seventeen summers, Noah told her they were leaving. He would have run off long before, but Jocelyn was too young to go. Slipping off in the middle of the night, they eventually found themselves on the streets of Oxford with no money. Noah had tried to steal his father's pouch of coins, but the big man slept with them securely beneath him. If he had awakened, the consequences would have been dire.

Trained to a craft, Noah's body was lean and strong. The serving girl had been eyeing him since they entered.

He had learned to work the forge with his father, but smithing was dirty and too much work. Whoring was far easier. Now a tall, handsome lad of nearly twenty summers, all the lasses, young and old, appreciated Noah's dark hair and his eyes with just a hint of wickedness. Unbeknownst to Jocelyn until later, there had been a few male customers as well. He had cuckolded many a husband, and more than a few openly wanted to kill him. And while his male customers paid for his silence, many secretly wished the same.

Lately, Noah had resorted to having sex only for sport. Despite his good looks and strong body, he quickly realized Jocelyn was the real draw. Willowy in stature with a fair complexion that tended toward milky, a hint of freckles, black hair to her shoulders, and generous eyelashes, Jocelyn turned many a man's head. She was one of the most popular whores in Gropecunt Lane.

To Noah, sex was a game, one of power, revenge and money. But, he knew that Jocelyn wanted affection, and that one day there would be someone who might offer her love and take her from him. Jocelyn could make more money than Noah. That was the main reason to keep her from leaving. And, Noah feared another reason she wanted to leave was due to the night he drank far too many pots of ale and tried to have his way with her as their da had done.

"Looking after you keeps me from having a proper wife," he had said. "It be only right."

Jocelyn's reply had infuriated him. "If you be having it off with me and not being paid," she had said, "then you want no wife." It took several days for the bruise on Jocelyn's face to fade, and some punters mistakenly thought that was what they were buying.

They might still be in Oxford if not for that William. Noah fumed to himself.

The youngest son of a wealthy cloth merchant visiting Oxford on business, William Fullecoppe had taken a liking to Jocelyn. He liked her so well he had become a regular customer. He always rented a room at the inn and paid for the whole night. Noah chuckled silently to himself and spat on the floor. Now the bloody fool thought all of her customers should take her to a room, but most never did.

When he saw that Jocelyn was showing feelings for William in return, and overheard them making plans for Jocelyn to run away, Noah became alarmed and knew he must do something. He vowed to scare him off; they left instead.

Noah sat pensively chewing his bread and sipping ale, resentments building in his mind over their current plight. Even the atmosphere of a tavern could not assuage his discontent. He gulped down the rest of his pot, stuck the bread between his teeth and headed out the rear door to relieve himself in the alley and then wait for Jocelyn to finish her business. Then they could find a place to sleep. Stepping into the darkness, he ran headlong into a lad wearing rags and smelling of goose dung.

"Watch where you be going," said Noah.

The young fowler just snorted, gave him a sneer, and entered the tavern.

Noah moved down the alley and around the corner near the stables and turned to face the wall. Untying his braes, he heard footsteps. Noah pressed himself against the wall, trying to disappear. Head turned and his cheek to the wall, he peered through the gloom and saw a tall man with long yellow hair emerge from the shadows and walk toward the street.

Noah's heart jumped. Satan's cock, it was the cloth merchant! What was William doing here? It didn't matter, he would take care of this now, once and for all. He scanned the surrounding ground, spied a stout stick, and picking it up followed after the man.

Just as the merchant was about to enter the tavern Noah called out to him. "William!"

The man stopped short and turned."You!" he said, staring at Noah. "What are you doing here?"

"Leave her alone," Noah said. "You cannot have her." Noah raised his stick menacingly.

William closed the distance between them and grabbed Noah's arm. "Put that down and be quiet, you fool. Someone may hear you. Be off! My brother and father await me inside." With a mean look in his eye, William suddenly let go of Noah's arm and backed up a couple of steps. "Where is Jocelyn?" he asked.

"That be no business of yours," Noah replied.

William scanned the street and appeared relieved that no one was about.

"You mean she plies her trade here? She is with someone, now?"

"So it was lies you told her." Noah's words grew louder.

"Keep your voice down." William glanced at the tavern door then back to Noah. "You both must leave town." He could not hide his desperation.

"You told her lies, said you would take care of her."

"I will pay you handsomely," said William, pulling at his hair. The look of desperation on his face was rapidly turning to terror. "You must find her and leave, now!"

"Sad part is she believed you."

Noah took a step forward and, swinging the club, caught William with a heavy blow to the side of the head just behind his ear. The merchant crumbled to the ground. Noah could not breathe, just stood there and stared down at William, waiting for him to move. He waited several moments. He still did not move. Noah felt the panic rise within him. Had he just killed a man? He took two tentative steps closer. Slowly he knelt on one knee and laid his hand on William's chest, pressing over his heart. William's coate was too thick; Noah could not feel his heart beating. His chin quivering and his eyes welling with tears, Noah bent over and put his ear to William's chest. Nothing. Holding his breath, he pressed his ear harder to listen. His breath came rushing out just in front of a sob as he heard the faint but steady thumping of William's heart.

Noah heard the squeaking hinges of the tavern door. He jumped to his feet and ran into the alley.

"Help! Someone, help me!"

Noah peeked around the corner and saw William's brother shouting toward the door of the tavern. He turned and ran past the stables and around the back of the building.

Jocelyn and the man in the green tunic were under the jetty of the second floor room of the tavern. The mark was pulling up his hose and straightening his tunic when Noah grabbed Jocelyn, and without a word started to drag her away.

"Wait!" said Jocelyn a bit too loudly. Noah clamped a hand over her mouth. As Noah continued to pull her away, Jocelyn stuck out her hand, and the man dropped a penny into it. With the transaction complete, Noah hurried along the back alley, Jocelyn in tow, past the smell of the middens. Noah did not stop until they were several buildings away.

"We gots to leave."

"But Noah, where will we go? It is dark and cold."

Noah clenched his jaw. "I done a bad thing, Joss. We gots to leave. Now!"

SIX

Hewrey burst into the hall.

"Master!"

Tristan sat by the hearth, deep in thought, Ernulf asleep beside him on the bench. He looked up as the young man slammed the door and ran across the room.

Hewrey called out again.

"What has you in such a lather?"

"The Saxon," Hewrey panted, bending over, hands on his knees, gasping for air.

"Slow down, lad," said Tristan. He waited for the lad to settle. "Now, what of the Saxon?"

"I think he knows the babe be here," Hewrey said, still short of breath.

Tristan sat up straight, a scowl spreading across his face. "What makes you think this?"

"Alma, down at the Saint George." Hewrey straightened up and nervously started pacing about as he talked. "She were serving them and heard one of his men say something like 'we should just go get him.'"

"That could mean anything," said Tristan. "Stand still!"

"Yes, master." Hewrey stopped moving and stood in front of the knight. "But she also said they was asking questions about your wife and child.'"

The groaning hall door drew their attention. Rhonwellt and Ciaran entered the hall, stomping the snow from their shoes just inside the door.

"We saw Hewrey come running up the lane, a mangy harrier at his heels," said Rhonwellt. "They both looked as though they felt the foul breath of Satan on their necks. All is well?" The two monks crossed the floor, Rhonwellt rubbing his hands and blowing into them.

"Hewrey suspects that Wulfric knows Ernulf is here." Tristan watched as Rhonwellt cast his eyes to the floor, his face clouded with trouble.

"What has you so convinced, Hewrey?" Rhonwellt asked, raising his head to look at the youth.

Ciaran dragged a bench closer to the fire and the two monks sat down. Hewrey squatted on the floor and relayed the incident at the inn, and what Alma had overheard.

"Do ye think they seen the babe in the doorway when they was riding up the ramp?" asked Hewrey.

"Perhaps," said Tristan. "It would explain the questions about a wife and child."

"What do you think they will do?" said Ciaran.

Tristan slowly shook his head. "Wulfric is a dangerous man. It shows in his eyes."

Rhonwellt poked absently at the fire. "Do you think they would try to take him by force?"

"There are only three of them," said Tristan. "I have eight men-at-arms and a whole village under my charge, plus all the area farms. That is over one-hundred fighters."

"A moment ago, you said he was dangerous," said Ciaran.

"Wulfric is dangerous, but no fool. It would be reckless for him to try force against so many." Tristan could see the worry lines in the monk's face grow deeper and, after a slight hesitation, reached out a hand to Rhonwellt's shoulder. "Worry not. I shall let no harm befall the lad. I give you my word."

Rhonwellt peered into Tristan's face, then nodded.

"Do you think Wulfric and his men killed the members of Ernulf's caravan?" Ciaran said, nodding his head toward the boy.

"Who can know? But, they definitely knew the travelers."

"Brother Rhonwellt says Ernulf called the big one uncle," said Hewrey.

"Well, if Wulfric is Ernulf's uncle," said Ciaran, "why would he not declare it? Why pretend they were strangers?"

"That he did not admit kinship only strengthens the case we should not trust him. I believe Rhonwellt is right. Ernulf may truly be in danger."

"What can God be thinking?" said Ciaran, signing the cross, bewilderment creeping into his voice. "How can He allow someone to wish harm on a child owning only three summers?"

"You have led a sheltered life, Brother," said Tristan, "shut away from the world. The things I have seen tells me God thinks very little of us. He has a strange way, indeed, of showing His love for mankind. It is as though we are contemptible in His eyes and not worth the trouble. I know I shall never fathom it." There was more than a hint of venom in his voice. He stared across the room.

"Well, he be safe here," said Hewrey, "and feels it enough to sleep sound,"

All eyes turned to the child sleeping contentedly beside Tristan. "And we shall see that he remains so," said the knight.

"I will kill any man tries to harm him," boasted Hewrey as he mimed the act of slitting someone's throat.

"Such talk," warned Tristan, pointing a finger at his servant, "could get you killed, my lad. It would seem you are already lucky to be alive after your attempt at gallantry in the tavern. I grant you have pluck, but do not be so quick to put yourself in harm's way unless you are prepared for the outcome. You may be ready to kill. But are you as ready to die? Always consider that."

"Yes, master, I am."

Tristan searched Hewrey's face. There was passion and determination in his fiery eyes.

"I believe you are," Tristan said more gently. "Let us pray it does not come to that. It would grieve me immensely to lose you due to some recklessness I should have prevented." Tristan paused, feeling a bit embarrassed. Then, he puffed himself up. "And I thought I told you to get rid of that bloody dog!"

† † †

JOCELYN RELAXED AND LET THE MOVEMENT OF THE CART gently rock her on the seat next to the driver. Brother Simplicius clucked to the mule as the cart rattled along the muddy road. A gradual thaw, precipitated by a slight rise in temperature, had turned the track into a thick ooze that caked the cart's wheels and the mule's hooves. The hogshead of wine and the weight of the four passengers caused the cart to sink down into the mire, sludge filling the ruts left in the wake of the wheels as the cart passed. The going was slow and arduous.

Brother Simplicius, a stockily built monk of nearly fifty summers, accompanied by Brother Gregory, a young lad new to the novitiate, was delivering wine from the priory cellars at Saint Cattwg's to the Saint George and the Dragon in Ryd Lliw. He said their journey had begun long before dawn. When he stopped to pick them up, nearly ten furlongs from town, Brother Simplicius dispatched the novice to the rear of the cart to sit with Noah, while Jocelyn sat on the plank across the front with the older monk. His rough hands snapped the reins to encourage the mule to move a little faster.

"*Habetis at propinqui Ryd Lliw?*" Simplicius asked.

Jocelyn gave him a blank stare in response.

"*Me excusatum.* Please excuse such rudeness. I find I now think in Latin as I teach it at the priory. I asked if you and master Noah have kin in Ryd Lliw."

"No, Brother," replied Jocelyn. Why did people ask so many questions?

"Then, what takes you there?"

Jocelyn looked out over the landscape. She shrugged. "It is just a place we have never been."

"You are so young to be on the road alone."

"I have eighteen summers," she answered. "And I am not alone. I am with Noah."

Simplicius smiled. "Eighteen. Why is a comely lass like you not yet *nupta*, married? With babes?"

She did not answer right away. Jocelyn nervously scratched at the back of her hand then picked at her finger nail. "No one will marry me," she said, her voice quiet.

"Perhaps, someday. You are young still."

"What is this Ryd Lliw like?" she asked, changing the subject.

"Small village," replied Simplicius, "attached to the hall of Sir Tristan Cunniff. We shall bide the night with friends at Saint Tysilio's. The priest and his assistant were members of our community until a four seasons ago."

"Can we find work there?"

"Ryd Lliw is *praedium prosperum* — a prosperous estate," said Simplicius. "If you possess skills that are in demand, you may find positions." The monk paused before asking the next question. "Is there anyone looking for you?"

"You mean are we on the run?" Jocelyn asked.

Simplicius nodded.

"Why does everyone always ask that?"

The monk offered up a small chuckle. "Forgive me, young lass. I probe too much. Ascribe it to the curiosity of an old man who spends far too much time shut away from the people of the world."

An uneasy silence followed. Out of the corner of her eye, Jocelyn saw the monk turn toward her. She kept her face impassive.

After a moment, he continued. "Still, I have to ask myself. Why would these two striplings be on the road, in the dead of winter, and headed only to a place they have never been, if they were not on the run?"

"We are no striplings." Jocelyn was defiant. "Noah has twenty summers and I have told you I have eighteen."

Simplicius raised his hands in surrender, an easy grin still plastered across his face.

"Brother Simplicius tries to play the fool," said Brother Gregory from the back of the cart. "Do not be misled by it. He is crafty. He will not let up until he knows all. You might as well tell him and be done with it."

"This might be an opportune time to sit in silence, Brother Gregory," said Simplicius, his voice retaining a good-natured ease.

"You have been warned, my lass," said the novice. "Resistance is futile."

Jocelyn began to feel irritated at the monk's persistence.

"So you are either runaways, or criminals, or both," continued Simplicius. "In either case, someone is probably looking to find you. Can you not go home?"

"No," she said. A moment passed. "You ask too many questions, monk!"

"*Apologiis*, mistress." Simplicius clucked to the mule again. "*Ambulado*, Molly. Walk lively." Simplicius paused a moment. "If you were in the town yestereve after compline, you must have heard the excitement."

"Excitement?"

"A man was killed in the street in front of the tavern. I believe it was the cloth merchant's son."

Jocelyn's blood ran cold and she felt her heart skip a beat. "No brother, I had not heard." She could barely get the words out. Jocelyn turned on her seat to look in the back of the wagon. "Noah, did you know about this?"

Noah kept his eyes down and shook his head.

They passed the rest of the journey in silence, Jocelyn fretting at the news there had been a murder and fearing Noah had something to do with it. After traveling another score-and-four furlongs, Simplicius pulled the cart to a halt in front of the Saint George and the Dragon and went in. Jocelyn was climbing down from her perch behind the mule when Noah jumped from the back and came around front.

"Not much here," said Noah.

Jocelyn stepped in close. "Noah, what happened in Cydweli? What did you do?"

"You gots to set yourself up in the tavern. Go on." Noah turned and made a great show of looking the town over.

Jocelyn grabbed the sleeve of his tunic and spun him around. "What did you do to William?"

Noah yanked his arm away. "Sit in the back like you always do, out of the light."

"You said you did a bad thing. What did you mean?"

"The monk was right, the village is small but there be men who will fancy you, I wager."

Jocelyn seethed at his evasion. She grabbed his hair and jerked his head back. "What...did...you...do?" she said through gritted teeth.

"Ouch, Joss! I only hit him." Noah winced in pain. "I hit him with a club, a small one at that."

"You killed him!"

"No, Joss, I swears. He were breathing when I left him lying there." Noah paused, clawing at her hand to release her grip on his hair. "Least I thinks he were. Someone came and almost seen me. I had to flee."

"All is well here, mistress?" A young monk approached the siblings. They did not see or hear his arrival.

"Ye should be minding yer own business, monk," Noah said, the snarl in his voice matching the one on his face.

As Noah spoke, the door opened and Brother Simplicius and

Brother Gregory emerged from the tavern. "Brother Ciaran," said Simplicius. "God's peace to you."

"Good day, Brother Simplicius," said Ciaran.

"Bugger off, the lot of ye," said Noah.

"Good day, Brother," Jocelyn said to Ciaran. "I am Jocelyn, and he is my brother, Noah."

"Good day to you, mistress. I am Brother Ciaran, assistant to the priest at Saint Tysilio's."

"Seems everybody be having a bloody good day," Noah mumbled, but did not look at any of them.

Jocelyn glared at Noah, then turned her attention back to the monks.

"What brings you to Ryd Lliw, mistress?" Ciaran asked, his face turning a hot red.

"My brother and I have just arrived," she said, her voice sweet and her eyes enticing. "We seek a new life."

"You are free to travel?" asked Brother Gregory.

Jocelyn beheld Ciaran a moment longer and then turned to Brother Gregory. "Our father was a blacksmith and we were born free. We are indentured to no one."

"There are some here," said Ciaran, "who have means to retain a serving girl, and farmers who may need hands in the spring or workers in the stables."

"I be no farmer," said Noah.

"I did not mean..."

Jocelyn cut Ciaran off. "Pay no heed to Noah. He is ill-tempered most of the time. We will be happy for any work offered. Though he is right when he says he is no farmer."

"Did you acquire smithing skills from your father?" Simplicius asked.

Noah did not answer.

"Sir Tristan's smith may have need of help," said Ciaran. "There is also a town forge." He turned to Jocelyn. "Do you fare well with children, mistress?"

"I cared some for our younger brother after our mother died, before he went to live with our aunt."

Ciaran looked pleased. "I have an idea," he said. "Meanwhile, will you all please sup with Brother Rhonwellt and me? It will be the simple fare of monks. Lentils with bread and ale."

"No meat?" asked Noah.

"Not today, master Noah. But you are welcome, nonetheless. We shall partake right after Vespers. I trust you will be there, as well?"

"C-church?" Noah stammered.

"We will," said Jocelyn quickly cutting off any further objection from Noah. Her brother just scowled.

"We shall come as soon as we have concluded business with the landlord," said Simplicius. "I look forward to seeing Brother Rhonwellt. It has been many months. Come, Brother Gregory." He bowed and turned to enter the tavern, the young novice right behind him. Brother Ciaran headed toward the hall.

"What you think you be doing, you little bitch?" Noah growled when the monks were out of earshot. "I are no smith and no farmer. I eat meat, and I go to no church!"

"Well, tonight you will pray and eat lentils and be glad for it."

"Since when do you give the orders?"

"Since your greed addles your brain and you are likely to be accused of murder," said Jocelyn, trying to keep her voice low. She grabbed Noah's sleeve and pulled him away from the tavern door. "A whore in a small village like this will stick out like rotten meat at a banquet. All them Fullecoppes will have to do when they get here, and they will surely come, is ask about any new wenches in town. Well, they will not find one. Not this time."

"But church!" he said through clenched teeth. "You think a whore in church will go unnoticed?"

"No one but you and God will know that," Jocelyn spat. "Besides, you used to like church." Her tone had become cajoling.

"Yeah, until I learned their sinful ways," sneered Noah, "felt their roaming hands all over me and found out monks pays to roll with the likes of you when no one be looking. Then pretending to be all holy like and calling it a sin later."

"They are just men, brother mine, with the same needs as all men. And their money spends as well as any."

"I go to no church and they be no smithing," said Noah.

"You will do what needs doing, pet." There was menace in Jocelyn's voice as she used Noah's own words against him. "I nearly killed you once. Do not forget that, brother."

Noah clenched his fist in front of her face. She held his gaze as the muscles in his jaw worked with rage. They stood toe to toe in silence for a moment and then Noah spun and headed for the door of the tavern.

"I need a drink."

"You shall have to hustle it yourself. We have no money for ale."

SEVEN

For once, Rhonwellt did not have to struggle to keep up with Ciaran's hurried pace. He walked with determination and purpose as they ascended the rise to the hall.

"Are you sure you did not mention Ernulf by name when you spoke to this lass?" Rhonwellt asked, his tenor brimming with anxiety.

"No, Brother, I did not," said Ciaran.

Rhonwellt was not reassured. "What exactly did you say?"

The younger monk stopped, pulling his hands from deep in his sleeves and spreading them in front of him. "I merely asked if she was good with children," Ciaran said.

After taking a couple of steps, Rhonwellt stopped and turned to face him, chewing the inside of his cheek and staring at his assistant. "I am not so sure it is a good idea," he said.

They resumed walking.

"But, why, Brother? There is really no one to care for him. Sir Tristan has his estate to run and he needs Hewrey at his side. You and I are tending the church and visiting the sick. Yet someone must always stay with Ernulf because he cannot be seen outside the hall until we are sure he is safe. A nurse is the perfect solution."

"The lass is unknown to us." Rhonwellt stopped again. "How do you know we can trust her?"

"It is in her eyes..." he said wistfully. Suddenly, the look on Ciaran's face said he wished he could retrieve the words as soon as he said them. His face grew red. He plunged his arms back into the depths of his sleeves and lowered his gaze.

Eyes squeezed shut, Rhonwellt began walking again. It had begun. Ciaran's manhood was stalking him. Aloud, he said, "Being beautiful does not make a lass trustworthy." Still facing ahead, he opened his eyes and trained them to the right to glimpse Ciaran.

"I did not mean that, exactly," Ciaran replied.

"What did you mean, Brother?" Rhonwellt asked, keeping his voice even so as not to betray his concern.

"I do not know." Ciaran cradled his face in his hands, then slid them up and over the top of his head. "The words were on my lips before I knew my mind had formed them."

"Ah," replied Rhonwellt, more a breath than a word.

The monks continued to the hall without speaking further. They did not wait for Hewrey to answer their knock. Rhonwellt was reaching for the latch to enter when a mysterious dog appeared from nowhere and sat down beside them. A typical harrier, it was small, mostly white, with a brown face, rump, and tail. A saddle of black ran over its back. When Hewrey opened the door, Ernulf trotted over to greet them and the dog darted through the open door, jumping on the child, toppling his small frame to the floor.

"Rinc!" Ernulf squealed with delight, throwing his arms about the dog's neck. Rinc licked his face in return.

"Bloody hell," said Tristan who sat by the fire, cup in hand, focused on the flames.

"And how is our master Ernulf today?" Ciaran asked the child. "I see you have found a friend."

Ciaran reached out to pick Ernulf up when the dog growled at the young monk.

"Na!" Ernulf commanded the animal. "Rinc, eistedd..."

Rinc slowly sat, all the while keeping a keen eye on the strangers. Ernulf turned to Ciaran and held up his arms. The monk bent over and lifted him.

"You know this fellow?" Ciaran asked, looking toward the harrier.

Ernulf nodded, his face beaming, and laid his head on Ciaran's shoulder.

"The child may be happy now," said Tristan, elbows on his knees, sullenly twirling his cup back and forth in his hands, "but he spent much of the morning crying for his mother."

Ciaran sat down planting Ernulf on his lap. The dog moved over to sit on the floor beside the bench.

"What is it Rhonwellt?" Tristan asked, without looking up. "What worries you?"

The monk slumped down onto a bench blowing his breath out from puffed cheeks. "How can you know I am worried? I have said nothing."

"That is just it," said Tristan. "You entered the hall, crossed the room and sat down without uttering a word. Something weighs on you." Flames danced in the knight's dark eyes as he continued to stare at the fire.

"You think me a chatterbox?" Rhonwellt asked, feeling a bit insulted.

"No, but you grow exceedingly quiet when unsettled."

Rhonwellt sighed. "You begin to know me well," he said, relaxing a little, his hands on his knees.

"It was always thus." Tristan turned to face the monk. "So, what is it?"

Hewrey handed them cups of warm cider. Accepting his, Rhonwellt took a sip. "Ciaran has made a suggestion that, on the face of it seems reasonable, yet I am in doubt."

"What is your idea, Brother?" Tristan asked. He motioned for Hewrey to put more wood on the fire.

"A nurse," Ciaran said, feeding cider to the boy from his cup. "For Ernulf."

Tristan did not answer right away. Then he asked, "And why does this trouble you, Rhonwellt?"

"It means we must take others into our confidence. Someone else must know the lad is here."

"I think that be happenin' already," said Hewrey.

"Is happening already," said Tristan.

"Yes, Master. Is happening. Sorry."

"I think Hewrey is probably right," said Ciaran, putting his cup down and settling Ernulf on the bench beside him, arm around his shoulder. "And I can see you have not the patience for dealing with a child."

"I did not ask for your opinion on that, Brother," replied Tristan.

"You did not."

The knight glanced at him. "I am your liege and yet I allow you to speak to me thus."

"Because you know I am right, My Liege," replied Ciaran.

Rhonwellt had to smile at Ciaran's undaunted spirit. Was there a bit of a taunt in his emphasis on the honorific?

"Probably," replied the knight, cracking a tiny smile. He drained his cup and held it out for Hewrey to refill. "Who would perform these duties? Have you someone in mind?"

"There is a young couple," said Ciaran, "a brother and sister. They are new to the village, and are in need of work and lodgings."

"Who are they?" pressed Tristan. "Whence do they hail?"

"Their names are Jocelyn and Noah. Beyond that, I do not know...yet."

"Then how do you know she is trustworthy?"

"He says it is in her eyes," said Rhonwellt, pursing his lips, a twinkle in his eye.

Hewrey snorted with laughter and slapped his knee. Watching Hewrey, Ernulf did the same.

"A glowing recommendation," said Tristan, grinning, "especially from a monk." Everyone but Ciaran chuckled as he went red in the face. Rhonwellt managed a thin smile. Tristan asked, "Has she experience with children?"

"She has," said Ciaran, his irritation at being the target of teasing evident. "She cared for a younger brother."

"What of this brother?" asked Tristan. "What can he do? Could he hire out to a farmer?"

"Other than being somewhat ill-tempered, Noah looks strong. Jocelyn has him firmly in hand but says he has little knowledge of farming. Though she says he has some training at a forge."

"She says, she says," said Tristan. "Has this Noah no tongue to speak for himself?"

Ciaran did not reply but went on. "If he is at the forge and Jocelyn were at the hall, it would be easier to keep an eye on them." Had Rhonwellt heard something in Ciaran's voice when he spoke her name?

"You want me to employ them and yet you say we must keep an eye on them." Tristan's face was stern.

"Only until we know them to be trustworthy," said Ciaran. To Rhonwellt, the novice's defense was going badly.

"Did you not say that you found that in her eyes, already?" teased Tristan, his face impassive.

"With every word you dig the hole deeper, Brother Ciaran," said Rhonwellt. "You do not instill confidence. Cease now, whilst you are ahead."

Ciaran sat with a pleading look.

"Very well. Bring them to me and I will speak with them," said Tristan. "I shall decide then."

"They sup with us at the cottage this night," said Ciaran, breaking into a grin.

"They will?" said Rhonwellt, surprised.

"I shall bring them up after. Brother Simplicius and his new novice will join us."

"Simplicius is in Ryd Lliw?" said Rhonwellt, brows raised. "Your surprises have no bounds."

"They delivered wine from Saint Cattwg's to the tavern today. They will join us for Vespers, sup with us and stay the night."

"You seem to have it all arranged," said Rhonwellt.

"After your meal, then." Tristan drained his cup again.

"Thank you, My Liege." Ciaran said, still grinning.

Rhonwellt feared someday Ciaran would go too far, Tristan would object to such liberty and it would be no jest.

✝   ✝   ✝

CIARAN DRAGGED THE RAKE ACROSS THE FLOOR, GATHERING THE soiled rushes into a pile to be discarded. The recent thaw had turned all the roads and paths to mud, and when the faithful of the parish had arrived for morning mass, they had deposited large quantities of slime on the floor rushes, fouling them and requiring their removal.

The young monk rested his cheek on his hands atop the rake handle, his mind far from his task. Ciaran had fought to conceal his pleasure, but his pulse quickened at the thought of the willowy lass abiding close to him at the hall. He had only just met her, and yet visions of Jocelyn kept creeping into his thoughts with a disturbing regularity.

Needing solitude to sort these new feelings out, and under the pretext of making the necessary preparations for Vespers, he had excused himself from his friends and walked down the hill to the church. Entering through the side door, he went immediately to the steps leading up to the altar and knelt in front of it. He signed the cross, closed his eyes and began earnestly praying for forgiveness. A few words into his plea, he stopped.

Forgiveness for what? What had he done?

He searched his mind for evidence of some sin, but found none.

Not even the sin of thought could apply here. He had only envisioned Jocelyn's face.

Where was the sin in that?

A cold chill ran the length of Ciaran's spine, followed by a quick intake of breath as he recalled the time he had helped Brother Rhonwellt prepare Brother Mark's body for burial. That was surely a sin. Never having seen an unclothed body before, the sight of the captivating monk, naked on the table in front of him, within reach, had compelled him. He had reached out his hand, let it hover over the flesh and almost touched it. He remembered being filled with an expectant thrill. What would it feel like? He had no idea what should have come after the touch. Ciaran knew nothing of carnal acts, would not even know how to commit one. He only knew they existed since the church constantly warned against them. In an instant, the expectant thrill was gone, replaced with crippling guilt, shame that threatened to crush him. Yes, that was clearly a sin, and he had spent the remainder of the night, prostrated on the chancel floor in self-induced penance, begging forgiveness. He had never felt such terror as he had then and did not understand why.

Ciaran was drowning in confusion. Did he entreat the wrong thing? For what should he pray? He did not know why his mind was so distracted. Understanding? Yes, he should pray for understanding. But he found the effort to be of little use, for the vision of the lass's face kept intruding into his petition. If he could not achieve a result with prayer, then work was the answer. *Ora et labora*. It was every monk's direction. With a sigh, he crossed himself, then rose and went to replenish the spent candles in the chapel, and clear the floor rushes — routine tasks to occupy his mind and supersede his bewildering thoughts.

With a jerk of his body, Ciaran realized he had been gathering wool. With new determination, he resumed his chores. Piling the rushes, he picked them up and carried them out the side door, laying them on the pile to rot with the rest. He then went to the near-by shed, retrieved an armful of fresh reeds and took them in to distribute them across the floor.

He had nearly finished when he heard the bell toll Vespers.

Ciaran was busy lighting the candles on the altar when the front door opened. He turned to see Brother Rhonwellt enter followed by the two visiting monks from Saint Cattwg's, the siblings and a handful of villagers. He quickly turned his back to the rest of the chapel, not daring to look behind him, lest the sight of her distract him again. Simplicius and Gregory took their places at the front, while Jocelyn and Noah stood with the parishioners in the center of the room. The four monks knelt, sketched the sign of the cross, rose, and began to sing.

"*Deus, in adiutorium meum intende. Domine, ad adiuvandum me festina. Gloria Patri, et Filio, et Spiritu Sancto. Sicut erat in principio, et nunc et semper, et in saecula saeculorum. Amen. Alleluia.*"

The Latin invocation rang clear and bright, steam from the breaths of the monks visible in the chilled air, the small brazier in the corner having cooled since it was last used for Mass. Ciaran sang especially loud and forceful, the extra effort needed to keep his focus on his prayers. Suddenly, he noticed Rhonwellt's penetrating gaze boring into him from the side. Ciaran lowered his volume a little, closed his eyes and forged on. But this unusual zeal still found him racing a word or two ahead of the others. Rhonwellt discreetly brought his hand up and touched Ciaran's elbow, causing him to flinch and cease his chant. When he began to sing again, the young monk slowed his tempo to match the others.

With a shriek from the protesting iron hinges, the large front door groaned open, causing all heads to turn toward the sound and the monks to briefly falter in their song. Wulfric was the first to enter, hand on the hilt of his sword. Osgar and Leo followed close on his heel, the three judiciously crossing themselves but not bothering to kneel. Ciaran scowled at the sight of the swords strapped to their waists. He did not need to look to see the displeasure that surely would be on Brother Rhonwellt's face. Brother Rhonwellt did not permit weapons inside Saint Tysilio's. Apparently, the Saxon and his men were unaware of this decree.

Wulfric's eyes scanned the room, gazing briefly at each face in attendance. Leaning over, he whispered something to his henchmen, and again signing the cross, the three swept from the room with the same abruptness with which they had entered. While the congregants returned their attentions to the front of the chapel, Ciaran noticed Rhonwellt gaze intently after the three men as they exited, slamming the door.

✞   ✞   ✞

WULFRIC AND HIS MEN TROOPED AWAY FROM THE CHURCH, back toward the inn. The Saxon's mind was preoccupied with puzzles: the caravan, the knight, and the child. In the darkness of early evening, the light from a nearly full moon reflected in his eyes, giving him an otherworldly appearance, and made the puddles in the lane appear frozen. His attention was so engrossed with finding answers, he splashed into the middle of one only to find himself ankle deep in water.

"Shit!" he cursed as he felt the icy liquid seep through the seams in his well-worn boots, soaking his feet. Pulling them from the water, he stomped on the solid ground at the edge of the pool, and stood staring down at his wet boots. "Bloody Cunniff nor his servant attend prayers in the knight's own church."

"May not be religious," replied Osgar, veering to the side to escape the water. The height of his lanky frame proved a disadvantage. His feet flew from under him and he landed unceremoniously in the ooze. "Bloody Christ!" he snarled. Leo snorted with laughter.

"Everyone in the land is religious, you halfwit," said Wulfric in disgust, trying to ignore Leo. "At least they are supposed to be."

"Not me, master," said Leo, reaching out a hand to help Osgar up.

"Aye, and one day you shall burn for it." Wulfric grew still and pondered a moment. "Someone always stays at the hall. He is hiding something. I know it."

"You means the bairn?" Osgar asked as he turned to and fro wiping mud from his clothes.

"Yes, Ernulf is there, we know he is," said Wulfric stepping carefully now to avoid another large puddle.

"We seen him," said Leo, still chuckling.

"But why does he keep him hidden? And what else is he hiding?" Wulfric muttered, mostly to himself. "And where are the women?"

The three men turned and entered the inn. Stomping the mud and water from his boots, Wulfric held up three fingers to Alma as they plowed through the patrons to a table in the back. Their rough passage was met with much grumbling, however no one openly challenged them.

"No one has seen the child outside the hall," the Saxon continued. "No one we have talked to in the town seems to know he is there. Why? What is Cunniff's purpose in hiding him?"

"Why not just go take him, master?" said Osgar.

"Devil's plums, man!" Wulfric snarled, his voice a low growl. He glared at his man. "This is Cunniff's land. Hell's gates, it is his town. They outnumber us twenty-to-one before we ever draw sword. One word from him and we hang before sunset."

Looking toward the bar, Wulfric thumped the table and spat on the floor. "Where is that wench with my drink?" After wriggling her way through the crowded room, Alma soon appeared with three pots of ale. Osgar took a big gulp from his. Wulfric just stared into his cup.

"Perhaps," said Osgar, "if we had more men we could take him. Make the knight think twice..."

"Where would we gets more men?" said Leo, slugging down some ale. "How about Swansea? I wager we could get plenty men there."

"Not big enough," said Osgar. "But Cardiff could be. What you think of that plan, master?"

"Be quiet, both of you. Leave the planning to someone with a brain."

"Yes, master."

"Besides, it is not our job to take the lad. Only to find him. Once we have done that we are to return to Cydweli and tell Master Selwyn. He will decide what to do."

EIGHT

Under a cold, gray sky the following midday, Rhonwellt found himself seated next to Brother Simplicius on the wine cart headed to Cydweli. Brother Gregory lay napping in the box, with Rhonwellt's horse, Epona, tied behind. A canopy fashioned from oil-soaked hemp cloth stretched over a frame of bent branches protected them from the constant drizzle. Rhonwellt pulled his cloak tighter about him. Still, the damp had settled into his bones and chilled him through. Though constant motion probably kept the animals warm, both walked with their heads down and their ears out to the sides to keep the water out.

The wet, blustery weather matched the monk's mood. He had tried to find excuses to remain at Ryd Lliw, saying there would be no one to say mass, then tried putting it down to other matters needing his attention. The real reason, the dread in his heart, he kept buried.

The previous evening had started pleasantly enough. After a humble supper, Ciaran took Jocelyn and Noah to the hall for Tristan's consideration, while Rhonwellt remained behind to catch up on news from the priory brought by the visiting brothers. A small blaze burned in the hearth and reflections from a half-dozen candles danced lively on the walls lending a mellow atmosphere to the cottage. Rhonwellt had burned extra candles in honor of his guests, an extravagance seldom known while at Saint Cattwg's. Honoring God with anything other than meager simplicity was a concept he was slow to embrace. Tristan was generous, and the knight's insistence they live comfortably was winning Rhonwellt over. While life at Ryd Lliw was not opulent, neither was it spartan.

Simplicius had been gentle but blunt. "There is no good news to report, Brother," the monk said. "It is the reason Prior Alwyn sent me with the wine, instead of another." He took a deep breath and exhaled with a sigh. "It grieves me to say that Brother Anselm is dying."

Stunned, Rhonwellt stared openly, unable to speak for a few moments. His throat felt constricted and he struggled to swallow. "It cannot be his time," he said at last. "It is far too soon."

"Anselm has seventy-three summers." Simplicius reached out and laid a hand on Rhonwellt's arm. "The Almighty has been exceedingly generous in the seasons granted him."

"Time goes so quickly," said Rhonwellt. "It was the Feast of Saint John the Beloved one summer ago when I last saw him.."

"He is comfortable. Still, he grows weaker every day," said Brother Gregory. "Though compassionate, Brother Remigius knows there is nothing further he can do."

Again, Rhonwellt grew quiet. Simplicius withdrew his hand and went on. "If you would bid him Godspeed, Brother, you must visit soon."

The cart rolled over a large stone in the road, jolting Rhonwellt on his perch in the front. He grabbed the edge of the seat to keep from being thrust off into the muddy road.

"*Lacrimæ Mariae*," mumbled Simplicius.

Since leaving the priory, Rhonwellt had not allowed himself to think much about his old friend. Leaving him behind had been too painful. He missed Prior Alwyn and some of the other Brothers, but the absence of Anselm overwhelmed him completely. It had been necessary for Rhonwellt to put the old healer from his mind. Now, he was wracked with guilt.

Ciaran was the one to persuade him. "You must go to him without delay!" he had said. "You will surely have regrets if you do not." Ciaran was right. Rhonwellt's grief was immense. He would find no joy in visiting his old friend only to confront his imminent death. Yet, he knew he would come to rue his decision were he to forgo the trip.

Rhonwellt stared impassively at the scenery. Warming weather had caused the snow to melt, still the fields lay empty, the ground too wet to plow. Shy as a stripling's beard, sprigs of fresh grass peeked cautiously through winter's mat, turning the rolling pastures green. Clusters of sodden sheep grazed quietly, oblivious to the rain. A half-dozen crows squawking on a bare tree limb reminded Rhonwellt of a row of bickering monks, each chastising another over some perceived transgression.

How fickle life could be, how unpredictable even in the strictly governed routine of a cloister. Thirty years ago, Rhonwellt had been the contented son of a farmer and entangled in a love affair with Tristan. For the affront to his position, Tristan's father had Rhonwellt savagely beaten and left by a river to die. He never expected to see Tristan again.

Brother Anselm had pulled him to safety, nursed him for three days where he lay until he was well enough to travel, then took him to Saint Cattwg's to heal. There, Rhonwellt remained. Uncertain why God had redeemed him, he felt compelled to commit to the religious life and take his vows.

Anselm had been as a father to Rhonwellt. His bond with the older monk had become sacred and complete. Anselm had personally tutored him to improve his reading and taught him Latin, saving a lad of fifteen summers the embarrassment of being taught with much younger school-aged boys. How patient Anselm had been. Rhonwellt struggled to be obedient, failing more often than he succeeded. Anselm passed on all he knew of medicine to the young monk, yet lovingly understood when Rhonwellt said his calling was with brush and pen instead.

While Rhonwellt had grown up and into middle age, Anselm had grown old and was now ready to depart this life for the next. At this point in his life, Rhonwelllt keenly felt the impact of any death and though he had seen little of his old friend since leaving the priory, he knew where to find him should he need him. Rhonwellt fought back tears. He could not fathom a world without Anselm.

"You are *cogitabundus*, Brother," said Simplicius.

Rhonwellt was only vaguely aware that Simplicius had spoken. "Pensive?" he mumbled, wiping his eyes with the back of his hand.

Simplicius nodded. "What has you so *in vexationem*?" he asked.

Rhonwellt kept his own counsel and did not answer right away, but knew Simplicius would press the matter.

"There is much on my mind," he said at last.

"I know that you are *maximi afflicti* over Brother Anselm." Simplicius' tone was sympathetic.

Rhonwellt sighed and looked at the older monk, slowly inclining his head in agreement.

"Is that all?" Simplicius asked.

"For the most part," replied Rhonwellt, looking away toward the rolling hills. Afraid he might become overwhelmed with the emotions surging within him, he fought for control, clenching his hands and endeavoring to breathe evenly.

"But, there is something else."

"Sometimes..." Rhonwellt paused, uncertain whether he should go on. He turned back to look again at Simplicius whose raised eyebrows asked—what?

Rhonwellt was ill at ease speaking of his life with Tristan to others though the affection between them was known openly among the brethren at the priory. He even found it hard to confide in Ciaran on these matters despite the fact he was closer to the young monk than anyone.

"Sometimes, Sir Tristan can be so unreasonable."

"He certainly is *difficillima*, your knight," Simplicius replied, followed by a tiny chuckle.

Rhonwellt could feel his face grow hot and he was sure he must look crimson as he offered a faint, self-conscious smile. "He is moody." Rhonwellt concentrated on his hands folded in his lap. "A sennight is not such a very long time, but he seemed so against me going." He absently picked at some flecks of mud thrown up onto his robe by the horse's hooves. "He reminded me of my responsibility to my parish."

"Brother Ciaran should be able to lead *de officiis* while you are gone."

At this moment, Rhonwellt found Brother Simplicius' constant use of Latin irritating, but he knew it would be of little use to mention it.

"I said I would be back by compline for the Feast of Saint Bartholomew and could conduct mass the next morning. He nearly forbade me go. I should have been glad his reluctance matched my own and seized the chance to stay. But, of course, I could not."

"Perhaps he just wanted you *prope*, near at hand," said Simplicius, his eyes full of mischief.

"You speak as if you almost approve of...us." The last word was barely audible.

"I leave it to God to judge," said Simplicius, "at least for the most part. The church maintains that it is *peccatum est contra naturam.* Mostly, I believe that. But it is nearly universal in practice. That says something." He shrugged his shoulders.

Rhonwellt grew uneasy with the direction the discussion had taken, yet could not stop it. He had initiated it.

Brother Simplicius clucked for the horse to move along. After a moment, the older monk continued. "But I also know you to be a man of abiding integrity. I am confident you would not enter into such an arrangement lightly, Brother. For you it would be no simple case of *opprimo affectum.* I trust it is much more than that for you to consider abandoning your vows."

"Thirty summers ago," said Rhonwellt, his voice hesitant, "I could have blamed it on the ardor of lusty youth. Those fires burned out in me long ago."

"And, now *alterius flamma* burns within you."

Rhonwellt gave a simple nod. "It has been so long since I have felt anything like this, I find myself at a loss for knowing how to proceed."

"Then it would appear you have not," there was a short pause, "*processerant.*"

"No, not yet."

"I am gratified to hear it. For, it tells me it truly is a *materia cordis* and not just a *materia carnis*. And, I know when you do, it will be a move well considered."

Rhonwellt was struck by Simplicius's use of when and not if. He seemed more certain than Rhonwellt.

The older monk turned his attention to the horse and clucked again. "*Ambulado. Ambulado*, old girl."

Rhonwellt returned to the passing scenery, trying to sort through his conflicting feelings. Lifeless looking trees stood alone or in clusters behind low stone walls or wattle fences that lined the road. Nothing moved around the cottages they passed, save the smoke from hearth fires that laced its way up through the thatched roofs. They met no other travelers on the track. The only sound was the shush of the breeze.

The conversation with Brother Simplicius had been unnerving, but Rhonwellt marveled at this brother's ability to bring a person's thoughts to the fore. Having the opportunity to give voice to musings that usually only wandered around inside his head was gratifying. It sharpened the reality of this whole situation. Though some residual resentment lingered in his mind toward Tristan, Rhonwellt knew it would be short-lived. He could never sustain feelings of anger at him for long. Most often they were quickly supplanted with a confusing sense of warmth and profound joy. But Tristan's ever-changing moods meant they were often at odds for brief periods. Though hard to understand, he was getting used to them.

Suddenly, a wave of sadness washed over him as he recalled the reason for his journey—to bid Godspeed to a beloved friend. That emotion was clear. The manner of love he felt for Brother Anselm, or Brother Ciaran, he understood well. It was simple and uncomplicated. However, everything he felt for Tristan was, at its simplest, labyrinthine. Why did it feel so impossible when, for others, it appeared so easy?

✝ ✝ ✝

HEWREY WATCHED FROM THE BUTTERY AS JOCELYN TALKED softly to Ernulf, holding him on her lap in front of the fire. They had spent some time at hide-and-seek, Ernulf squeezing behind the wall hangings to hide while Jocelyn made a great show of looking for him. Hewrey laughed when the child's tiny feet, visible under the edge of the hanging, repeatedly gave him away. That, and the fact he always hid in the same place. Jocelyn would pretend not to find him and would have to beg him to reveal himself. Now, sitting quietly, the child laid his head on her breast. After a moment, he sat up, looked at her strangely, then rested his head there again. Whispering something in his ear which caused him to giggle, she smiled a distant smile then rested her chin on the top of his head.

From his first glance at Jocelyn, Hewrey schemed to get close to her, to win her over and bed her. He fantasized cornering her in the buttery, or in the hay down at the barn. He dreamed of fondling her breasts, which must be tiny for they hardly showed beneath her smock. Though he preferred a lass with a bit more meat to the bone, Jocelyn was pretty enough. He especially liked that she kept herself clean and did not smell, except for the lavender she put in her hair. He had gotten close enough to smell that.

He might even take a bath if he knew it would help. Bathing was taking a bit of getting used to, but his master insisted he do it regularly, at least once a week—every week. It was a custom Tristan had brought back from Persia. Even Brother Rhonwellt and Brother

Ciaran did it, and everyone knew monks never bathed. Still, he feared he would never get used to washing three times a week like Tristan. There were limits to his adventurousness. Though still unsure whether bathing could lead to terrible disease, he would not argue from fear of losing his position.

How different his life had become since entering into service to his master. He had swelled with pride when Jocelyn exclaimed she had never been in such a fine house, for in truth, neither had he. The floors were clean and unsoiled by manure since they did not have to share the space with livestock. They burned an abundance of wood harvested from Tristan's well-maintained copses so there was nearly always a fire to warm them. Hewrey ate more venison, mutton, and eel in one month than he normally ate in three seasons, and the wine and ale were the best Hewrey ever tasted. Though he slept on the floor, he had a soft palliasse with no fleas that he could drag near the fire, and enough brychans to be warm on the coldest of nights. Master had commissioned a scene depicting St. George slaying the dragon painted onto a very large wall cloth that hung opposite the solar that enthralled him. The startling realism filled his head with fantasies of heroism as a brave knight in service to the King like his master.

"Hewrey, fetch my dry cloak and pack some food."

The voice startled him. Tristan had burst suddenly into the hall and gone immediately up the stairs to the solar, shouting orders over his shoulder.

"What is it, Master? What be happenin'?" Hewrey noticed his mistake at once, but too preoccupied, his master did not correct him. Hewrey could hear Tristan's boots as he stomped around the upstairs room, first to one side, then the other, and back again. Soon the knight came down wearing his spurs and carrying his mail and helm.

"Help me into this," Tristan said, holding out the metal shirt.

Hewrey breathed roughly as he took the mail shirt and stood on a bench, "It be heavy. Is heavy." The knight quickly peeled off his surcoat and stood there in his braies, undershirt and padded doublet.

"A band of men tried to sell horses to the smith in Cross Hands—

horses beyond their means to own. The smith had heard of the attack on the caravan and became suspicious." Tristan held his arms aloft, while Hewrey hefted the heavy metal shirt over his master's head. Tristan fit his arms into the sleeves, and Hewrey let the shirt fall. "An attempt was made to take them into custody but they fled, leaving the stolen horses behind. A posse of townsmen have them cornered on a tor about twenty furlongs from there."

Hewrey then helped him back into his surcoat. "You will not wear your breastplate, master?"

"I shall be fine without it. These are brigands and thieves, not trained knights. They are likely the ones who attacked Ernulf's caravan. They will hang for their offense." Tristan fastened his sword belt and dagger around his waist.

"Let me grab my kit," said Hewrey. "Be just a shake."

"No," replied Tristan.

Hewrey felt crestfallen. "But, master. My place be...is...with you."

"Not this time, lad. With Rhonwellt gone, I shall need you to stay and keep the child and his nurse safe. It is a big responsibility. Can I rely on you?"

Hewrey's eyes grew wide with disbelief. "Me, Master? Are you sure?"

With this new role, Hewrey's dreams of heroism appeared to be much closer to reality though, in truth, the prospect was daunting and Hewrey wondered if he was up to the task.

As if his master had read his mind, he felt a reassuring hand land on his shoulder. "Remember," Tristan said, "the most gallant of men are always a little afraid. It is going beyond the fear that makes them brave. You are nearly a man, Hewrey. It is time to behave as one."

Hewrey looked up and returned his master's gaze, and with finality, nodded agreement.

"Good lad. Bar the door while I am gone and admit no one you do not know. Be especially on the lookout for that Saxon."

"The Saxon be gone, Master. I were down at the gate at daybreak and I seen him ride out with his lads."

Tristan nodded. "That may not be as good as it sounds." He paused, scratching his chin, a look of worry on his face. "In any event, I hope to be back on the morrow." He turned to Jocelyn. "Mistress, you and Ernulf are to obey Hewrey and not leave the hall until I return."

Before she could respond, Tristan spun about and strode quickly across the room.

Hewrey heard him mumble as he went out the door, "I bloody knew I should not have let Rhonwellt go."

NINE

Accompanied by his five men-at-arms and six villagers, Tristan rode out of Ryd Lliw in a drizzle and headed Northwest. At the hamlet of Pontarddulais, he recruited three Welsh bowmen and two swordsmen. A half-dozen fighters, riding plow horses and drag mules, joined them from the pit at Upper Tumble, grateful for a break from scraping coal. Late in the day, with darkness settling in, the company arrived at Cross Hands, a poor village near Nant Glas, a small tributary of Afon Gwili. Barely a town at all, Cross Hands was a motley collection of huts and cottages grown up around the remnants of a military encampment left from the Norman occupation and abandoned some thirty-five summers ago.

With only a shabby alehouse and no proper tavern or inn, the men had bed down in a small barn behind the smith's shop, heat from their horses providing some small degree of warmth against the cold. Offered a place at the alehouse, Tristan opted to stay with the men— the straw in the barn appeared cleaner. After a meal of coarse bread and a tasteless porridge washed down with barely palatable ale, Tristan lay down in the straw and listened to the voices of the men in his company telling tall tales and bawdy jokes about tavern wenches or errant monks and nuns, before settling down for the night. With his eyes closed, he could imagine clear desert skies brimming with stars overhead and sand beneath him, camping with his troops outside Acra or Jerusalem. It had been a long time and being on the move again, with a band of men under his command, felt gratifying. In a small way, he found he had missed it.

In his later years, just before leaving the Holy Land, scenes like this had been his favorite part of soldiering. Gone was the thrill and anticipation of impending battle. The smell of blood covering him so thick the sand stuck to him no longer held any allure. Over a score of summers had left him sick of wholesale slaughter in the name of two gods who vied for power over every grain of sand. It was the camaraderie of his fellow soldiers, the sounds and smells of the desert and the encampments he relished. Contentment from being in the open, away from the fetid towns and cities, spending nights with Amjhad, his Persian servant and lover, every bit as magnificent and glorious as the name signified, came to mean the most to him. But, the honor and glory of war quickly faded watching the life ebb from Amjhad's eyes as he lay mortally wounded in Tristan's arms. Soon after that, he took his leave and started the wanderings that eventually brought him home. Yet tonight he felt the familiar buzzing in his stomach that always heralded a skirmish. The familiar feeling of intoxication disturbed him.

Tristan arose the next morning feeling refreshed, having slept far better than he anticipated. Breaking their fast with more porridge, bread and ale, the men set out for Lletem Tor, about eight furlongs from town. The rain had stopped, and a muted sun shone between a few lazily moving clouds hung in a blue sky. The ground, however, was still a mire and the going slow until they reached the rockier ground spread out around the base of the outcrop.

The sheer face of Lletem Tor rose to the height of about eighteen men. The back was a rugged slope dotted with clusters of boulders, scattered trees, and shrubs and appeared to be the only route of escape.

"Who can tell me about this place?" Tristan asked the men who had spent the night on watch in a cleft at the foot of a rock wall at the bottom of the slope.

"I can, my lord," said a short, wiry villein in his thirties with a lazy eye, high forehead and no teeth. "I pulled me stray sheep out of there as a lad. I knows it good."

"Who are you, good fellow?"

"They calls me Henry, my lord. I were named after the King, God rest him." The man quickly signed the cross.

Tristan emitted a low chuckle. "God rest him, indeed, Henry. Tell me the lay of this place."

"Pretty much what you sees, my lord, but for one thing. There be a basin up the face there, right behind that wide cluster of rocks. Not deep, but good shelter. No seeing it from here, but it be there."

"Why did you not just go up and get them?" asked Tristan

"We would have," replied Henry. "Since they was ahead of us a bit, once we got here they had got high up and holed in. Arrows started flyin' down at us. One of them are a bowman and his aim be true. Morgan, there," he said pointing to a young man sitting on a rock near the fire, "was sore wounded by a shaft, poor lad. His horse shied at the last second or he be hit through the heart and dead sure. We are not afeared, my lord, but we be farmers and herdsmen, not fighters. We has no weapons against arrows."

Tristan's dark brows came together, the space between them wrinkling with displeasure, but he nodded. He understood their reticence at going up against an archer who held the high ground. "There are four of them?" Tristan asked.

"Five, my lord," said Henry.

"Five?" he said. "Who is the fifth?"

"Small. Long, full cloak, ridin' back of one of the others. Prob'ly a lad. Some reason, those two stayed back from sight when they tried to sell the cobs."

Tristan studied the steep incline running up face of the tor. Had there always been five, or had they picked up another along the way?

With the trees and boulders, there were plenty of places for an archer to position himself above and have a clear view of the empty fields below. Who were they that there would be an archer? It would not be easy to approach them unseen. With twenty-two men at his disposal, over half of whom possessed only willingness to serve a knight and very little fighting skill, he would need a plan—and a good one.

Tristan motioned to one of the bowmen, a tall, lanky Welsh lad of about seventeen summers with black curly hair and brown, sorrowful eyes. The lad hurried over.

"Yes, my lord," he said, bowing slightly. "Pwyll, sir."

"Your bow looks well made, Pwyll," Tristan said pointing to the man's weapon.

"Most any Welshman can make a passable bow, my lord."

"How close," said Tristan, pointing to the cluster of boulders hiding the basin on the face of the tor, "would a bowman have to be to hit a man up there?"

"Close, my lord," the lad replied. "Welsh bows be short, good for power, close-in, not for range. And we be shooting up hill. If we was above them shooting down, it be better."

"And you think there is only one bowman?" Tristan asked, turning to Henry.

"I only seen one," Henry replied.

Tristan rode along the front of the slope, from one side to the other. Keeping behind a line of trees, he examined the features of the terrain. To the left, it was nearly all rocks, only the faces of which stood out from the earth, providing little cover for anyone trying to climb to the top. Though most of the trees and brush in the center, the ascent there was much steeper than it was on either side and would involve climbing some boulders on the way. As he scanned the right side, he saw what looked to be another way up the face. He rode back to where the others waited.

"We cannot waste any more time," said Tristan. "We must get up there and bring them down."

"If you leads us, sir knight, we will follow," said Henry, others mumbling with varying amounts of enthusiasm.

"I know you will," replied Tristan. "But let us see if we can accomplish this with no one else being injured or killed."

"Pwyll, you and your bowmen follow me, and try to keep out of sight from those on slope." Tristan dismounted and led the three bowmen to the far side of the tor where they squatted behind a large boulder. "See that narrow path running right along the edge behind that line of rock? Do you think you three could get up there and take a position above the place where they are holed up?"

The three men, following Tristan's pointing hand, looked a little dubious, but slowly nodded assent.

"The rocks will offer little cover. They are less than knee-high and the path behind is perilously narrow. You would have to crawl on your face to get there unseen. If you move silently and are undetected, it would give us the element of surprise and we could capture them alive and have the joy of seeing them hang."

Pwyll turned to one of his companions. "Iolo. You for going?"

The doe-eyed Welshman nodded.

"Wyn here be wider than that path are in some places," said Pwyll, turning to the third short and stocky Welshman. "What say, lad? Can ye do it?"

Wyn squinted at the narrow path. "Aye, I can do it," he mumbled.

"Whichever of you can," said Tristan, "take out their bowman. Do not kill him. Just render him unable to shoot."

Tristan left the bowmen at the bottom of the slope and returned to the camp. He motioned for the men to gather around him as he laid out his plan.

"At my signal, Pwyll, Iolo and Wyn will scale the hill by that path on the far side, each delaying his start from the one in front of him by several moments to spread them out. Once they reach the top, they will remain concealed and will fan out with one in the middle and one on either side and eliminate the threat from the archer. We will call for their surrender. Once we have no worry from arrows, the rest of us can climb up and take them. Remember, these men slaughtered five people, perhaps six. We must see them hang. Are we ready?"

Tristan looked around at the faces in front of him. A couple of the coal miners looked absolutely gleeful. Others returned his look with anger, some with fear and uncertainty. But he knew they would all follow him.

"May God protect us all," said Tristan, signing the cross. The men followed suit and Tristan noticed some offering up prayers.

The wait was interminable. Tristan wanted to watch their ascent, but had need take care lest he alert the fugitives to the climbers. He made a show of spreading half the men across the bottom of the outcrop to block any attempt at escape, placing Henry on the far side to watch the bowmen, ready to signal him when they reached the top. Meanwhile, he prepared those with blades to climb when the order was given.

They waited, anxious eyes trained on the outcrop. There was no movement anywhere, and the world grew silent. Time crawled, and it appeared all of nature awaited the signal to advance.

"Bowman!" cried a miner. All eyes went swiftly to where the man pointed just to the left of the basin. An outlaw had quickly stood, loosed an arrow and immediately hid again. A muffled cry came from the direction of the climbers. To everyone's horror, about a third of the way from the top, Wyn rose from behind the low rock line, an arrow through his neck. He staggered, turned in a circle clutching his throat and then disappeared soundlessly over the side of the cliff. Audible cries came from several of the men below. Then all grew quiet again.

"Christ's blood!" spat Tristan. "His size betrayed him."

The knight started to move toward Henry, but the man stealthily motioned for him to stay put. They waited the time it would take to say ten Hail Marys until Henry finally nodded, a gesture Tristan nearly did not notice. His eyesight was not what it once was, and he had difficulty seeing great distances.

Tristan stood up. His voice broke the silence. "We shall accept your surrender."

They waited.

A loud, raucous laugh echoed from above. "And end up danglin' from a gibbet? No thank you, my lord."

"It is your last chance," Tristan responded. "I shall not ask again."

"No, my lord, if you come to kill us, then be done with it. My neck was not made for no rope."

"Do you speak for them all?" shouted Tristan.

"No. The rest will give their decision when ye gets here. For ye will have to come get us. We will not be comin' to you."

Tristan gave the signal. The men assigned the assault began the climb. Funneling through a break in the rocks at the bottom covered with trees and in deep shadow, they emerged into the open about sixty feet up the incline. With very little cover, everyone was on the lookout for a brigand to loose an arrow from his bow that could end a man's life before ever he saw it coming.

Suddenly, they heard the buzzing of an arrow overhead. It passed close to a Pontarddulaisman, nearly close enough to crease his scalp. An inch lower and the man would be dead.

Where the bloody hell were Iolo and Pwyll? Tristan quickly scanned the top of the cliff. He saw Iolo stand, aim and shoot. His shaft ricocheted off a rock above the outlaw bowman's head. The Welshman disappeared, emerging moments later farther to the right. Tristan watched the fugitive turn to peer at the top of the tor, raising his bow to shoot. Just as Iolo loosed another arrow, Pwyll stood and let fly. Both shafts found their mark in the middle of the brigand's chest.

"That be for Wyn, you son of a whore," Iolo yelled, disappearing behind a rock.

Tristan urged his men to climb faster now that he knew the outlaw bowman posed no further threat. They scrambled up the slope and approached the rock formation that rose in front of the basin. Tristan leaped out in front, drawing his sword as he slid down the loose rock lining the sides of the shallow depression, riding to the bottom on an avalanche of small stones. Once on the floor of the basin, he charged forward. Hearing the clang of steel behind him, he glanced over his shoulder. The others were in place and the fight was on.

Other than himself, Tristan figured there was not a real swordsman in the lot. There was more circling and feinting than actual blows struck. Displaying skill that surprised Tristan, a Pontard-dulais swordsman quickly relieved an outlaw of his weapon and had him pinned to the side of the basin in surrender. The other two fought stubbornly on. A second soon surrendered. In a last valiant attempt at victory, the man who swore not to be taken, charged at Tristan. His sword sliced from right to left, then right again, followed by a high downward blow intended to cleave the knight's skull. Though Tristan blocked and deflected with ease, he found he must reassess the skill of his opponent.

Then it happened. The world receded, and a buzzing in his stomach took over his whole being. All noise ceased except for the pounding of his heart and the sound of his own breath rasping in his ears. Even the clanging of steel on steel failed to reach him. Tunnel vision set in, eliminating all but that which was right in front of him. His movements became automatic.

The outlaw advanced a step, raised his weapon high to the left and delivered a downward blow to the right. Tristan blocked it low. His opponent immediately followed with a downward slice to the left. Stopping it in the middle of the swing, Tristan raised his sword, carrying the outlaw's blade up and out of the way. The outlaw countered with a quick thrust to Tristan's midsection and turning his wrists, delivered a horizontal cut. The blade sliced empty air as the knight sucked in his stomach and hopped backward. Both men countered deftly strikes to the left and right.

Guessing his opponent to be younger by ten summers, Tristan became conscious of the effects of his own advancing age. Feeling winded from his exertions, he knew he needed to end this quickly.

Whether sensing Tristan's fatigue or a last-minute surge, the outlaw charged fast and hard. Delivering crossed blows the knight had difficulty fending off, the murderer forced him back to the side of the basin. His feet hit the loose stones on the incline and Tristan lost his footing, sending him sprawling to the ground. The outlaw moved in fast for the kill.

Raising his sword above his head, the fugitive brought it down in a sweeping arc aimed at Tristan's face. Tristan rolled away from the direction of the intended blow. He could feel the breath of the steel as it shushed the air where his head had been a moment before. Arms gripping his sword straight over his head, Tristan rolled twice more and staggered to his feet.

"You grow old, my lord," the villain taunted.

Tristan did not answer. Gritting his teeth, he let out a growl and lunged forward, delivering a downward slice to the right. Raising his sword as if to slice to the left, he came down again on the same side. Striking the man on the right arm as he parried to defend his left, Tristan nearly severed his opponent's hand at the wrist. Sword clattering to the ground, the outlaw let out a cry, grabbed his bleeding arm and sank to his knees. Tristan stood panting, his breath rasping from his lungs, his sword pointed at the man's throat.

It was true: he had grown too bloody old for this!

"My lord!" Pwyll's voice penetrated Tristan's cocoon of silence. The knight looked to the top of the basin to see the Welshman pointing his bow, the string drawn back, ready to shoot. "There!"

An outlaw tried scrambling up the loose stones, cloak billowing out behind from a slight breeze. Pwyll let fly his arrow. The shaft slamming into the ground in front of him, the escapee stopped and slid back to the basin floor. Tristan strode over to the cowering form.

"Just where do you think you are going, my lad?" demanded Tristan, blade out in front of him. The figure stood and turned to face him.

"I am no lad, sir knight," came a firm, high voice from inside the hood.

TEN

In the glow of a lone candle, Brother Rhonwellt stood at the foot of Brother Anselm's cot and watched the life-force slowly ebb from his old friend. In the time Rhonwellt had been gone from Saint Cattwg's, the old monk had become thin to the point of emaciation, had become almost unrecognizable. His breathing was shallow, punctuated by occasional, incoherent mumblings. His face was ashen and Rhonwellt realized that if not for his utterances, one could easily assume Brother Anselm was already dead.

The monk marveled at how peaceful the old man appeared. It reminded him of the first time he had seen that face, kneeling beside him, compassionate grey-green eyes staring down at him from a ruddy face, his chin nestled in a cowl.

"Am I dead?" Rhonwellt had asked, gazing into a fringe of tonsure that glowed from the sun shining behind it. "Are you an angel?"

"No my son, you are very much alive," Anselm had promised him in a deep resonant voice, "and I am far from an angel."

Rhonwellt winced as his body recalled the searing pain. Agony so intense as to change his mind. He must be dead, forbidden entrance into heaven, relegated to eternal damnation for his sin, and the face before him was actually the Dark One, come to collect his soul. But, Anselm's voice had been gentle and persistent. It kept his mind from the torment in his body until the effects of the poppy juice lulled him into a blessed sleep. When next Rhonwellt woke, he found himself transported, as if by magic, to the top of the river bank, next to a warm fire, the monk praying silently beside him.

Rhonwellt did not have to wonder at his fate if Brother Anselm had not stumbled across him that day so long ago—he would be dead. There would have been no vocation as a monk as Saint Cattwg's. His days would have ended long before the ink stains that defined his life there would appear on his hands. Stains that would not fade and told him who he was, a brother in Christ in a family of monastics, an illuminator of manuscripts, and a soul in search of love and redemption. None of this would ever have existed, and though he had always been acutely aware of this, he did not dwell on it.

The thought he seldom allowed himself to consider, however, was what his life would have been like if those events had never happened. Who would he be? If Declan had not betrayed him and Tristan, would the feelings they shared have endured? Could they really have forsaken the expectations of society, faced the judgment of the church and the possibility of death, to cleave to each other?

Deep in his heart, Rhonwellt realized that, even then, he had never really dared hope there could be a future for them. He had fully presumed Tristan would do what they expected of a man of his rank: to forsake him, marry to advance the family fortunes, and provide heirs to carry on the line. Yet, Tristan had confidence things would work in their favor. He carried the presumptions of youth and privilege. People with position had faith that though life was largely prescribed, things would always work out for them. Rhonwellt's station in life held no such expectation for happiness. Any such future seemed remote since he had never held much interest in women and there was no inheritance at stake. His hands would have remained the rough hands of a farmer, with dirt under his nails instead of ink stains. The clothes on his back, rags instead of woolen robes. He would have learned nothing beyond simple reading or writing or simple numbers. He would likely have remained a single man, tilling the soil and caring for his parents as they grew old and died. Life would have been predictable. What had been unforeseeable was that a score-and-ten summers later they would find themselves reunited and, though it held no certainty, contemplating a future that neither could have imagined. After nearly a lifetime of wondering just whose side God was on, Rhonwellt found it hard to accept that maybe the Almighty had finally decided to smile on him.

And there was the crux of it. He did not trust God. He did not trust anyone, save for the old man who lay dying before him in the near-darkness of the infirmary, the man who had given him back his life. From the moment he opened his eyes on that riverbank, Rhonwellt had trusted Anselm like a father, had even called him that for a while, until Anselm had convinced him that despite the great difference in their ages, they were brothers, bound together through Christ and that should bring them closer than any earthly family connection.

Lost in another skirmish of the mind, he started at a hand laid on his shoulder, and turned to see Brother Etheldrede behind him.

"Brother Rhonwellt," Etheldrede whispered as they embraced and exchanged the kiss of peace. "Praise God. I heard you had arrived."

To Rhonwellt, the joy in Etheldrede's voice could not mask the note of sadness in the brother's eyes.

"I sought out Prior Alwyn upon my arrival just before compline," answered Rhonwellt. "I asked his permission to forego the office that I might have time alone with him. He is unresponsive." Rhonwellt's chin began to quiver. "I am not sure he knows I am here."

Etheldrede looped his arm through Rhonwellt's and the two monks stood looking at the breathing corpse before them. "He has been thus for two days now."

"Then he is unable to take nourishment?"

"We tried to spoon water between his lips," said Etheldrede. "It would trickle down into his mouth but he could not swallow."

"Without water," lamented Rhonwellt, "he will not survive for more than another day or two."

"So says Brother Remigius." Etheldrede paused. "You know, he has asked for you. Many times."

"And when I have come, he knows me not."

"Sit with him. Hold his hand. Talk to him. Say what it is you need to say. God will see to it he hears you."

How strange it felt to be back where the name of God was readily on everyone's lips daily, hourly, moment by moment, an atmosphere he found diminished since leaving the priory and moving to Saint Tysilio's.

Rhonwellt went to the side of the bed and sat on a small stool.

"His end is near," said Brother Etheldrede, "and it is time we started vigil for him. Shall I tell Prior Alwyn you and I will take first watch?"

Rhonwellt nodded silently, his focus on Brother Anselm as he took the old man's hand in his.

Brother Etheldrede signed the cross in a blessing to the dying monk, tucked his arms in his sleeves and left.

Numb with grief, Rhonwellt sat holding Anselm's hand. What could he say? Though he wanted to say what was in his heart, he was not sure he knew what that was. The words 'thank you' were there, but his heart felt so much more. Three simple words that lay on his heart were stuck in his throat, and could not get past his tongue. He had never said those words to any living soul, not even Tristan. He was not sure he could now. Yet if not now, when?

"Father...I..." His mouth was dry, his tongue stuck to the roof of his mouth. He prayed, and taking a deep breath, he tried again. "You have been dearer to me than anyone." He cast his eyes toward the ceiling as though he might find the words there. Blowing out his breath with puffed cheeks he stumbled on. "You have...loved me like a father...and... treated me as a beloved son. No man could receive greater blessing than your affection." He brought his gaze down to rest on the thin, ragged face cradled in the pillow. "I have always sought to make you proud of me. And though pride is a sin, I hoped you felt it toward me." Bringing the fingers of the old man's frail hand to his lips, he kissed them and gave a gentle squeeze. He prayed for Anselm to return the gesture, but there was nothing.

The door opened and Rhonwellt heard footfalls behind him. He turned to see a man of about forty summers, tall, lanky, and moderately dressed. His long hair was the color of straw, his beard wispy, like that of a youth.

"Forgive me, Brother," he said. "I did not mean to disturb you."

Rhonwellt did not speak, merely stared at the man.

"I am Selwyn Gyffard. While traveling from the North, I took ill. The brothers kindly put me up until I could recover."

Rhonwellt nodded.

"I have just come to collect my things. I will lodge at the inn this night and leave for Ryd Lliw on the morrow."

"May I help, my lord?" came a voice from the doorway.

Rhonwell froze at the familiar sound.

"No, Wulfric, I can manage."

Rhonwellt lifted his gaze to meet the face that carried the name and locked eyes with the Saxon.

☦   ☦   ☦

STEAM FROM HIS BREATH QUICKLY DISSIPATED INTO THE COOL air as Rhonwellt strolled the cloister. A half moon peered out from the edge of a slow passing cloud casting an eerie light over the garden. He inhaled deeply, but the fragrance from the lavender and rosemary, so prevalent through spring and summer, was sadly absent this time of year. Rhonwellt loved the serenity of the priory cloister and had not realized how much he missed his time there.

He walked to shake the numbness that had settled over him since witnessing Brother Anselm take his final breath a short time ago. His death had been a simple, quiet occurrence, he just stopped breathing. Gripping his arms inside his sleeves, Rhonwellt wept. He secretly feared that when the grief did finally manifest itself openly, it would cripple him. Instead, he absently put one foot in front of the other, extracted an arm and began fingering the simple wooden cross around his neck, praying for Anselm's soul and for his own deliverance.

Out of love for Brother Anselm, Rhonwellt had tried to help wash and prepare the old monk's body for burial; one last act of devotion to the one who had saved him. Though an undertaking he had performed countless times on both stranger and friend, it proved one he could not fulfill for one so dear. He was simply too close to the emotion, unable to detach himself from the intimacy. Having allowed himself the comfort of thinking Brother Anselm would always be there, preparing his body for burial was too final an act. Not up to the task, Rhonwellt decided to walk.

Beginning his walk at half-Matins, he lost track of time and was surprised when he heard the bell toll Lauds. As the clanging of the bell subsided, he heard the familiar drone of the monks drift over the cloister wall, chanting the Prayers For The Dead. They would transport Brother Anselm's body in the front door to lie in state in the presbytery until his funeral.

He thought he might take a trip to the jakes but reconsidered, deciding to join in the end of the procession accompanying the body. Wiping his face, he hurried along the arcade and in through a door to the *cellarium*. Threading through the barrels and tuns, he exited the door that led outside. The precession was just a few yards ahead to his left. He stepped to the right and stopped to relieve himself against the wall of the *cellarium*. A practice unheard of among the monks, it was another bad habit he had picked up from Tristan who, like most men, pissed most anywhere he pleased. Yet, he could not shake the feeling of vulnerability when doing so, and pissing out in the open always seemed to take longer to empty his bladder. Uneasy that someone might see him, he often had to shake the feeling he was being watched.

If he hurried, he might make it to the end of the line before the monks entered the large front doors to the church. He was just finishing up and straightening his robe when Rhonwellt heard footsteps. The distant chanting of the brothers had nearly covered the sound. Grabbed roughly from behind by an arm about his neck, he felt cloth being forced over his head. Everything went black. Something pressed against his throat through the fabric. He knew it was the blade of a dagger. A harsh voice whispered in his ear and the stench of putrid breath assaulted his nostrils. "Not a sound, monk, or it be your last." He thought he recognized the voice with the clipped accent of the North.

No one else spoke, but if he was correct, he knew his captors numbered four. They wound a leather thong around his wrists, and led him away like a tethered animal, one man on either side to guide him. They walked for a few yards and made a left turn. The ground was dirt, not gravel. They were going behind the infirmary. But where? He started counting his steps to keep his bearings. After one hundred paces, they went left again and stopped. He could smell horses and fresh manure and was sure they were behind the dorter near the monk's graveyard.

How could this happen again? Rhonwellt began to panic. It felt like a reliving of events before being rescued by Brother Anselm, except this time he was fully awake and walking instead of half dead and being carried. His whole body shook and he began to hyperventilate.Though he fought to hold it back, he felt a whimper escape his lips.

"Calm down, brother." A different voice, more refined than the other. "We shall not harm you. You are worth nothing to us dead."

"What do you want with me?" asked Rhonwellt. He could barely get the words out.

"You shall know soon enough," said the second voice. "Right now we must be on our way."

Suddenly, hands seized his legs and threw him up and over a horse's back. Groping the darkness for something to hang onto, he grabbed for a lock of hair from the mane. The animal felt familiar. Had they stolen Epona as well? How did they know?

The party started to move.

The brothers would surely notice he was absent. Or would they assume his grief so great he found he could not attend? Would they search for him, perhaps raise a hue and cry? He knew the brothers would be at prayer until at least a quarter Lauds. By the time they could raise an alarm, they would be far away. Suddenly, any hope of rescue disappeared.

The band rode on until Rhonwellt thought it must be well past Prime, perhaps nearly Terce. He could see daylight out the bottom of the covering over his head, but nothing else. To quell his fear, concentrated on where they were and where they might be going. The muffled sounds from the horse's hooves said they traveled off the beaten path, but he could not tell if it was just to the side of the road or cross-country through open fields. However, since their travel had been over fairly level ground, he knew they had not gone into the hills and were likely near some road and headed toward some other town. Yet, would they not have to avoid being seen? Leading a bound and blindfolded monk would surely create suspicion and draw scrutiny.

As Rhonwellt's mind flitted from one thing to another, he noticed them change directions. They had turned left. Something struck him in the face. Even through the cloth covering his head it stung, making his eyes water. The suddenness of the blow startled him and made his heart skip. A tree branch. They were entering a woodland. He breathed in the odor of damp and decaying leaves and could hear the faint trickle of running water. The sound was not large enough to be a river, it must be a stream or spring. Again, he plunged into the darkness of that other time.

His horse stopped, and the sound of creaking leather told him the others had dismounted. Almost immediately they dragged him to the ground, led him a few paces and guided him to sit. Putting his bound hands between his legs, he felt a large rock.

"If ye needs a piss," said a guttural voice he recognized at once, "we shall not molest you this time." As the hood was snatched from his head, he squinted in the light and looked into the face of the Saxon, standing in front of him with Osgar, Leo—and Selwyn.

Rhonwellt turned to the man he had seen in the infirmary. "Master Gyffard, what is the meaning of this? Are you in charge here?"

"Actually," said Selwyn "you are at the mercy of Wulfric. I am here to see he does not run afoul of the law. Such things matter little to him."

"Since when does kidnapping not run afoul of the law?" Rhonwellt asked. He wondered at Selwyn's congenial manner and if it was false. He did not sense the same malice from him he did from Wulfric.

"Let us say," replied Selwyn, "you are a reluctant guest."

"Where are you taking me?" demanded Rhonwellt, trying to put grit into his words.

"Why home," answered Wulfric.

"I apologize for all this," Selwyn continued, indicating the bindings at Rhonwellt's wrists and the hood in the Saxon's hand. "Wulfric thought it necessary, and he usually gets his way."

"Necessary for what? And what do you mean you are taking me home?" Rhonwellt tried to stand, but Wulfric pushed him back down with enough force he nearly fell backward over the rock.

The big Saxon stepped closer to Rhonwellt as he spoke. "It was necessary because you knew us and we could not take the chance you might call out our names."

"I think you remedied that when someone threatened to slit my throat."

"Osgar is nothing if not enthusiastic," Wulfric chortled. "He does get into the spirit of a thing."

Osgar grinned and spat on the ground at Rhonwellt's feet.

"What I said before is true," said Selwyn. "I wish you no harm. Wulfric wants what he wants. Despite his methods, you are worth nothing to us if you are dead."

"Worth?" spat Rhonwellt. "Surely you do not think anyone would pay for my return." He fought back waves of doubt.

"Perhaps the knight at Ryd Lliw...?" Wulfric said, more of a question than a statement.

"When the ale have their tongues, some says he be most fond of your arse," said Osgar.

Rhonwellt snapped his head to look at Osgar. The sneer on the lug's face showed more titillation than condemnation.

"Osgar!" snapped Wulfric.

Osgar chuckled and stepped back.

Wulfric turned to Rhonwellt. "Osgar is crass but right." Wulfric paused. Rhonwellt looked directly at the Saxon and saw a twinkle in his eye. "A couple of pottles of ale will always pry tongues loose. Folks say the knight...favors you. That must make you worth something."

Rhonwellt's stomach felt queasy. "I am just a priest," he said. "He will not pay for my return."

"Perhaps," said Wulfric as he put his foot up on Rhonwellt's seat, his arm on his knee and leaned in. "I happen to think differently. In any case, it is not coin we seek, brother."

"Then what is it you hope to gain?"

"A trade." Wulfric's eyes grew deadly earnest.

"Trade?" said Rhonwellt, thoroughly confused.

"Yes."

"Trade for what?"

"The knight has something I want, and I have you."

Immediately the situation crystalized in Rhonwellt's mind. Wulfric did not mean something. He meant someone.

ELEVEN

Arms tucked into his sleeves, Ciaran scurried along the road and over the small bridge spanning the mill race, glad to feel the sun shining on his face and warming his woolens. Though he could see storm clouds in the distance, the brief sun break was a welcome respite from the cold and the rain. Except in the highest elevations, the snow was gone and unless he walked on the very edge of the track, he would have found himself ankle deep in mud created by the slight thaw. The warmer temperatures had brought the sleepy town bustling to life, the locals trying to get ahead with chores left undone due to the freeze.

With Brother Rhonwellt and Sir Tristan both gone, Ciaran was alone at Ryd Lliw and feeling apprehensive. Even with Jocelyn there to care for Ernulf and sure of Hewrey's loyalty and that of the other servants, he was still nervous. He knew Tristan had worked hard to put his villeins at ease and overcome the rumblings throughout the estate that the lord of the manor was a sodomite. But, he made no effort to garner friendships in the village—because in reality the knight's heart belonged to the ginger-haired, green-eyed monk—and their suspicions eventually waned and they gradually became fiercely loyal to the moody, yet generous lord of the manor. So Ciaran had faith he could rely on the villeins in case of any trouble. Still with all these reassurances, the young monk knew he would feel better when everyone was back where they belonged: Brother Rhonwellt in his church and Sir Tristan at the hall. Especially now with murderous brigands slaughtering travelers on the road and that hulking Saxon poking his nose into the affairs of the estate. Though Wulfric had left two days ago, Ciaran was sure they had not seen the last of him and his men.

He paused at the intersection in front of the gate. One direction led back to the hall—and Jocelyn—the other, down the road and into the village. It was still some while until Sext and he should prepare the church for the office. With thoughts of Jocelyn causing a fluttering in his chest, there could be no doubt the church was the better choice. He turned toward town.

About to enter the gate to the churchyard, a commotion in front of the tavern caught his attention and filled him with curiosity. He could spare a little time and started to walk toward the disturbance.

Two horsemen were in the middle of the street, their well-bred mounts dancing around a figure wedged between them. Even from this distance, he could see the figure trapped between the horsemen was Noah. A small crowd had gathered and everyone was shouting, Noah loudest of all.

"Who are you?" shouted Ciaran as he rushed toward them. However, with the din of the crowd, no one heard him. "Be still!" he yelled, clapping his hands to gain their attention. "Everyone, please... be still."

Slowly, the raucousness ebbed into a low murmur, all eyes on the young monk. Ciaran turned to the strangers on horseback. "Now, who are you and why do you harass this man? His master will not be pleased."

"No one be my master," shouted Noah at Ciaran.

"Hush, Noah," said Ciaran. "As long as you work for Sir Tristan, he is your master." Ciaran turned to the stranger. "Well?"

"This cur murdered my brother," said the younger of the two outsiders. "I mean to see him hang."

The older man sat his horse, impassively watching the scene unfold.

"Noah, is this true?" asked Ciaran, astonished at the accusation.

"No, Brother, I swear," said Noah, his eyes so wide with fright that the whites shone all around his pupils. He moved back and forth, spinning around like a trapped animal. "I never done it!"

"He lies," sneered the stranger, jumping down from his horse. He was dressed head-to-toe in dark brown leather with a sword and dagger strapped to his waist. "I saw it with my own eyes." He grabbed Noah by the front of his jerkin and pulled him close. "I shall see your body twitch from the end of a rope until your eyes bug. And when they toss your carcass into the pit, I shall piss on it with relish."

Some bystanders shouted in agreement. Mustering his courage, Ciaran held up his hands to quell the noise. "Well, until he is tried and found guilty," said Ciaran, wedging his way between the lad and his accuser, "Noah will remain here." Ciaran realized he was shaking with fear but hoped no one noticed. He worked to keep his voice even and tremor-free. "In the mean time, you shall piss on nothing unless it is your own shoes."

"Do not vex me, monk," said the man, so close to Ciaran that spittle showered the young monk's face as he spoke.

"He has his way," shrieked Noah, pointing at the stranger, "there be no trial."

"Good idea," said the stranger. "Why waste the time?"

The crowd started to grow noisy again.

"See! I got no chance." Tears started to form at the edges of Noah's eyes. He quickly wiped them away with his sleeve. "The rich always gets their way."

At last the older man spoke. "Brother. I am Walter Fullecoppe." He gestured to the younger man. "My son, Thomas." About fifty, his neatly trimmed hair and beard were gray. His clothes were in shades of murrey, well-made and costly. His appearance clearly indicated wealth, but with no trace of ostentation.

The crowd grew still. When rich men spoke, people listened.

"I am Brother Ciaran, assistant to the priest here at Saint Tysilio's." Ciaran fought for calm. Even now, he wondered that he found the courage to speak with such force to a man who smelled of danger.

"Well, Brother Ciaran," Walter said, his voice even, "we mean to take this man with us. Be a good lad and do not try to stop us. I would not see you hurt."

"I am a man of God. You would not dare." Ciaran's mind raced. He looked around the crowd to see if he could read their mood. These people did not know Noah. Would they support him or turn on him? The looks on their faces showed their feelings were mixed. What was he going to do? If he let them take him, Noah's fate was certain. Where was Sir Tristan?

In that moment, Thomas took a step toward Noah. "You murdered my brother," he spat, his voice a low growl. "You and that whore of a thing you call your sister. Where is she?"

"Do not call her that!" Ciaran shouted back, arms down at his sides, fists clenched in rage. "What you say is a lie and that is a sin!"

"Thomas!" Walter glared at his son. "Forgive my son, Brother. William was my eldest, and he and Thomas were closely bonded. Witnessing his brother's murder has unhinged him."

Thomas spat in the mud and glared back at his father, then at Noah. "My wits are sound and it is no lie. William was a godly man and his whore-of-a-sister tried to lead him into a life of wickedness and depravity."

"Jocelyn is not a whore!" said Ciaran through clenched teeth. He felt his control slipping away.

Thomas taunted Ciaran, his lip curled with contempt. "She has besotted you, young monk." A perverted smile played across his face. "Have you tasted sin, Brother? Have you fallen prey to that creature?"

Ciaran stood rooted, unable to move, his chest heaving as his rage grew. He must think. Thomas's claims could not be true. Why was no one defending Jocelyn? Without a word, he flew at Thomas, his fists flying, landing a blow to the man's chin. Ciaran grabbed at his jerkin. Thomas put a hand to his mouth, and upon pulling it away, his eyes narrowed when he saw blood on his fingers. The crowd erupted. Thomas pulled his dagger from its sheath and reached for Ciaran. The monk took a step backward. Thomas advanced another step, putting Ciaran within reach again. Grasping the front of his robe, Thomas pulled Ciaran close, the tip of his dagger touching the young monk's throat.

"What the bloody hell is going on here?" All eyes turned toward the sound of the voice. The clamor had been so loud, no one had noticed Tristan ride in hard and fast, followed by his makeshift posse comitatus and the string of outlaws. The knight's horse skidded to a stop as he threw himself out of the saddle, grabbed Thomas from behind and threw him to the ground. Before he could get up, Tristan had drawn his sword and had it pointed at the man's heart as he lay sprawled in the mud.

"Take the prisoners to the tithing barn and chain them fast to the walls," Tristan said.

"That one too?" asked one of his men-at-arms, pointing to the mysterious outlaw in the cloak and hood.

"For now." Agitated, Tristan turned to the strangers. "Well?"

"Praise God you are back," said Ciaran, his throat hoarse with fear as he let out a big sigh of relief.

Without moving his sword, Tristan turned to address the older man on the horse. "Sir! I await an explanation."

Walter looked long and hard at Tristan before he spoke. "You are lord of the manor here?"

"I am Sir Tristan Cunniff, knight in service to my King, bound to the Earl of Gloucester and this is my manor. Now explain...this," said Tristan looking around.

"First, your monk attacked my son."

Ciaran looked at the ground, but could feel Sir Tristan's eyes on him.

"And what did he do," Tristan said with a nod of his head toward Thomas, "to provoke this attack? Brother Ciaran is a peaceful man." Tristan paused a moment. "Who are you, sir?"

"Walter Fullecoppe. The one at the end of your sword is my son, Thomas."

"State your business in Ryd Lliw."

"This man, my lord," said Walter pointing at Noah, "murdered my firstborn, William. I mean to see justice done."

Tristan looked at Noah.

Noah, hemmed in by the crowd, looked terrified. "No, my lord," he said, his voice quavering. "I never done it, I swear. "

The knight turned back to Walter Fullecoppe. "The lad says he is innocent."

"Thomas says he is guilty," answered Walter.

"I saw him do it," said Thomas from his place on the ground. "Now, let me up!"

Tristan moved the tip of his sword away from Thomas' chest, but did not put it away. Springing to his feet, Thomas' eyes burrowed into Tristan, who glared back.

"Did you also witness this crime, Master Fullecoppe?" Tristan asked, eyes still on Thomas.

"No, my lord. I did not."

"Then we have only Thomas' word that Noah is guilty."

Thomas reached for the handle of his sword. Walter held up his hand to stay his son.

"Do you name my son a liar, Sir?"

Tristan slowly turned his gaze on the elder Fullecoppe.

"I do not, Sir. I merely say that grief often clouds one's perception."

"An eye-witness account is not mere perception, my lord."

Tristan worked the muscles of his jaw but his face showed no emotion.

"And where did this murder take place?"

"In Cydweli, my lord," said Walter. "I have a business there."

"I grew up at Saint Cattwg's," said Ciaran. "I know everyone in town and I have never seen you before."

"We have been there less than four seasons," he said dismissively to Ciaran and turned to Tristan, "I believe that is outside your demesne and your estate."

"It is Maurice deLondres, Lord of Cydweli's jurisdiction."

"And we shall take him there to be tried," said Walter.

"It is true the crime was committed outside my jurisdiction. However, what are my assurances Noah will ever reach Cydweli alive much less stand trial?"

"What are you saying, my lord?"

"It is well known accidents plague the transportation of prisoners and is often unsuccessful. Many times they meet their deaths before they ever reach trial."

"You insult me sir!" shouted the elder Fullecoppe.

"Perhaps I do, Master Fullecoppe. Do you demand satisfaction?" Tristan tapped the flat of his sword across the open palm of his other hand. "Will you face me?" He turned to the son. "Thomas?"

Fullecoppe remained silent, looking around the crowd of villagers.

"I think it best Noah stay with us for the time being."

"You cannot do that!" Thomas bellowed, grabbing hold of Noah by the shirt and dragging him toward his horse. "He returns to Cydweli with us."

Noah tore loose from Thomas' grip and started to run.

"Noah, the church!" Ciaran yelled, as he placed himself in Thomas' way. "Grasp the altar and claim sanctuary." If he could do that, Noah would be temporarily beyond the reach of the law. Noah clawed his way through the crowd of onlookers and sped for the chapel.

Thomas sent Ciaran sprawling to the ground with a blow and started to give chase.

"Master Fullecoppe, halt!" said Tristan. "Or shall I have my bowman let fly?"

Thomas stopped and turned. Pwyl, his bowstring pulled tight, had a shaft knocked and aimed directly at Thomas' chest.

"You have attacked a man of God. I could arrest you for that."

"Thomas, do not be foolhardy," said Walter. "Let the swine claim his sanctuary. We have the law on our side."

"I will not see him abjure the realm and escape punishment." Thomas' face twisted with fury.

"The way is set, Thomas, unless he forfeits sanctuary by leaving the church. In which case he will hang, anyway."

"I will make sure someone is here," said Tristan, "to see that he does not."

"Thirty days is not so long a wait to see justice," said Walter.

"Sanctuary at Saint Tysilio's is forty days, Master Fullecoppe," said Ciaran, rubbing the side of his face as he picked himself up out of the mud.

"By whose decree?" demanded Walter.

"Mine," said Ciaran. He turned to walk after Noah.

TWELVE

Ciaran winced at the pain in his hand as he put the skin of his scraped knuckles to his lips. He muttered to himself in rebuke on his way to the church, not bothering to avoid the mud or the puddles. He had struck another person—in anger. It was an automatic response, before he had time to think. How could he let it happen? Only one other time in his life had he done something like this, the time he slapped Sir Tristan when the knight had gotten drunk thinking Brother Rhonwellt was dead. Tristan had come close to killing Ciaran for it. Now, it had occurred again. Surely, the blame fell to Thomas Fullecoppe. The man should never have said the things he did about Jocelyn.

Close to tears from a heavy heart, Ciaran fought to contain his fury. He was a man who had pledged his life to serve God, to do good, and he had committed a violent act against another, a sin. He had shed blood. To make matters worse, he had committed one sin in response to another. He tried to deny it, to force her from his mind. If he just prayed hard enough, he thought the feelings would go away and he could be redeemed. Instead, his sin lurked there, an ever-widening stain, growing blacker every day. If he could not conquer it, he knew he would face damnation.

What made it even more diabolical was that his sin brought him profound joy. Was that not the very nature of sin? Prior Alwyn had always said the Devil never sleeps, that evil was cunning in its allure. Suddenly, Ciaran knew firsthand the prior was right. His temptation always was strongest at night under the cover of darkness when Satan's imps wandered about and he was alone in his bed. One need not be in the company of another to sin when one had his own body at hand. It took his whole will to resist. It not only kept him from sleep, but dominated his waking hours as well. The feelings of shame overwhelmed him. And because of his wickedness, he had resorted to violence. It was true, one sin did lead to another.

The gate to the churchyard stood open. Ciaran crossed the enclosure, entered the nave and peered into the gloom as the heavy door fell closed behind him. He knelt and crossed himself, stood and moved toward the chancel. Ascending the steps to the altar, he struggled to clear his head. There was a much more urgent problem at hand and it fell to him to deal with it. He scanned the room.

Taking in a deep breath, he called out softly. "Noah?"

"Brother?" The reply was low, tentative, however, the voice did not belong to Noah.

Two figures warily rose from behind the altar and peered in the dim light. Jocelyn had her arm around her brother's shoulder. Noah looked at Ciaran with bulging eyes and his body shook with terror.

"What can we do, brother?" Jocelyn asked, her voice full of uncertainty.

Ciaran tried not to look at her lest he show his feelings, but could not help himself, convinced the lust he carried in his heart for Jocelyn would be his undoing. If only she had never come to Ryd Lliw.

✝   ✝   ✝

"IT IS ANOTHER HALF DAY'S RIDE UNTIL YOU ARE HOME, brother," taunted Wulfric. "Eat now. We shall not be stopping again."

Sitting in the large wood copse, dim gray light from a cloudy sky struggled to penetrate the tree canopy. Rhonwellt had hardly noticed the food beside him. They had given him some bread and dried fish and watered wine to wash it down. In his state of high anxiety, he had given no thought to hunger. But when he started to eat, his mood calmed and he realized he was starving.

"I would fare easier if you unbound my hands," said Rhonwellt.

"You will fare just fine as you are," replied Wulfric, no sympathy in his voice.

Though Selwyn had said nothing to confirm or deny their intent to trade him for Ernulf, his silence on the matter said plainly that Rhonwellt was right. So, why? What could they want with the lad? He did not know if he should consider their interest benign or malevolent, but Rhonwellt needed to find out without letting on that Ernulf was at the Hall.

Selwyn and Wulfric were in charge. Whatever should happen, it was their plan, and they showed a determination to see it through. Men used to being in charge seldom showed any doubt as to the rightness or righteousness of their decisions. Wulfric had carried out Selwyn's orders in his absence, proving Selwyn could count on him. Rhonwellt expected he could sway neither of them.

That left Osgar and Leo, the hapless pawns. With no likely investment in the outcome of their master's plan, Rhonwellt wondered, if he could crack the shell on either of them, would he find anything sensitive underneath? He sat for a moment, chewing his bread and looking toward the ground. Washing it down with some watered wine, he took a breath but did not raise his head.

"It is a sin, you know," he whispered, with a sad shake of his head.

"Did you say something, monk?" asked Wulfric.

Rhonwellt raised his head and repeated it, a little louder. "I said, it is a sin."

"What are you prattling on about?" Wulfric took a heavy swig from his wineskin and cocked his head as he looked at Rhonwellt.

"You have all committed blasphemy."

"How so, brother?" replied Selwyn, a slight smirk on his face.

"Blasphemy is to show..."

"I know what blasphemy is!" said Selwyn. "What I want to know is how you think it applies here."

"I am a man of God, dedicated to His service. By taking me against my will, you have shown disrespect for His holy representative, thereby expressing contempt for God Himself." He paused for a moment and perused all their faces before he added the final blow. "You could all be excommunicated then hung. You would receive no absolution. You would die with unforgiven sins on your souls outside the state of grace, and would spend eternity in Everlasting Fire." He let this sink in. Wulfric showed no reaction to the remark while the smirk never left Selwyn's face. Did they know he had stretched the truth a little and were wise to his game, or were all Saxons just non-believers? No matter, it proved he adjudged Wulfric and Selwyn rightly. He would not persuade them.

Osgar hesitated for a moment at Rhonwellt's declaration, his ever-present sneer growing stiff. Rhonwellt stared at him. Had he seen a flicker of doubt in the man's eyes? Before the thought had fully formed in Rhonwellt's mind, Osgar recovered, the sneer returned to his face and he chuckled softly to himself.

At the mere mention of hanging, Leo's mouth fell open and his hand went quickly to his throat. Rhonwellt could see him stop breathing for a few seconds. He looked toward his master and then back at the monk, but he said nothing. In that moment, Rhonwellt knew Leo was the one. The man had a very real fear of burning in Hell. If there was any information he might glean, it would come from Leo. The problem was, Rhonwellt had to pry the information from him without his masters or Osgar knowing, all the while reminding Leo of the danger to his eternal soul. The look on Leo's face said the second part would be easier than the first, that his fear of God was far greater than any fear of his earthly master.

Rhonwellt was applying his mind to a strategy when Wulfric yanked the wineskin from his hand. "Well played, monk, but it will avail you naught. Be still. It is time to go." Wulfric yanked him to his feet and pushed him toward his horse. Epona stood quietly as the Saxon heaved him into the saddle, so forcefully he nearly went over the top and off the other side. Grasping the pommel, he righted himself and shoved his feet into the stirrups. His face turned crimson and he fought to control his anger. He had barely gained his equilibrium when Wulfric slapped Epona's rump and she took off with a start.

This time, they decided to forego the hood. Rhonwellt would no longer have to struggle to stay upright in the saddle now that he could see. Perhaps luck would present him an opportunity for escape. Epona was a docile creature, not prone to running. His captor's spirited coursers would overtake her before they got far. No, his best bet was to pry information from Leo.

Leaving the wood, the party rode along the edge of the road, Rhonwellt riding between Osgar and Leo in the lead, while Selwyn and Wulfric guarded the rear. Rhonwellt was instructed to keep his sleeves low about his wrists to conceal his bindings and to say nothing if they encountered anyone on the way.

"Your master," began Rhonwellt, "seems sure Sir Tristan will trade me for whatever it is they think he has. And they seem sure that he does, in fact, have whatever they seek."

"What the hell you on about, monk?" replied Osgar. "You speaks in riddles!"

"I stated it plainly enough," said Rhonwellt, gratified he had confused the oaf. "But I shall make it clear enough for even you. What does Selwyn want from Sir Tristan and is your master sure the knight has what he wants?"

"He be sure, alright," said Osgar.

"How can you be so certain?"

"Because we seen him."

To Rhonwellt's surprise, it turned out to be Osgar who was the fount of information.

"Saw what?" asked Rhonwellt, snorting through his nose, trying to give the impression there had been nothing to see.

"Not what," said Osgar, with a note of triumph. "Who."

Rhonwellt looked at Osgar, nothing registering on his face.

"The bairn," said Osgar.

"The child," exclaimed Rhonwellt. "What child?"

Osgar's eyes became slits and his jaw muscles tensed. "Are you having me on, monk? The bairn I seen with me own eyes, standing in the doorway to the hall."

"There is no child," said Rhonwellt, shaking his head and evoking a smile. "Ask anyone in the village. Sir Tristan has never wed and has no children."

"We asked. It be right what you says. But I knows I seen a bairn, no matter what anyone says."

"Osgar, be quiet about master's business," It was the first Leo had spoken and his voice carried an air of uncertainty. "Brother, do you think God will forgive us for what we done?" Leo trembled sightly but did not look at Rhonwellt. He gripped his horse's reins so tightly his hands were white.

"Shut it, Leo," spat Osgar.

"Osgar. He be a priest and we done wrong takin' him. God will..."

"Bollocks, you fool!" Osgar glared at Leo. "The priest be having you on. Pay him no mind."

"Your salvation is at stake, Leo," said Rhonwellt. "However, it is not too late."

"I fears Hell, brother," said Leo as he crossed himself. "Pray for me."

"I shall." Rhonwellt leaned in toward Leo. "If you could free me, there could be hope for you."

Leo hesitated, scratching his cheek. As he watched Leo's face,

Rhonwellt saw evidence of the conflict going on inside the man, and knew the choice was not so simple for a lowly man like Leo. No matter his fear of burning in a far off Hell after death, the swift and brutal consequence for displeasing his master loomed in the here and now. Rhonwellt wondered which fear was stronger for Leo. He leaned in again to say something more when Osgar's fist flew, catching him on the ear and the side of his head. Rhonwellt had been so focused on Leo, the blow caught him unawares. Firey explosions went off behind his eyes as he felt himself slip from the saddle and sink slowly to the ground between the horses. The animals danced nervously around, coming within a breath of trampling him.

"Master!" exclaimed Osgar, licking his lips, the pitch of his voice rising. "He were trying to set Leo against you... to set him free. I were going to tell you."

Wulfric rode forward, moving in close to Leo. Grabbing the front of Leo's tunic with one hand, he unsheathed his dagger with the other and pulled Leo nearly off his horse, until they were eye-to-eye. Pressing the edge of the blade to Leo's face, the Saxon put a small slice in the man's cheek, causing a trickle of blood to run down and into his collar. "Do not forget who is master here," Wulfric hissed.

Eyes wide in terror, Leo could only tremble. Wulfric stared at the lackey a moment more and released him.

"Get him up," hissed Selwyn, his teeth bared in anger, the cords in his neck standing proud. He pulled his horse up close, pushing the other mounts away from the stunned monk lying on the ground. "Get him up now!"

Osgar and Leo dismounted in a rush and, grabbing Rhonwellt under the arms, hauled him upright. Seeing double, the monk shook his head to clear it. There was a ringing in his ear.

"Wulfric, your temper will get you killed one day," said Selwyn.

"Not if I kill them first." The big Saxon stood, feet planted firmly, breathing heavily, his lips pressed into a thin line.

Selwyn continued. "The monk is of no use to us dead and will be a poor bargaining chip if badly injured. Now, walk away and calm yourself." Selwyn turned to the other two. "Set him down and give him a drink. When he regains his senses, get him back in the saddle."

"And you," he said walking toward Wulfric, "you bloody, hot-headed fool. Is it any wonder Merwenna would have naught to do with you?"

THIRTEEN

Rhonwellt's head still throbbed from Osgar's blow, his wrists chafed from their bindings and his buttocks ached from being in the saddle all day. The muscles in his face tightened as he and his captors topped a rise that looked out over Tristan's estate, its many fields laying fallow in winter. A weak sun hung low in the sky near the horizon, straining with the waning of day to break through a light cloud cover. Smoke wafted up through the thatch of the nearly two-score cottages that dotted the land, spreading a light haze over the valley. In the distance the church bell summoned the faithful to Vespers, its doleful toll reminding Rhonwellt that his capture had kept him from his turn at sitting vigil with Brother Anselm's body and attending his funeral on the morrow. In that moment, Rhonwellt determined to return to Saint Cattwg's if he lived through this ordeal and offer prayers in the chapel and at the grave of his long-time friend.

"There," said Selwyn. "That one there." He pointed to a dismal-looking cottage sitting atop a small mound just off the road. "It sits alone. We can keep an eye on the manor and it will give us a good vantage point to see anyone approaching." Wulfric nodded as he and Selwyn turned their horses and rode off.

A barely noticeable smile flitted across Rhonwellt's face and quickly disappeared.

The sun lingered, balanced on the horizon, about to dip below it as they quickly covered the five furlongs to the hut. No sound greeted them and the tiny window was dark but for the faint dancing light from a lone candle or small hearth fire. Wulfric and Selwyn dismounted and, drawing their swords, approached the door. The two men nodded at each other. Wulfric raised his foot and thrust it forward, sole flat in front of him, toward the door. At the moment it should have contacted the wood, the door flew open, throwing the Saxon off balance. Selwyn chuckled as the big blonde lurched forward through the opening, narrowly missing the old woman standing there. Osgar and Leo were mute, their mouths hanging open.

"No need be kicking Esyllt's door down when it be open to all," said the old woman through a toothless grin. Esyllt watched as the others dismounted, Osgar tying the horses to a rickety fence enclosing the small yard in front of the cottage. "By the gods, ye be a big'un," she said, looking up at Wulfric, who stood half again her height. The Saxon growled as he regained his footing. "Come in, my lords," entreated Esyllt, bowing low. "Come in. Ye do honor to Esyllt's unworthy hovel," she said. "Not often does such lofty lords as yourselves visit the like of this pitiful old woman." As the men entered the hut, the crone cast a glance in Rhonwellt's direction. "Friends of yours, brother?" she asked, closing the door.

He raised his hands slightly, allowing his sleeves to fall away and show the bindings at his wrists.

Her tongue darted across already moist lips as her eyes narrowed. "I see," she said, shaking her head from side to side. "Has dancing with the devil caught up to ye at last? I always knew you would burn."

The old woman's words came as a slap to Rhonwellt, feeding the guilt that always lay just below the surface of his conscious thoughts. Head lowered, he could only stand and stare. Her clinging to the old ways and eschewing Christianity had fooled him into thinking she did not look on him in disapprobation. Had he misjudged the old woman utterly? Until now, she had treated him with open regard.

"Then you are no friend to the monk," said Selwyn, leaning slightly forward, his head tilted and eyebrows raised.

Without looking in Rhonwellt's direction she answered, "Esyllt's only friend be Esyllt. The monk be naught to me."

The look of surprise on Selwyn's face grew with each moment.

"What about the knight at the Hall?" Selwyn asked.

"A master cannot be friend to any under him," the crone replied, making a great show of snatching small linen cloths that hung drying in the eaves and covering the seats of two rickety stools in front of the fire. "Sit. Sit. Would not have your fine clothes be soiled by Esyllt's dirty old stools." She kept bowing as she talked and worked. Turning toward Osgar and Leo, she said, "Yer hounds can stay inside to warm, but they must stand or sit on the floor." She quickly went about stoking the coals and fed more dried dung to the fire.

Osgar shifted his feet, looking sullen, then squatted on his haunches, his back leaning against the door. "I be no hound," he muttered.

Leo stood quietly, shoulders drooping with a look of profound fear, mixed with a little sadness.

"Have you any food and drink, old woman?" asked Selwyn. "And stop bowing and scraping!"

"Aye, my lord," she said, bowing again, even lower. "Apologies, my lord. Old Esyllt be flustered, not knowing how to act in the presence of someone so grand."

Rhonwellt grew more confused by the old woman's behavior. That old harridan feared few and was subservient to none. Why did she grovel so? What was she up to?

"Give us drink," demanded Wulfric. "Do you have ale?"

"Aye, my lord. But old Esyllt's ale not be fit for your ilk. I have something more to suit."

Now, Rhonwellt felt sure something was amiss. Esyllt's ale was known throughout the estate and adjudged to be among the finest.

What was she playing at?

She reached for a jug sitting on a shelf near the fire. Just out of reach, she turned to Osgar and Leo, cocked her head, and hunched her shoulders.

"Osgar, get the jug down," said Wulfric.

"But master..."

"Get the bloody jug!" Wulfric shouted.

Osgar rose, crossed the small room in three steps and reached for the jug.

"Your kindness to an old woman have earned you both a drink," she said with an unctuous tone, pointing at him and Leo. As Osgar brought it down and handed it to her, she caught his eye. "Your master must be very kind. Such cheek should earn ye a beating." As she turned away, Rhonwellt noticed a slight twinkle in her eye.

Having only three cups, she emptied the herbs from one of the bowls onto the table nearby. With her back to them she began pouring a thick amber liquid into the vessels. "This be a fine mead from the monastery in Cydweli. It were just sitting on a cart in front of the tavern a few days past, not looking like it belonged to nobody." She let out a high cackle. "Now Esyllt have it to serve to you fine sirs." She fussed over the cups a moment longer and began to pass them out.

"Some for the monk, too," said Selwyn when he saw she had passed him over.

"Waste good mead on the like of him?" the old woman sneered.

"We need him in good shape for the trade."

"Then he not be for the gibbet?" she asked.

"Nay. He is but a business transaction," said Selwyn. "When we have rested and eaten, we shall send a message to the knight stating our terms."

"Then ye wish to sell him back to the knight."

"Enough questions, old woman," snarled Wulfric. "Now give the monk his drink and be on with our food."

"Apologies, my lord. Just the curiosity of a feeble old mind." Esyllt picked up a bowl from the floor and flashed a cold smile. As she turned to fill it, Rhonwellt saw the inside. The grime covering it made him shudder. He could only imagine what had been in there. She poured a meager amount into the bowl and facing Rhonwellt, started to hand it to him when she hesitated. She looked at it for a long minute and raising an eyebrow, she spit in it, stirred it with a dirty finger and looked him in the eye as she handed it to him.

The monk swallowed hard, dropped his chin and closed his eyes as he took the bowl. The spittle had already blended with the mead. Had he not seen her hurl it in, he would not know it to be there. She had pointedly let him see her do it. Rhonwellt's heart sank as he stared into the bowl, but he did not raise it to drink. He lifted his head and looked at all their faces. Selwyn stared into the fire while Wulfric watched the crone. Osgar grinned broadly. Still sullen, Leo would not meet Rhonwellt's gaze, and did not drink his mead.

"Somethin' wrong, monk?" teased Osgar.

Despite his thirst, Rhonwellt would not drink. His disappointment made it too hard to get any words out. The bowl lay in his lap, his eyes glued to it as though it were penance and he was not allowed to drink it or put it down, but must only hold it.

Selwyn lifted his gaze from the fire and silently appraised the old woman as he sipped from his cup. Wulfric downed his in one gulp and thrust his cup forward for more, but Selwyn stayed the big man's hand and shook his head.

"There be plenty, my lord," said Esyllt, moving toward Wulfric's cup. "Perhaps a little more for all of ye." Without waiting for permission, she refilled all the vessels. Seeing Leo's still full cup, she said, "Drink up. The like of you may not taste the like of this again." Leo raised his cup to his lips. As Esyllt turned away, Rhonwellt noticed Leo take a mouthful from his cup. "Now Esyllt be warmin' the stew," said the old woman.

She swung the pothook on its pole embedded next to the hearth so that the large iron kettle hung directly over the flame. "Toby snared a rabbit t'other day, so it have meat," she said with satisfaction. "It be warm soon." Stirring the pot with a long wooden ladle she began to hum softly to herself. Then, as if struck by a revelation, she snapped her fingers. "Young Toby could take a message to the knight for ye."

"Who?" asked Selwyn, absently.

"A feral ragamuffin latched onto me a while back. Nobody owns nor claims him. He helps old Esyllt and Esyllt feeds him."

"We shall handle our own affairs, old woman," said Wulfric. Esyllt stared wordlessly at him and almost imperceptibly nodded her head. Turning back to the stewpot, she resumed her humming.

The room grew silent but for the soft crackling of the wood burning on the hearth, the smacking of greedy lips from thick, sweet mead, and Esyllt's low humming. She continued to stir the pot. Lulled by the warmth and the quiet, Rhonwellt was suddenly startled as Leo smashed his cup to the floor, grabbed his throat and exclaimed, "She's killed us all!"

As Rhonwellt looked up from his bowl, Esyllt let out one of her high cackles. "Seems his thirst was greater than he thought," she said.

Rhonwellt scanned the room. All but Leo were asleep or dead, he was not sure which. He looked at Esyllt, then to his bowl and back at her.

"They only sleeps," the crone said. "Just a little juice of the poppy. They be harmless enough now, eh." Rhonwellt's eye went back to his own cup. "It be good mead. Shame ye did not wish to drink it," she said with a wink, her gums clearly visible within her broad smile.

Rhonwellt's head bobbed of its own volition as everything became clear.

Tossing her head toward Leo, she asked, "What about him?"

"Leo will be fine. Will you not, Leo?" said Rhonwellt, holding up his bound wrists. Esyllt reached for a small knife lying on the table. The lackey, still slack-jawed, only nodded as his eyes began to get heavy. "He will cause no trouble. I believe he contemplates his soul."

✝   ✝   ✝

THE TEMPORARY GAOL IN THE TITHE BARN WAS FILLING rapidly. To the prisoners already there, Tristan was about to add four more. As the great double doors swung open, the cart carrying Wulfric, Selwyn, and his men rattled to a halt inside. The captives, barely unconscious from the drugs Esyllt had put in their mead, and tossed around, bouncing off each other and the floorboards of the cart for the entire journey, were sure to be in a foul temper when they awoke. The driver had hit every stone and rut in the road on the way, and Rhonwellt grinned at the idea his actions appeared deliberate.

The monk was pensive since Tristan's arrival at Esyllt's cottage. The knight had entered and scanned the room, his hand rubbing the back of his neck, the muscles of his jaw visibly rippling beneath the skin of his face. Without a word he walked to Rhonwellt, folded his arms around him and drew him close, then quietly sighed. Instinctively, Rhonwellt had tried to pull himself loose but the knight held him fast. Esyllt busied herself with her back to them. Gazing at him, Tristan searched his face, wordlessly asking if he was all right. Rhonwellt silently nodded. The monk melted into him. It was only a moment, but all they needed.

Though the embrace had been reassuring, Rhonwellt felt relief when Tristan released him and turned to Esyllt. The knight cleared his throat, stared at the floor as though something had caught his interest, and with a stern voice said, "You have rendered me a great service, mistress. I shall not forget it." Before she could respond, he snapped his jaw shut, spun and left the room, barking orders at Hewrey to have the men load the miscreants into the cart. About to follow Tristan out the door, Rhonwellt stopped and stared at the old woman. He did not know what to say to her. It was clear her actions had brought about his release from his captors. Still, her words to him earlier had been most cruel, and the difference between her actions and her words confused him. He could not be sure they were simply a ruse to throw Wulfric and Selwyn off their guard, and his indecision must have been clear.

"It be a shame ye did not get to try Esyllt's mead," she said, her eyes shining, her voice soothing. "I bid ye come back and try it."

Relieved, he merely smiled and sketched the sign of the cross in front of her. "God keep you, mistress," he said.

She waived her hand dismissively. "God have no interest in old Esyllt, but I thank ye just the same." His face broke into a smile as her high-pitched cackle filled the room.

During the ride back, Tristan said nothing, but continually stole glances in Rhonwellt's direction. The monk could not be certain if the knight was angry or just reassuring himself he was still there— probably a little of both. As they passed Saint Tysilio's, Ciaran stood in the darkness, watching at the gate to the churchyard, a lantern held high in his hand. In its glow, Rhonwellt saw the young monk's brow knitted with worry, his other hand idly fingering the cross that hung about his neck. Though too dark to be certain, he thought he saw someone else, behind Ciaran, peering out the chapel door.

"I shall be at the church," Rhonwellt said as he slid from the saddle, handing Epona's reins to Tristan.

"Very well," said the knight. "Come to the Hall when you are finished." It was not an invitation.

"Compline will be upon us soon," Rhonwellt rebutted.

"There will be time."

"After prayers." Rhonwellt would not back down.

Tristan's eyes narrowed as he spurred his horse forward.

How different Tristan had become, no longer the easygoing lad. Rhonwellt had often heard that war changed men, made them hard. Tristan had gone beyond hard; he had become brittle. Seldom did

Rhonwellt see the ready smile, so familiar then, that was always on Tristan's face in his youth. Rhonwellt walked with weary steps to the gate where Ciaran waited.

"Brother Rhonwellt! What has happened? A filthy urchin came to summon Sir Tristan, and he left without a word, taking several men with him. They sped from here and his countenance was most dark. And who was in the back of the cart?"

"Slow down, lad. The urchin is Toby. He has somehow attached himself to Esyllt. I am exhausted. I need a moment or two of prayer and then I shall tell all to you." They headed for the door of the church where Noah stood.

"It be them?" Noah asked.

"Who?" replied Rhonwellt.

"No, Noah," said Ciaran. Then to Rhonwellt, "The Masters Full-coppe. Our Noah stands accused of murder and has taken sanctuary here in the church."

Rhonwellt gasped.

"I never done it, Brother. I swear."

Rhonwellt closed his eyes and uttered a long, slow groan. His shoulders drooped and his arms hung to his sides. Dear God, what else? "Give me a few moments," he said to Ciaran. Passing the stoup, he dipped his fingers into the water and sketched the sign of the cross, then went to the altar and wearily knelt before it. He had no particular prayers in mind, rather he needed a few minutes to gather himself.

So much had happened in just a few days, Rhonwellt felt overwhelmed. An old woman had turned up dead at the church gate, they found Ernulf crying next to the body and, though a few days had passed, he was no closer to knowing who they were or how they had ended up outside Saint Tysilio's. And why could he not get rid of this niggling thought Ernulf and the old woman did not just end up here, but were headed here? Then, Wulfric and his men appeared, the smell of danger clinging to them like some rancid perfume and giving Rhonwellt nothing but unease. Why had they asked so many questions about Tristan and his affairs? Wulfric and Selwyn were here for Ernulf, Osgar had admitted as much on the ride from Cydweli. Although Rhonwellt still did not know if their intentions were for good or ill, one thing he knew for certain, he did not trust Wulfric. Selwyn remained more of a mystery.

Noah and Jocelyn's arrival and their refusal to reveal their history seemed curious. Everyone had secrets and, these days, it grew harder to trust the face anyone presented as real. Ciaran's reaction to the comely lass filled troubled Rhonwellt. The day he long dreaded had finally come. The young monk had reached the age when an emerging hunger would assault him demanding attention. He was about to reach an awareness that the entire world was a banquet available for sating new appetites. Every monk who entered the cloister before reaching their majority faced it, and many could not resist, causing them to question their choice of vocation or to partake of the feast clandestinely. It felt remarkably like the decision Rhonwellt faced.

Returning to find Noah accused of murder only raised more questions about the siblings' past. The lad was a bit hardheaded, but Rhonwellt would never have taken him for a murderer. And, with Jocelyn now caring for Ernulf, Rhonwellt felt the need to know their story without delay.

All these events notwithstanding, it was the death of Brother Anselm that had shaken Rhonwellt the most. The fact his kidnapping had prevented him from taking part in the mass or attending Anselm's burial proved almost more than Rhonwellt could bear. They had wrested from him his one chance to pay tribute, to acknowledge all the old monk had meant to him.

He knelt before the altar, ignoring the ornate and costly carvings, focusing instead on the plain gold cross. Drawing in deep breaths and blowing them out between puffed cheeks proved only partially successful at clearing everything from his mind. Finally, he sat back on his heels in frustration, hands folded in his lap and staring at the floor. It was no use. If clearing his mind would not work, then he must occupy it with something useful. Both he and Ciaran needed answers: Ciaran, the details of his journey to Cydweli and subsequent kidnapping, and he needed the story of the accusations against Noah. And, then there was this issue of sanctuary.

Rhonwellt rose to his feet with difficulty, sketched the sign of the cross and turned to Ciaran.

"While we prepare some supper for Noah, we can talk." Ciaran quickly knelt, crossed himself, and followed Rhonwellt out the back door.

Once inside their cottage with the door closed, Rhonwellt collapsed onto a bench in front of the hearth.

"Sit and rest, Brother Rhonwellt," said Ciaran. "I will prepare our supper while you tell me everything."

Without raising his head, Rhonwellt looked up at Ciaran through his eyebrows and nodded. While the hour-candle burned down part way between one line and the next, they ate and traded their stories, each being duly shocked or horrified, depending on what they heard.

With his stomach full of food and some ale, Rhonwellt found he felt much better.

"It is nearly time to ring Compline," he said. "However, first we must discuss Noah and his request for sanctuary."

"I am sure he did not do it," said Ciaran.

"That is not the issue."

"Then what is the problem?" asked Ciaran, his head cocked to the side as he looked at Rhonwellt.

"Saint Tysilio's may not be eligible to offer him sanctuary."

"What do you mean not eligible? I do not understand"

Rhonwellt put his hands on his knees and pursed his lips before he spoke. "The Right to Sanctuary," Rhonwellt began, choosing his words carefully, "has always been controlled by the Church. The Crown thinks this gives the Church too much power. In and around London, the King has already declared that only churches chartered by the Crown may offer sanctuary. Not all will be chartered, manor churches may not."

"But the Right to Sanctuary is centuries old," said Ciaran. "How can the King change that?"

"It is about power. The fear is His Holiness is more powerful than many kings."

"But, he is the Pope and next to God!" stuttered Ciaran, the palms of his hands out in front of him.

"Kings rule nations. Rome is no longer an empire. Therefore, many think the Pope should stick to leading the faith and stay out of politics."

"But he is the Pope!" said Ciaran again.

Rhonwellt laughed softly. "It is complicated, and really does not matter. If Noah's accusers find out about the changing future of sanctuary, they may contest it and insist we abide by the coming new custom."

"Would we have to surrender him?"

"I do not know."

"What can we do?" asked Ciaran.

"We must find the truth or falsehood in the accusations against him and be prepared should sanctuary be challenged." Rhonwellt stood and stretched his arms over his head, yawning. "Now go, ring Compline, and pray God nothing else happens this evening."

FOURTEEN

Conflicting moods elicited a quiet countenance from Tristan as he and his makeshift band escorted the prisoners to the gaol set up in the tithe barn. Eyes straight ahead, the knight sat stiff in the saddle. He was in no mood to join in either the banter of the men celebrating a mission well accomplished or taunting the captives on their impending doom. The villeins greedily expected the rousing spectacle that an execution would bring to this otherwise uneventful season of the year, and Tristan would not begrudge them their show. Yule and the Feast of the Epiphany had passed, and other than the few minor feast days celebrated in this area, the next major event in Christendom was the beginning of Lent. A public hanging would help fill some of that time nicely and stave off a bit of the restlessness of winter.

The big Saxon stepped off the cart and walked sullenly into the barn by torchlight. The eerie yellow glow of the flame barely pierced the gloom of the interior as the guards led him to a far corner and secured them all to one of the iron cattle rings embedded in the wall.

"Lay a thick bed of straw," Tristan said to one of his soldiers.

"They may be felons, but they are my responsibility and I will not see them freeze to death before we can hang them."

"Prisoners die all the time, my lord," said the soldier.

"These prisoners will die by the noose and nothing else," said Tristan.

While his men were dealing with Wulfric's band, Tristan lit a second torch and walked to the opposite end of the immense structure to check on the prisoners they had brought down from the tor. The smallest outlaw, a woman if Tristan had guessed correctly, still refused to speak, to defend herself, or explain her presence. Dressed similarly to the men, she appeared every bit the ruffian. Yet, Tristan felt certain she was not in their company of her own will. He could not guess why she would not explain herself or distance herself from them.

Lost in the mire of his own thoughts, Tristan stood in front of the outlaws, his unseeing eyes staring off into the darkness beyond the torchlight. Awakened by the glare, the felons squinted, their eyes blinded by the blaze. Holding the torch high above his head, Tristan could see them clearly. Though he had never been a prisoner, he knew from fellow soldiers who had: men in custody always waited in fear that at any time someone might drag them out into the night or murder them on the spot before they had any chance at a trial.

The clamor of rattling chains and muted voices drifted from the other end of the barn. While the fugitives from the tor craned their necks to look past the stores piled in the center of the cavernous space, unable to see what the ruckus was, Tristan turned his focus on the woman cowering in the back, nearly out of sight in the blackness.

"Move her away from the others," said Tristan, leaning in and thrusting the torch forward to see her more clearly.

The woman gripped the chain that bound her to the wall with both hands, her eyes darting back and forth as her mouth opened to gulp some air. Exhaling, she breathed the word no.

"It is for your safety, mistress," said Tristan, seeing her distress.

"Safety from whom?" Her voice quavered, still she attempted to sound bold. "Men are men and much the same."

Her remark caught Tristan by surprise. Was that defiance he heard creep into her tone? "You have nothing to fear from me, Mistress," he said.

"She sure were soft and most agreeable, my lord" said the leader of the outlaws with a loud guffaw. "Wished I could taste it now." When he received no response, he added, "Unless, of course, she not be to your taste." Caught by the torchlight, the gleam in the rogue's eye taunted Tristan.

He turned and covered the three steps between them in a trice and thrust his foot forward; the blow catching the man on the side of his head as he lay in the straw, propped on one elbow. He flew backward; the grin evaporated into a grimace as he glared up at the knight.

"If I find you have forced yourself on her," snarled Tristan, teeth bared as he spoke. His words came slowly as he enunciated distinctly, "the last thing I will do, as they place the noose about your neck, will be to cut your cock from your body. I will then wrap your fingers around it to give you the pleasure of holding your useless member in your hand one more time as I kick the bucket from under your feet and the rope yanks tight." He leaned in for emphasis. "I am the law here. No one will forbid me do it. I pledge to God it shall be so!"

All sounds at that end of the barn ceased, replaced by a stunned silence. No one moved. Had they known the knight's past, they might have understood his violent reaction. As it was, they could only stare, mouths agape. Tristan fought to gain control, to calm the tremors in his body and steady his legs so they would hold him up. He took several deep breaths to balance his humors. Turning to the woman, he said, "My apologies, Mistress."

The whites of the woman's eyes showed all around the color. She did not speak immediately, rather stared at the knight. Tristan felt compelled to turn away. A moment later, he turned back and saw her eyes were still on him. After a couple failed attempts at sound, she cleared her throat and her voice returned, though not so strong.

"You jump to defend my honor," she said. "Are you so sure I still have any?"

"I could not say, mistress, but regardless, you have no reason to fear me."

"No reason! You are a man. Are you not?" Her eyes grew hot with anger.

Tristan bit the inside of his cheek. "I am. If my word as a man has no value to you, you have my word as a knight."

"Ah, yes. That most holy institution of elevated manhood." She curled her lips into a snarl and her nostrils flared. "More often, knights pretend to be saviors, but prove to be scoundrels, instead."

"How well I know it, mistress," he said, ugly memories of his first lord careening through his mind. "How good one is as a knight depends on how he conducts himself as a man." He stopped for a breath or two, letting the words he had just spoken sink into his own mind as well as hers. "Bad men cannot be good knights."

The woman's eyes stared as if seeing into some far off place. "That is how it ought to be," she replied with a sigh.

"I am fairly certain I am no scoundrel," Tristan said, his tone softening, the wrinkles disappearing from his face and forehead. "Just as I am positive you are no outlaw."

"How can you be so assured?" Her tone was not exactly defiant, nor was it conciliatory.

"For one thing, Mistress, your speech. It is that of one who has dwelt safely within the confines of a hall, reading or talking with the women."

"Maybe I just be good at deceivin' men who thinks they be me betters."

Tristan closed his eyes and slowly shook his head from side to side, a small grin trying to force its way across his face. He pursed his lips and bit it back. "Attempting to sound like a kitchen wench will do nothing to persuade me, Mistress. Besides, I have seen your hands." At the mention of them, the woman attempted to bury her hands in her lap. "They are hands made for pretty needlework. The hard scrabble life of a true ruffian would render them rough and scarred. The nails are neither torn nor cracked, and the dirt under them is recent and not the indelible grime of the poor. Your hands are delicate and beautiful and would become clean with but a light washing."

The woman said nothing.

"Still you offer nothing in explanation?" He waited. "Who are you? And, why were you with these men?"

"She be with us because she likes us," said the cocky leader.

Tristan's foot flew forward again, this time catching the outlaw in the shoulder. "Say nothing until you are spoken to," he said to him.

The woman remained mute.

"You have only to say," said Tristan.

The woman kept her head down. Her hands fidgeted in her lap.

"Why do you hold back? Surely, they must have taken you against your will."

Nothing.

Tristan's patience wore through. "God's teeth, woman, as you will confirm or deny nothing, you shall remain a suspected felon, and I shall treat you accordingly."

He spun about and headed for the door, demanding his men obey and separate her. He said quietly to one of his men, "See to it the straw under her is extra thick. Her cloak is fine but thin, and she is spindly with no fat to keep her warm." Tristan scratched his chin as he took a moment to look toward her. "Perhaps another night in chains will loosen her tongue."

Handing his torch to one of his men, he exited the barn and started trudging up the rise to the hall still wondering at the stubbornness of the woman. Why would she not say the words that would free her? It was unfathomable. He had limited experience with the temperament of women—his mother, a brief encounter with a young woman years ago and a few of the whores that followed the camps. It meant he would probably never comprehend the inner workings of their minds. Few men did, and he was not sure he even wanted to.

Women were not rational. Men were much more straightforward and less complicated.

Except for Rhonwellt.

As if it were not enough to worry about what to do with eight felons and an orphaned child, Tristan must also deal with his high-strung monk who unsettled his emotions. Usually mild-mannered and compliant, Rhonwellt possessed the ability to be extraordinarily obstinate at times. Tristan was still learning that the monk would not always bend to his will. Not that the knight needed to dominate, but during his time on the battlefield he had become accustomed to being obeyed without question. As lord of the manor, his word was law, but Rhonwellt would not be ruled.

No longer the robust lad Tristan had known, Rhonwellt had softened over the years. Though not at all womanly, neither was he one of the hardy kind of man the knight found himself surrounded by as a Crusader. Most soldiers were hard men, brutal and unforgiving of spirit. Nothing at all like the gentle monk who spent his days at his writing desk and who held Tristan's heart. The knight related to hard men. Men like Rhonwellt were outside his experience.

That Rhonwellt was rescued unharmed should have filled Tristan with joy and relief. Instead, he endured a tightness in his chest and found no occasion to rejoice. Tristan could not shake a sense that he had still failed, that somehow he had let Rhonwellt down, that his efforts to keep him safe had, once again, been inadequate. Though Tristan had not wanted him to travel to Cydweli to see Brother Anselm, it had nothing to do with apprehensions over Rhonwellt's safety. The real reason was that he did not wish Rhonwellt gone for long. Yet, despite his selfish reasons for wanting to keep Rhonwellt close at hand, it had turned out to be an issue of his safety, after all.

It was understandable that Rhonwellt would need to gather himself, to spend some time in prayer giving thanks that he was safe and sound. However, the monk's actions when he left him and went to the church made Tristan very much doubt he would see him again for the rest of the evening; disappointing, when all he wanted was to spend the end of the day eating and drinking his fill while basking in the sight of Rhonwellt alive and well at home—where he belonged.

Tristan paused to catch his breath, wrapping his cloak around him against the cold. At the moment, the way up to the hall seemed longer and steeper. Looking down the hill in the darkness, the twinkling lights of the demesne and the town beyond resembled many a soldier's camp. Even the sounds were similar: the noisy and lively voices spilling out onto the street of men carousing or arguing at the tavern, the hammer of the smithy as he worked late into the evening, the screeches of playing children who should have been in their beds log ago. Though the sounds were the same, the camps were in the past and best left there.

Tristan turned, looked up toward the hall and restarted his climb, the weight of his troubles far heavier than his boots. Since his time with Rhonwellt years before, Tristan had avoided emotional entanglements. Their relationship had been intense until morality and sense of family responsibility imposed on them by others tore them apart. Nothing was ever the same for Tristan after that, and the experience taught him he could not trust his own feelings.

The only other time he had given anything of himself was during his time in the Holy Land while on Crusade with Amjhad. His feelings for the Persian beauty had differed greatly from what he had felt for Rhonwellt. Though technically his squire and servant, the flirtatious youth had maneuvered himself into Tristan's bed, and the knight had gone along willingly. The olive-skinned lad intoxicated him.

Amjhad had been a natural warrior which meant they were very much alike and Tristan saw him as his equal. They depended on each other both on and off the field. Amjhad did not merely attend his master in battle, they fought side by side, each guarding the other's back. It was how they stayed alive so long. They wandered far into the desert away from the camps to lay together under a million stars, their furtive couplings battle-weary diversions to dissipate the pent up energy brought on by the blood baths earlier in the day. It was only when kneeling on sand soaked with Amjhad's blood as the young man lay dying in his arms that Tristan had realized the powerful emotional bond they had formed together in just two summers. It was the second time someone he cared for deeply had been taken from him. The first time had soured him on life. The second had taken the joy out of fighting.

Combat got under a man's skin. What started out as a mission to honor God and spread the message of Christ soon succumbed to the sheer thrill of killing. Amjhad's death made him reconsider the justifications for war and its wholesale slaughter. The youth's death reminded him about a distant God, one who could be cruel and uncaring. Left to wander the desert in search of who he was or might be thereafter, two long summers passed before his roaming eventually led him home.

Coming home was to come full circle—finding Rhonwellt still alive and living less than one-hundred-sixty furlongs from the estate where he grew up. However, it was not a step back in time. Too much had changed. Rhonwellt had given his life to God. Had Tristan held out even the slightest hope that Rhonwellt still lived, it proved a development he could never have envisioned. In the eyes of nearly everyone, most especially the Church, this unholy fellowship and the feelings they held for each other, were a sin whether carnal or not. The knight did not know what God Himself thought and did not really care. Since Christ had likely never known the warmth of another, how could He think to judge such things?

Topping the rise, Tristan stopped and stood before the hall door. Too much time had passed for him to have any real memories of the feeling of Rhonwellt's body next to his. He just knew he ached from the want of it, longed to create new memories of it. Tristan knew Rhonwellt's struggle was real and not just indecision. Could he work through his fear and reconcile the inconsistencies in the teachings of the Church with the feelings that dwelt in his heart? If not, the knight feared his beloved monk might never be wholly his. Gritting his teeth, Tristan suppressed a growl trying to force itself from deep in his throat.

He pushed the hall door open with such force it banged against screens wall. Hanging his cloak on the peg he looked around for Hewrey. The lad was not in the great room.

"Hewrey, pour me a bloody drink!"

✞   ✞   ✞

THOUGH THE GENERAL MOOD AT THE HALL THAT EVENING WAS genial, Rhonwellt could not fully embrace the spirit. He sat staring into the fire, his face empty of emotion. It was hard for him to remember a time when he felt so exhausted, yet he knew sleep would not come easily. Tristan was drinking heavily, his earlier dark mood growing lighter the more wine he consumed. With each cup, he put in less water, until soon he drank it nearly full strength. Hewrey kept offering to dilute it, but Tristan would only wave him off with a scowl. Ernulf sat contentedly on Jocelyn's lap, while the worry lines on the young lass's face showed the accusations against Noah were taking their toll. Ciaran sat quietly, saying very little and stealing furtive glances at Jocelyn. Though aware, Rhonwellt paid scant attention to any of it.

The ordeal of the kidnapping was over, and yet Rhonwellt could not shake the lingering millstone of emotion it had placed on him, and he was having difficulty putting his finger on what, exactly, those feelings were. There were many individual occurrences within the larger context, each demanding their own reaction.

Being grabbed, bound and blindfolded violated his being, it felt intimate and personal, too close to detach from or regard from a distance. It was immediate and visceral. The third such incident in his life—the first a lifetime ago and the second only the summer before, neither of which was he intended to survive—brought into play all his doubts about his own value. Once again, he wondered if he were cast as the fool in some divine jest.

The words from both Osgar and Esyllt, attempting to debase him and Tristan, cast doubt on his freedom to love or be loved. Even after Esyllt made it clear the words held no truth for her, uncertainty lingered. How could they—outsiders—pretend to know the nature of their relationship when he was still trying to fathom the ins and outs of it himself? There was no doubt he felt love for Tristan, but he had not yet allowed himself to consider what that really meant. The first time he had given himself over to love, it had nearly gotten him killed. Could he even do it again?

Then, there was Tristan's reaction. Though the knight had never favored Rhonwellt's trip to Cydweli, did Tristan really blame him for what had transpired? Was he not the one who suffered this indignity? Was he not the victim? Or was anger the only way the knight could deal with what he really felt? No matter, Rhonwellt believed it was of his own doing, and he felt responsible.

There was the true heart of the matter. He felt to blame; and for that, he felt guilty. Not only at fault for this latest set of circumstances, he suddenly realized that guilt was the feeling he attached to nearly everything, and had as far back as he could recall. Unlike the pain of a festering sore or ill-fitting shoes, it was not that searing, immediate guilt which resulted from some event he felt he had caused. Instead, it was a steady, ever-present pang of conscience, relegated to the background like the ache of bones in winter, always present, but only acutely noticeable whenever one attempted to move, rendering them reluctant to stir.

No matter how often Rhonwellt acknowledged his guilt and sought forgiveness, his burden never lifted for long. Each time, it weighed down on him, like stones being added one at a time by an executioner pressing someone to death for their crimes. If it did not cease, Rhonwellt knew he must soon suffocate.

Gathering his strength, the monk rose slowly from the bench and stood in front of the fire. He had no sense of time. Conversation around the hearth must have been sparse, for whenever he came to the present, there was silence. Even Ernulf was quiet.

"I must have rest." The company turned to look at Rhonwellt. "I bid you God's peace until the morrow," he said. With those words, he turned and shuffled toward the door. Rhonwellt had gone but half the distance when he heard unsteady footfalls approach from behind. Rhonwellt stopped and turned to face Tristan, watching him weave back and forth from the copious amount of alcohol he had consumed. "Tristan, you are drunk."

"I bloody well am!" Tristan replied, slurring his words.

"It is late," said Rhonwellt with a sigh, searching the knight's face. Their eyes locked. Rhonwellt saw more than one emotion staring back at him, coming from somewhere deep, a place he sensed Tristan allowed few to see. The intensity of it buffeted him like a strong wind. His inner self staggered. Was he seeing this because Tristan could not hold it back? Or had the knight ceased to care? Was this his soul being laid bare? Suddenly Rhonwellt felt like a voyeur.

Without a word, Tristan cupped Rhonwellt's face in his rough hands, pulled him close, stared at him with eyes the monk was sure could not focus, and kissed him. Not a gentle kiss, but hard, it mashed Rhonwellt's lips painfully against his teeth. It was a kiss empty of desire, beyond passion, borne from desperation. It was a kiss that said Tristan might be losing hope.

Rhonwellt's first impulse was to fight against it, to push Tristan away. But the knight's powerful grip held his face like a trap. The monk felt his heart race though he was uncertain whether from dread or want. The monk was glad he felt no desire in it. That would have intimidated him more. The intensity alarmed Rhonwellt, but his uneasiness stemmed from the emotion, not the man. He had never been afraid of Tristan, only the brooding warrior inside him, the fighter who lived his life constantly at war, his needs and wants seen as battles he must win, his doubts as enemies he must eliminate.

Unable to resist Tristan's strength, Rhonwellt's resistance ceased, his body went limp. He let it happen. Just when he thought he might want to return the kiss, Tristan released him, spun and walked away. Gasping for air, the monk realized he had stopped breathing. There was a slight taste of blood on his lips. His head grew light. Rhonwellt grabbed for the stones that framed the doorway and closed his eyes tight, glad for the opportunity to compose himself. After a couple of calming breaths, he opened his eyes. Watching Tristan as he crossed the room, the knight's legs more sure, his steps steady, Rhonwellt saw all other eyes in the room turn discretely away as he looked in their general direction. There was no reaction from anyone but Ernulf who stared openly. Jocelyn gently took the child's chin in her hand and turned his face toward her. She began to talk softly. Not able to hear her words, Rhonwellt felt his stomach tighten.

The last thing the monk saw as he turned, before he touched the latch and began to push the door, was Tristan approach the sideboard and reach for the wine jug.

"Oh, master, it is late. No more," said Hewrey, trying to stop Tristan from filling his cup again.

The knight ignored his servant, replenished his drink, and walked silently to the stairs leading to the solar. Deliberately, he began to climb.

The outer door to the hall opened readily. As Rhonwellt walked through, he was mindful of another, that inner door that would not breach so easily. Entry there had been shut and bolted fast for so long, every time he stood at the threshold he panicked. He could not clasp the latch and wondered if his only way in was for someone to open the door from the other side.

Suddenly, Rhonwellt realized he may wish to see what lay beyond that portal.

Had the bolt just been thrown back?

FIFTEEN

Tristan lay in his bed, staring at the barely visible rafters of the solar roof. The dim light of dawn made its best effort to sneak through the cracks in the shutters that covered the small opening cut into the wall. Although he could hear no rain hitting the roof, the near constant drumming that had penetrated his restlessness in the night and the weakness of the morning gloom assured him this would be another sunless day. With eight prisoners chained and under guard in the tithing barn to deal with, the weather would be no match for the stormy mood already taking shape in his head.

The knight's mouth was dry and the taste of stale wine lingered on his palate, a taste he hated but seemed ever-present of late. Tristan lay motionless, fearing any movement of his roiling stomach would cause him to retch. A thin sheen of sweat covered his face and forehead. If the room would stop spinning, he might attempt to get out of bed. When he tried to raise his head, his guts heaved. He belched. Fetid air traveled up his windpipe and into his mouth, forcing him to swallow hard, glad there was nothing in his stomach to force back down. Perhaps he needed more time before trying again.

The over-abundance of drink had disturbed Tristan's sleep and invaded his dreams, leaving him to toss and turn through the night. He awoke not at all rested but grateful that he had not conjured the nightmare that often plagued him during his frequent drinking binges, visions of Amjhad's death in the heat of battle—or the one-time wrinkle in that scenario where the face of his Persian lover was replaced, at the moment of death, with the face of Rhonwellt. That time, the dream had foretold a threat to Rhonwellt when Fulke had nearly killed him at the priory. There was no warning of the monk's latest brush with danger and Tristan fretted over it.

Tristan must have dozed off, for upon waking the second time he found he had no idea how much time passed. Maybe this attempt at arising would be successful. With a groan, the knight threw back the covers, swung his legs around and put his feet to the floor. He sat for a moment to get his bearings. Head pounding, he leaned forward, pushed himself off the bed and slowly rose to his feet. Wobbling on unsteady legs, Tristan realized he had slept in his clothes. He had Hewrey to thank that he slept warm at all. The lad would wait until he lost consciousness, then creep up the solar stairs and into his room and cover him. Without complaint, Hewrey did it and so often he required neither torch nor candle in the pitch black room. Tristan felt both regret and gratitude.

"You are a good lad," murmured Tristan.

Tristan dragged his feet across the room to the chamberpot. Bracing one outstretched hand against the wall, he pissed with a great yawn, then tucked himself inside his braes and he went to the wash-basin. He stared at the water in the bowl. God be praised for tiny miracles. There was no ice to break. The knight splashed his whole head, gasping at the bitterly cold water. It afforded little relief. He leaned on the washstand, letting the water drip from his face and hair. After a few deep breaths, he splashed his face again and reached for a linen.

"I am too bloody old for this!" he growled under his breath—a recurring sentiment these days.

The quiet clanking of dishes and shuffling footsteps drifting up from below stairs told him the rest of the household was already awake and he needed to pull himself together. Closing his eyes to steel himself, a curious scene played behind the lids; images of him walking up to Rhonwellt, grabbing the monk's face with his palms, and kissing him on the lips. The realm where dreams resided must be unreliable for surely that could not have occurred. Yet, somehow it seemed real. Dreams were a bloody waste of time, at least most of them. He shook his head, opened the door, and headed for the stairs.

"Good morrow, master," Hewrey called out as Tristan descended to the hall. "There be..." the lad stopped. "There is," he said, "hot porridge. Come. Eat. Break your fast."

"Just a cup of ale," Tristan answered, "with plenty water."

"Now, master," Hewrey said, "you must eat."

A flash of pique ran through the knight every time his servant tried to argue with him. No use being angry. That spirit was what Tristan admired most about him. Taking a deep breath, he relaxed his shoulders. "You are a good lad, Hewrey. Maybe later." While Hewrey filled his cup, Tristan stood in front of the hearth and looked around the room. "Where are Ernulf and Jocelyn?"

"Took a walk," said Hewrey. "Down to the church."

Tristan spun his head, his brows pointing skyward.

"Now master. The bairn been locked up in this old hall for days. Since them what sought him harm was caught, we seen no danger."

Tristan regarded Hewrey long and hard. He took a gulp of ale, swirled it around in his mouth and spat it toward the fire. It missed and hit the floor.

"With me," growled Tristan. "Now!"

The knight emptied his cup, grabbed his cloak from the peg by the door, and went out into the morning. The air outside, damp from a thin fog, was crisp and fresh. The knight breathed it deep into his lungs as he muffled himself inside his wool wrap and waited for Hewrey to catch up. Then, keeping a brisk pace to ward off the chill, Tristan led the way down the bailey rise, quickly covering the furlong and a half to the makeshift gaol.

An impressive building, the tithe barn stood between gatehouse and the church. A single room about twenty by forty paces, its stone walls stood about twice the height of a man on the inside, appearing to be half that on the outside due to the deep eaves of the thatched roof. The interior was expansive, its ceiling rising to the lofty height of eight or nine average men. Any one of the remaining majestic old oaks that dotted the nearby grazing meadows could have fit inside. A massive set of double doors, able to admit the tallest of wagons, pierced the middle of the longer, front wall. About one-third of the winter stockpile of goods remained, spilling from the back wall nearly to the doors, effectively cutting the room in two. The eight prisoners were chained in the barn, four at each end, the two groups obscured in both sight and sound from each other by the piles of stores.

One of the large doors stood ajar. As Tristan approached, he tersely acknowledged a group of five soldiers huddled around a fire just outside the barn.

"My lord." Their greetings bounced off each other in a jumble as they clambered to their feet as Tristan approached.

"They are quiet?" Tristan asked.

"They are, my lord," said a stocky Welshman, "though the loud one keeps complaining of the cold." He grinned and spat into the fire.

"Well, perhaps, after a night in a cold barn, a warm fire will entice a confession," said Tristan. "Haul them all out here, separately, to thaw by the fire, but leave the woman there to fret awhile longer." He turned to Hewrey. "Go to the village for bread and ale. Get enough for all eight." He dropped a few pennies into the lad's hand.

The door creaked open and the three men taken from the tor shuffled out, their eyes squinting in the gray gloom of the morning. Each prisoner wore a pair of iron cuffs on his wrists, each cuff joined by a long bar with a chain passing through a ring at the center, binding them all together.

They sidled up to the fire, blowing on their hands, then held them out over the flames, stamping their feet. The pounding in his head, his uneasy stomach and his memory of their crime left little room for Tristan to feel any pity for such men as they stood shivering in the cold air.

"I trust you were comfortable with your accommodation." The knight did nothing to stem the sarcasm.

"Like the finest of inns, my lord," said the brash outlaw, "though the linens was a might scratchy." He made a great gesture of bowing to Tristan. "What would my lord be servin' to break our fast? Mutton stew? Fine cheese?"

"Bread and ale," said Tristan, "and be glad of it."

Though he had initiated it, the knight's taste for the banter proved short-lived, and he bit back further retort. He knew the felon's attempt at bravado was all for show. While the murderer had claimed his neck was not made for a rope, there was no doubt the wretch would hang, so the man had nothing to lose. Ernulf had been spared the fate of the others. If Tristan's hunch was correct, so had the lad's mother. Who had lived and who had died mattered only to God at this point. Regardless of the number of killings, they had stolen horses, a crime with only one punishment. It was a shame a man could only hang once.

The other two outlaws remained mute, the prospect of hanging had stilled their tongues. Were it not for the four dead travelers, each might have looked forward to a long life after forfeiting a hand for thievery.

Tristan edged up to the fire, longing for a drink. With a heave from his troubled stomach, the thought quickly flew from his mind on the heels of regret. He stood there, eyes closed, hands out in front of him over the flames, indulging his misery. Damn this whole business. Had he earned no peace yet?

The clink of chain and shuffling of feet pulled Tristan from his morass of self-pity. As they led Selwyn and his men outside, they shielded their eyes from the light. They stopped on the opposite side of the fire from the outlaws. Silent, the two groups faced each other.

"It seems not just the poor lead lives of crime," said the outlaw from the tor with a chuckle. A dark-haired, handsome man with a cocky, confident smile, he exuded an air of deceit and danger. It made him seem roguish in every sense of the word.

"We have committed no crime," snarled Wulfric.

"And yet, you be in chains, same as me," said the rogue. Wulfric growled and strained at his bonds. The rogue chuckled, a twinkle in the corner of his eye. "If ye wants a piece of me, ye better hurry. I think our knight means to hang me."

"If I were not in chains," said Wulfric, "I would make short work of you on the end of my sword."

"You could try. But we will probably never know 'cause of..." He mimicked a noose being pulled tight around his neck as he stuck his tongue out.

"None of it really matters," said the knight, belching more stale wine. "You will all die. You lot for the blasphemy of kidnapping a monk," he said, pointing at Wulfric and his men, "and you for murdering the travelers in the caravan." He nodded toward the men from the tor. "You all should make your peace."

Wulfric and Selwyn looked at each other with dazed expressions. As Tristan watched the light of comprehension spread across their faces, their mouths fell open. Wulfric stammered, "A young woman and her child accompanied by an old man and an old woman and three men at arms?" No one said a word. Tristan stared back and forth between the two groups of prisoners.

"Not hardly worth the trouble," said the brigand. "A few jewels and very little coin. Only thing worth anything was the horses."

Wulfric paled. "All dead?" he asked, his hands balled into fists so tight his fingers went white. A look of profound sadness covered Selwyn's face.

"All except the woman," said the rogue. "A comely lass, and most compliant she was." He made a tsking sound as he winked.

In an instant, Tristan was in front of the outlaw and a back-handed blow sent him reeling. The impact with the man's jaw sent a jolt of pain through the knight's hand making him wish he had worn gloves. He shook his hand, moved his fingers, and then rubbed it with the other to ease the throbbing, smearing a trickle of blood that oozed from one of his knuckles.

Selwyn and his men came to immediate attention. The look on their faces said they did not know whether to believe the outlaw.

"Merwenna?" said Selwyn directly to Tristan. "My niece lives?"

"He lies," said Wulfric. Doubt in his voice betrayed the surety of his statement.

"Her body was not with the others," said Selwyn. "That must mean something."

"Neither were those of Ernulf and Myfanwy. It does not mean they live."

Tristan realized this was the first time Wulfric had said Ernulf's name.

"Merwenna lives," breathed Wulfric, looking back and forth between the outlaw and Tristan. "And you have her?"

"I do not know who I have," said Tristan.

"Where is she?" said Wulfric, his voice full of menace.

"Our host have her chained in the barn," the outlaw responded. "Keepin' her for hisself, I wager."

The big Saxon took a couple of steps toward Tristan, nearly dragging Selwyn into the fire. His chains stopped him short. Tristan looked at the outlaw, then at Wulfric. Without a sound, he turned, skirted the prisoners and strode to the barn. For the first time since waking, he was sure-footed and his head was clear. As he approached, the woman lay cowering in the straw.

"Merwenna, the time has come. Tell me the bloody truth. Now!"

SIXTEEN

Merwenna's hood fell backward when she snapped her head up at the sound of her name. Disbelief and more than a little fear covered her face. The outlaws had crudely cropped her hair, leaving it uneven with more than one bare spot. Though filthy and matted, when clean her shorn locks would be the same color as the straw stuck to it. Exposed, she put her hand up and self-consciously pulled at it.

Feet spread apart in an aggressive stance, Tristan's face betrayed no emotion, while his voice contained much. "Tell me the truth. I have run out of patience and am in no mood for your games."

"How do you...?" Before she could finish her question, a throaty voice from outside the barn called her name. She sighed. "He has found me, then."

"Who has found you?" asked Tristan.

"Wulfric." Her shoulders sagged, a look of defeat on her face. "That was he, was it not?"

Tristan nodded the affirmative. "They are in chains and cannot harm you."

"Then my uncle, Selwyn, is here, as well."

Tristan nodded again.

She looked up at him. Her eyes said his words had sunk in. "In chains? What has he done?"

"To begin with, he kidnapped my priest."

Her eyes grew wide. Her lips parted to form a word. She stopped, tilting her head. Then her eyes narrowed. "Whatever for?" she asked.

"He has not said." Tristan studied her face. "Does he mean you harm?"

She waited before replying. "No." She let her eyes drift away. "In his way, he is a good man. He may be stubborn and a bully, loud and uncouth, but he would never harm me." She looked back, directly at Tristan. "Nor would he have harmed the priest. I am sure." She shook her head slightly from side to side. "Stupid man! Why would he want a priest?"

"Not any priest. My priest."

"I do not understand."

"In time you shall."

The bellow of Wulfric's voice came again. "Merwenna!"

Tristan turned and strode to the door that stood ajar. "Shut him up! Now!" He was half-way back when he returned and called out, "Someone come in here and remove these chains. And bring food and drink."

As he returned to the woman in the straw, he could hear the distinct sound of a gloved fist striking flesh and bone outside the barn. A soldier appeared in the doorway, a grin on his face. "He be quiet now, my lord. One of the lads needs to go to the smithy's for hammer and chisel. I told him be quick about it." The man disappeared as quickly as he had come.

Merwenna grew still and Tristan sensed her retreat to someplace deep inside herself. At hearing footsteps behind him, he turned to find one of his soldiers approaching with bread and ale. The man looked to Tristan for direction. After the knight nodded, the soldier threw the bread onto the straw and set the cup of ale down just out of Merwenna's reach.

Tristan's face twitched. "Hand it to her," he said.

"My lord?" the soldier replied.

"I said hand it to her!"

The man bent to retrieve the cup, all the while his eyes darting between Tristan and Merwenna. He stood there holding it, the trembling of his hand causing little waves on the surface of the liquid.

"Now, pick up the bread and hand them both to her."

The guard followed Tristan's order, averting his eyes. "Mistress," he said in a voice barely audible.

Merwenna accepted it. Her hunger was conspicuous as she tore off a chunk and stuffed it into her mouth.

"Drag that crate over here," said Tristan, pointing to a large box laying nearby.

"Yes, my lord." The man scurried to comply.

"Now, go from my sight," said Tristan through a clenched jaw and waving a dismissive hand as he sat. "Do not cross my path or come within my sight again this day."

"Yes, my lord," said the man, casting his gaze to the ground. He bowed, backing away from the knight all the way to the doors.

Merwenna shifted positions so she could lean against the wall. She ate greedily and gulped the ale. Tristan watched her features soften as her body began to relax. Despite her present appearance, she was not unattractive, and somehow familiar. Yet, he was sure he had never seen her before.

Facing her, Tristan hoped she would be more forthcoming with information now that she was no longer hungry. "If they mean you no harm, then why do they pursue you all the way across England and Wales?"

She lowered her head as she mumbled her answer. Tristan could scarcely believe his ears. "He what?"

She raised her head. "He wants to marry me." This time her voice was full and overflowed with defiance.

Tristan exploded, his face twisted in disgust. "Of all the...! And you called Wulfric a stupid man. Woman, have you no brains? You journeyed for weeks across England and through the hostile Marches, you forfeited the lives of those with you, all to escape a marriage?" Tristan's words hit her like a slap. "That is stupid! How could you be so callous?"

Merwenna's eyes welled with tears and her chin began to quiver. "Do you think I have not been punished? God has had His retribution. He took my son away." She began weeping so hard her whole body convulsed. Yet, she made no sound. She pounded her legs with her fists until the wave of grief subsided. Tristan gave her time to compose herself, deciding she should live with her pain and remorse a little longer. He would tell her later that Ernulf was alive. She wiped her eyes with a corner of the cloak.

"It is not just Wulfric. I do not wish to marry anyone, though in all probability I shall. I just needed to postpone it for a while."

"Postpone it. Why? All women must marry," said Tristan, trying to comprehend her rebelliousness. "It is what gives them legitimacy."

"Legitimize me! Men!" Her face grew hard. "Why do you men all think we women need a man to validate our existence?" She raised her hands to point at him, her chains rattling. "Besides, I am a widow. That legitimizes me and gives me certain privilege. I have done what they required of me. I am not obliged to marry again."

"Only if your husband left you with means."

"Ranulf was a good husband and provided well for me. I have land and some little money."

"Norman or Saxon?"

"Norman. He died in France in service to the King. I observed my year of mourning and now I am free." She eased a little. "My journey has another purpose."

"And that is?"

"I cannot tell you, at least not yet."

Tristan was about to insist when two soldiers entered the barn and scurried over to where they sat. One carried a large hammer and an iron chisel, the other an iron ingot the size of a man's shoe. Laying the ingot on the dirt floor, they used it as an anvil to chisel open the rings about her wrists. When the bands were finally off, she massaged where the skin had been rubbed raw.

"Rhonwellt will have a salve for your wrists." Still angry, it took effort for Tristan to sound sympathetic.

"Thank you, my lord," she replied, her voice tight with anger of her own.

He leaned forward with his elbows on his knees. Deciding to let the question about her purpose lay for now, he tried another avenue. "Tell me what happened on the road."

Biting her lip, Merwenna cast her eyes downward. She grabbed a fistful of the cloak covering her with one hand and began to twist it with the other. She remained silent for many moments. Her shaking shoulders betrayed the fact she wept again, silently.

Tristan was ill-equipped to handle women crying. They often used it as a ploy and could cry readily. Men almost never cried. He could easily count, using each digit on his free hand only once, the times he had done so. Crying made him feel vulnerable and that made him angry. But something told him anger would be of no help, that another response was needed now. He sat up straight and gripped the handle of his sword, something familiar and comforting, a sign of strength. He allowed his anger to flow into it, relaxing his demeanor that something gentler might come from his mouth. "Come child. Tell me all of it."

Without raising her head, she said, "I am no child. I have been wife and...mother." She fell silent for a moment and let out a great sigh. "Now I am neither."

"You did not accompany those men willingly." Though delivered as a statement, it was really a question.

She shook her head. "They attacked us." She stopped wringing the cloth of the cloak and smoothed it out on her lap, her hands sliding over it repeatedly, almost obsessively.

"The caravan?" he said.

She nodded.

"Merwenna. Look at me."

She turned her head away, then around, taking in her surroundings, though there was little to see in the gloom of the cavernous barn. Tristan sensed she was stalling. He waited.

"They killed everyone," Merwenna said at last. "An archer picked off two of my guardsmen before we knew they were there. Then they came at us from out of a wood." She looked up. Even in the darkness, Tristan saw eyes full of raw grief tinged with anger. She worked her mouth as though it were dry. "Hrodulf tried to get us away, but the cart hit a rock and overturned." She swallowed hard, her voice quavering. "Ernulf and nurse became pinned beneath it," she paused, "and left to die."

She squeezed her eyes shut as though trying to block out an unspeakable vision. Her breath came in shuttering gasps but her eyes remained dry, her supply of tears apparently exhausted. "They ran my last guardsman through with a sword and..."

Tristan waited a moment. "And..." he said.

Merwenna drew in a deep breath. "And they cut Hrodulf's throat. All the while laughing at his efforts to protect me." Tristan let her ramble on, mostly because he did not know what to say to her. "Hrodulf had seen over sixty summers, had served my family since before I can remember and still tried to stand for me. They cut him down with no more regard than for a rabid dog." She shot a glance at Tristan, her anger having reached full measure. "They made me watch them murder him. As the life faded from his eyes, they pleaded for something from me. I think forgiveness at not being able to save us. It was I who should have asked his pardon."

"Were you subjected to anything untoward?"

"You mean did they...?" She inhaled and blew her breath out through puffed cheeks. "Thanks be to God, no! The one in charge said they needed to get far away while time was on their side."

Glad to hear that the outlaws words might have been empty boasts, in his heart Tristan was not sure he believed her. The answer to that could wait for another time. Pieces of the tale began to take shape in the knight's mind. Merwenna had just given him all the players, but not the why and how.

"You come from the far north."

"Aye," she said. "Near Halifax."

"A long way, indeed, mistress. I passed through the place once as a lad." Tristan's mind drifted for a moment, conjuring distant memories. "I experienced kindness there in a dark hour. An experience both happy and sad," he said sounding wistful. Shaking the thoughts away, Tristan probed again for an answer as to the true reason for her journey. "What brings you to southern Wales?"

She narrowed her eyes. "It is personal and I cannot tell you, not yet. In the meantime, I am in need of a garderobe. Would that be permitted?"

"We are no grand castle, just a simple hall. A privy will have to suffice."

✟   ✟   ✟

THE THREE GUARDS STATIONED AT THE CHURCH DOORS HUDDLED in front of a small fire in the yard, eating the hot pottage Ciaran had brought them to break their fast. Ciaran sat talking with Noah while they ate.

"Noah, Brother Rhonwellt has told you, you cannot leave the church. Is that correct?"

Noah nodded.

"If you do, you will have broken the rules of sanctuary and are subject to arrest. You realize this, do you not?"

"Why so many guards? I just be one man."

"They are here to see you do not leave," replied Ciaran. "One is Sir Tristan's man. The other is a Fullecoppe man."

"But, I did not kill him. Why must I leave the country?"

"You will be forced to leave only if they cannot prove you innocent of William's murder."

"But, I are innocent."

"Then we must prove that. Meanwhile, if you flee from this place, they will hunt you down. You do not want that to happen. Only if God smiles on you, will they not kill you outright as a fugitive and never bring you back to stand trial."

"They always finds folk like me guilty."

"Sir Tristan and Brother Rhonwellt will do all they can to see that does not happen."

Ciaran did not want to tell him that if he were forced to abjure the realm, he would be unlikely to reach the port of departure, that someone would likely trick him into leaving the road and kill him. Or that if he ever tried to return, he would suffer the same fate.

Leaving Noah to ponder his situation, Ciaran walked outside. He found Rhonwellt standing by the churchyard wall, gazing toward the barn next door.

"Where is Ernulf?"

"At the hall," the young monk replied.

"We must keep the child secreted away," said Rhonwellt. "I still fear for his safety."

"But the men are in chains, Brother," said Ciaran. "Surely, they pose no danger now."

"Ernulf does not like the big Saxon," Rhonwellt answered. "We shall keep him here, out of sight, until they are safely back in their gaol."

"Clearly," said Ciaran, "it was the men they took from the tor who attacked the caravan, for they had the stolen horses. Do you really think both groups of men were out to kill them?"

"At this moment, I only know the Saxon and his men pursued them. I do not know why, and that is what troubles me. If Wulfric means him no harm, why does Ernulf dislike him so?"

The monks stood on the porch just outside the church, keeping close attention to the movements in front of the barn. The stone and thatch building sat further back from the street, with a porch raised enough for them to see over the wall enclosing the yard, affording them a clear view of the activity. Huddled in their woolen robes, they watched as the prisoners shuffled out into the morning air to warm around the fire, their heads down, eyes squinting at the brightness of the light outside. The metallic clink of chains drifted across the chill air.

"They look very cold," said Ciaran, shivering against the chill, "and very sad."

"They do not build gaols for comfort, Ciaran. Those men are felons, they committed murder. If they look sad, it is because they know they shall hang for their crimes."

Ciaran quickly sketched the sign of the cross, his other hand absently fingering the crude wooden one that hung from his neck.

"Your prayers are likely to no avail," said Rhonwellt, glancing over Ciaran's shoulder. "I believe them to be unrepentant."

"Brother look," said Ciaran, stepping out further onto the stone porch, "Sir Tristan has just gone into the barn. And the Saxon has called out."

"Someone is missing." Rhonwellt peered around Ciaran, resting his hand on the younger monk's shoulder. "There are seven where there ought to be eight. One outlaw is missing. He must still be in the barn. Three men accompanied the Saxon. All four are there," said Rhonwellt.

"The big blonde is hard to miss," said Ciaran. He craned his neck as he looked down the street.

"Sir Tristan brought five outlaws back from the tor."

"Yes, one was a corpse thrown over a horse, the other four alive." Though already tall enough to see well, Ciaran stood on tip-toes.

"Only three stand around the fire," said Rhonwellt. "The fourth has either died or is still in the barn."

"Why do you suppose Sir Tristan has kept him there?"

"Fie! You are like two old janglers tattling at the gate behind your husbands' backs." The sound of Jocelyn's voice behind them gave both monks a start. Neither had heard her approach.

"Mary's teeth, lass!" exclaimed Rhonwellt. "Do not creep up on a body like that! I do believe I felt my heart stop." The monk patted his chest. "Furthermore, I heartily reject the appellation."

Jocelyn wedged herself between the two men. "Surely there is room for one more at the gate." With an impish grin, the young girl cast her gaze in the direction of the barn. "There is talk in the town that one of them is a woman."

"Surely not," gasped Ciaran. "Women cannot be outlaws. Can they, Brother Rhonwellt?"

"Alma, down at the tavern, says that even with her head buried deep in her cloak when she rode by, what little she saw plainly said it was a woman."

The three fell silent, continuing to peer over the wall at the activity next door. The sound of small hands clapping accompanied by childish giggles drifted out from the interior of the church. Rhonwellt turned to look uneasily over his shoulder toward the sound.

"Noah has finished breaking his fast," said Jocelyn, "with nary a complaint about the lack of meat. Now he plays Pick The Hand with Ernulf." Rhonwellt looked at the young lass with a blank stare. "Which hand is the pebble in?" Both he and Ciaran nodded by lifting their chins slightly, but Rhonwellt remained skeptical. "Do monks never play games?" she asked.

"There was seldom time for such activity at the cloister," said Rhonwellt, wistfully. "*Ora et labora*. Prayer and work was our lot."

"Brother Oswald used to play it with me," said Ciaran, "when I first arrived there as a child."

"Did he, indeed?" Rhonwellt was surprised. "I never knew."

"He did. He saw that I was lonely and frightened and it put me at ease. But when I assumed the duties of novice, Prior Alwyn put a stop to it."

Rhonwellt thought he knew most everything about Ciaran, but this simple fact had escaped him. It was two complete changes of the seasons after Ciaran arrived at the priory before Rhonwellt gave him any notice — not until the lad had begun to help the scribes in the scriptorium by filling ink pots and sharpening quills. Drawn to his innocence and utter openness, almost immediately they were inseparable.

"Brother Rhonwellt, how has so much strife come to our little village?" Ciaran asked. Wrinkles furrowed his forehead as he thrust his arms deep into his sleeves. He peered down at his feet, his gaze lingering there a moment, and then raised his head to look at Rhonwellt. "First, the old woman dies in this very yard having escaped death after all of her companions are murdered." He sketched the sign of the cross. "Brutal ruffians who seem to have some reason to pursue Ernulf, kidnap you. And men accuse our Noah of a heinous crime." He cocked his head to the side. "Is God displeased with us?"

Rhonwellt, reluctant to mention that those thoughts had entered his mind also, tried to give an answer that would set the young monk more at ease. "Some may believe such," said the older monk. "I prefer to think God has brought these problems to us because He is confident we will know how to deal with them." He had to keep thinking that even if he did not fully believe it.

"Noah did not kill William," said Jocelyn. "I am sure of it."

"Two quite powerful men say that he did." Rhonwellt was matter-of-fact. "Experience should tell you who they will believe and who they will not." Rhonwellt stared at the action in front of the barn for a few more moments. "Tell me about William and his family," he said.

"William was a..." she paused, "...a friend."

Rhonwellt put his hand on Jocelyn's shoulder, turning her to face him. He said in a calm voice, "Lass. Noah is in very serious trouble. It is time for the plain truth."

"I do not..."

Rhonwellt cut her off. "William was a gentleman who paid to... spend time with you."

Jocelyn's face went ashen. She swallowed hard, burying her face in her hands.

Ciaran breathed the word no, his face becoming a mask of disbelief.

"Though I have lived most of my life sheltered from the world," said Rhonwellt, "I am not incognizant of what happens there. A young woman, unmarried, traveling with a brother who seems unwilling to work, and no other means to support them, well, one need not be a seer to know that which lies hidden."

"Please do not hate me, Brother Rhonwellt."

"Lass, God constantly reminds me that I have laid forfeit any right to judge another's character."

"Please do not tell Sir Tristan." She grabbed the sleeve of his robe, her eyes beseeching him. "He will surely cast me out."

"Sir Tristan has enough on his mind at present. We need not bother him with such matters, now. But, in time he must be told. Doubtless you know that already."

"Thank you, Brother." Though she fairly whispered her thanks, she still looked worried.

"I must go." Ciaran's words were almost indiscernible as he turned and scurried toward the door, his feet shuffling across the stones of the porch. He carried his head low, staring at the ground. Jocelyn looked after him as he walked away, making motions as if to go after him.

"Leave him be, lass."

"He looked so hurt, Brother Rhonwellt." Anguish creased her brow in deep wrinkles. "I fear I have disappointed him."

"He will recover," said Rhonwellt as he watched his young friend walk away, the burden of disillusionment dragging at his heels. "Until last year, he had lived in the confines of cloister since his tenth summer. He still knows little of human nature with all its many faces. This conversation will go easier without him present."

"I guess I never realized. He is a monk. Is he not bound by vows to avoid attachments that could turn...you know?"

For a moment, Rhonwellt retreated far away. He breathed in long and deep, letting it out slowly. "Ciaran has entered his seventeenth summer. His body betrays him, demanding he confront urges and sensations he has never known." Rhonwellt stopped, pretending to concentrate on the activity at the barn, while thinking of similar feelings that had recently been reawakened in himself. He shook the musings away. "Life in cloister is never without sin, as many would believe. He knows that monks sometimes act on their carnal desires. However, he has not as yet been burdened by those yearnings, himself."

"You call desire a burden, Brother Rhonwellt. Do you see those feelings as such?"

"Being confronted by that which is forbidden is much more than just a burden, especially feelings as natural as love and desire. It can be an agony one is not sure they will survive."

Jocelyn silently watched the door of the church as Ciaran disappeared inside. She wrapped her shawl tightly about her as though suddenly aware of the morning chill.

"Now tell me, lass, about William Fullecoppe."

Jocelyn thought for a moment. "We met at the tavern in Cydweli. We had been together a few times when he began to seek me out regularly." Her voice took on a dreamy quality. "He was very handsome, tall, built like a knight with hair the color of oat straw at harvest." Her eyes began to dance as she remembered. "There was a cleft in his chin I thought made him look interesting. He said he hated it." Closing her eyes, with her arms crossed in front of her she hugged herself. "He treated me kind and told me I was beautiful."

Rhonwellt could see that the story she told was about to overwhelm her. "You loved him?" he asked.

She shrugged her shoulders. "I have known many lovers in my life, but not much love." She turned away and would not meet Rhonwellt's gaze. "I am not sure I would know it. Not really." Her body seemed to deflate, giving the appearance she was shrinking. "He said he loved me." Her voice shook.

"You must have known he could never marry you." He thought the futility of his own situation should make it easy to feel compassion, yet Rhonwellt struggled to sound sympathetic.

"Yes, I knew," said Jocelyn. "Even so, someone like me still has dreams."

"How does Noah figure into it that they should accuse him of his murder?"

"I told Noah of William's feeling for me. It scared him."

Rhonwellt stood with his arms folded, the thumb of one hand cupped under his chin, the first finger crossing his lips and touching the tip of his nose.

"William posed a threat," said Jocelyn. "Noah is frightened that I may one day leave him."

"People will think Noah killed him to keep that from happening."

"But he did not, brother. Noah is brave in talk only, not in deed. He could easily have argued with William, even threatened him, but he would lack the courage to do more than that. I have never seen him more frightened than he is now," said Jocelyn, motioning toward the interior of the church with her head. "He is terrified of hanging, and he would never last from one full moon to the next even if he were able to successfully leave the realm. He cannot survive without me."

"You are saying he needs you," said Rhonwellt, "and not the other way around?"

"It has always been that way," replied Jocelyn, "though he is careful to make it seem otherwise."

The look on the monk's face asked if she teased while he wondered if what she said could be true. Though sure that Jocelyn possessed uncommon strength and resourcefulness, he felt certain she and Noah each depended heavily on the other to survive.

"Then," said Rhonwellt, "we must see to it he is not forced to abjure and does not hang."

"How?"

"Prove his innocence."

"You and Sir Tristan?"

Rhonwellt shook his head. "Sir Tristan has enough on his mind at present, lass. We should leave him be to sort it. I fear Noah's fate has fallen to us. Pray God we are up to the task."

Jocelyn crossed herself. "What should we do?" she asked.

"First I must hear Noah's side to the story."

About to return to the church, a flurry of renewed activity caught their eye. The Saxon and his men were led back into the barn, followed shortly by the outlaws from the tor. As the last man disappeared through the door into the black interior, two figures emerged from a small opening in the end of the building and headed for the hall. Sir Tristan led the way, followed by a smallish figure with a delicate step. Rhonwellt and Jocelyn looked at each other.

"It is her!" whispered Jocelyn. "It is the woman."

"Sir Tristan is taking her to the hall." Rhonwellt ventured to the edge of the porch. "Apparently she is no longer a prisoner."

SEVENTEEN

As he approached the church, Rhonwellt ran his hand over the top of his head. The stubble there reminded him that his tonsure was long overdue for a shave and a trim. He often feared it was the sin of vanity that made him want to shave the top of his head almost monthly rather than twice yearly according to custom. Yet, stroking the short stubble produced a soothing effect when he found himself deep in thought.

Rhonwellt bent slightly to clear the doorway and stepped into the gloomy interior of the small nave, Jocelyn close behind. Noah sat with his back propped against the wall, partially hidden from view behind the altar. Ernulf, cross-legged on the floor was pointing to one of Noah's hands held in front of him, fists closed. Noah his fist to reveal the sought-after pebble in his palm.

"Good lad," he said. Ernulf's face broke into a wide grin.

They stopped in front of the game players. Ernulf turned his face upward, flashing an open smile. Rhonwellt bent slightly to squeeze his shoulder with affection, then turned to address the young man.

"Noah," said Rhonwellt, "I need you to tell me everything that occurred between you and William Fullecoppe."

"I never killed him, Brother Rhonwellt. I swear, I never done it."

"Noah!" Jocelyn snapped. "Stand up when Brother Rhonwellt speaks to you."

"Joss," he replied, his head coming up with a defiant snap, his usual surliness returning. "I told you not to be talking to me like that. You scold me like I were a child."

"Then stop behaving as one, Noah." Jocelyn's tone was sharp, her arms folded in front of her. "You are in serious trouble. Try to act like you understand that."

The lanky young man struggled to his feet. Despite Noah's outward demeanor, the fingers of one hand picking at a small hole in the thigh of his worn hose told Rhonwellt much about the young man's state of mind: Noah was worried.

Ernulf rose and went to Jocelyn, clinging to her skirt.

"I never done it, Brother," he repeated, squarely meeting the monk's gaze.

"So you keep saying, lad," replied Rhonwellt, "again and again. If I am to believe you, you must tell me all. Do you understand me? No matter how damning it may sound."

Noah nodded slowly, his features frozen and expressionless. His only movement was the twisting of his finger in the ever-widening hole in his hose.

"You cling to God's altar, lad," said Rhonwellt, "whereupon stands the cross. It would be a grave sin to utter falsehoods under the rood while touching His Holy Table."

Rhonwellt could see his words were having an effect. The lad's eyes flitted back and forth, the clouds of doubt in them turning to fear. Suddenly animated, Noah licked his lips and blurted out, "I only hit him over the head, once, with a stick."

"Noah!" Jocelyn screamed, her face twisted in fury, tears beginning to well. "You lied. You did kill him." The young woman lunged at her brother, grabbing a handful of his hair. Ernulf staggered as Jocelyn spun away, his eyebrows arched high in wonder. The child backed away and stood against the wall.

"No, no, no," Noah protested. "He were alive, Joss, I swear."

Rhonwellt stepped between the siblings, prying Jocelyn's fingers from her brother's hair before she could tear it from his scalp. "Enough!" he said, holding them apart with a hand on each of their shoulders. Rhonwellt looked from one to the other, chewing the inside of his cheek to keep his annoyance in check. "This affords us nothing."

Jocelyn turned and walked to a small bench along the wall and sank down onto it. "You will hang!" In a heartbeat, her voice grew nearly breathless and had no volume. "This is bad, Noah." Her chin quivered.

Rhonwellt grabbed the young man by both his shoulders and peered into his face and asked a simple question. "Why did you strike him?"

Noah broke away from Rhonwellt's grasp. His answer was direct and equally simple. "He were trying to take Joss away."

"Christ's blood, Noah!" said Jocelyn. Rhonwellt closed his eyes at her expletive and signed the cross. "William was nice to me. First man in a long time to treat me gentle. Do you even remember what that is like?"

"We be a team, Joss. Just you and me. Ever since ma died and da took to drink."

"Ma did not die and you know it. She run off with a bloody tranter. That be why da drank. He was a cuckold."

"Aye. And he seen to it we paid for her sin. His hatred brung us together. William wanted to part us."

"Is that the best we can hope for?" Jocelyn asked, regaining herself. "Just the two of us? For the rest of our lives?"

Looking bewildered at her words, Noah's face flushed as though he struggled to keep some repressed emotion at bay. Having lived for so long in survival mode created an interdependence between them. The direness of the present situation had given rise to animosities never resolved. Rhonwellt caught movement out of the corner of his eye and glanced in time to see Ciaran disappear through the back door that led to the cottage. He had Ernulf by the hand; the child staring wide-eyed over his shoulder.

"You only make it sound bad, Joss. We can make it, you know, just us two."

"It is bad, Noah. And if you cannot see that, then you are more like da than you know."

"I be nothing like him. I never done to you what he done."

"You tried."

Merciful God, thought Rhonwellt as he closed his eyes, sketching the sign of the cross. The idea that fathers could do such things to their own daughters sickened him. The demands of the flesh were wicked indeed.

Noah grew quiet, his fists clenched at his sides, the hole in his hose apparently forgotten. "Only once. Da beat me for it." His face flushed. "I seen how da hurt you. I tried to keep him off you and then he beat me for that. He hurt me bad, Joss."

"I know he did. Da never wanted for reasons to thrash you." Her tone eased a little and her features softened. "That, and the fact you are my brother ties us together for eternity." The siblings stared into each other's faces. Rhonwellt could only guess at the pain each saw in the other. "But there has to be more," she said, "more than going from town to town in search of dull-witted, drunken men with purses to fleece, trying to keep one step ahead of the local reeve."

"It were good, Joss." Noah had a pained look about him. "Just you and me."

"But not forever," replied Jocelyn. "I want more." She paused for a moment. "Noah, you should want more."

"We come from nothing, Joss," said Noah, his hands in front of him, palms up as though seeking alms. "Will always be nothing. I know what I be, and I knows there be no escaping it."

Jocelyn straightened her back, smoothing the skirt of her tunic with her hands. "I know what I am, Noah. Men see fit to remind me of it nearly every time." She paused. "All but William." Jocelyn opened her mouth to speak further, but said nothing. She sat motionless, her hands resting again in her lap and her face downcast. Rhonwellt took advantage of the emotional lull to get back to the task of extracting Noah's story.

"Tell me what happened leading up to your altercation with Master Fullecoppe."

"Old Willie, he were sweet smelling, with fine clothes and fancy talk. Always giving me the eye. I says no. He went off me after that."

"A great many people do not like you much, Noah," said Jocelyn. Her declaration was non-accusatory, matter-of-fact.

Noah winced at her words but kept on talking. "Then he settles on Joss. Not sure what he likes, I reckoned. He took to buying Joss two, three times a sennight, filling her head with all kind of foolishness."

"It was not foolishness, Noah. William was gentle," said Jocelyn. "He was clean and he tasted good."

Rhonwellt's face grew hot at the mention of the taste of a man. Was there a memory of his own there? Images rose in his mind that filled him with terror. Thrilling sensations in his body caused him to tremble to his core. His head swimming, Rhonwellt swallowed hard, trying to dislodge the lump that had formed in his throat. He clutched the wooden cross at his neck so tightly he could feel the edges of it dig into his hand.

Jocelyn's tone suddenly grew reflective. She stared down at her hands. "He liked me, Noah."

Allowing a few moments of silence to collect himself, Rhonwellt tried to speak. His voice nearly failed him. "Noah?" he said, indicating the lad should continue with his story.

"He comes into the *Thorn and Thistle* looking for Joss. She were with someone else, I tells him. He not be liking that."

Rhonwellt's unease grew the more Noah described the intricacies of Jocelyn's vocation. Such directness on matters of the flesh were unheard of at the priory. In his discussions with Prior Alwyn, the old monk couched such issues in vague references often spoken of in Latin and never touched on any specifics. But, he needed to hear the story, so he pushed on. "He became angry when she went with another man?" asked Rhonwellt.

"Not so much another man" replied Noah, his words coming in a rush as he raced to get the story out. "More like on account of she were whoring in Cydweli."

"Noah!" Jocelyn whined.

"It be true, Joss. He were only afraid someone would find out about him. Offered to pay us to leave."

Jocelyn buried her face in her hands and let out an agonized moan.

"Did you know he were here, Joss? That how we end up here? You was following him?"

Rhonwellt needed Noah to finish his story. "And that is when you struck him?" he said.

"Aye, brother," he nodded, "that be when."

"You struck him only once?" said Rhonwellt, palm caressing his tonsure.

"He never come after me, so once were enough." Noah's eyes grew wide as though in shock. "He folded up like a corpse cut down from a gibbet."

"Then you knew he was dead?" Rhonwellt was struck by the young man's use of the word corpse.

Noah was slow to answer. "I feared he were. But I swears to not hitting him hard enough to kill him."

"Did anyone see the two of you argue?" Rhonwellt had been pacing. He stopped with his back to the lad.

"Some in the tavern may have seen me follow him out the back, but not a soul were in the street when we comes around."

"Could they have heard you argue from inside?"

"Noise in the tavern were too loud."

Rhonwellt resumed pacing.

"Is it real bad?" Noah asked, his finger once again probing the hole in his hose. "Am I going to hang?"

✞   ✞   ✞

SOMETIME LATER, A SOLDIER RELAYED THE MESSAGE.

"Sir Tristan says you are to come to the hall now, girl."

The order came as a surprise to everyone. Jocelyn eyed the soldier, then shrugged her shoulders.

"Very well. Come Ernulf," she said holding out her hand to the boy.

"My lord says the child stays. He will call for him later."

Jocelyn tried to protest. "But Ernulf is in my charge." She then cast a worried glance toward her brother.

"My lord was most clear. He remains with the monks until sent for."

Rhonwellt nodded to her, trying to give reassurance. "Run along, lass. You have duties to perform and cannot always be here with Noah. Apparently we are to be summoned later." He attempted some levity to mask his worry over the strange order. "He will not stray. The guards will see to it he remains here." Jocelyn put a smile to her lips that appeared forced and followed the soldier out the door and across the yard. Waiting at the gate stood Esyllt, blowing warm air into her hands, the handle of her large basket slung over her arm. At the sight of the old woman, Rhonwellt's brows shot skyward. He wondered at her presence and hoped there was not another body to deal with at the hall. This whole episode had suddenly turned downright mystifying. He watched the three exit the gate and start up the lane.

When their time came to make their way up the hill to the hall, Ciaran walked in front carrying Ernulf, whispering in his ear, while Rhonwellt remained a little behind. The hour approached half-sext and a weak mid-afternoon sun lurked behind the gray fog that had rolled in low to the ground, barely clearing the top of the bell tower on the peak of the church.

The conversation at the church had unnerved everyone. Ciaran had been broody throughout the office of sext, only mumbling the words, his voice barely audible. He forgot to sign the cross several times, and never raised his head, rather kept his gaze cast to the floor, his eyes wide open, but focused on nothing.

His head bowed, deep in thought, Rhonwellt found he could not shake Jocelyn's words from his mind. Her frank mention of the taste of a man had given rise to a remembrance both unsettling and compelling — the time he and Tristan stood face to face, naked on the bank of the river over four seasons ago. His body tingled at the recollection. Save the corpses he had prepared for burial, stiff and cold to the touch, seldom had he seen another living soul naked or been himself unclothed in the presence of another. To see Tristan had aroused and without shame discomfited and inflamed him. At that moment, Tristan offered him that which he most desired and feared, and he had almost refused it—almost, until his own needs overwhelmed him. He could not think about that now.

Adrift on the waves of his own musings and unaware of where he placed his feet, Rhonwellt stumbled and fell to one knee, hands in front of him in the mud. Ciaran was about to turn back when Rhonwellt motioned for him to continue on. Picking himself up, he wiped his hands on his robe, all the while chastising himself for such clumsiness. With all the thoughts swirling in his head, and the accompanying stirrings in his body, he would have preferred to avoid Tristan until he could will them away. The summons made that impossible. Walking slower would only delay the inevitable. He took a deep breath, and steeling his resolve, quickened his pace to catch up with the others.

Falling in beside Ciaran, Rhonwellt could only imagine the profound confusion and disappointment his young friend must be feeling. Arms jammed far up into his sleeves, Ciaran walked with a heavy step, Ernulf beside him, clinging to his robe. Never looking to the right or the left, his usual chatter was ominously silent. The future held the promise of a conversation that must take place, one Rhonwellt had tried to broach at the cottage earlier as they prepared for sext. But, Ciaran had been sullen and unwilling. Yet, he knew the task of explaining the awakened sensations in Ciaran as he grappled with the onrush of manhood, yearnings the vocation would prohibit him from fulfilling, would fall on him.

Chastity was the sacrifice expected of every monk who dedicated his life to serving God, and not all monks could or would make the choice. It was always hardest on those who reached their maturity while already in service, realizing there were avenues in life they were not meant to explore, joys only available to other men. Carnal cravings clouded their vision, making it harder to see that service to God could hold profound joy more than equal to the fleeting plea- sures of the flesh; or so Prior Alwyn had said, and he had always believed. Now, he was not as sure. If the conversation with Noah had aroused such intense yearnings in Rhonwellt, knowing full well the profundities they held, he could only imagine the turmoil they aroused in Ciaran, who would have no inkling of their full measure.

Rhonwellt moved closer and placed a reassuring hand on Ciaran's shoulder. The young cenobite looked up briefly, moisture at the corners of his eyes that Rhonwellt knew would be free-flowing tears were he alone with the full weight of the burden on his heart. Rhonwellt wished he could send Ciaran back to the cottage to deal with the matter in his own time and in his own way; however, the summons to attend was clear.

The would-be tears at the corners of Ciaran's eyes tugged at Rhonwellt's already overplayed heartstrings. Had he been too harsh in the way he revealed the truth about Jocelyn? Rhonwellt could have sent the young monk away to spare him the heartbreak, for he would have learned the truth soon enough. But he had not. He feared the conflicted feelings within himself had left him so unnerved as to deprive him of any compassion. Surely, Ciaran was as disconcerted by the war raging inside him as Rhonwellt was about his own strug- gles, and just as worried that he might lose the battle. Ciaran's misery was already acute, and any thought he could have compounded it caused Rhonwellt genuine grief. Why must man's cravings bring such torment? Many would lay it to the curse brought down by the daughters of Eve. And, while that may be the case with Ciaran, it did not apply to Rhonwellt's situation. The monk swallowed the lump he felt rising in his throat. Could it be that Rhonwellt was jealous? Resentful that, though considered wrong for a man called to serve God, the world of men would see Ciaran's yearnings as acceptable, whereas Rhonwellt's would always be an abomination. Had he secretly wished for Ciaran's torment to equal that of his own, or surpass it? His own heart must have become devoid of simple kindness. Why was it that every time he thought about his feelings for Tristan he felt no happiness there? And why did he still want it so badly?

Before Rhonwellt had the chance to recover any inner balance, they arrived at the hall. Ernulf bore all his diminutive weight against the heavy oaken door, pushing it open with a great creak and a sigh. There would be no use pondering the motives for their summons now.

Though not yet evening, the hall was very warm, the fire in the hearth burning brighter than usual. Ordinarily, Tristan would be content with a small blaze, just enough to ward off the chill where his face would be pleasantly warm while his back would still feel the cold. To Rhonwellt's wonder and amusement, between the large blaze in the hearth and over a dozen candles and lamps burning, the room was nearly a firestorm. Ernulf ran immediately to Hewrey who, wearing his best clothes, carried a jug from the fire to the sideboard where he stood poised to pour them warm drinks. Rhonwellt and Ciaran strolled across the floor to stand by the hearth. Hands in front of him over the flames, Rhonwellt glanced around. Jocelyn and Esyllt were nowhere in sight. The relief on Ciaran's face was clear as he too looked about the room.

"Well, we are here," said Rhonwellt, still agitated from the turmoil of the day.

"You seem unstrung, brother," observed Tristan. "Perhaps some warm cider will balance your humors. Or, maybe something stronger?"

"Cider will be fine."

Tristan seemed in a playful mood, quite a change form his demeanor the past few days.

"Where are Jocelyn and Esyllt? And why have you summoned us?"

"Patience, my friend." Tristan rose from his seat to stand opposite Rhonwellt at the edge of the hearth. Suddenly, his gaze focused on something behind Rhonwellt's back. "Do relax and sip your cider," he said softly. "We are about to witness the miracle of God's grace." Tristan held his cup high as in a salute as he called across the room, "Mistress. Come you down and join us."

EIGHTEEN

Ciaran sat on a bench facing the hearth, his back to the stairs leading up to the solar. At Tristan's words and the gesture with his cup, he turned with the others to see the reason for the salute. In the doorway at the top of the stairs stood a woman, unknown to him, young and comely. She was dressed splendidly in a fine kirtle of deep murrey, belted at the waist with a narrow braided leather thong. Showing above the low-cut top of the dress was a clean white linen tunic, gathered and tied at the neck, the cord forming a large drooping bow. A simple gauze veil covered her head, held in place by a circlet fashioned from delicate ivy trailers laced with crocus flowers hardy enough to survive a brutal winter. A wool shawl, the color of deep amber ale, hung loosely around her shoulders. Though her face was radiant, Ciaran could see a tightness around her eyes that betrayed a deep sorrow. Ciaran stared at her. Surely, this woman was not the one who Sir Tristan captured with the outlaws. Yet, who else could it be?

Ciaran watched the woman descend to the great room below, Jocelyn and Esyllt emerging from the solar behind her. Despite the mesmerizing appearance of the mysterious guest, from the moment she came into view, Ciaran only had eyes for Jocelyn. Not the equal of the woman in front of her, he still found her simplicity to be more alluring. He tried not to look, admonished himself for wanting to. Although his mind still reeled from the revelations he had learned about her, she still captivated him. Ciaran could not force his eyes from her.

Disillusioned and confused, the young monk swallowed hard as nausea tried to overtake him, threatening to make him retch. Jocelyn a...whore... He could barely bring himself to think the word, could never say it aloud. If Prior Alwyn knew, he might not allow her to enter the church to pray as long as she remained unrepentant. The church was unwavering on the issue; it denounced them as unclean, sinful women. Righteous men were to have no relations with them.

Yet, here he was, completely enthralled and unable—perhaps unwilling—to put her from his mind. There could be no doubt he would be condemned. He was no different from most men. Evidently, sin and hypocrisy existed unchecked even within the Church.

Ciaran buried his face in his hands. How had he become so corrupt? He breathed out a low moan. None of those things could be true of Jocelyn. It was not possible. She was but a simple girl, not a doxie. Had Noah forced her to sell her body to men that they might eat or have shelter? Was this what life was like outside the safety of the cloister? Where was God in all of this, and how could He allow such things to exist in His creation? Brother Rhonwellt was right. The Almighty, though omnipotent, was not always fair.

He had spent many a sleepless night on his knees beside his cot, trying to pray these feelings away. Yet, they persisted. The battle waged on and he thought his heart might break, that he would not survive. Why was it all so complicated? Could he not love God and Jocelyn at the same time?

He began to tremble and rock his body back and forth on his seat.

✟   ✟   ✟

RHONWELLT WATCHED THE WOMAN MAKE HER WAY DOWN THE
stairs. Jocelyn and Esyllt followed discreetly behind the former
captive, now miraculously transformed, as she glided down the stairs,
each step filled with grace and confidence. That Tristan had arranged
for the young nurse and the old crone to attend her said he must hold
her in high esteem. She had arrived a prisoner, bound in chains, and
now he treated her like an honored guest. What had happened to
change his mind? And, whence did this new-found esteem come?

The monk regarded her more closely. She was slight of build, no
more than five stone, yet did not appear fragile in any way. He put
her age at around thirty summers. Her mouth was small with thin
lips, her nose straight, and slightly upturned. Her face, especially her
mournful eyes, displayed an intelligence not always found in women.
At least, so he thought.

Rhonwellt had little understanding of women, especially those of
higher birth. Most of his practical experience was with poorer
women, like Master Gwillim's wife, Mistress Wen, and Milisandia
the fowler from Cydweli, or Esyllt from Ryd Lliw. Even the experience of his own mother, whom he had not seen in over thirty
summers, was not available to him. It saddened him when he thought
about how quickly the image of her had faded from his memory after
joining the cloister. His impressions of her now were like murky
shadows and but painful recollections.

The ghosts receded and Rhonwellt was once again in the hall.
The unknown woman continued down the stairs. Esyllt, struggling to
manage the steep descent, lowered herself one painful step at a time,
stooped and balancing herself with a hand on Jocelyn's shoulder as
the young woman came down ahead of her. The procession fascinated Rhonwellt. The varied faces of womanhood there before him;
from the young and vibrant to the old and infirm, ordinary and plain
against the exceedingly beautiful, the higher born who held the
power and the low who held none. And all had one thing in common;
each was mysterious in her own way. Like the Fates, three different
and individual women, each with her own story.

He had learned some of Jocelyn's history in the last few days and what he had yet to discover would most likely be as disturbing as that which he already knew. To have endured so much in her few short years would surely have created scars that would be forever with her.

He was not sure it possible to persuade Esyllt to relinquish the details of her life. The truth about the crone, though possibly full of wonder, would probably remain as elusive as the nature of her concoctions. Had she once been as beautiful as she was now wise, and did her wisdom come with age or had she always been so? Esyllt held her own kind of power, and he could not help but grin at the thought of how she frightened Ciaran.

Now, it appeared they were to find out about the ex-prisoner soon. Was she married, or at thirty, had she ever been? There was no doubt she would make someone a good wife. Any noble not in need of a large dowry would be glad of her. For though she carried herself well and was certainly higher born, he doubted she carried a title; perhaps a wealthy merchant's wife or lady to a knight.

Rhonwellt froze. Could that possibly be the reason she was here? Despite the heat in the room, chills ran down his back and he could feel gooseflesh rise on his skin. Had Tristan realized he needed to take a wife out of concern for producing an heir? Most men were. It had never arisen in discussion, other than the solitary dialogues he often had with himself in his own head, but it made perfect sense. She was young, at least still young enough to bear him children. She was presentable. And if she were found to be as formidable as she was sturdy, she could prove herself a worthy foil to Tristan's fits of temper and drunken silences.

Despondency crept over Rhonwellt. If this were all true, had he missed his opportunity? His inability to act on a clear indication that Tristan's feelings remained the same as they had when they were lads may have cost him any future happiness. Tristan said he would not pressure him, that there was time. How could he think that having lived for well over forty summers he still had all the time in the world? If he could not commit himself to Tristan, the knight might choose instead to sire children, and then where would he be?

The woman had stopped midway down the stairs but he only caught part of what she was saying. "...heartily gratifying," he heard her say, "to be clean and once again dressed in my own clothes, my lord. I am most grateful to you for retrieving them. When last I saw them, they lay scattered in the snow and mud."

Suddenly the truth illuminated his mind like a candle piercing the blackness of a darkened room. It was so obvious, he could not believe he had not thought of it before.

"I ordered all traces of..." Tristan stopped and thought for a moment, "...the incident obliterated, my lady," said Tristan. "The bodies were prepared and await proper burial after the thaw. For now, they lay atop the ground, covered with stones. However, a mass was said, and your goods stored away."

Hewrey, having disappeared into the buttery, reappeared in the doorway to the great hall carrying trenchers of cold meats, cheeses and dried fruit. Ernulf peered out from behind Hewrey's leg, his tiny fingers clinging to the lad's hose. Tristan rose and went to the child and guided him forward with his hands on his shoulders.

"My lady," said Tristan, his face beaming. "Behold, your son."

Silence crept over the room like a specter, the only sound the crackle from logs burning in the hearth. All motion stopped, everyone suddenly frozen in place like lifeless statues in a graveyard. Rhonwellt watched the woman's face change from relaxed to eyes open wide in shock, saw it twist and warp with that look of pain common to both inconceivable joy and unimaginable grief, her eyes welled with tears. She sank slowly to her knees, her lips moving but making no sound. Mouth open and wearing a blank expression, Ernulf took tentative steps toward the woman kneeling on the far side of the hearth.

Then, as if suddenly released from the influence of a spell that had rendered them both unable to feel, recognition filled their faces. Their excited voices broke through the hush, filling the hall with their unrestrained joy. Ernulf ran to the woman and threw himself into her arms.

"Mama!" he cried.

"Ernulf," she said, her voice trembling as she drew the child to her breast, "my darling boy."

Profound emotions of his own welled inside Rhonwellt as he signed the cross and prayed silent thanks to a capricious God who showed He could also be benevolent. Tristan had said they were about to witness God's grace, and they all bore testament to this unfathomable miracle.

After allowing mother and son a few private minutes together, Tristan stepped to the hearth and opened his mouth as if he was about to speak. The woman cut him off, her eyes flashing deep anger. "Why did you not tell me my son still lived, my lord?"

"I needed to be sure of you first, my lady." Tristan replied.

"And when you became sure of me," she said, her voice rising, "why not then? Why did you not bring him to me at once?"

"It would not have been appropriate, my lady."

"Not appropriate! He is my son." Ernulf looked up at his mother, his eyes wide.

"Would you have really wanted him to see you for the first time as you were, my lady, filthy and in rags, lying in the straw and chained to a wall? Was it not better for him to greet you as he remembered you? In a hall, freshly bathed and in your own clothes, smelling like his mother instead of like cattle?"

Merwenna took a breath, held it and then let it go.

"Must everything always be a battle with you?" Tristan asked. When she did not answer, he continued. "Now, if you will permit me, Mistress Merwenna," he said, gesturing towards each of the monks in turn, "may I present Brother Rhonwellt and Brother Ciaran? They tend our flock at Saint Tysilio's."

"Ah, your priest," said Merwenna, composed once again. She turned to Rhonwellt. "You are the one taken by my brother and Wulfric?" Rhonwellt admired the woman's command of herself.

"I am, Mistress," Rhonwellt replied.

"Accept my apologies for Wulfric's rash behavior, please." Her words appeared to be said in earnest. "I know the deed was of his doing. Sometimes, he proves he is just an ass. It is gratifying to see that you were not harmed."

"Thank you, Mistress." Rhonwellt tipped his head, slightly. He forced a smile though he was yet unable to completely forego the resentment of his ordeal. "The one called Selwyn is your brother?"

Merwenna nodded.

"He exhibited kindness to me, mistress, as did the one called Leo."

Her eyebrows furrowed and released. "What will become of them?" This time she directed her words at Tristan.

"I am as yet undecided. There is still the matter of kidnapping Brother Rhonwellt." Pique had quickly supplanted his congenial attitude. "The Church considers it blasphemy."

"And, what is it to you, my lord?" she asked.

"I take it as a personal affront," said Tristan, his ire increasing. The knight flung his arm out holding his cup for Hewrey to refill it. "They arrived here under the pretense of obeying the law and doing their Christian duty by notifying me of murders committed on my land." Tristan took a drink from his cup and scowled. "Never did they disclose their connection to the victims in any way. Nor did they offer to assist in the capture of those responsible. Therefore, my lady, I am not favorably disposed towards them."

Merwenna hesitated. "I would ask you to show mercy, my lord. But perhaps another day in chains would have a humbling effect on them. Wulfric could certainly use it."

"That is easily accomplished, my lady," said Tristan. "As for mercy, I must need think on it."

Merwenna started to speak again. Tristan put his hand up, stopping her. She lowered her eyes, tilted her head slightly to one side. The room went quiet again. Merwenna stroked Ernulf's hair. His muffled sobs began to subside as she held him close, his little hands clinging to her. After nuzzling Ernulf and whispering in his ear for a few moments, she asked, "Myfanwy?" The question was directed to no one in particular.

Tristan shook his head, his eyes downcast.

"How?" she whispered while signing the cross.

Her chin quivered and Rhonwellt thought she might begin to cry.

"I can answer that, mistress," Rhonwellt said, recovering himself. "Carrying the child proved too taxing for her heart. It simply gave out."

As she looked at Rhonwellt, questions filled her eyes. "What do you mean, brother?"

"I was trained by the medicus at the priory, Mistress. There are signs. It is my belief she used the very last of her strength to get your son to safety." Rhonwellt related the events of the morning he and Ciaran found the old woman and the boy outside the church.

"She and Hrodulf were with me all my life. And now they are both dead. He died trying to protect me, she trying to protect Ernulf." Her face took on a faraway look, her features down-turned. She said nothing for a moment. Rhonwellt felt moved, watching her as she struggled with her emotions. At last she said, "I should like to see where they rest. Perhaps on the morrow."

Tristan nodded. "Whenever you are ready, my lady."

Rhonwellt studied the woman. She seemed so familiar. There was a look about her he felt he should know well. Yet, searching his mind he could not remember seeing her before. Feast days and market days in Cydweli had caused many hundreds of people to pass through in his years there. Surely it was possible to have seen her before, as just another face in the crowd, one easily forgotten until another one similar would cause him to take notice. She looked strange with her hair cut short, like a man. Had the outlaws done it to disguise her? He thought how different she would appear with long locks peering out from under her head cloth, cascading down to her shoulders. Perhaps that was why he could not place her. Then again, he had never been prone to looking at women, and it seemed reasonable he would not remember her or where he had seen her.

The room grew quiet, Rhonwellt soaking in the peacefulness around him. At the moment, his own troubles seemed to have lost some of their sting. Listening to the quiet hum of voices and basking in the fire's warmth, Rhonwellt's eyes grew heavy.

NINETEEN

Finding sleep impossible, Noah's exhaustion reached to the bone. Numb from slouching on the hard church floor, he shifted to make himself more comfortable. Huddled inside a brychan given him by the monks, the cold from the stones still permeated his wiry body and he could not control his shivering. He carried no fat, and sinew could not keep the chill at bay. Except for the small noise of a rat skittering back and forth somewhere in the dark, the eerie silence was unnerving, occasioning the hairs at the nape of his neck to stand proud. Despite the lack of warmth, sweat trickled down his back.

He was not usually afraid at night, even knowing it to be the time Satan's minions wandered about preying on unprotected souls. Knowing his soul already lost, that had posed no real threat to him. But this was different. Someone very alive and from the world of men could await him in the shadows to lure him from his refuge and kill him. Though supposed to represent safety, sanctuary offered no guarantee one would live through it—not if the accuser was determined.

Jocelyn said she would come ahead and bring him food before the rest came down the hill for compline. He would be glad of some time alone with her. His sister would talk calmly to him, taking some of his worry away. It bruised his ego to know how much he depended on her strength. Though he could never tell her, she was his rock.

Noah sat, unable to shake the fear that a gibbet and noose awaited him for a crime he did not commit. The image appeared behind the lids every time he closed his eyes. He could not have killed William Fullecoppe even though the brother had accused him. He had not hit William hard enough to kill him. Though a bit foppish, William was a hearty man and the blow would have rendered no serious damage. He was only trying to send the man a message, to stay away from Jocelyn.

The squeal of the courtyard gate hinge drifted in through the side window opening. Noah sat up straight, listening for Jocelyn's footfall. He was hungry and hoped his jittery stomach would not rebel if he tried to eat. Above all, he hoped there was meat. A good mutton stew or eel pie would do much to fortify him and calm his nerves. Noah looked toward the window and leaned in its direction. Instead of footfall, he heard voices. Jocelyn had not come alone as he had hoped. He strained to recognize the voice and hear what they were saying, but could only tell that they were not engaged in ordinary conversation. They were arguing.

Noah got to his knees then stood so he could look out the opening. One of his legs had gone dead from sitting and he crumpled back to the floor, hitting his head on the corner of the altar. He hissed a breath at the pain. Putting a hand to his head, he rose again, this time testing the dead leg before putting his whole weight on it. He still did not have its full use, but he limped to the window and looked out. There was no moon and a thick ground fog had obscured everything, even the courtyard wall only a dozen paces away. The walls of the church were thicker than the length of a man's forearm. Noah had to lean far into the opening to see out. He looked to the right and the left but could not see Jocelyn or who she was talking to. The sounds came from a place hidden from his view, closer to the door.

He shook his leg and rubbed it to urge the feeling back. Once it felt more like he owned it and would bear his weight, he shuffled toward the door. Careful to make no sound, he lifted the latch and pulled the great oak slab open just enough to see through the crack. Barely visible through the fog, he spied Jocelyn, ghostly and ill-defined, carrying a trencher with his supper. An unknown man grabbed ahold of her arm, spilling the food onto the ground. Noah's heart sank. He was so hungry.

"Let go of me!" Jocelyn said. The crisp air carried her voice easily. She swung a foot upward toward the soft spot between the legs of the compact but sturdy mountain-of-a-man who held her.

"Ah now, none of that, lass," said the man, laughing and turning to the side. "You tussle like a lad. I like that." He let go of Jocelyn's arm, grabbed the front of her dress and pulled her close, his other hand closing around her throat. They stood nose to nose, neither of them moving.

"Come on, Joss," Noah breathed, rooted in place. "Get away from him. You can do it."

Aided by a slight breeze, the fog thinned for a few moments, allowing Noah to see the figures in the courtyard more clearly. The man let go of the front of her dress and slid his hand down her body and began to lift her skirts.

"No, Joss," Noah whispered. "Make him stop."

"I needs to see it for myself," said the man.

"Why are you doing this?" asked Jocelyn. "What do you want?"

"I needs your murdering whore-of-a-brother to come out of the church. Why not have fun whilst I waits?"

"He will not come."

"He will, for you, his precious…sister. Wait and see."

Noah froze in fear. What should he do? If he left the church, he would break sanctuary, would be vulnerable to capture, perhaps worse. If he stayed within the safety of the building, Jocelyn could be seriously hurt, even killed. Noah squeezed his eyes shut, tried to control his breath. "Joss, you got to get loose," he whispered.

"Come out, lad," the man called out, inching Jocelyn's skirts up further.

"Noah, stay there," Jocelyn cried, clawing the hand that held her throat.

A thick patch of fog blew through and obscured the courtyard again for a few moments. Though the feeling had fully returned to his legs, now they were just weak and his body shook so violently he was not sure they would hold him up. Jocelyn had to break free. It was the only way. He could not help her. The fog cleared again, bringing the scene outside back to clarity. The man had Jocelyn's skirt almost to her waist. He had a twisted grin on his face as he looked toward the door where Noah hid. Noah sensed the man knew he was there, watching, cowering, every inch of his skin raised like goose flesh. Jocelyn probably knew too. She knew he was not as brave as he pretended to be.

Jocelyn struggled against her assailant. Noah gripped the edge of the door, his fingers turning white. His sister clawed again at the hand on her throat as the man turned back to sneer at her. Suddenly he pulled her close and licked her face from her chin to her brow. Noah sucked in a breath, saw Jocelyn go rigid.

She was silent for a moment then calmly spit in his face.

"Bitch!" he growled.

She spit again.

Noah held his breath.

The man held her out at arm's length, still by the throat. In one swift movement he let his hand drop from her throat to her chest, drew a fist with the other hand, and punched her in the face. The sickening sound of the man's fist hitting her soft flesh made Noah's stomach jump. Jocelyn crumpled to the ground. The man dropped to one knee and yanked her skirts up. Drawing a knife from his waist, he leaned over her.

"Abomination!" he cried. "Time to correct God's mistake."

Eyes wide, Noah burst through the door and into the courtyard. He could hear someone yelling and, after a moment, realized it was his own voice. He stumbled toward the two figures. Noah had no idea what he would do when he got to the man, but knew somehow he must stop him. Closing the distance between them, Noah stretched his body, about to leap through the air, aiming for the man's back. Before Noah's feet left the ground, the man's arm shot straight out, a powerful blow catching him square in the chest, just below the rib cage, stopping him in his tracks. The blow forced all the air from his lungs. He could take no more in. The muscles in his chest would not work.

Noah kept trying to breathe. He felt no pain, only burning in his lungs. Everything else went numb. It was not until the man pulled his hand away that he noticed the knife. He had forgotten about it. The man had twisted the blade as he pulled it free. Then the pain came. Noah grabbed his stomach and bent his head down. His guts were on fire. Blood oozed from between his fingers—already, so much blood. He could smell it, taste it in his throat. Vertigo began to overtake him like when a child twirls until they are too dizzy to stand. The earth bucked and lurched and he staggered. The world around him became a blur and, through the haze, he saw his sister laying on the ground, not moving, exposed, and vulnerable. Now, both legs had gone dead. Noah was but a step away and yet he was not sure he could reach her.

His knees began to buckle. He was going down. There was no stopping it. Noah's mouth had filled with blood, too full to swallow. It spilled out and ran down his chin. He could not save Joss after all. His eyes began to close. He turned, hoping for one last glimpse of Jocelyn before she faded from sight. With his remaining strength, he lurched in her direction. Sinking slowly to the ground, his world turning black, he felt her soft body beneath him, safe from further harm.

✟   ✟   ✟

CIARAN PULLED THE HEAVY HALL DOOR SHUT BEHIND HIM AND looked out over the demesne and the town beyond. A low ground fog covered everything as far as his eyes could see. Only the bell tower and top-most roofs of the tithe barn and the church were visible peeking out of the mist. The air felt brisk on his skin and, having no lamp, Ciaran buried both hands deep inside his sleeves as he began to descend the manor rise.

Having felt too downhearted to sup with the rest at the hall, his empty belly now grumbled from the lack of food. He would go straight to the cottage for some bread and cheese before heading to the church to ring compline. Skirting the puddles and patches of mud churned up by foot traffic, he picked his way carefully down the lane lest a slip of foot rattle his already delicate emotional state. He only needed to get through prayers, then he could retire to his bed, bury his head, and be alone with his confusion and suffering.

Ciaran mouthed a greeting to the guards at the gatehouse, but proceeded through without stopping, and headed directly toward the cottage. He noticed the gate to the churchyard stood ajar. Perhaps the guard had gone to relieve himself as Brother Rhonwellt had told them not to piss in the yard. Entering the cottage through the postern gate, Ciaran collected his bread and cheese, gulped down a mouthful of watered wine from the skin and went out of the cottage and into the church through the side door.

The sanctuary candle flickered in the dark. Using a taper, he lit the brazier near the front of the altar.

"Noah," Ciaran said. "It is nearly compline. Sir Tristan and the rest will be here shortly. Have you finished your supper?" There was no answer, he heard no movement. A full belly must have made Noah sleepy. "Noah," he called again, more softly. In the unlikely event Noah had drifted off, he would let him rest a bit longer, at least until he rang the bell. The shrill peal of the bell could rouse the dead.

But, where had Jocelyn gone?

Head down, the monk went to the back of the church and sat on a bench near the bell rope absently chewing a mouthful of his supper. With nothing to drink, the dry bread went down slowly. He waited patiently, running his tongue across his teeth to clean them. A breeze wafted across the room and he lifted his chin to let it wash over his face, closing his eyes and inhaling the crisp, damp air.

Allowing himself a few moment's indulgence, he rose and grabbed the bell-rope, giving it a hard tug. The alto song of the bell called out like a ghost through the fog. He pulled the rope seven more times, then made his way to open the door in welcome.

"Noah, time to wake," said Ciaran, swinging into the door niche.

The oak-and-iron slab already stood partially open, fog curling in along the floor only to dissipate quickly before reaching the center of the room. How had he not noticed it before? Ciaran peered outside. Where was the guard posted to watch Noah?

Ciaran tentatively called out, the faint rush of water and steady creaking of the mill wheel next door his only response. A cold chill ran the length of his body. Ciaran swung around and went straight to the altar. He had hoped to find Noah sleeping behind it, propped against the wall. The lad was not there. Ciaran hurried back to the door, stepped onto the porch and called out again.

"Noah!"

He waited.

"Jocelyn!"

Still no answer. He narrowed his eyes and attempted to stare through the fog toward the churchyard gate. Though his vision was unclear, about half the distance between the porch and the gate he spied something on the ground. He took a few tentative steps toward the spot. What was it? A few more steps and a vague shape came into focus. It looked like a body. He squinted more. No, it was two bodies. Ciaran went rigid, recalling the time he found Brother Rhonwellt lying on the ground at the Priory and thought he was dead. He shook his head, not sure he could bear such an experience again.

He ran the last few paces to the bodies. Noah lay on top, face down, with Jocelyn beneath him. Both lay covered in blood. Ciaran's stomach retched. He turned his head and heaved up the bread and cheese. What should he do? He bent down and, as he had seen Brother Rhonwellt do, laid two fingers on the large vein in Noah's neck. There was little warmth to the skin and he could feel no throb beneath his fingers. He reached out to do the same with Jocelyn. He let his hand hover over her face. No, he could not. It would be a sin to touch a woman. But if Noah was dead, surely Jocelyn must be as well.

Tears welled in Ciaran's eyes and a sob escaped his lips as he rose and ran to the church. He grabbed the knots in the bell-rope and pulled and pulled causing the bell to ring out—not the slow peals proclaiming prayers but each desperate ring rapidly following the last to say distress. He pulled until his arms ached. When he could no longer feel them, he let go and began a slow trance-like walk back to where the bodies lay.

Stepping through the door, he could see the others had already arrived and rushed over to Brother Rhonwellt who stood looking down in horror. Sir Tristan and Hewrey were just pulling Noah's body off of Jocelyn, exposing the nakedness of her lower body. A whispered gasp escaped everyone's lips.

Ciaran stared in disbelief. He wanted to look away but could not.

"Brother Rhonwellt, I do not understand," he said. "Jocelyn's body looks the same as mine."

TWENTY

The faithful who had gathered to pray compline stood as unwilling witnesses to the aftermath of murder instead. Some looked in an uneasy silence, mouths agape, others whispering speculations behind their hands. No matter, Noah was dead and Jocelyn lay covered in blood, exposed and subjected to ogling eyes full of judgment.

After rolling Noah's body gently off to the side, Tristan rose and looked around the churchyard. "Where are the bloody guards?" Had Fullecoppe's guard killed Noah or simply abandoned his post to provide opportunity to another? Where was his own man? He circled the front yard then peered down each side of the church. The ground fog obscured anything farther than a few paces away. Tristan doubted the perpetrator was still near but the action of looking for him gave the knight a few moments to gather his thoughts.

"This is Fullcoppe's doing," said Tristan. "There were two guards and one was his man. Now neither are to be found."

Rhonwellt knelt and, showing great care, covered Jocelyn, and tested for a pulse. The monk nodded. Jocelyn still lived.

Tristan laced his fingers through his hair and ran his hand over the top of his head, pausing at the crown. He stared with unseeing eyes. Noah had claimed sanctuary on his demesne. According to the law, he was responsible to see that the accused lived long enough to abjure or be proved innocent. He had failed.

"Hewrey, fetch my sword!" Tristan could not bite back his pique. If it were not for Rhonwellt's rule against weapons in the church, he would have it on him now. Tristan motioned for two of his soldiers to attend him. "Take Jocelyn to the barn and chain him away from the others. Then..."

"No," said Rhonwellt through a clenched jaw. "Jocelyn has done nothing to warrant chains."

"You do not give the orders here, Brother," said Tristan. "He has deceived us through omission and will go to the barn until we can discover what else he has kept from us. Now, send these folks home. Prayers are canceled."

"I meant no defiance," said Rhonwellt. "You are master of everything for as far as the eye can see. However, within these walls, God is master. One does not cancel prayer. In fact, it seems to be the best remedy for the situation. We are to provide them place and opportunity, and we shall."

"While you are else-wise occupied with Jocelyn, who shall lead them?"

"They will be fine on their own. Please, do not argue with me. Besides, Jocelyn may be injured. What he has done is probably a grave sin, but he has broken no law but that of God. At least that we know of." He turned as if to look at Jocelyn, then shook his head and faced Tristan. "Put him in the cottage that I may tend him. Post a guard. Post two."

Tristan regarded Rhonwellt for several moments. Once his monk had settled on a thing, he would not easily be dissuaded. "Very well," said Tristan, and headed for the gate calling over his shoulder to the soldiers. "You three, with me." Once in the lane, he looked toward the hall. "Where is Hewrey with my bloody sword?"

"Why, Brother Rhonwellt?" Ciaran asked.

Rhonwellt could not look at the lad. He had no answer to offer him. It was beyond belief how they had not known. Such things may be more common in places like London, but would be much harder to conceal here despite the lack of sophistication in the local villeins. Rhonwellt could hardly contain his surprise that it had not come to light before this. Jocelyn had looked and played the part to perfection. His voice, his movements all spoke to him being a young woman. It was all an illusion. Ciaran was right, the question was why.

"The ground is cold," said Rhonwellt. "We must get him to the cottage."

"Would that be proper?" asked Ciaran, taking a slight step back.

"Since there is proof beyond any doubt," replied Rhonwellt, "that Jocelyn is a young man and not a young woman, I cannot see any harm in it. Help me lift him."

The monks struggled to get Jocelyn off the ground to carry him through the church to the cottage.

"If we are to find out why he has done this," said Rhonwellt, panting from his efforts, "better the questioning come from us than Sir Tristan. There is too much at stake for him to be gentle in his interrogation."

"What Jocelyn has done must be a sin," said Ciaran. "Surely, the Church condemns it."

"It is safe to assume it does," replied Rhonwellt, "since the church condemns most things." He stopped to catch his breath and gazed off into the fog. "Yet, Saint Eugenia and Saint Pelagia lived as monks centuries ago. No one discovered they were women until their deaths, still the Vatican canonized them. So, once again, the church is not consistent in its condemnation."

"Saints? That cannot be so," said Ciaran, grunting under his burden.

"Were they not part of your lessons with Brother Daffyd?"

"They were. However, I am sure he did not teach us they were women. I would remember."

Once inside the cottage, they deposited Jocelyn on Rhonwellt's cot and covered him with a brychan.

Rhonwellt straightened his back with a grimace. "Well, as I recall," he said while lighting a candle with an ember from the hearth, "the lessons about the saints were less than riveting and given in spring, a time more conducive to woolgathering than sitting with rapt attention to a droning monk."

"You cannot compare Jocelyn to a saint! It is devilry, and she... he...bewitched me."

"Jocelyn deceived us all," said Rhonwellt, "made every one of us look the fool. Though I do not think that was his intention."

"Noah was also part of the deception," said Ciaran.

"True," said Rhonwellt "The fact they both lied to us makes it seem criminal."

"It seemed so unfeigned." Ciaran cast his gaze toward the bed. "Noah acted as though she was actually his sister, not like they were playing a role."

"My thoughts, as well," replied Rhonwellt. "Noah is dead," he paused and signed the cross. "Now Jocelyn is the only one with the answers we seek."

Jocelyn emitted a low groan and rolled his head around on the pillow. Rhonwellt and Ciaran moved closer to the cot. With a deep breath, his lids fluttered open, he stared straight up, then slowly let his eyes wander down to where the monks stood staring down at him. He moved his mouth and licked his lips.

"What has happened?" Jocelyn said through a groggy voice.

"Someone has killed your brother and attacked you," said Rhonwellt. "We know why. Now, we would hear your explanation."

"Noah is dead?" Jocelyn asked, struggling to sit up.

"He is, lad," said Rhonwellt.

At these words, Jocelyn's hands went immediately to cover his lap, his eyes closing so tightly they nearly disappeared from his face.

Rhonwellt and Ciaran waited through a long silence.

The only reaction from Jocelyn was that his face relaxed a little. "How did he die?" he asked at last.

"We hoped you could tell us that. We found you both on the ground; you unconscious, Noah dead on top of you, both covered in blood."

Jocelyn eased the brychan back to reveal his blood-soaked clothing and slowly opened his eyes. It took a moment for him to respond to what he saw. Then, using his feet and hands, he began to push himself backward on the cot as if trying to distance himself from the blood. Jocelyn let out a low cry, sprang from the cot and began to tug at his clothing, shouting for help to get the tunic off. He pulled at the fabric, trying to extricate himself until a loud rip rent the garment down the front. Wriggling his arms free, he let it fall to the floor and kicked it out of the way. The under-sheath stained as well, Jocelyn pulled it up and over his head and discarded it. Rhonwellt turned his face away from Jocelyn's nakedness while Ciaran gaped openly. Jocelyn dove onto the cot and trembling, pulled the cover up to his chin.

"The truth of you is no longer secret," continued Rhonwellt. "What do you have to say?"

Ciaran's lips began to move long before he uttered a word. "Why?" was all he said.

His chin resting on his chest, Jocelyn's hair fell across his face. Nervous fingers picked at the woolen fibers on a frayed edge of the brychan.

"Was it just a lark fooling me into believing you were a young lass?" Ciaran asked.

"You would not understand," said Jocelyn, his voice muffled into the bed covering.

"So far, you have told me nothing that I might decide."

Standing off to the side, just out of the glow of the candle, Rhonwellt began to sense Ciaran was not just questioning Jocelyn as one might probe the answer to a mystery. This was personal. Ciaran needed answers for his own reasons. Rhonwellt had known the flame for Jocelyn burned bright in Ciaran's heart, but cruelly dowsed, it now flickered on the edge of going out. Suddenly, Rhonwellt felt like a windowsill snoop, listening in on something intensely private, not meant for his ears. The facts revealed would be the same no matter who heard the confession. Tristan would be angry that he left it to Ciaran, but Rhonwellt had dealt with the knight's ire before and could again. Slowly he backed to the door, lifted the latch with as much care as he could and stepped through, closing it behind him without a sound.

☩   ☩   ☩

HEWREY HASTENED TO KEEP PACE BESIDE HIS MASTER AS Tristan veered into the lane bound for the *Saint George and the Dragon,* their boots pounding heavily on the packed dirt.

"Master," said Hewrey. "What was that? Is Joss a him or a her?" He chewed on a dirty fingernail while his other hand gestured wildly at the air in front of him. "Bugger, I almost fancied that one. Lads is not to my taste," he whispered, leaning near as they walked, "not like you." Hewrey meant no harm. It had not been an issue between them since their first meeting. "What does it mean?"

"It means nothing," replied Tristan. "Jocelyn was not what he seemed. You believed in what you thought you saw, nothing more."

"He sure were like a real lass, not like a lad at all. How could he do that?"

"In the East, there are men called mukhannathun who cast aside their sex to live as women."

"And folks just lets them do it—be women? Why?"

"The Saracens believe it is their true nature," said Tristan. "Some rulers hold them in high regard."

"Does the King have any of them?"

Tristan chuckled softly. "No, Hewrey, it is unlikely."

"Be nothing funny about this, Master."

His master stopped chuckling and grew serious again. "There is not. And there is nothing funny about Noah's death, either. If the Masters Fullecoppe had aught to do with it, I mean to know. Now step along and watch yourself if there is a fight."

"You not be thinking of leaving me outside, Master."

"No, you are with me. Just be careful."

Arriving at the tavern, Sir Tristan threw the door open with such force it slammed up against an empty bench setting just inside. The room bustled with excited patrons as the news of Noah's death had already arrived. The ale flowed and speculation was high, especially at the possibility of a hanging should the perpetrator be caught. Despite the size of the crowd, the landlord had not bothered to bring out extra candles. Hewrey squinted his eyes to bring his vision more clearly into focus in the dim light. He could not see them anywhere in the room.

"Fullecoppe!" Tristan shouted.

The room went silent and most faces turned toward the open door.

"Where are the Masters Fullecoppe?" he bellowed, striding to the counter.

"They are within, my lord," said the landlord, pointing to the rooms above. Even in the near darkness, the landlord's pallor was noticeable. The taverner scurried from behind the counter, nervously wiping his hands on his greasy apron, forcing an obsequious smile across his face.

Hewrey loved watching men grovel to his master.

"Right this way, my lord." Grabbing a lantern, the landlord led them up a short flight of stairs that emerged into a narrow hallway at the top. "There, at the far end, facing south, our best room, away from the noise that drifts up the stair." The landlord bowed and took a step back to allow Tristan and his men room to pass.

Hewrey took the light from the man's outstretched hand and led the way. The floor shook as the five men tramped down the hall. His stomach fluttered as he gripped the handle of the dagger. He was about to slip it from his belt when his master stayed his hand.

"Let us hope there is no need," said Tristan.

Stopping in front of the last door, Tristan stood with his feet apart, hands at his sides. Hewrey watched his master's fists clench and unclench. An anxious jolt seized his stomach, and he began to sweat from nervous excitement. He had seen his master in action before and had never doubted his own bravery. But, this was not a street skirmish. It was official business, beside his master acting as an enforcer of the law. He hoped he would do well if there was a fight.

"Master Fullcoppe," Tristan called out. The taproom below was still quiet, allowing them to hear boots cross the floor. The door opened.

Walter Fullecoppe stood inside, a slight smile on his face that slowly melted away at the site of the armed men at his door. "My lord?" he said.

Tristan pushed past him and went into the room. Thomas Fullecoppe was just rising off the bed, his hand hovering around the hilt of his dagger, an open frown on his face. Hewrey moved to stand closer to Tristan.

"What the..." Thomas sputtered. Walter held his hand in front of his son indicating that he should remain quiet.

"What do you want, my lord," said Walter, "that you barge into my room?"

"You know very well, sir," said Tristan.

"You mean the death of the murderer."

"Then you admit it."

"I admit to nothing, my lord." Walter turned and casually walked to a bench and sat down.

Hewrey's breath caught in his chest. The affront to his master would not go unnoticed. But, to Hewrey's surprise, Tristan only pursed his lips for a moment, then returned his face to calm.

"You could not wait for a trial," said Tristan, "so you killed Noah rather than take the chance on him being found innocent or forced to abjure the realm."

"I did not kill him," replied Walter. "Though I admit no small pleasure in knowing he is dead. He killed my son."

"And it was you who attacked Jocelyn. Did you know his secret? Were you going to kill him, too?"

"Him?" said Thomas, stepping forward. "What do you mean?"

Hewrey sensed his master's body stiffen at Thomas' approach.

"Are you trying to tell me you did not know Jocelyn was a man?"

Hewrey's stomach tightened upon hearing it said out loud.

"Preposterous!" said Walter, suddenly rising to his feet and rushing toward Tristan.

All the men in the room came to high alert, hands hovering over their weapons. In an instant, Hewrey's dagger was in his hand.

"What kind of trickery is this?" Thomas licked his lips, his eyes darting back and forth. "It is a lie."

"It is the truth, and you tried to kill him. My guess is Noah intervened and paid for it with his life."

"Do you realize what you are saying, sir, what you are saying about my firstborn? You besmirch his name." Walter's eyes went wild, his breath became rapid. "I should kill you for that."

A chill went the full length of Hewrey's body. Was this it? Would there be blood? He gripped the handle of his dagger until his fingers felt numb and looked toward his master.

Tristan appeared calm. "You could try," was all he said.

TWENTY-ONE

Ciaran took a hesitant step toward the cot and stopped. What should he do? The situation was unimaginable. Which emotion should take precedence, anger or confusion? Trying to decide, he took two more steps until his legs rested against the edge of the bed. He lingered in the uneasy silence, waiting for Jocelyn to speak. Weighing his feelings, the confusion proved stronger and came to the fore.

"Can you not look at me?" Ciaran asked. "Is your shame so great?"

"It is not shame," Jocelyn replied, toying with the frayed edge of the coverlet and staring as though he spoke to it.

Ciaran's voice was barely a whisper. "Then what is it?" He kept his head down and, forcing back tears, wiped his nose with his sleeve.

Jocelyn drew in a breath then blew it out through full cheeks. "Disappointment, sorrow, bitterness—I am not sure."

Ciaran tilted his head a mite and raised his eyebrows.

"Me...this...my life." Jocelyn waved a hand around at nothing in particular.

"How can it bring anything but disappointment and sorrow if it is a life filled with deceit?" Ciaran turned to focus on the door leading to the back room he and Rhonwellt used on occasion as a Scriptorium. He wished he were there now, bent over a manuscript, quietly lettering, instead of here having this conversation. The reality was bad enough. Would knowing why make it any easier to accept? "You pretend to be something you are not. Your life is a lie, and that is a sin."

After a moment, Jocelyn faced Ciaran and snorted a laugh. "Most lives are a lie. Mine is a curse."

The young monk lowered himself down until he sat on the edge of the cot, his eyes focusing on the door. "What is the difference?"

"People lie of their own free will, are happy to do it, and then beg God for forgiveness," replied Jocelyn. "A curse is God's lie thrust upon them and they rage at Him for bringing it down on them."

"Do you rage against God?"

"Do we not all rage against God? Only kings and fools are free from that by virtue of their stations."

"Being rich offers no shield, nor does being senseless. They can rage as well as any."

Jocelyn let out a groan. "God makes no sense."

"He does not have to," said Ciaran. "We are not meant to question God. He is a mystery."

"And, I am one of God's greatest mysteries," Jocelyn said, his voice full of sarcasm. "I am a mistake."

"God is infallible and without error."

"Well, he erred when he made me." Jocelyn spat the words. "I am a woman."

"I have seen..." Ciaran paused, his heart thumping in his chest. Taking his time, he turned his head around to look directly at Jocelyn. "I may not know much of these things, but with mine own eyes I have seen you as God made you, and He made you a man."

"Then God made me wrong."

"You may feel He made you wrong, but you are wonderful as you are." Ciaran swallowed hard. Where had those words come from? He knew the truth and yet, looking at Jocelyn lying there, only his face visible on the pillow framed by his long black hair, Ciaran saw only a miracle.

"He cursed me with this body. It is not the right one and there is nothing I can do about it."

Ciaran signed the cross, his face pinched. "That is blasphemy, or heresy, I am not sure which one. But I know both are sins." Ciaran's stomach lurched and sweat stood out on his brow in spite of the chill. He could not comprehend how he could see her...him...as both miracle and sinner. Or that knowing him to be a man, Jocelyn still held the same allure.

"That may be so," said Jocelyn. "Yet, I know it to be true in here, and in here," he said, pointing to his head and his heart, "and it is the only way this makes any sense."

"It makes no sense at all." Ciaran shoved his hands into his sleeves and dug his nails into the flesh of his arms. Jocelyn seemed so convinced. "Has Satan possessed you?" Ciaran asked, leaning away and extricating a hand to cross himself. He could not hide the anguish in his voice. "God made you a man. Why can you not just accept that," Ciaran hesitated a moment, "as I must?"

"I said you would not understand and, it is obvious you do not." Jocelyn's body shuddered and he hugged the brychan closer. "Mama was the only one who did."

"Your mother knew this?"

"She knew, but could do little to help me. Though she did keep da from cutting my hair, I screamed so loud when he tried. I always was spare-built and soft. Early on I knew I was a lass. Never did men's work, always helped mama."

"Not all boys are rugged," said Ciaran.

"And da hated me for it. Said it made him look bad as a man."

"Being soft did not mean you were a lass."

"I wanted to wear female clothes since ever I can remember." Jocelyn took on a faraway look and a small smile spread across his face. "When I was about five summers, some of us youngsters was splashing in the river shallows, our clothes in a pile on the bank. I heard mama's voice calling me home. I hurried to put my duds on and in the rush to sort mine from the others, I pulled a shift from the pile. Nothing much of a thing, coarse, rough-sewn, no more than a sack with arms. I wondered what it would feel like to wear it, to actually have it on my body. So, I slipped it over my head and let it fall down around me. I cannot describe what it was like. I was wearing a tunic meant for a girl, not a boy. For the first time ever, I felt..."

Ciaran studied Jocelyn's face, waited for him to finish. Jocelyn raised his head to briefly look into Ciaran's eyes and then looked back down to stare again at the edge of the brychan. It was several long moments before he went on. "I wore it home."

"No one said anything about you wearing a shift?"

"Da said nothing, just got real quiet. But, his refusal to speak and the look on his face scared me, scared us all. Mama said I had to give it back. Said the child I took it from, it was probably her only one, would be hard on her family to replace it, they was so poor."

As Jocelyn grew still again, Ciaran continued to gaze at him lying in the bed, covered to the neck. Jocelyn's secret was revealed, yet his feelings had not changed. Though Ciaran knew what lie beneath the brychan, he could only see Jocelyn, the beautiful, soft, feminine girl. Was he seeing only what he wanted to see, ignoring the truth? Had he truly been bewitched as he had told Rhonwellt? Was this what the Church meant by sins of the flesh? Jocelyn was just Jocelyn, but yet what his body looked like made so much difference—made it the difference between right and wrong, between the light of new discovery and the utter darkness of sin. A cold chill gripped him and he hugged himself inside his sleeves and fought to drive these troubling thoughts from his mind.

Ciaran suddenly realized Jocelyn was speaking again. "No one really spoke through supper and while we all went to our beds, da went drinking. I was in that drifting place between sleep and awake when I felt a hand cover my mouth. There was the smell of charcoal, iron, and ale and I knew it was him, and he was mean-drunk. He yanked me off the straw that was my bed and carried me out the door into the night. I tried to scream, but he tightened his hand over my mouth. I knew he meant to kill me. He carried me a ways from the cottage and threw me to the ground. He kicked me a few times and then picked me up by the front of my shirt and punched me in the face, without saying a word."

Ciaran sat motionless, only half-listening as Jocelyn told his story. Somehow, he felt he should not be hearing it at all. His mind told him he should just get up, walk out the door and leave Jocelyn to the consequences of his own actions. That was exactly what he should do. However, his confused heart kept him rooted in place.

"Do you think he truly meant to kill you?"

"Mama seemed to think so," Jocelyn replied. "She had heard him take me and followed him. She told him that if he hurt me, he would need to give up drinking or never know a sound night's sleep again, that when he was drunk, she could murder him while he slept. She promised da would never know until it happened. He dropped me to the ground and walked away. He never knew a sober day after."

"I do not believe you," said Ciaran. "I want to, but cannot. It is too unbelievable."

"That you do not believe it does not make it any less true."

Growing up at the priory had shielded Ciaran from the harsher realities of life. Only since moving to Ryd Lliw had he seen the world for what it could be, that sometimes it was a place of unfathomable cruelty, teeming with injustices based on your position in the order of things. He never imagined there could be people like Jocelyn in the world. He was still getting used to knowing there were people like Sir Tristan and Brother Rhonwellt and the nature of things between the two men. So far, it involved only emotions. As far as Ciaran knew, they had not yet engaged in sin. He also knew it was only a matter of time before they did, and when they did, he would need to decide how to handle the knowledge. This situation with Jocelyn was entirely different. Was it a sin to think or wish you were something you were not? Though he knew the Church would surely condemn it, did it actually constitute sin?

Jocelyn was still talking. Almost as if Ciaran was not there, he kept telling his story, as though he needed a witness. "When mama died, da said that if I wanted to be a woman, then I could be his woman. I must keep his house and warm his bed."

"What are you saying?"

"He meant that I should take the place of his wife."

"You could not be a wife."

"I can cook, I can tidy a cottage and I can pleasure a man. What else is there?"

"But, he was your father!"

"And, I had only twelve summers! As you said, I am not rugged. What was I supposed to do? He would have been happy to see me dead. With mama no longer around to keep me safe, what could I do?"

"What about your brother?"

"Noah tried. God knows he did. Da's hands were big as the hoof on a heavy horse. He would only need one to kill Noah. After a few drunken beatings, I put a stop to it, said I would do as the old man wanted." Jocelyn paused, the skin of his face rippling under a clenched jaw, a look of anguish turning his eyes hard under a knit brow. "Noah was a good lad. Even though da was seldom sober enough to use me as he intended, it was the start of my brother's ruin. Me being how I was confused him. He wanted a brother. Still, he did not mind so much I was not rough-and-tumble. It was him not being able to protect me, you see, made him feel less of a man." Jocelyn raised his head. "Still, he was all I had, and now he is dead."

Jocelyn seemed to drift off to somewhere inside himself as Ciaran sat there, grappling with all he had heard. It was all too much and, for the moment, he could hear no more. He would need time to sort through all Jocelyn had said. He carefully stood and made his way to the door. At the last minute he turned back to look at Jocelyn lying on the cot, blankets to the chin. He looked so frail and alone, all the surety and strength he had shown as a woman, gone at the moment. The sight tugged at Ciaran's heart, tempting him to return to the bedside. He could not. With a shake of his head, he pulled up his hood and went outside, nodding to the man guarding the door before he went into the church.

Ciaran's conversation with Jocelyn had taken longer than he realized. Compline had ended, and the church sat empty and silent when he passed through. The distant voices of the villagers who had stayed for prayers drifted over the air as they made their way to their cottages or to join the others at the tavern. For certain the conversation would be lively concerning Noah's murder and the truth that had come to light about Jocelyn. He rejoiced that he did not frequent the tavern and would not have to bear the derisive gossip.

The air was brisk, and the fog had all but dissipated, giving way to a partly cloudy sky. Ciaran glanced to the North toward the tithe barn and the hall beyond. Where had they taken Noah's body? Perhaps they had put it in the barn, temporarily. It would be cold there and out of the elements. Soon, they would move it to the church where he and Brother Rhonwellt would wash it and prepare it for vigil and burial. Since they had yet to prove Noah had committed any crime, Ciaran hoped Brother Rhonwellt would afford Noah all the respect due the deceased. The trials thrust upon Jocelyn and Noah in their short lives had been tragic and Ciaran prayed God would show Noah the mercy after death that had eluded him in life. Noah was dead, his fate settled. The question that remained was what would become of Jocelyn?

Ciaran crossed himself and was about to leave for the hall when movement caught his eye in the graveyard on the North side of the church. The monk froze, his skin prickling and raising the hairs on his nape. He craned his neck and peered into the night. At first he saw nothing. His mind must be playing tricks. He started to look away. There it was again, and this time it was moaning, a horrific sound to Ciaran's ears. A black shape was rising out of the darkness from behind a gravestone near the churchyard wall. The monk's hand flew to his mouth, stifling a scream. He fell to his knees, squeezed his eyes shut, crossed himself, then clasped his hands in front of him as a prayer for mercy tumbled from his quivering lips. It was happening. His feelings for Jocelyn had been so wicked, one of Satan's minions had risen from the grave and was coming for him. He cautiously opened his eyes and saw the black shape emerge from behind the gravestone and make its way on unsteady legs straight for him. He let out a sob and crossed himself one more time. He pressed his lids closed again. He could hear the footfalls as it staggered closer. Footfalls! Why did it not float through the air as demons should? He heard the footfalls stop. It was right in front of him. He could hear it breathing. Ciaran fell backwards onto one elbow, shielding his face with his other hand.

"Brother Ciaran," said a very earthly voice. "Are you well? Whatever is wrong?"

A hand seized his shoulder and shook him. Ciaran screamed.

"Brother Ciaran, it is me, Ercwiff."

Ciaran slowly opened one eye and peered around his hand. It was Ercwiff, Sir Tristan's man, the one he had left to guard Noah, and there was blood running down the side of his face.

☨   ☨   ☨

TRISTAN WAITED. WHAT WOULD BE THE FULLECOPPE'S NEXT move?

His face ashen, gripping his dagger, Hewrey stood close, Tristan's soldiers fanned out behind him. Tristan put out a hand, pushing Hewrey's blade toward its sheath. An outward calm belied the knight's frayed nerves. His other hand resting casually on the hilt of his sword, Tristan prayed for a resolution that would not involve more bloodshed. He had little hope. Violence seemed to attach itself to him, unbidden. Though he hated it, he understood it. His life had been full of it.

Walter Fullecoppe faced Tristan, his eyes narrowed in fury. His breath rasped in his throat. "You are saying my son was a sodomite?" The words shot through the air on droplets of spit.

"I have said no such thing," replied Tristan. Only the muscles surrounding his mouth moved.

"You said that filthy whore was a man. What other explanation is there?"

"It would depend on the extent of his relationship with Jocelyn and whether your son knew the lad's true nature. There are many ways a whore can relieve a man." Tristan shifted his weight slightly. "William is your business. I am not here to judge him. God will do that. You and Thomas, on the other hand, are my business if you had aught to do with Noah's death."

"We did not!" Walter waved his arms wildly through the air. "Thomas was here with me in this room since darkness fell. Ask the landlord. He will vouchsafe the fact we took supper here and remained the evening."

"I shall do exactly that when I am finished here," said Tristan. "You would not have to kill Noah yourself to merit blame. You would only have to order it done. Where is the man you left to guard him?"

"Leslie? I saw him last at his post, talking to your man. Why?"

"He was not there when we found Noah, and none has seen him since. My man is gone as well."

Walter stood motionless, head bowed. He did not speak for a moment. "Leslie would have greater cause than any to kill him and I would not blame him. He had served William since they were small lads. They grew up together. Leslie loved him as a brother and William's death hit him hard. He was first to vow vengeance. Perhaps it is why he volunteered to stand guard outside the church." Walter raised his head to look at Tristan. "I wondered why it was not he who brought the news of the guttersnipe's death."

"Until he is found, you are all suspect. I am glad you enjoy this room, for you may be in it for some time."

"You cannot force us to stay!" Fists clenched, Thomas's eyes raced around the room like a caged animal looking for escape. With a scraping of boots on the wooden floor and the clinking of mail and steel, Tristan's soldiers became alert at Thomas's display of fury.

"I am master and the law here," said Tristan. "You will stay here until such time as this crime is resolved. When you are proved innocent, then you may leave, not before."

"Then solve it in all haste," said the elder Fullecoppe. "I have a business to run and have been too long away."

"We still have no answer to the question who murdered your son," said Tristan.

Walter snapped his reply. "That is not your concern. William's murder did not occur in your demesne. Besides, I have already told you. That guttersnipe murdered my son."

"You accuse Noah and he was murdered here, that makes it my concern. You offer no proof. Did you actually see him commit the deed?"

"Thomas and I saw him flee from the place where William's body lay in the street. That is evidence enough for me."

"It may satisfy you," said Tristan, "but it does not fulfill the law. Was his man Leslie with William when he was killed?"

"William had sent Leslie to the tavern to tell us he would join us there shortly. So, no, Leslie was with us. When, after a long wait, William did not appear, Thomas went to the door and searched the lane for him. It was then he saw him lying in the street."

Walter went to the bed and sat down. His shoulders slumped and his whole demeanor said he was exhausted. He bent forward, elbows on his knees and rested his forehead in his hands.

"I held him as he died in my arms," said Thomas, his voice catching in his throat. "And now, the one who murdered him is dead. I only wish I had killed the filthy cur myself." Thomas paused. "However, wanting him dead is not a crime. I did not kill him, nor did my father."

To Tristan, while it seemed logical to suspect the father and son of Noah's murder, he still had his doubts. If the landlord substantiated their claim to be at the inn at the time of the murder, then they could well be innocent of the killing itself but could still have arranged it. Or had a dedicated manservant done it of his own volition? He stared at the Fullecoppes for a moment to see if their movements or manner held hint to any hidden truth.

"With me," he said, motioning to Hewrey and his men with a gloved hand as he pivoted and went out the door.

TWENTY-TWO

Tristan's mood grew worse with every step.

All the way back from the tavern, Hewrey had kept his own counsel while the knight brooded, wallowing in self-pity, yearning for a cup of strong wine. Misfortune had his scent and ill winds seemed to dog him, relentlessly biting at his heels, keeping him on the run; not only on the battlefields of Outremer but in the quiet rolling hills of home. The knight was tired and wanted to spend his waning years in quiet with his monk and caring for his land and his people.

Instead, he had a barn full of prisoners, half of which were guilty of thievery, kidnapping and murder. The other half were engaged in the folly of men pursuing women. Worse, though, was the fact they had kidnapped Rhonwellt as a bargaining chip for the return of Ernulf. Tristan seethed at their impertinence. The punishment for kidnapping was harsh and since Rhonwellt was a man of God, a priest, and what is more, his priest, Tristan could have them hung. Short of that, they must pay some price. Though sure they never intended the monk any harm, they had placed Rhonwellt in fear for his life. In truth, the real source of Tristan's anger was he had to face the fact that, once again, he had not been there to protect him.

It was clear to Tristan Wulfric was born for battle. He might need every fighting-man available at his disposal now that he had a fresh murder and an unmasked imposter to contend with; an abundance of problems and a shortage of patience. It was time to turn the Northerners loose from their confinement in the barn. Unless he pressed the issue of kidnapping Rhonwellt, he had no reason to hold them.

One question that loomed large was whether any of these events were connected. He still could not tell if the outlaws who murdered the travelers were at all connected to Wulfric and Selwyn. It seemed unlikely, but not impossible. Had Wulfric enlisted them to follow the travelers who then saw the opportunity for their own gain, robbed and murdered them and fled? There was Merwenna. Why was she running away from a man she did not fear and who had no hold on her? The issue of marriage made no sense. And, why was she on her way here? Though he seemed to have some answers, he still had many questions.

Then, there was the separate incidence of the murder of William Fullecoppe and subsequent slaying of Noah the smith and Jocelyn's pretending to be a woman. How had these dramas and their myriad players ended up in his demesne? He would give anything to hand these problems off to someone else, such as a local reeve had there been one. Perhaps the time had come to fill that job. It would be fitting and proper for a town growing as fast as Ryd Lliw.

"Master, look!" said Hewrey, pointing toward the churchyard as they approached the gate.

"Ercwiff?" Tristan recognized his man bent over a prone Ciaran sobbing, his face buried in his robe. "What happened? You are bleeding." Giving a nod in Ciaran's direction, he asked, "What is wrong with him?"

"My lord," Ercwiff said, with a quick bow, "One moment I was talking to the other guard, and next thing I knows I am waking up behind a gravestone." The soldier rubbed his head and when he pulled his hand away there were traces of blood. He winced. "As for Brother Ciaran, I comes from behind the stone and walks toward him, he drops to the ground and screams. He been sobbing ever since and making no sense."

Ciaran picked himself up from the ground and started toward the door of the church.

Tristan stopped him with a hand on his shoulder. "Brother Ciaran?"

"I will be fine, Sir Tristan," Ciaran said, wiping his eyes with the heel of his palms and sniffing loudly to stay a dripping nose. "Just leave me be." The monk continued on until he disappeared through the church door.

"Hewrey," said Tristan, "take this bloody fool to the hall and have Brother Rhonwellt see to his wound. I will be there shortly. Tomorrow we search for the Fullecoppe man. It is clear he murdered Noah. Whether it was at the behest of his masters is no matter. He will hang for murder—if I find him."

"Yes, Master," replied Hewrey.

"If Merwenna is at the hall, tell her to stay there until I arrive. You men, with me," Tristan said to his soldiers and stomped off in the direction of the tithe barn.

Selwyn, Wulfric, and his two henchmen sat wrapped in their cloaks, their legs and feet buried in the straw, their backs against the wall, looking cold and wretched. Holding a torch aloft, Tristan approached, stopping a few paces away, and ran his gaze over the lot. Patches of light and darkness danced across their faces and steam from their breath rose ghost-like through the gloom. The creases on Wulfric's brow furrowed into deep shadow.

Tristan prayed this was the right thing to do.

"Have I your assurance you will be of no further concern to me if I turn you loose?"

"Why in the name of Heaven would we do that?" replied Wulfric, lips curled in a sneer, baring his teeth.

"You are guilty of kidnapping my Priest. To the Church that is blasphemy and you could be excommunicated. Then, according to law, you could be tortured and hung. And having lost any hope of salvation, damned far worse than for being a mere felon."

"If we do not swear?"

"You would be less trouble to me if you were dead. I would not feel obliged to watch my back. But, you are Merwenna's kin, and she has been through enough sorrow."

"What is Merwenna to you?"

"She is naught to me but a widow in need of shelter. She is, however, something to you, and I understand you acted out of concern for Ernulf when you thought she was dead. It is why I am inclined to be merciful. Do I have your word?"

"You have my word," said Selwyn, straightening his back and sitting upright. "I am grateful for your kindness in rescuing her and Ernulf. I am in your debt and will cause you no further concern." Selwyn tossed his head toward Wulfric and his men. "They will cause you no trouble either, or they will answer to me. And, unless I miss my gauge, Merwenna will have something to say in the matter."

Tristan gave a short nod to Selwyn, then turned his focus to Wulfric. "What say you, Saxon?"

Tristan and Wulfric locked eyes and stared long and hard. The knight could sense the hatred seething behind the Saxon's outward demeanor and it made his skin prickle. Finally, the big blonde gave his chest a half-hearted thump with his closed fist and said, "I swear." The gesture told Tristan the man would be true to his word however reluctantly given.

"Unbind them," said Tristan, "and take them to the fire to warm."

The band of brigands at the other end of the barn appeared more miserable than the Saxons. The warmer weather had not made them any more comfortable, and with only two cloaks between the four, they lay huddled together, buried as deep in the straw as their bonds would allow. Their heads hung low, only the leader deigned to look up as Tristan approached. His false aura of bravado was gone, replaced with a dull-eyed resignation that his future was death on the gallows and public display on a gibbet.

"Sir Knight," said the outlaw, squinting against the glow of the torch, "your gaol is cold."

"I must needs only keep you alive long enough to hang," replied Tristan. "The law says nothing of keeping you warm. Be of good cheer. A fiery place awaits you upon your demise. Imagine an eternity many times hotter than if the whole of London were ablaze and you sat in the midst of the flames. Think it a blessing. You will never feel cold again."

Regaining some of the old defiance, the outlaw spit in Tristan's direction. "And I shall see your black heart there, knight, when you pass through those gates and join me."

In two strides, Tristan stood in the straw with one foot planted in the middle of the brigand's chest, the torch lowered to within inches of the man's face. "A welcome relief," said Tristan, "for, after thirty summers in the desert, I find Wales to be damp and disagreeable. In the meantime, it is home and everything I desire is here."

Tristan turned on his heel and left before any response came.

"Sir," said Selwyn as Tristan drew near the Northerners warming around the fire, "I wish to see my niece."

His mind still on the outlaws, it took Tristan a moment to focus in on the request. The knight's initial reaction tended toward irritation, but Selwyn's tone was calm and had come as an appeal and not an order. "I shall take you to her without further delay. All of you, walk with me to the hall."

Wulfric puffed himself up as if to say something. Selwyn held a hand up in front of the Saxon. "We gave our word," he said. "Be still."

All remained quiet as Tristan led the company up the rise to the hall. Wulfric walked doggedly with heavy steps, his countenance sulky and ill-tempered. The warrior had given his word, but Tristan knew he bore watching. The man could be trouble without ever breaking his oath.

The harrier was the first to greet their arrival as the heavy hall door swung open.

"Rinc! God has seen fit to spare you too," said Selwyn, as he bent to give the dog a pat on the head.

"Uncle!" Merwenna rose with Ernulf in her arms and crossed the room.

Selwyn engulfed them both in an embrace. "You are well?" he asked, putting a hand to her cheek.

"I am for the moment," Merwenna said as she walked back to the hearth, an arm entwined with her uncle's, Wulfric and the servants close behind. "And you," she said over her shoulder to Wulfric, "are a bloody fool."

Selwyn peered closely at her with narrowed eyes. "Child, what have they done to you? Your hair, it is gone."

"It will grow back," said Merwenna turning to lay a kiss on her uncle's shoulder. She then turned to Tristan. "Tell me, have I reason for concern? They robbed my caravan, murdered my soldiers and two of the dearest people I know, and the brigands who assailed us took me against my will. Now, another murder has occurred in the church-yard, and I find a man masquerading as a woman; what kind of wild place is this Wales?" Though her face suggested her words had been said lightly, her dark eyes flashed a subtle fury when she looked at Tristan so he could not tell her true mood. "Have I traveled from the farthest Northern reaches to the other end of the kingdom only to find myself adrift in a sea of wickedness?"

"That sea is vast, Mistress," replied Tristan. "Are people so pure in the North? This remote corner of Wales is not the only port of call for vessels of sin. However, I think you will find the ship of justice calls here as well."

Indulging an overwhelming need to be near Rhonwellt, Tristan went straight to where the monk was tending the wounded guard. Having the Saxons in the hall reminded Tristan of their trespass against his beloved green-eyed monk and the knight's discomfort renewed his determination to keep him from harm.

Peering over Rhonwellt's shoulder, Tristan's nose lightly caressed the monk's hair and inhaled the familiar scent. Rhonwellt shifted slightly and stole a quick glance in Tristan's direction. The knight breathed in Rhonwellt one more time, then straightened to take off his sword belt. Hanging it on a hook, he gestured to Selwyn and Wulfric. "Sirs, you have no need for arms while in my hall."

Selwyn stood for a moment. Then, with a small bow he loosed his sword and went to the wall to hang it. Wulfric held back, staring intently at Tristan. Was this to be a challenge? Tristan held his breath and placed himself in front of Rhonwellt, but remained where his sword was still within reach. No one moved. The air in the hall crackled from the silence.

"Wulfric," said Merwenna, "just do it, please. Do you not think you have caused enough problems? You forget yourself. You are a guest."

Wulfric did not move, only licked his lips and regarded Merwenna. "A guest who was recently a prisoner."

"You kidnapped my priest!" said Tristan through a clenched jaw. "Now, hang up your sword or use it." Taking a step toward his own weapon and drawing it from its scabbard, he moved menacingly toward Wulfric. "You have size, Saxon, but I fought my first battle when you were still at your mother's teat. Do you intend to challenge me in mine own home?"

"Wulfric, you bloody fool!" said Selwyn, fists balled tightly at his sides, his voice bellowing about the room. "You gave your word. Are you about to prove it worthless?"

Setting Ernulf down on a bench, Merwenna moved close to Wulfric, stood toe-to-toe with him and looked up into his eyes. Laying her hand on his chest, she leaned in close. Tristan could tell she was whispering to him, but was unable to hear what passed between them. The muscles of the Saxon's face rippled under the skin. He ran his off-hand through his scalp, the fingers of his sword hand twitching near the hilt. Suddenly, the big blonde's eyes grew round, his mouth fell agape. She placed a finger on his lips to still any response he might make. Slowly, Wulfric's gaze shifted from Merwenna to Tristan and he blew a gust of air from flared nostrils.

"Osgar," he said turning and heading toward the door.

"Aw, Master, it be warm here."

"With me, now!"

Osgar rose and followed his master as Wulfric strode out the door.

Tristan made to follow when Merwenna stopped him. "Leave him be. He will not disobey me," she said. "The price would be too dear."

"What price?" Tristan asked.

"Why, my ire."

The corners of Tristan's mouth curled up into a small smile, the first since discovering Noah had been killed. "What did you tell him?"

"All you need to know for now," said Merwenna, "is that I sent him to secure rooms at the inn and to tell the landlord that you would pay for it. It will give him time to cool his temper."

"Mistress, you presume..."

"I presume only that you are a good host and that since your modest hall is full, you would accommodate lodging them there."

Tristan slowly shook his head from side to side, the small smile still on his face. "I think I would do well not to risk your ire, either."

"A trait from my mother," said Merwenna, a twinkle in her eye, lips pressed into a sly grin. "Wise and brave, Sir Tristan. You could prove a good catch. And this place could use a woman's touch. It is no more furnished than a camp."

"It suits us," replied Tristan, looking around. "And my heart has already found grace in another." Resisting the urge to look in Rhonwellt's direction, Tristan instead aimed his gaze at the floor. Hoping to thwart any further comment along those lines, he instructed Hewrey to refill their drinks and bring some bread and cheese.

Ever since Wulfric's steamed departure, Selwyn had remained quiet, almost pensive, all the while staring into the bottom of his drinking pot. "You mentioned ships of justice. Do you say the King's law is meted out here?" he asked, lifting the cup to his lips.

"They will feel God's justice," said Rhonwellt, crossing himself and sending Ercwiff on his way with a wave of his hand. "It will prove more awful than any punishment the law could inflict and will last for eternity."

"Will there be a trial?" asked Merwenna.

"There is no need for one," replied Selwyn, snorting into his cup before taking a drink.

"Then we goes ahead and hangs them." Hewrey poured wine into Tristan's outstretched pot. "What a day that will be. Eh, Master? The whole village be turning up for that."

"To hang them with no trial is murder," replied Tristan.

"What about Trial by Water?" said Hewrey, beaming with excitement. "That be a right spectacle, waiting to see of they floats or sinks."

"Trial by Ordeal," replied Rhonwellt, "is to determine their guilt or innocence. Their guilt has readily been established."

"It will be but a formality and need not be long, but there will be a trial." Tristan downed half his pot of wine. "Merwenna will testify and that will put an end to it. Then, yes Hewrey, they will be hanged and the whole village will turn up for it."

"What if you were to only threaten Trial by Water?" said Selwyn. "Then, perhaps they would confess to escape the ordeal. Merwenna would not have to testify and the outcome would be the same."

"Whatever is done," said Merwenna, "you must see it accomplished soon. For what they did to Myfanwy and Hrodolf, I would watch them die with relish and see their bodies left to rot."

"Harsh sentiments for a woman," said Rhonwellt.

"You know little of women, Brother," replied Selwyn. "Some are as ruthless as any man. Merwenna is very like her mother. Ceolwyn was her own woman, one who refused to be dictated to by men. It dismayed Merwenna's father greatly."

The mention of the name Ceolwyn sparked a recognition in Tristan he could not quite place.

"The size of her dowry more than made up for it," said Merwenna. "And, though betrothed to father, she was already with child when they wed."

"A healthy marriage settlement has persuaded many a man to swallow his pride." Tristan held out his cup for Hewrey to refill.

"Niece, you know not what you say." Selwyn slapped his hands on his thighs and leaned forward. "You father was a man of honor. He would never have taken advantage of Ceolwyn."

"You are right. His honor was beyond reproach. And he loved my mother above all others."

"Child, this is not a discussion for the ears of strangers. It is family business."

Tristan agreed and grew uneasy. Why was she baring family secrets in front of people she hardly knew?

"Still, she told me before she died, the seed was already within her when she married—and father knew it."

"Hush, Merwenna! I will hear no more, at least until we are alone."

"We are alone. The only others here are servants, a child, and a monk. It is my story to tell and there is one here who must hear it."

Merwenna's dismissal of Hewrey and Leo as insignificant was nothing out of the ordinary. Servants were nobody. Ernulf was a child and would not understand, anyway. But, for her to view Rhonwellt as inconsequential rankled Tristan. He would tell her so—later, when Rhonwellt had gone. For the present, he would not interrupt her story.

"Are you saying you are the child of another?" Selwyn began to pace in a tight circle, gesturing wildly with his hands.

"I am," said Merwenna. "Though she did not love father, she did not object to him or the marriage. But she had already tasted the flesh of another man."

"It cannot be true." Selwyn sat heavily on a bench and put his head between his hands. "Did she tell you who?"

"She did. She said it was a visiting squire, young and barely a man. His master was acquainted with grandfather, though how she did not say. Grandfather despised the master but would not refuse him hospitality. Being so young, uncle, you were not allowed near the knight because of his carnal tastes for young boys."

Tristan's head snapped up and his breath caught in his throat. It had become clear.

"The man shamed his young squire by calling his manhood to question in front of the whole company at supper and then sent him from the room in humiliation. Mother found him later near the lake, despondent and in need of a friend." Tristan felt her eyes upon him. "I understand the master did not survive the wars."

Tristan's stomach knotted into a ball and he could not feel his heart beating. A bead of sweat ran down the side of his face. His head was spinning with distant images of a painful memory from long ago and his moment of deliverance. "I was but fourteen summers," he mumbled. "It was the first time I ever lay with a woman. It had been months since I had known any kindness or gentleness. I had nearly forgotten what it was like." He openly stole a glance toward Rhonwellt. "I never forgot it."

"You are saying it was our host?" said Selwyn, waving a hand toward Tristan. "He is your father?"

Merwenna nodded.

TWENTY-THREE

Rhonwellt's clay drinking pot slipped from his hands and tumbled to the floor, shattering the strained silence. His gaze went immediately to Tristan, looking for some kind of denial, a gesture or response that would tell him what he just heard was not true. Did Merwenna accuse him falsely? Tristan had just confirmed he knew Merwenna's mother, even admitted to lying with her, but that did not mean she had borne his child. However, it was a death-bed confession. People did not lie in their final moments if they wished to unburden their souls before meeting their Maker.

"Could she have been mistaken?" Tristan's voice sounded muted as if crossing a great distance.

Merwenna handed Ernulf to Hewrey and went to sit next to Tristan.

"I believe my mother," Merwenna said. "I knew the first moment I saw you. You are exactly as she described you. Older and more care-worn, but recognizable."

"Why would she remember someone so utterly forgettable?" said Tristan, his voice barely audible.

"The circumstance then made you quite memorable. She was a

virgin and betrothed. You were the first man she lay with and, though she did not say, for that one night, she probably loved you. These things can happen. To a young woman, that is significant."

Merwenna took his hand in hers, turned it over and examined it from all sides then lay it back in his lap.

"Now, all this time later, you appear to be no less remarkable. For a man owning more than a few summers, you accounted for yourself well on the tor when you rescued me. I am certain you served the king well in the East. They still speak of your encounter with the beggar in Cydweli. He hunted you for over thirty summers. So it would appear that, for good or ill, people remember you."

Merwenna put her fingers up near his face and began to trace the jagged line running down his cheek. When Tristan recoiled slightly, she let her hand fall back into her lap. "Obviously, this scar came later as she did not mention it."

Merwenna continued to gaze at him for some moments before she let her eyes fall to the fire.

"Though handsome and robust, she said the most notable thing about you was the overwhelming melancholy in your eyes. She remarked it was unusual in one so young. You carry it still. Sadly, that was what convinced me I had found you."

Rhonwellt knew whence some of Tristan's sadness had come and it weighed on him. Would that he could just acknowledge that he had already lost his heart to Tristan and vanquish some of the pain in the knight's dark eyes, ease the ache in his heart of never being sure. It was fear, almost terror, that held the monk back. And though Rhonwellt realized that, he could not put his finger on its source. Though it may not be rational, Rhonwellt knew it was very real, and it paralyzed him.

Rhonwellt hugged himself tightly inside his sleeves. He could feel the stone walls of the hall close in around him, as though the room was suddenly shrinking. His heart pounded in his ears and there was not enough air. Inhaling deeply and repeatedly, his struggle to fill his lungs made him dizzy, caused his fingers to tingle and the muscles of his hands to contract. He tried hiding them in his sleeves. The room was spinning, and he prayed he would not lose consciousness. He looked up through his brows and caught Selwyn staring at him. Immediately upon meeting Selwyn's eyes, the man looked away. The monk tried to seem relaxed. Thankful for the dimness of the light, he prayed his emotional distress was not evident.

"I will take my leave, sir," said Selwyn, rising and giving Tristan a bow. "I must see to it Wulfric has caused no trouble. When his ire is up, he does not think clearly." He nodded at Merwenna and Rhonwellt. "Niece, Brother." Selwyn started for the door. "Leo, come." The all-but-forgotten servant rose and followed his master out.

Though his body felt numb, Rhonwellt sensed a tapping sensation and wetness on his feet. He looked down to see Hewrey kneeling in front of him, gathering shards of clay and rearranging the rushes on the floor. The hem of his robe had become soaked from his spilled drinking pot and the liquid was dripping onto his toes.

"Not to worry, Brother," whispered Hewrey. "It are only a little wine." Hewrey kept his eyes lowered as he worked.

To Rhonwellt, the wine resembled blood, fresh from a cut before it turned dark. How fitting, as the news had come to him with the impact of an arrow leaving him feeling wounded. He looked on passively and lifted his feet as Hewrey moved dry rushes to cover the spoiled ones.

Rhonwellt tried gazing into the fire to occupy his mind, to ease his anxiety and escape this moment, to get lost in the sedative effects of the dancing flames and their irresistible movement. His efforts proved fruitless, for his eyes found their way back to Tristan time and again. Though Rhonwellt looked at him with the same eyes, he saw Tristan as different. Tristan was a father—and a grandfather—and this gave the knight new dimension, made Rhonwellt see him in a new light.

Or, were these thoughts only folly? Tristan was the same man he had always been, was he not? He had been a father and grandfather for a score-and-ten summers. The facts were not new. Only the knowledge of them was new. But knowledge held significance. Would what he knew change things? Would it reshape who and what they were to each other? Or, worse, would it define them? Would it show them what must be and what Rhonwellt now knew may never be?

Extracting his hands from his sleeves, Rhonwellt gripped the edge of the bench to steady himself, swallowed hard and squeezed his eyes shut. It was only a matter of moments before he found himself staring at Tristan again. Rhonwellt sat there wishing he were invisible. He knew people were talking around him but felt like a ghost, hearing their words while not really there at all. He desperately wanted to get up and leave, to fly to the church in hopes of the solace he could not find here, or better yet retreat to the comfort of his cottage and the familiar loneliness of his bed. He willed his feet to move. They would not. He doubted his legs would carry him even if he succeeded in the attempt to stand. There he remained, gripping the edge of the bench, stuffing down the misery welling in his heart and climbing into his throat. He had been foolish to believe it could ever be any different, that he could truly have what Tristan had to give him.

"I am prosperous but not wealthy." Tristan lifted his pot to his lips and tipped his head back. Scowling, he thrust his pot toward Hewrey who filled it with a scowl of his own. "What do you want from me?"

"Only to know a little of my father." Merwenna leaned in as she spoke, tilting her head to look at him.

"Nothing else?" Tristan took a gulp from his replenished pot then sat with his head down and face to the fire. His brows narrowed. Rhonwellt knew Hewrey must have put too much water in it.

"I have enough money and land left me by my husband," said Merwenna. "I need no more."

"The man who raised you was your father, not me," replied Tristan, holding his pot in both hands and running his thumbs along the rim. "I am a soldier. I know nothing of being a parent nor am I suited to it."

"Being widowed and a mother, I am raised and no longer need parenting." Merwenna placed a hand on Tristan's arm. "But I carry your blood. Is that not something?"

"That is the extent of it. I mean you or Ceolwyn no disrespect, but I was naught to your mother nor was she anything to me. Ours was a furtive coupling borne out of pity from a kind young woman for a young squire who was loathed by his master. There was no time for feelings. My master and I were gone a day later."

"It was not pity," said Merwenna, "compassion more likely."

"They are one and the same," said Tristan, "though I do believe one is born of a kinder thought and easier to take in."

"She wanted to remind you there was still kindness to be found in the world. Your master had turned your disgrace into dinner conversation to further humiliate you and she hated him for it."

"Many would have agreed I deserved such condemnation."

"Those sentiments arrived on these shores with the Normans. We Saxons never believed such tripe."

Rhonwellt began to squirm on his seat, uncomfortable with the turn the conversation had taken. If Tristan felt the same discomfort, it was not evident. What Merwenna alluded to should never be spoken of aloud. Why did Tristan not put a stop to such talk? The monk tried summoning all his will to leave.

"You were headed off to war and not likely to return." Merwenna hesitated. "She thought you should know the warmth of a woman at least once."

"She need not have worried," said Tristan, clearing his throat. "There is no army on earth that does not have the warmth of women close at hand." Tristan turned from staring into his cup to face her fully. "Why would your mother tell you all this? Why not carry the truth to her grave rather than name you a bastard?"

"She was dying and thought I deserved to know the truth. She valued truth above all else and had nothing to lose. Since I had been securely married and widowed, nor did I. My marriage to my husband legitimized me. The Normans had come but twenty summers before. My father was one, and my mother was a trade secured by my grandfather to gain favor with the conquerors and avoid the diminished circumstances suffered by most of us Saxons at the time. They took his land but did not reduce us to servitude."

"I really must retreat to my bed," said Rhonwellt, willing himself to rise on shaky legs, at long last finding the resolve to leave. "Matins will soon be upon us." Perhaps the monk's desire for invisibility had succeeded for Tristan and Merwenna looked at him as though he had appeared from nowhere.

"Apologies, Brother," said Tristan, rising, his movements awkward, his voice unsure. To Rhonwellt, the knight's eyes begged forgiveness, but also something else, though Rhonwellt could not divine it. "I fear we have been rude and grievously ignored you."

"I find the turmoil of the last two days has exhausted me." Rhonwellt sighed as he began to cross the room, Hewrey already ahead of him to open the door. He stopped and turned to face the hearth. "God grant us clarity to make sense of it all," he said, signing the cross toward Tristan and Merwenna. "I wish you God's Peace and a restful night."

✝   ✝   ✝

TRISTAN WATCHED RHONWELLT LEAVE. HE HAD NEVER forgotten for a moment that Rhonwellt was there, only surprised at the suddenness of his exit. The knight did not think he could have gotten through listening to Merwenna's story had his beloved monk not been close at hand, to even him out and somehow give him strength. Several times he had caught glimpses of Rhonwellt's discomfort and knew the monk had wanted to go, but selfishly, Tristan was glad Rhonwellt had remained.

Following his nature had been far easier for Tristan in the East than here at home. Persians did not view love between men with the same shame Christians so righteously attached to it. Here, nearly everything was a sin. Among his fellow Crusaders, men like Tristan were not rare, and it was easy to turn a blind eye. Every soldier knew death stalked them relentlessly, could find them at any time, and that any chance for a moment of tenderness could be their last. Many were willing to dance with the devil for it.

Here, he found that the farther away one was from the hardscrabble struggle for survival, either through wealth or a perceived closeness to God, the harsher the judgment. The lowest of the orders was too busy staying alive to care much about such things.

"You regard him fondly, your priest." Merwenna's tone was not accusatory, rather matter-of-fact.

Still staring at the door after Rhonwellt, Tristan paused before turning his attention to her. If the young woman was truly his daughter, then they might as well have it all out in the open, and now would do as well as any time. There remained one swallow of wine in his pot. He raised it thoughtfully to his lips to drink, forming the words in his mind before he spoke. Lowering the vessel, he took a breath and shifted to face her fully on.

"You know what I am," said Tristan, at last, "how it has always been with me." He paused and looked at the door and then back to Merwenna. "I was not made for women."

"You have chosen a hard life."

"I did not choose it." Tristan picked up the poker and started to stir the embers in the hearth to bring the dying fire back to life. "It is who I am."

"How can you be so sure? You lay with my mother."

"I did, and I have lain with other women since. It is not that I am incapable."

"Then what is it?"

"It would be a lie. I could take a wife and am yet young enough to beget more children, but there would be no passion in it. It would not be for love. It would be a ruse."

"No one gets to marry for love, least of all women." Merwenna gathered her skirts, rose, and walked to the side table where the scraps of a light supper remained. She took up a small chunk of bread and a slice of cheese and began to nibble. "To marry would keep you safe." She returned to the hearth and stood in front of Tristan,

He raised his head and searched Merwenna's face. "You are very like Ceolwyn. She was easy to talk to, and I soon found I confided to her things I would never tell another soul." He paused a moment, deliberated whether he should have more wine. He decided against it. "Would it surprise you to know this estate once belonged to that same master who caused me such misery?"

Merwenna's face could not contain her surprise as her hand froze midway to her mouth. She stopped chewing.

"I asked Lord Robert for it."

"Whatever for?" she said, recovering.

"There are many reasons. Though I found it run down upon my return, it had once been a prosperous demesne surrounded by fertile fields. There was a certain poetic justice to be found, as well. Grenteville would twist in his grave to know I was now lord here. However, its greatest asset is that it is remote, far from the scrutinies of civilization. The village had been all but abandoned for many summers. I can grow it the way I choose. The people are uncomplicated, they wish to work, feed their families, have shelter against the rain and cold, and know some joy. If they feel I am a good master, neither harsh nor untrustworthy, and mean them only to be safe and prosper, they will feel no need to judge me or each other in order to survive."

"I feel you give them too much credit. Are you not afraid they could turn on you?"

Tristan thought for a moment. "I am very careful never to give them reason." Tristan lowered his head and clenched his jaw. "It is late and has been a trying day. Go to bed and we shall speak more on the morrow. Hewrey has provided for you in the room next to mine in the solar. He has already taken Ernulf up."

"Father?"

"Do not call me that!" The words were out before he could stop them and his reaction much harsher than he intended.

Merwenna recoiled. Her tone had been reticent. Perhaps she was only testing the waters.

He forced himself back to calm and went on in more civil tones. "I only mean that it is too early yet for me to be addressed as such. I have only just found out. Give me a little time to adjust."

"Have I said something to offend?"

"Please, child, just go to your bed and be with your son. All will be well." He spun on his heel and went to the jug on the side table and filled a clay pot. "Hewrey, show Merwenna up and go to your bed as well."

"Yes, master." The lad scrambled to his feet from where he had been sitting, dozing up against the wall.

Keeping his back to the room, Tristan listened to the footsteps recede across the floor, heading for the solar stairs. He was exhausted, a little frightened, and not nearly drunk enough. Hewrey had judiciously watered the wine this evening. Tristan downed the pot and poured another. Had he said too much? Merwenna was so very like her mother. He remembered his night with Ceolwyn and that he had told her all of it, the whole tale, told her of his love for the ginger-haired lad with the sea-green eyes. Had she told the tale to her daughter? Perhaps Merwenna already knew the lad had been Rhonwellt. Could he really trust her? Or, had he already set in motion the downfall of his life and Rhonwellt's as well?

Tristan slowly turned and shuffled across the room to the door. Stepping outside into the night, he pulled the door closed quietly behind him and started down the hill. The sky was clear and the weather had turned brisk. He had not brought his cloak. He crossed his arms, huddled against the cold and trudged toward the gatehouse. Passing through, Tristan said nothing to the guards, only nodded, and turned into the lane that led to the village. The night was quiet, and the street deserted. Even the usual noise from the tavern was subdued. He was glad, for he did not want to encounter anyone due to the state in which he found himself.

The gate to the churchyard stood open, so it made no noise when Tristan entered. Gravel crunched under his feet as he crossed the yard to skirt the church and head for the cottage behind. Tristan had been to Rhonwellt and Ciaran's cottage so few times it felt awkward. He was not sure what he intended to say or do, but needed to see Rhonwellt, to make sure he was all right. The dwelling came into sight and Tristan stopped, suddenly realizing Rhonwellt would not be alone, that Ciaran and Jocelyn would likely be there. He stared through the darkness at the small flicker of a candle showing between the cracks in the window shutters. He stood there, motionless, torn between leaving and going to the door.

Then, the light went out.

TWENTY-FOUR

Rhonwellt rose before dawn, careful not to wake Ciaran and Jocelyn. He would rely on the young monk to officiate morning prayers, for if he did not leave now, before anyone else was about, Rhonwellt might lose his resolve. He had slept not a wink, his mind spinning from all he had learned the previous evening. Compounding it all was his arrival at the cottage to find Ciaran and Jocelyn asleep together, Jocelyn's arms wrapped tightly around Ciaran from behind. That Ciaran was still chastely robed did little to quell Rhonwellt's alarm, or still his imagination as to the many possibilities or outcomes of such an arrangement. But, he would have to deal with all that later. That was, of course, if he ever came back.

Determined to take his leave unannounced, he decided to forego the chamber pot and relieve himself outside. He had gone to bed still in his robes so he had only to don his shoes before tiptoeing out the door and into the early morning. Though the night had been clear and a chill still hung in the air, clouds visible in the grayish pre-dawn light at the edges of the horizon promised rain during the coming day. Smoke from rekindled fires would soon settle over the village like a low-slung fog, saturating the air with the dirt-and-ash smell of burning peat.

The hostler was already awake and about his chores when Rhonwellt entered the stable and asked that Epona be saddled and readied for a trip.

"You must be going far, Brother, to be needing your horse."

"Yes, Ronan, a bit further than I care to walk." Rhonwellt thought it best not to reveal his destination, though he knew Ciaran would figure it out quickly enough if given the chance to think it through. He was not sure anyone else would care enough to wonder.

"Weather coming in. Hope you gets to where you are bound before it is upon you."

"As do I, Ronan. That is why I am off early, in hopes of beating the rain." Rhonwellt prayed God would absolve his lie. And, he hoped Ciaran would forgive him for leaving such a great responsibility on his shoulders when the young monk himself was in such emotional turmoil. Rhonwellt knew he should be there to help Ciaran sort out the confusion about Jocelyn. But his own turmoil had so preoccupied him, he doubted he would be of any real use.

"Must be a day for traveling," said Ronan, leading the docile mare out into the yard and helping Rhonwellt into the saddle. "The Masters Fullecoppe left a short while ago on their return to Cydweli. If you be heading that way, you can most likely still catch them and travel safe."

"Thank you, Ronan. That is good to know." Rhonwellt signed the cross in the hostler's direction. "May God's peace be with you."

Rhonwellt was not sure he would travel with the Fullecoppes, though he planned to keep them in sight in case of trouble. Directing Epona out into the lane, Rhonwellt turned his back on the rising sun and headed down the road toward Cydweli.

The rocking rhythm of the horse's gait began to ease the anxiety plaguing Rhonwellt's mind, a tension he only now realized had set every muscle in his body on edge. Time immersed in the steady routine of the priory was what he needed now: a few days with his brothers, of being fed and housed as a matter of course, the tolling of the bells telling him when and where he needed to be next and what he was to be doing, sitting at a desk in the scriptorium, pen in hand, his mind focused solely on the shaping of the letters on the parchment, all in the safety of the familiar. And prayer, much prayer. It would help to set his mind right, bring the clarity he hoped for.

Knowing Epona would keep to the track, Rhonwellt pulled his hood up, allowed his eyes to close and tried to relax the knot that ran from his neck down to the space between his shoulder blades. It was the place he carried his worries. He was about to remark to himself that perhaps Brother Anselm would have a draught to ease his tension when he remembered the old monk was dead and that the last time he had gone to Cydweli was to say goodbye to his friend, only to be kidnapped most unceremoniously before he could attend Anselm's funeral mass. Now, he journeyed there again with great sadness once more burdening his heart.

Rhonwellt was shaken to the core. He had been on the verge of accepting that he and Tristan might find some happiness at last when this latest revelation landed in their midst like a rock falling from a tor. It reminded him of the words in Job from scripture, about the Lord giving and the Lord taking away. How much more did God want from him and how much more did he have left to give? The Almighty expected a hefty tithe. Would there ever be a time when he had sacrificed enough?

Soon, Rhonwellt's mood was darker than the approaching storm clouds. Unless he distracted himself, it would likely become dour.

"Let us catch up to the others, old girl," he said as he opened his eyes, clucked to Epona, and encouraged the mare to pick up her pace with a gentle nudge of his heels. Since he had not glimpsed them since starting out, Rhonwellt hoped he had not allowed them to get too far ahead. Topping a small rise, he saw father and son only a furlong ahead, still close enough to catch, and urged the mare into an easy trot. The sound of Epona's hooves must have alerted them to his approach for they turned in their saddles and watched him close the distance. As soon as they did, he rued his decision to give up his solitude and join them, wishing he had continued to stay behind but keep them in sight. But, it was too late now. They had stopped and were waiting for him to catch up.

Walter Fullecoppe sat atop his saddle, an impassive air about him, whereas Thomas greeted Rhonwellt with a knit brow and suspicious leer. Rhonwellt forced a smile to his face.

"Good morrow, sirs," said Rhonwellt, keeping his tone light to hide his dismay at having made his presence known. "We travel in the same direction, I see."

"We are if you are bound for Cydweli," said Walter Fullecoppe. "You are most welcome to join us."

The look on Thomas's face said he did not share the same enthusiasm for adding a traveling companion. The younger man clucked to his horse and moved out ahead, leaving his father and Rhonwellt to ride alone. Was he just the solitary sort or was there more to his unfriendliness? Or was the sadness over his brother's death that acute?

"It appears as though Master Thomas' grief is all-consuming," said Rhonwellt.

"It comes as a bit of a surprise to me," replied Walter. "They were always close as boys, but had grown apart more recently, especially on the part of Thomas."

"Is that not common as boys become men?" He thought of the rift between Tristan and his brother, Declan, before Declan took his own life.

"Sometimes." Walter turned his face to Rhonwellt. "Have you no brothers of your own?"

"I have been with the church since my childhood, and known no family since attaining thirteen summers."

"For that, I am truly sorry, Brother. The bond between siblings is like no other and can last a lifetime. It was like that for my sons when they were younger. Thomas worshipped William, as boys often do their elder brothers."

"What changed?" Rhonwellt asked.

"I often wondered," replied Walter. "Neither would say." The elder Fullecoppe turned and stared straight ahead into the distance, his eyes becoming hard, moisture collecting in the corners. "Now, I think I may know."

Rhonwellt nodded but said nothing as they settled into an uneasy silence. He would make inquiries while at Cydweli about the Masters Fullecoppe.

✝ ✝ ✝

THE SOUNDS OF A DAY WELL UNDERWAY DRIFTED IN THROUGH the window opening of the solar wall rousing a reluctant Tristan from a restless sleep. As soon as his wits cleared enough to let him know he was still alive, the pounding in his head began. The knight had tired of waking every morning to the misery caused by too much wine the night before, yet his attempts at moderation had fleeting success. He groaned as he rolled onto his back and tested the morning light by opening his eyes just a crack. Even in the gloom of a cloudy day, the light was painful. He slammed them closed and groaned again.

A full bladder began to pressure him to rise and seek relief. Tristan pushed back the bedcovers, pivoted, put his feet to the floor, and bent over to feel under the bed for the pot. He found nothing.

"Bloody hell." Tristan forced his lids open to search the room. In the dim light, he could see the vessel where it lay, overturned, in a puddle near the outer wall. It would seem he had used it some-time after climbing to the solar to retire. Then, in yet another drunken stupor, he must have spilled the contents either by kicking it or stepping in it. Tristan looked down at his feet and with relief he noticed his hose were dry.

The knight combed his fingers through his hair, greasy and tangled from sweating through the night, and slid his hand down to rub the back of his neck. With shaking fingers, he tried rubbing his temples. It brought no relief, Tristan's head still throbbed. He closed his eyes. His tongue stuck to the roof of his mouth and tasted foul, like stale wine. Why had he drunk so much?

He need not ask the question for the answer, this time, was plain enough—Merwenna. Over the brief extent of a single evening, everything Tristan thought he knew about his life had changed. He now had a daughter and a grandson. More to the point, he was a father and grandfather. How he considered the situation somehow made a difference. Being a parent created a different consequence than merely having children. It changed who or what he was. He could not help but wonder if his life would be transformed by this fact, and how. Would it make a difference for him and Rhonwellt and the life he hoped they would build? Would Merwenna accept or reject their relationship? Tristan grabbed his head between his palms and moaned, exhaling through clenched teeth. Such serpentine thinking was making his headache worse. And he had to piss.

Clenching his fists on either side of him, Tristan pushed his knuckles into the mattress, raising his body upright onto wobbly legs. He waited a moment to be sure he would not topple, then moved toward the overturned chamberpot. Setting it to rights, the knight relieved himself, his unsteady stance causing him to piss mostly on the floor. Tristan felt bad for he knew Hewrey would grumble at the prospect of cleaning it up but would do it, nonetheless. In that moment, Tristan had the realization that his drunkenness had as profound an impact on those around him as it did on himself. He needed to do better.

On his way to the washstand, Tristan caught his hose on a raised splinter in a floorboard and swore when he heard it tear. Once there, he stood leaning on the stand, staring at his face reflected on the surface of the water in the bowl. What did he know about being a father? How did one go about being a parent to a grown woman beyond the age of parenting?

He remembered stumbling down the hill in the dark and ending up at the cottage Rhonwellt and Ciaran shared, only to stare at the window, lacking the courage to knock at the door, to go in. One thing stood out clear in his foggy recollections about yestereve: Rhonwellt's distress at Merwenna's news seemed to surpass his own. Rhonwellt had put forward a valiant effort at concealing his heightened emotions, but Tristan knew. The evidence was clear, spoken in how the monk moved his body and the sadness in his eyes, sadness that resided there because of him.

Voices came floating up from the hall below, and Tristan realized the rest of the household was up and about. He knew he would have to go down soon. Were Hewrey the only one there, the knight wouldn't care. The lad had seen the aftermath of his master's heavy drinking many times. Since there were others, Tristan felt the need to be presentable. He splashed water on his face. It was cold enough to make his breath catch in his throat. He splashed more water, this time over the top of his scalp. Letting his hair drip into the basin, he felt his mind clear a little. Morning after morning, the same thing and he had become weary of the repetitive routine. He soaked his head a third time.

The knight felt his wandering into those labyrinthine thoughts only agitated him and never gave him any clarity. The idea of Merwenna and Ernulf was new territory, and all the thought in the world would not provide him with knowledge he did not possess. The solution would be to forge ahead and hope he could stumble onto doing the right thing. However, there were other matters having to do with Merwenna before him he already held the knowledge to resolve. He must punish the outlaws who had sought to do her harm. He had a trial and subsequent hanging to arrange.

Tristan changed his tunic and hose, put on his boots and headed for the hall. Pausing at the top of the stairs, he ran his fingers through his hair, took a deep breath, and began to descend, wearing his most confident pre-battle face.

"Master. You are up," Hewrey called out. "There is porridge, hot and thick and sweet. Will you be needing some raw eel?"

Tristan felt his stomach lurch at the thought of food as he crossed the room to stand beside the hearth.

"Since when do you keep raw eel?" Tristan replied. Hewrey quickly turned his back but not before Tristan saw his shoulders shake from laughter.

"Good morrow, sir," said Merwenna, looking up at him with uncertainty on her face. "The porridge is quite delicious and will do as much to cure morning pottle-ache as any raw eel. May I get you some?"

"Hewrey knows I cannot eat so soon after rising," he replied with a wave of his hand. Tristan was quiet for a moment, trying to form the words into a thought to ensure it came out right. He raised his head. "I fear I am out of my depth here," he said to Merwenna. "I only ask for your patience."

"It is not my intention to cause you distress," Merwenna said.

Hewrey sidled up to Tristan's side holding out a drinking pot. If Tristan was correct, it contained far more water than ale. He accepted the pot and put it to his lips, sipping it. The knight was searching for an answer when the door opened and Ciaran peeked around into the room.

"Brother Ciaran," said Hewrey, "you be wanting porridge, right?"

Ciaran slipped in and shut the door and scanned the room. "I am looking for Brother Rhonwellt. Is he not here?"

"No, brother," Hewrey replied, "no sign of him yet today."

The young monk walked to the fire, spreading his hands over the flames. "I fear I have been negligent in my duty and did not ring the bell for Lauds. Nor did Brother Rhonwellt."

"Well, Master has just rose," said Hewrey with a smirk, "and none of us has seen him."

"I can find him nowhere. I fear he has gone."

"Gone?" Tristan was suddenly all attentive and rose to his feet. "Where has he gone?"

"Yestereve, he arrived at the cottage quite late. I...we...were asleep, but I heard him come in. He was muttering to himself like he does when he is upset though I could not understand his words. Then he tossed most seriously in his bed. I must have drifted off for when I next awoke, it was light, Lauds had long passed and Brother Rhonwellt had gone."

"Have you checked with Ronan to see if he has taken his horse?" Tristan made as if to head for the door, then stopped.

"No, sir, I have not," said Ciaran. "But if he has, I think I may know where he has gone."

All eyes turned to Ciaran and waited expectantly.

"I am quite sure he has gone to the priory."

"Why there?" asked Tristan.

"He will bury himself in a manuscript at the scriptorium. It is where he goes to think."

"I shall send someone to bring him back," said Tristan.

"He will not come until he is ready," said Ciaran. "That, you know to be true."

"I believe I know why he has gone," said Merwenna to Tristan. "And, when the time is right, if anyone goes for him, it must be you."

TWENTY-FIVE

After their brief conversation, he and the Fullecoppes had ridden in near silence for the remainder of their trip which suited Rhonwellt well. With all that weighed on him, idle chatter would have been difficult. He was glad for traveling companions who made no demands on him. Other than stopping to water the horses thrice, they remained in the saddle for the whole day. Rhonwellt even broke his fast with bread and some cheese while rocking gently to Epona's gait. When they were yet fifteen furlongs away, it had started to drizzle but never progressed into a full rain. It was past Nones and nearly supper-time when Rhonwellt had finally reached Saint Cattwg's damp, but not soaked through.

Now, Rhonwellt sat next to Prior Alwyn at the head of the table, the place reserved for guests of the priory. He stared down the rows of monks seated on each side of the long trestle. This new vantage point felt odd, since Rhonwellt had been used to his old seat in the middle along the right side. The dull tunk of wooden spoons clacking against wooden bowls was the only sound in the refectory aside from wheezing and the occasional cough. He had quite forgotten how different it was to eat in silence. He seldom did it these days, and never when he ate at Tristan's hall.

Immediately upon arriving, Rhonwellt had gone directly to the prior to secure permission for his stay.

"Brother Rhonwellt," Alwyn said, showing joy and surprise in equal measure to see his brother before him. He reached for Rhonwellt and pulled him close, bestowing the kiss of peace on each cheek. "I had no idea you were coming. God be praised, it gladdens my heart to see you."

"And you as well, Father Prior," answered Rhonwellt, blushing toward the floor.

"You look very well indeed." Alwyn motioned to a bench. "Please, sit and tell me what brings this happy reunion."

Rhonwellt could see that the prior had visibly aged since he left. The old monk still looked reasonably fit but the dullness and fatigue in his eyes were still there.

"Things are well at Saint Tysilio's? And our Brother Ciaran, how is your young assistant?"

Rhonwellt hesitated before answering. How much should he tell his old teacher? So many things had brought him here, some too personal to share—at least not now.

"You are reticent to answer," said Alwyn, his brow knit with concern. "Are things that grave?"

"Where to begin," said Rhonwellt, after another, longer, hesitation. He absently picked at the skin on one of his fingers.

"Why, commence at the beginning, of course."

"I am not sure there is one. It is not just one thing, but many. But they are somehow intertwined."

"Then start with the least of them."

"Each is significant in its own way." Rhonwellt's words felt like an understatement, bringing a thin smile to his lips. "However, there is some joy attached to one. Sir Tristan has recently discovered he has a daughter and a grandson." He would not admit to the prior that this was the gravest of all the things that troubled him.

"That is...surprising," replied Alwyn. Alwyn's gaze bore into Rhonwellt. "You do not seem to share in that joy, and I suspect that troubles you more than you let on."

Rhonwellt shrugged.

"Yet, you may find benefit to that revelation beyond your knowing at this time."

Rhonwellt was about to ask the prior his meaning then decided against it. The only one who could benefit from it was Tristan. He did not want to think about that.

"Excuse me," said the prior as he rose, went to the door and flung it open. "Ailiet, surely there is work you should be about rather than loitering with your ear pressed to my door."

"Apologies, Father Prior."

A young boy peered around the prior, his eyes scanning the interior of the chamber. Tall for a boy and strikingly thin with alabaster skin, blue eyes, and no hair, the lad appeared to be a ghost.

"We have discussed this before, have we not?" The prior's voice was not harsh or unkind.

"Yes, Father Prior. I just wanted..." Ailiet peered at Rhonwellt again. "They are about to ring for supper," he added.

"Then, you will meet our guest at the evening meal. Now, off with you."

"Yes, Father." The lad hung his head and left, sneaking one last glance at Rhonwellt.

"You have a new novice," said Rhonwellt as Alwyn closed the door and returned to his chair.

"He is not a novice yet. Still a schoolboy. He has only nine summers."

"And yet, he already takes joy in anything that disrupts the routine." Rhonwellt knew well how the monks craved anything that would pull them out of the doldrums of the sameness of the everyday. "He looks like he could use some time in the sun. He is so pale."

"It is not for want of sun. His skin lacks all color as does his hair.

What hair he has is purest white. His head was shaved when he came to us and we try to keep it so."

"What is wrong with him?"

"As far as we know, nothing. His father dropped him off here last spring. The family is large and the father said the boy's appearance frighteed the others in the village. They thought him possessed with some kind of demon and his father feared they might harm him out of ignorance. It seems he is just a sweet, bright boy to whom God has handed a strange and heavy burden. At first, missing his family, he cried daily. He seems happy now, he is quick and will do well here. Most of the brothers have embraced him. Those who have not, are afraid but will come around eventually." The prior shifted and leaned to the back of his chair pausing for a moment. "Now, you were telling me the reasons that brought you here."

Rhonwellt did not want to dwell on the subject of Merwenna and Tristan and broached another. "My traveling companions as I journeyed here were a man named Walter Fullecoppe and his son Thomas. You know of them?"

"I do," replied the prior. "Cloth merchants who arrived here just after the Feast of the Ascension. Walter is, I believe, a good, devout man. His older son much like him..."

"William," Rhonwellt interrupted.

The prior looked at Rhonwellt with confusion.

"William was the name of his older son."

"Ah, yes." Prior Alwyn cleared his throat. The interruption appeared to have thrown him off his thought. "Yes. Anyway, his younger son is arrogant and most disagreeable."

"Thomas is not so very different from many who chafe at the lot of second sons. But, you are right. It has made him disagreeable."

"It is said William was murdered. A young brother and sister if I remember correctly."

"That is what the Fullecoppes say. Noah and Jocelyn, the brother and sister, fled to Ryd Lliw with the Fullecoppes in pursuit. Noah claimed sanctuary at Saint Tysilio's. Then, someone lured him from the safety of the church and murdered him. We believe it to be the Fullecoppe's servant who disappeared right after and has not been seen since."

The prior crossed himself, then was still for a few moments. "I can tell by the way you speak, you are not so sure of the truth of this Noah's guilt."

"I am not," replied Rhonwellt.

Alwyn cradled his chin between thumbs and steepled fingers, his gaze burrowing into Rhonwellt. "I know you, Brother Rhonwellt, have done so since you were a boy. You have burdens weighing you down. And when in such a state, you withdraw into yourself. When you lived among us, you would sequester yourself in the scriptorium at every opportunity, the thoughts inside your head your only company. You seldom spoke even when permitted. You thought you were in search of answers. In truth, you avoided answers that might frighten you and wallowed in self-pity. It did not work then, and it will not solve your problems now." Alwyn rose, walked around his desk and stood looking down at Rhonwellt. "For as long as you are lodged as a guest with us, brother, I am still your prior. This is what I am asking you to do. Occupy yourself with finding the truth of this matter. Do what you do well. Talk to people. Find out all you can, and when you have all the facts, deduce their meaning and work out the solution." Alwyn placed a hand on Rhonwellt's shoulder and squeezed gently, the personal nature of the gesture taking Rhonwellt aback. "And while you are occupied with that, trust God to give you the answer to that which burdens your heart the most. Though you fear what you desire most is slipping away, I think you will find that, in truth, nothing has changed."

☦   ☦   ☦

CIARAN TOOK HIS TIME WALKING DOWN THE HILL, HIS LARGE

feet slapping the path. He carried the bundle with Jocelyn's belongings under his arm. He had done his best to carry out the office of prime, but he sincerely wished Rhonwellt were here. It was so unlike him to leave and tell no one. As the thought struck him, he came to an abrupt halt.

"God no, I pray he has not been kidnapped again," he muttered. He shook his head as if to fling the thought away. Surely, it was as he had said at the hall, Rhonwellt had gone to Saint Cattwg's.

Clutching his bundle in both arms, Ciaran started down the hill again, this time at a run. He slid to a stop in the doorway of the stables. Rhonwellt's horse was not in her stall.

"Ronan, where has Epona gone."

"Why, with Brother Rhonwellt, of course," the hostler replied, startled by Ciaran's sudden appearance.

"Where have they gone?"

"No idea," said Ronan. "He come early for her. Said they was going further than he cared to walk. That be all I knows."

"He was alone?"

"Far as I knows. Is anything amiss?"

"No," replied Ciaran, "I am sure he has just gone to Cydweli."

Ciaran turned on his heel and headed toward the cottage. It would not do to have Jocelyn naked in his bed any longer. The idea was too disturbing and was surely a sin. A lump formed in his throat as he recalled waking to find Jocelyn snuggled up behind him, arms wrapped tightly around him, her breath warm and moist on the back of his neck. The sensations that had gone through his body had frightened him, and he had not known what to do. Even though the truth was clear, it was not possible for him to think of Jocelyn as a boy—a young man. To Ciaran, she was still a young woman. But it was not true. Jocelyn had a cock. Young women did not have cocks. Whatever the case, Jocelyn must get out of his bed and dress.

He was about to push the door open when Ciaran heard the shuffling of feet inside. Jocelyn was out of bed and moving about the room. If he entered now, he would see her...him...naked. He should not, yet to his shame found he very much wanted to. No one had ever aroused such feelings in him before and it left him greatly confused. Ciaran knew these feelings were sinful but found, to his added confusion, a part of him did not care. His heart thudded in his chest as he signed the cross and asked God to remove this temptation. He waited until the sound of movement inside had stopped and he was sure Jocelyn was back in bed and under the covers before he knocked softly and opened the door.

The cottage was warm, almost comfortable, more welcoming than he had ever known. As monastics, he and Rhonwellt were used to the cold and seldom had a fire any longer than was necessary to take the chill off. Ciaran looked toward the bed. It was empty. He had been wrong. He quickly scanned the room and found Jocelyn standing by the brasier blowing on the coals and adding more peat. The young monk closed his eyes, tried not to look but found he could not resist the urge to open them again. Jocelyn stood motionless as Ciaran took in the sight before him completely.

A prickling sensation shot up his spine and exploded in his head. He thought he might reel. He stumbled forward a step, his eyes locked firmly on Jocelyn as he held the bundle out. Jocelyn turned and stepped toward him.

"Ciaran, do you need to sit down?"

He opened his mouth to speak but only shook his head.

Jocelyn took the bundle from him and laid it on the bed, but made no move to cover himself. Ciaran went numb, not even sure his heart was still beating. It must be, however, for the pounding in his ears threatened to deafen him.

"I have never..." He faltered. "You are so..." He could not say the words. Jocelyn was beautiful, but he could not bring himself to say it out loud.

Jocelyn stepped in close to Ciaran, but did not touch him. He had never been this close to anyone naked who still lived. His breaths became uneven, and he trembled with every inhale. He found he had to breathe through his mouth to keep from passing out.

"Close the door," said Jocelyn, softly.

Ciaran turned and pushed the door shut. He did not turn back around, but stood staring at the wall. He felt Jocelyn take his hand and guide him back to the center of the room. Ciaran determined he would keep his eyes averted.

"Keep your eyes closed," said Jocelyn, a soft but firm command.

Ciaran turned to face Jocelyn, eyes about to spill over with moisture.

"Good, now keep them closed."

Still holding Ciaran's hand, Jocelyn raised it to his lips and kissed each of his fingers, one at a time.

Ciaran could not remember the last time he felt anyone's kiss. He had forgotten how it felt. He only knew this was not like a mother's kiss. It was not the same at all.

Jocelyn reached down and lifted Ciaran's other hand. Holding one in each hand, Jocelyn lifted them up and placed them on either side of his head. Jocelyn's hair was clean and soft, almost silky. Slowly he led them down his head and onto his shoulders. One at a time, Jocelyn moved Ciaran's hand over his shoulders, down across his smooth, hairless chest, across his nipples and then down his sides. With his eyes closed, to Ciaran Jocelyn was a young woman again. Soft and pale, skin so hot he thought it might burn his fingers. Jocelyn continued to push Ciaran's hand lower, drawing them across his stomach and still lower until he felt the edge of the hairs over that forbidden place. No matter how much he tried to will against it, Ciaran could feel his own cock stiffen and push against the front of his robe, throbbing with the same rhythm of his pounding heart. The sensation of it rubbing against the wool sent shivers up his spine. Satan was relentless and could make him sin even when he did not want to.

"Please," Ciaran pleaded, "stop."

Jocelyn paid him no heed but kept moving Ciaran's hands lower. The forbidden hairs tickled the inside of his palms. His cock jumped. He squeezed his eyes tighter. A sob trembled from his lips.

"Please. I cannot do this."

"A part of you wants to, does it not?"

"Yes." More than a word it was a breath.

Jocelyn stopped moving Ciaran's hands, brought them back up and kissed them again. "Open your eyes."

Ciaran shook his head.

"Please, Ciaran, open your eyes and look at me."

Ciaran slowly let his eyes open, but kept his gaze to the floor. It took him a moment to focus. Still holding his hands, Jocelyn took a step back.

"Look at me, Ciaran."

Reluctantly, he raised his head. He let his eyes wander over Jocelyn's body one more time.

"This is what I am, Ciaran. I cannot be what you want me to be, only what I am."

"I do not know what I want you or anyone to be."

"Perhaps not. But one day it will become clear to you. I may not know a lot about monks, but I do know you would break your vows to lie with me. And you deserve more. If the time ever comes, it should be with someone worthy of you."

"I am no one special."

"Ah, but you are." Jocelyn turned to his bundle of belongings and pulled out some clothes. "What you are is rare. And you deserve more than someone whose only lot is to be another man's sinful secret. I had deluded myself with William. But now I know the truth. And with Noah gone I am on my own."

To Ciaran's surprise, the items Jocelyn pulled from his bundle were the clothes of a man. Jocelyn began to dress himself.

"Do not say such things, please."

"It is true," replied Jocelyn. "That is why I must leave, for your sake and for my own."

"Leave! Where will you go?"

"Some place larger, where people do not know me. Perhaps, London."

"London is so very far away. It would be dangerous."

"I will travel as a lad. Without Noah, it will be safer. But when I make it there, I can disappear into the shadows and be who I am again, a lass with a cock. I have always lived my life in the darkness. It is what I know."

TWENTY-SIX

Word of the trial had gone out only the day before and the number of strangers milling about Ryd Lliw this early on such a crisp morning surprised Tristan. It only proved that even the weather would not deter those bent on attending the spectacle of a hanging. They came on foot, on horseback, in small carts, and even a large hay wagon that carried several families from a village a couple of dozen furlongs away. Most brought food and drink. Those who did not would bring much business to the tavern and the widow who made meat pies. If trade was brisk enough, the local ale-wife would most likely be forced to serve some of her greener brew to keep up with the demand. And though most women of the village would bake extra loaves of bread to earn a few pennies, by the end of the day, not a loaf would be available for the asking in the whole area.

Small wagers were already being placed on whether they would discover, when they took the bodies down, that the condemned had pissed and shit themselves at the moment of death. However, the serious money was on whether their cocks would stiffen and release seed from the shock of the drop and the tightening of the noose. Although such an occurrence was rare and most wagers on that particular outcome would prove fruitless, eager hands still parted with hard-earned coin on the slimmest chance of winning more.

The huge double doors to the tithe barn stood propped open and the earliest arrivals had already staked out their places for the best view of the trial. Near one end of the cavernous storeroom, in full view of the condemned and affording them the opportunity to contemplate their fate, soldiers dragged a large empty wooden crate to the center of the room and placed a hastily fabricated chair on top for Tristan to use while overseeing the proceedings. The nearly two-hundred spectators would easily fill the remainder of the space.

Rhonwellt had been gone since yestermorn, and Tristan fought desperately against every urge to get on his horse and go after him to bring him home. At this point, Tristan wondered if Rhonwellt might refuse to return if he did go to fetch him. He quickly tossed such thoughts from his mind and returned to the day's task. The one thing to keep him from going was to stay busy.

Tristan ordered a meal brought from the tavern for the prisoners. It would be their last and he wanted them to eat it early enough that their stomachs would be mostly empty when they were executed.

With the uprights for the gallows already in place, the village carpenters and his sons sat perched on the crossbar nailing it on. Three ropes lay on the ground waiting to be slung over the top; a small box lay next to each rope. This was Ryd Lliw's first hanging since Tristan had become lord of the manor, and he intended to make it memorable, not only as entertainment for his villeins but as a deterrent to any who would attempt to commit crimes on his estate. Letting the bodies hang from gibbets along the main road for weeks after would further fix the message that, though remote, the King's justice was alive and well in the outlands.

With Rhonwellt gone, the task of confession and absolution for the condemned would fall to Brother Ciaran. Tristan turned from the activity at the barn and headed next door to find him. The cottage was quiet as he knocked gently on the door. When it creaked open, Jocelyn stood there, staring at him with a blank expression.

"So, you have decided you are a man, after all," said Tristan, gesturing at Jocelyn's male attire.

"I am until I get to a place where I do not have to be," replied Jocelyn.

"Then, you are leaving."

"I must. The truth about me will no doubt have spread quickly in such a small place. I cannot stay with everyone knowing."

"Wherever you go, they will find you out sooner or later." Thumbs hooked behind his belt, Tristan moved past Jocelyn and to a bench near the bed.

"Then I must go someplace where it will not matter," said Jocelyn, "a place like London. I know a bawd there who will take me in."

"That is a dangerous life," said Tristan. A moment of sadness came over him. For all their brutality, the Saracens were far more accepting of life's peculiarities. At least they made a place for people like Jocelyn.

"It is the only life I am allowed," replied Jocelyn.

"It is remote here," said Tristan, "but word has spread about the knight at Ryd Lliw who lives without women. Something like that draws people who need to escape from something. They are less likely to judge others as harshly. There could be a place for you here."

Jocelyn walked to the bed and sat down, eyes on his hands folded in his lap. He sat motionless for a few moments before he turned his head to look at Tristan.

"Though there are reasons to stay," said Jocelyn, taking a breath and letting it out slowly, "the reason I must go is greater."

Tristan waited for Jocelyn to say more. "You mean Ciaran?" he asked at last.

Jocelyn nodded.

"Are your feelings for the lad so great?"

"I am fond of Ciaran. He is sweet and kind and so very innocent." Jocelyn glanced at the bed. "His feelings for me are the problem."

"Did you bed him?"

Jocelyn flinched at the accusatory tone in his question. "Bedding men is what I do!" he responded, voice icy with defiance. Then he softened. "But, no, not him, though he would have gladly enough."

"You are his first skirmish with lust...or love. It was bound to happen, eventually. Lads fall in love every day."

"That is why I could not lay with him. When he thought I was a lass, to him it made sense. When Ciaran found out the truth and still felt the urge to lie with me, his confusion and terror could very well have broken him. I could not do that to him."

"I thank you for taking pity on him," said Tristan.

Jocelyn leveled his gaze at the knight. "It was not pity."

Tristan and Jocelyn sat silently together for a few moments. "Where might I find Ciaran?" Tristan asked.

Jocelyn shrugged. "Try the church."

The knight was nearly out the door when he turned back. "Consider the offer to stay," he said.

✦ ✦ ✦

TRISTAN STOOD AT THE GATE TO THE CHURCHYARD LOOKING UP and down the street. Ciaran had not been in the church as expected. He ground his teeth. Why were neither of his monks where they were supposed to be today? He turned right toward the tithe barn and headed down the street. The crowd at the barn had grown to about fifty people, and there in the middle stood Ciaran, staring up at the gallows.

The crowd parted to let Tristan through.

"They are to hang today?" asked Ciaran.

"They are."

"But, they cannot. Brother Rhonwellt is not here to hear their confession and offer them absolution."

"He should be here," replied Tristan. "But, since he is not, you shall have to do it."

Ciaran looked over at Tristan, his eyes wide. "I cannot. I am not a priest. I do not know the words.The church is most specific. Their souls are at stake."

"They have no souls," replied Tristan. "They are thieves and murderers."

"They do, and you know it, Sir Tristan. Their souls may be black, but if they confess, they can still be saved."

"Well, if they are to be cleansed, it will have to be you who accomplishes it. I have seen men die on the battlefield having confessed their sins to their comrades. Do you really think God would send them to Hell because there was no priest present to hear their last words? Is that the God you worship?"

"That is the God we all worship," said Ciaran, "and I have to believe He is merciful."

"Then hear their confession. You know the words. Trust in God's mercy. Seeing your robe and tonsure will give them some peace. The condemned will have enough on their minds they will not notice if you do not do it perfectly."

Ciaran said nothing, only crossed himself and folded his hands. Tristan could see the monk trembling and put a gentle hand to his shoulder.

"I believe your faith to be strong, Brother, and I know your heart is pure. I trust you would never knowingly do their souls harm."

"But, I am not pure. I carried lust in my heart."

"There has never been any man who lived who did not feel lust at some time. Even many saints have confessed to it. It has not stained you forever. Now go to them and hear them. We shall begin the trial soon."

✞   ✞   ✞

OVER A DOZEN TORCHES LIT THE TITHE BARN AS TRISTAN climbed up to his seat to begin the trial. It was past nones, and an even larger crowd than he expected filled the storehouse. Over two-hundred enthusiastic villeins from near and far stood shoulder-to-shoulder, from wall-to-wall, eager to get on with the show. The trial was only a precursor, as the hanging was the most significant event of the day, and the one for which the crowd held the greatest amount of anticipation.

Tristan held his hands up and waited for the noise to die down. "Bring the prisoners forward," he said over the hushed murmurs.

All heads turned at the sound of clinking chains as the three condemned men emerged from the shadows into the flickering light. Though the leader's bluster had waned some, he still tried to present a brave countenance. The other two had melted into puddles of fear and regret. The three stood facing Tristan, heads down. The slightest movement caused their chains to sing their eerie song.

"The three of you are charged with horse theft, kidnapping, and the murder of five people." The murmurs of the crowd rose and then died down again. "What is your name?" he asked the prisoner on the left. Tristan saw the man's lips move but could not hear him over the noise. He jumped to his feet and shouted, "Silence!" As the room grew quiet, Tristan sat down and asked again. "And speak up this time."

"Allen, my lord," the prisoner replied, his voice barely audible.

"Have you a second name?"

"No, my lord." The man kept his eyes to the floor.

"What did your father do?"

"He were a farmer."

"Well, Allen Farmer," said Tristan, "you have heard the charges. What say you?"

"I done it, my lord." His voice was hollow and showed no emotion.

Tristan then addressed the man in the middle. "Your name?"

"Reggie, my lord. And my pa were a carter."

"Reggie Carter, you have heard the charges against you. What say you?"

The man nodded, but said nothing.

"You must say it aloud," said Tristan.

Clearing his throat Reggie said, "Yes, my lord."

Last was the outspoken leader. "Name?"

"Most calls me Percy, my lord."

Tristan waited but a whit. "Well, Percy what?"

"Never knowed my pa, my lord. But some calls me Percy Lightfingers."

The crowd laughed and the prisoner's face broke into a wide grin. Tristan bit his tongue while he let the laughter die on its own.

"Percy Lightfingers, what say you to the charges?"

"I could say I never done it, but then again that pretty lass in the back will likely say I did. I could never call a pretty lass a liar."

Tristan let his eyes linger for a moment on Merwenna standing at the back between Selwyn and Wulfric, Ernulf in her arms. His nostrils flared as he fought to control the urge to beat the life out of the man. Instead, he let his gaze wander over the crowd.

"Charges are levied, and they have admitted their crimes. Is there one here who will speak on their behalf?"

No one spoke.

"Since no one will speak for you and you have admitted your guilt, you shall be taken from here directly to the gallows where you shall hang by your worthless necks until you are dead. And may God have mercy on your black souls."

A hearty cheer went up from the spectators at the verdict while Reggie quietly sank to his knees, loosed his bladder, a puddle forming under him.

"Pick that one up," said Tristan pointing toward Reggie, "and take them out."

Already the crowd had was flowing out through the door and gathering around the gallows in the yard in front. The prisoners squinted as they stepped out into the light. At the sight of the gallows with the ropes hanging from the crossbar, Reggie began to sob and his legs threatened to buckle under him. Two of the guards nearly carried him. Allen crossed himself, his wide-eyed stare never leaving the ropes. Percy smirked as he chewed the inside of his cheek, then turned and gave the crowd a wink.

"Ye wasted your coin if you be betting on me pissing meself," he taunted. The crowd roared its pleasure at his defiance. "As for ole Reggie, he done it already. Lost your bit there, too. No telling with Allen, here. Guess your only real hope lies in one of us getting a stiff cock. All you lasses watch close. If I does, it be just for you." Percy winked again.

"A lot of good it will do any of us, pet," yelled a woman's voice from the middle of the crowd, "not with you hanging from a rope and getting colder by the moment."

"You men, last chance to place your bets."

"Get on with it!" An impatient voice from the din.

Tristan's soldiers helped the three to climb atop their crates, placed the ropes around their necks and drew the nooses tight. In an instant, a hush fell over the crowd. At Tristan's signal, the crates were kicked away. As the bodies fell and snapped the ropes taut, the crowd cheered. Allen and Reggie went quietly to their deaths with only a tiny jerk and a few spasms. It was Percy, the defiant one who seemed most reluctant to leave this world. His body bucked and pitched at the end of the rope for a significant amount of time before growing still.

✝   ✝   ✝

THE EXECUTION OVER, THE ROADS FILLED WITH SPECTATORS making their way home. There was still plenty of daylight so most would be home before dark. His pack thrown over his shoulder, Jocelyn closed the door to the cottage, filled with sorrow at having, once again, to leave a place and people of whom he had grown fond. Most sorrowful of all, he was leaving without Noah. His brother had always been there, and Jocelyn found it hard to imagine a world that did not have Noah in it. Jocelyn felt a sting in his eyes and a thickness in his throat. He pressed his lips into a thin line and tried to blink away the strong emotions that threatened to overwhelm him. He had never given much thought to any feelings he might have held for his sibling. Noah was an assumption, someone who would always be. And, now he was not. Jocelyn had never relied on Noah for anything but his continued presence. But everything would be different now. In a world where the future held no certainty, his only constant had vanished in a moment.

Most of the time Jocelyn felt only anger and frustration toward Noah. It was surprising to him that he might feel something different now that his brother was dead. So crippling was Noah's fear of hanging, he had clung desperately to the idea of sanctuary as readily as he clung to the altar that made it real. The images of Noah running into the churchyard to help him stayed vivid in Jocelyn's mind. Noah's action had changed everything Jocelyn knew about their relationship. Surely her brother had known his life would be forfeit, yet he did it nonetheless. Jocelyn could not help but think he had underestimated his brother all along.

Emotion was so unreliable.

Jocelyn wended his way through a sparsely wooded area to a small glade behind the monk's cottage and outside the graveyard. There stood a lone grave with a simple wooden cross marking the place of Noah's final rest. It was more than Jocelyn could have hoped for her brother. Jocelyn stood over the small grave, fighting back tears. This might be the last time he would ever see the place where his brother rested. Jocelyn bit his lip to keep from breaking down. He would not cry. There was no time for such nonsense. Swiping a sleeve across his face, Jocelyn turned from the grave and made his way out of the churchyard.

Leaving Noah behind, Jocelyn's thoughts turned to Ciaran as he melted into the mass of travelers heading out of town.

TWENTY-SEVEN

The chancel sat eerily quiet following Terce. Rhonwellt had not realized how filled with noise his life had become.

He went immediately to his old bench in the choir. Now assigned to another, he chose an empty place and knelt down, sketched the cross and leaned into the bar, his forehead resting on folded hands.

When the brother left, he moved to his old seat, resumed his contemplative position. He would spend his time in reflection before sext, prayed at the fourth hour, followed by dinner. The place felt familiar, the routine soothing. For the first time since leaving Ryd Lliw two days before, the inescapable numbness he had carried with him had begun to subside, replaced by simple disappointment. Now, he could admit that feeling something was preferable to feeling nothing.

Yet, however soothing the familiarity, the serenity Rhonwellt sought eluded him. With a sigh, he dutifully signed the cross, rose and exited the chancel. Perhaps he should take Prior Alwyn's advice and set his mind to other tasks—such as exploring the murder of William Fullecoppe. He was told they had called Brother Remigius to tend William after the assault. Perhaps Rhonwellt could glean some information from the infirmarian's recollections of the incident. Despite all indications, Rhonwellt continued to doubt that Noah Smith was a murderer. Rhonwellt believed Noah when he admitted he accosted William Fullecoppe but stated the man was still alive when last he saw him. Noah was dead. If he was truly innocent, that he would be remembered as a murderer chafed at Rhonwellt.

The infirmary was unoccupied save for one old man from the village downed by a bout of ague. A lack of any living family and his advanced age earned him regular meals and a clean, warm bed; near luxury compared to his usual existence. He looked so content, Rhonwellt prayed that if it was God's will, the old man be allowed to die where he lay when his time came.

Brother Remigius sat by the old man's bed, quietly reciting from a Psalter.

"God's Peace be with you, Brother," Rhonwellt said from the doorway.

"And also to you, Brother," replied Remigius, a smile brightening his face as he raised it from his text.

"Are you able to leave your duties here for a while? I would have you walk with me that I might ask you some questions."

"You look troubled, Brother Rhonwellt. How may I help?"

Rhonwellt tipped his head toward the patient and raised his eyebrows.

"He is likely sleeping," said Remigius, "and will not notice my absence if it is brief."

"Is his condition dire?"

"No, it is but simple ague exacerbated by age." Remigius leaned over the bed and put his hand on the old man's forehead, waited a moment and gave a satisfied nod. "His fever steadily grows weaker. But, he is lonely and enjoys company at his bedside."

"Then I shall return you to him quickly." Rhonwellt gestured toward the door. "Shall we walk?"

They exited the infirmary and Rhonwellt turned toward the fish ponds beyond the cemetery behind the dorter. He stopped short at the sight of a wall under construction.

"I do not know if I shall ever grow used to this portion of the priory being enclosed. Work on the new perimeter wall goes slowly, I see."

"Masonry is expensive. The work advances as we have the money." Brother Remigius put his hand on Rhonwellt's arm. "You are not known to chatter idly, brother. What is on your mind?"

"The death of William Fullecoppe."

"Ah, yes, an untimely sorrow for certain."

"Can you tell me what it was you saw as you came upon the scene?"

"There is little to tell, really," Remigius replied. "As I approached the tavern, I noticed William lying in the street, Thomas Fullecoppe cradling his brother's head in his arms and covered with blood."

"What was the wound?"

"A knife wound under his arm toward the back."

"This was fatal?"

"If the blade were long enough. According to the location of the wound, it could have pierced his heart. That would explain the amount of blood."

"Were there any other wounds?"

"Yes, there was also a blow to the head."

Rhonwellt nodded, stroking his chin. "That is in keeping with what Noah said. He also said he only struck him with a club, nothing else."

"The Fullecoppes have spread the word that young Noah is dead," said Remigius, signing the cross. "They have declared his death justice for William's murder."

Remigius and Rhonwellt stood at the edge of the pond.

"Did Thomas have a weapon?"

"He did. He carried a dagger. When asked to show it, they found his blade was clean."

"How are the Fullecoppes regarded in the village?"

"They are new to the town, arriving after you left us. Neither liked nor disliked, they are prosperous but untested. But, there are rumors about William, that he was..." Brother Remigius hesitated, casting his eyes to the ground, "...a sodomite," he concluded with a weary sigh.

Rhonwellt pressed his lips into a thin line and gripped his arms inside his sleeves. Remigius's tone was like being brought face-to-face with the Almighty's condemnation of his own feelings for Tristan. Rhonwellt grew tense and an uncomfortable moment passed between the two monks.

"Apologies, brother," said Remigius, "I meant no disapprobation."

"Worry not, my friend," replied Rhonwellt. "You only mirror what is in my own heart. I still wonder if such profound feelings are truly the work of Satan. But, your point is well taken. Master Fulle-coppe's lust for men ultimately led to his murder."

Remigius knit his brow, his face twisted into a grimace. "I thought it was the young lass traveling with this Noah that was the issue."

Rhonwellt thought for a moment. Should he reveal the truth about Jocelyn? "In truth," he said at last, "Jocelyn was a young man, not a woman as he presented."

Rhonwellt heard a sharp intake of breath. Remigius's eyes grew wide. "Christ's teeth!"

Rhonwellt's hand flew up to cover his mouth and the grin forming there.

Remigius hurriedly signed the cross. "God forgive such an outburst!" He put a knuckle between his teeth and bit down hard. His eyes began to water.

"Ears have an easier time in hearing such words than the mouth that says them. I spend much time with a knight and his soldiers," said Rhonwellt. Reaching up, he gently pulled Remigius's knuckle from his teeth before he drew blood. "God seems reluctant to prevent my ears hearing blasphemies far worse on a daily basis. I find them no longer remarkable."

"What you say is so astonishing, I have no other words. Yet, that would tend to strengthen the validity of the rumors about him," said Remigius. He rubbed at the teeth marks on his finger. "I suggest you talk to Glyn, the fowler's boy."

Rhonwellt ran his hand over the top of his head; the stubble of his tonsure tickled his palm. "The lad who played a part in solving the riddle of the beggar two summers ago?"

"The same. There is little that transpires in this town that escapes Glyn's attention," replied Remigius, "and he is eager to tell what he knows for a pint."

"For one confined to the priory grounds, you seem to know much on the happenings in town."

Remigius gave a sly wink. "I have my sources."

"The lad seems so young to have such a taste for ale," said Rhonwellt, with a small shake of his head.

"Owns no more than fourteen summers, but could out-drink any man in town before he had twelve. Folks pay him little mind as much of what he has to say is exaggeration if not pure fish story. On this, he has a tale to tell as well. He lives out the road to Glanyfferi with his mother and younger brother, but you are more apt to find him at the tavern. It is early yet. You may find him still be sober."

"Thank you, Brother. I shall leave you to return to your patient."

Crossing the bridge to town, Rhonwellt paused mid-span to look over the edge at the turbulent water below. Though the tide was out, the Gwendraeth still ran fast and deep from winter rains. A small barge used to carry goods from ships anchored downstream where the river entered the bay strained at its moorings as the powerful current attempted to carry it back to the sea. In the summer, the barge would rest tilted to the side, its flat keel resting in mud waiting for the tide to float it again. The brown surge closely matched Rhonwellt's agitated state of mind. He could as easily drown in his own misery as he could in the angry flood waters, with no hope of swimming to safety. It was one thing to struggle with his feelings for Tristan and whether to give himself up to them. But this investigation forced him to view the whole subject with more wary eyes. Thin as a razor's edge, the line between love and lust was easily crossed. To the church, the line did not exist at all.

Rhonwellt turned from the water and continued on his way toward a tale he was not sure he wanted to hear. Traffic on the road was light, and he encountered almost no one. Two young lads skipped by, dutifully signing the cross as they passed Rhonwellt.

"Glyn the fowler," Rhonwellt called after them, "is he in the tavern?"

"Like always, brother." They both laughed.

Rhonwellt elbowed his way through a small crowd milling about in front of the South gate into town and on up Bailey Street to the *Thorn and Thistle*. Though the door stood open, the air inside the tavern was stale at this early hour. Fewer than a dozen patrons sat scattered about the room. He crossed to a table in the back where Glyn sat alone, staring into a pint.

"What do you want?" said the boy without looking up from his cup.

"I am Brother Rhonwellt. I wish to talk to you, if I may."

Glyn raised his face to look at Rhonwellt, his eyes narrowing when he saw who stood in front of him. "Not be needing no preaching, Brother. Ma says I be a lost cause."

"I do not think anyone is truly lost. But that is its own matter and I am here for another purpose."

"What then?" A bit of the wariness left Glyn's eyes.

"I wish to talk to you about the Masters Fullecoppe."

The wariness returned ten-fold. "What about them?"

"Someone murdered William."

"Everybody knows that. Happened in the street right out in front of this very tavern."

"Well, some of the circumstances seem very odd. I am trying to find out why."

Glyn drained his cup and Rhonwellt motioned for the girl to bring the lad another and one for himself. After she brought their drinks, Rhonwellt waited for her to leave before resuming. He raised his cup in a toast.

"To the truth." said Rhonwellt. Glyn raised his cup in return. "It is said William cared little for women, that he favored men," said Rhonwellt, leaning in toward Glyn. He saw the lad's knuckles turned white as his grip tightened around the clay pot in his hands.

Glyn stared straight ahead, his nostrils flared, breathing shallow like he hoped no one would notice. "That has naught to do with me."

"I was told you have a tale to tell."

Glyn put his head in his hands, his fingers clenching and releasing his hair. Rhonwellt thought he heard a small sob, but when Glyn looked up, his hard eyes were dry. "Who has been saying what about me? I will cut their lying tongue out."

"None has accused you of anything."

"That old fuss-pot Brother Remigius and his spies, I wager."

"Much like you, he has an ear to the ground for the happenings here. But he told me nothing. Only to ask."

Glyn bobbed his head. "Not here," he said. "Out the back where none can hear."

Benches scraped the floor as they pushed back from the table and rose. Glyn quickly ducked out the back door and disappeared through the postern gate in the stockade wall near the middens. Rhonwellt's sandals slapped on the mud as he struggled to keep up. Glyn had stopped at the edge of the bluff overlooking the Gwendraeth and the priory lands on the opposite bank.

"Them Fullecoppes is a bad lot, Brother. He shamed me and now I will go to Hell, sure."

"Tell me what happened," said Rhonwellt, standing close so they could speak in quiet voices.

"Not sure I can say such things to a monk."

"My ears hear the same as any," said Rhonwellt. "If your words are true, God will not condemn you for saying them, nor will I."

"He were always eyeing the lads, never the lasses except that Jocelyn, so I knowed he were bent like that. See, a couple of us, we knowed about Jocelyn but never said nothing. Bawdy lads knows the smell of a woman. Wanted to see who would go with her. After they finished, them what did, come all quiet. Made us laugh. It were a great joke, Brother." Glyn's shoulders shook as he gave a soundless chuckle, then became serious again. "One evening I were drinking a pot and Master Fullecoppe comes lurching up to my table and falls onto the bench."

The lad grew quiet and Rhonwellt gave him time to continue with what he already knew was coming. They stood in silence for several moments, Rhonwellt's heart pounding as he awaited the words.

"It were wrong, I knowed it," said Glyn. "He said he would give me three pennies to...to do things to him. Three whole pennies! I asked him what was I to do." Glyn clenched his fists and pressed them to his eyes, his face twisted in anguish. "He said I was to shove my cock up his arse." Glyn opened his hands and covered his mouth. His eyes bulged. "God forgive me, Brother. Filthy mouth!"

Rhonwellt pressed his eyes shut.

"But, I done no such a thing, Brother. I swear!"

Rhonwellt opened his eyes and looked directly at Glyn, unable to determine for sure if the lad was telling the truth.

"Why would he think that about me, brother? Why would he think I were bent like him? Do I look funny like that?"

"Men," Rhonwellt paused, "like that, look much the same as any other. They could even be a knight or a monk. He would have no way of knowing if you were any different from other men."

Glyn seemed to ponder that for a moment. "If I done it, will I go to Hell? Even if I lied and it were only the once?"

"As someone who is also a sinner, that is not for me to say."

"Even if he gave me two more pennies to keep quiet?" Glyn spoke so low, Rhonwellt almost did not hear. "Said he would hurt me if I ever told. Never could figure why he picked me. He always seemed interested in the younger lads."

"Younger than you?"

Glyn nodded. "Offered the butcher's lad money, but he would not take it. The lad threatened to tell. He roughed him up a mite on account of it."

"William Fullecoppe used his greater wealth to take advantage of those of lesser means. He knew that, being poor, you would not refuse. God will not fault you for that."

Rhonwellt hoped that was not a lie.

"William? No Brother, you mistake me. William only had eyes for that Jocelyn. It were Master Thomas what plagued me. Him, not William."

TWENTY-EIGHT

The bodies swayed in a light breeze that blew the smell of the deteriorating flesh well away from town. Hunched inside his cloak in the gray light of dawn, Tristan listened to chattering crows who, once they had feasted on the corpse's eyes, remained now only to taunt them in the loneliness of death. Any clothes that remained after the rag pickers had their choice of the best sagged from drenching rains in the night and clung to the lifeless frames. Gibbeted a furlong beyond the last cottage at the edge of town, they hung as sentinels, a warning to all with villainous intent. Tristan had not slept well the night before and was not sure what had drawn him there to gaze into the blank faces; only that he felt compelled to come, and he stared with a mixture of emotion.

Tristan felt his jaw tighten, bile rising in his throat. In life, these men had been no better than animals, their every breath a waste of God's good air. They had set out to murder indiscriminately, young and old alike, for a few baubles, some coin, a cart horse and a few soldier's mounts. Five lives for so little gain. But they were as careless as they were ruthless. They had not realized Ernulf and Myfanwy still lived and left them for dead. They would likely have done the same with Merwenna when they finished with her, had they not been so busy running and not had an opportunity to act on their plans for her. It meant there were witnesses who could identify them if needed. And that failure had made it possible for Tristan to meet the daughter and grandson he never knew existed, the extraordinariness of which amazed him yet.

Tristan knew little of miracles since he had long ago ceased to believe in them, but fate had certainly intervened when it delivered Ernulf to him out of a clear blue sky and Merwenna only days later under equally baffling circumstances. If these events, added to finding Rhonwellt still alive after all this time, did not count as miracles, they came very close to any definition Tristan had ever heard and showed perhaps this rarely predictable God was far more capricious than he knew.

Rhonwellt had been gone three days. The executions were over. The aftermath hung there for all to see. Now that Merwenna had found Tristan and made herself known to him, she and Wulfric were being prodded into reconciliation by Selwyn, suddenly eager to seal the match. Noah was dead and buried and Jocelyn had quietly left town in search of that place where he could be himself. There were no more distractions to keep Tristan from mounting Ambisagarus and riding to Cydweli to bring Rhonwellt home. Would he even come? What if he would not? Tristan felt his courage waver.

As a soldier, he had never run from any battle, but this crusade for Rhonwellt's love left him unnerved. Uncertainty of victory had rarely played any part in his decision whether to engage an enemy. So, why did he hesitate now? Because he knew his sword would be useless in this fight. He would need to forge a new weapon lest he find himself in battle unarmed. He only had his heart as his shield. Yet, many a shield had proved useful for more than protection after a sword was lost or dropped. It would have to do.

He could wait no longer. To delay further might send the wrong message, that he did not care if Rhonwellt came back. Tristan cared and he must make Rhonwellt see just how much. If Merwenna had shown him one thing in her rash journey from the top of the country to the wilds at the bottom, it was to pursue what you want and not stop until you achieve it. A trait, it seemed, they shared.

After a final look at the corpses, Tristan began the short walk through town and back to the hall. The streets had been deserted when he walked out to view the corpses, folks still lolling in the warmth of their cottages breaking their fasts. In the time he had been at the gibbets, the villeins had begun to emerge, to turn their animals loose and go about their daily chores. Hats came off, heads bowed as he passed. Voices greeted him with, "Good morrow, my lord." Surprised, he looked into the faces, some familiar, some not. He could see a new pride, looks that said they had a new-found and growing respect for their lord-of-the-manor. Overnight, Tristan had changed Ryd Lliw from a gathering of cottages and their inhabitants that served an estate, to a real town where the King's Justice was alive, a place to feel safe. As he returned their greetings, Tristan began to realize things would differ greatly from this day forward. He felt his confidence surge; a courage he sorely needed.

Strolling through the gatehouse, he was headed for the stables when he noticed Sag, standing at the rail, fully saddled and ready to go. Ronan was bent over, a hind leg between his knees, cleaning a hoof and checking the shoe.

"Who has ordered him readied?" asked Tristan.

"Hewrey did, my lord," said Ronan, letting the hoof fall to the ground. "Said you be traveling this day. That were the last foot. Sag be fit and in good spirit, eager to be on the road with his master."

With a nod to Ronan, Tristan looked toward the hall. What was Hewrey up to? How could the lad have known if Tristan had only just realized himself?

Tristan entered the great hall. Merwenna sat by the fire engaged in conversation with Ciaran, Ernulf smiling on the monk's lap, fingering the rope-like cincture about his waist. He could hear Hewrey banging about in the buttery. The big iron pot used for heating bath water sat over a bed of coals, steam rising from the open top.

"You are having a bath?" Tristan asked Merwenna. "We shall give you the hall for privacy when it is ready."

"The bath is not for me, my lord. I believe it is for you. It is you who shall need the privacy." Merwenna's face glowed and her eyes twinkled.

"I have polished your other boots," said Hewrey, emerging from the buttery with a full jug of ale, "and have laid out a clean tunic and hose. There is just enough clove-oil for your hair. You can bring back more when you return."

"Return from where?"

"Why from bringing Brother Rhonwellt home, of course. Today is the day, is it not?"

Tristan stared from person to person, his expression blank, his mouth slack. "But, how...?"

"I knowed as soon as you rose from your sleep. Showed plain on your face, it did."

"There is nothing to keep you from it, now," said Ciaran, smiling at Tristan while tousling Ernulf's hair and lifting the boy off his lap to set him on the floor. "It is time he came back, even if he does not know it yet."

"And the bath, and the clothes...?"

"You want him to come with you, do you not?" Merwenna rose, came around the hearth and stood next to Tristan. "Entice him. Look your best." She put her hand on her father's arm. "Let him know you put forward the effort. Make him realize how important he is to you."

"You not be going to buy a cow, master. This be...is... Brother Rhonwellt. You wants him back and so do we."

"You are a knight," said Merwenna, "and this is your quest. Do what needs must to win."

"Just bring him back," said Ciaran, his voice barely above a whisper. "I need him. We all need him."

"I shall," said Tristan. He choked back a surge of emotion and walked to the side table to fill a pot with ale so he could have his back to the room until he could regain his composure. He took a drink of the ale, swishing it around in his mouth before he swallowed it. With his next sip, he took a deep breath and turned. "While I am gone, Hewrey, I have a job for you and Merwenna."

"I am to stay behind again," replied Hewrey, his body sagging with disappointment, his expression stony.

"Only to make it possible for you to accompany me in the future."

"Master?"

"You once said this hall was spartan as a soldier's camp," he said to Merwenna. "I took no pleasure in hearing it, but you were right. It is. We have existed as bachelor knights, with few comforts. Lived as though we could break camp and leave at a moment's notice. It is what I am used to, how I like it. But it is not really a home."

"It suits us," said Hewrey.

"It does," replied Tristan. "But we are not going anywhere, not anytime soon. If you are not to be left behind all the time, Hewrey, then we need someone to run the manor."

"You saying I runs it bad, master?"

"I could not ask for anyone to run it better. You are loyal, attend me well, especially when I am at my worst, and are a passable cook. But those things should be your job only when we are away. You and Merwenna shall find us a cook and someone to serve."

"Women? In your house, master?" Hewrey's mouth fell agape.

"Women, men, I do not care as long as they can do the job. We shall need more furniture as well. A trestle about thirty hands in length. And benches. And a bed for the second room in the solar for Merwenna and Ernulf."

"Are you so sure I am staying?" Merwenna replied.

"There will always be a place for you here, whenever you like for as long as you like. Now that I know of you, I will not let go so easily." Tristan looked at Merwenna for a long moment. "It would bring me great joy if you would stay and run my house, permanently or only for as long as it takes to sort out your feelings for Wulfric." His face took on a scowl. "If anyone can keep that lout under control, it is you."

Tristan took another drink from his pot. "But, whoever shall run my house, I am determined to bring Rhonwellt back to a home this time."

✞   ✞   ✞

Rhonwellt paused, his pen suspended over the parchment, watching the bead of ink at the tip grow larger with each passing breath, threatening to drop with a splash onto the page in progress. The bead disengaged from the quill tip and floated downward until Rhonwellt's other hand flew out to catch it before it ruined his morning's labors. He was lettering simple text instead of the colorful and intricate illuminations he preferred. Text required far less concentration, allowing his mind to gather wool, but the wayward ink-drop reminded him necessity compelled closer attention. It also afforded him a distraction from that which really held his thoughts hostage—Merwenna. Tristan's daughter was the last thing he wished to think about. He would have to deal with it eventually, but not until he had gained clarity on how he truly felt about her arrival, especially on how it might change things between him and Tristan.

The odor of tallow filled the air, each candle glowing like a single ember in the dim light. Though five other monks sat at their desks absorbed in work, the room was silent but for the rustling of parchment and the sound of scratching quills, punctuated from time to time by a whispered oath brought on by an errant stroke of the pen and followed by the scraping sound of a knife eliminating the offense.

Despite the brazier burning nearby, Rhonwellt could still see his breath as it floated ghost-like on the chill air in front of him. He had forgotten how cold it was at the priory and missed the warmth of his little cottage at Saint Tysilio's. The priory had been his existence for nearly all his life. What had been so commonplace before, at moments seemed strangely foreign now—recognizable, but not. His brothers seemed the same, and he felt warmth in their company again. The companionable silence was soothing, though he had grown accustomed to engaging in casual conversation, especially with Ciaran. But the longer he was at his old home, the differences between the small church he shepherded and the priory became more evident.

There were the little, noticeable, but benign ways in which they were dissimilar: the silence, the routine of faithfully observing all the offices, having the structure of one's life dictated by the ringing of a bell. On the other hand, Rhonwellt found the things he did not miss in the least were seldom having meat to eat, never bathing more than once in two fortnights, and the petty arguments among men living so closely confined.

However, the most profound distinction between the two churches was how each functioned from day-to-day. Intended as religious outposts, the purpose of monasteries and priories was to spread the faith to all areas of the realm. Yet, most often they ended up serving mainly as refuge to the religious cloistered within the walls. The brothers had very little contact with the people of the nearby villages beyond daily mass, hearing of confessions, caring for the sick, and market days. The monks remained secluded and protected behind their walls, squabbling among themselves, and generally oblivious to the plight of the souls in their care.

Manor churches like Saint Tysilio's, on the other hand, proved vital to the people of the village and outlying areas where they stood. Rhonwellt interacted with his parishioners daily. He felt needed, useful. With Ciaran's help he had learned nearly all their names. He found he cared for the villeins, and they seemed to care for him. And, it appeared they did not mind their priest seemed overly fond of the lord of the manor. They were becoming an extension of the new family he had claimed for himself, for that was how he now saw Tristan, Ciaran, and even Hewrey.

And that was the best thing about his new life at Saint Tysilio's—

Tristan abided there. And it came as little surprise that Rhonwellt found the last half-sennight absence from his knight left an aching hole in his heart. Lately, memories kept presenting themselves unbidden. His confusion upon seeing Tristan after all that time and his fear at the implications, the first time they talked after the knight's return, the faint scent of clove from the knight's hair reminding him of a far-off time, being in Tristan's arms near the priory pond. There was Tristan's drunken kiss one night at the hall, the taste of wine on his lips, the smell of it on his breath, the rough way Tristan held his face between his hands, his breath rasping in Rhonwellt's face, and the fact he could not kiss him in return. All these thoughts had set him awash in feelings of joy, yet untempered fear and shame at how close he was to losing control each time.

But the most troubling was a memory from one of his early visits to the manor before moving there. He had gone down to the river to bathe. Tristan had caught him naked, kneeling near the water, peering at his own reflection. Before Rhonwellt could settle on what he was feeling, Tristan had disrobed and stood before him. The sight of Tristan's nakedness left him both thrilled and terrified. The splendidness of Tristan's body, shaped and toned and hardened from years of the action of battle and living rough, plus the vulnerability that his nakedness lent it, sent a thrill coursing through Rhonwellt. Tristan's eyes had held nothing back as they feasted on the sight of Rhonwellt's body, saying that the knight wanted him, thrilled him even more. When Rhonwellt realized they stood face to face in equal states of arousal, he thought he would tip over the edge.

He had always put what followed down as an accident, that it had been unintentional. Only now could he admit he had wanted, with all his being, to embrace Tristan in that moment, to hold his body against his own, skin to skin, to feel the knight's muscular arms around him, his warm breath on his neck as he held Rhonwellt, their erections rubbing between their bellies, their lips pressed together, and finally their seed dripping to the ground between them.

Whenever the memory came, Rhonwellt experienced either

unbridled joy or uncontrollable fear. Never knowing which it would be, he dreaded that memory most. The thrill was obvious. The terror came from how easily blurred the line between love and lust could become.

Rhonwellt gasped, thrust his hand into his lap to hide the obvious evidence of his lustful thoughts while he furtively signed the cross with the other. He looked up through his eyebrows and glanced around the scriptorium, sure he would find all eyes staring at him, aware of his sinful thoughts. He pushed his hands further down into his lap. His body tingled and his face burned hot. He tried to stifle his staccato breathing. He had come so close to that moment of no return. His tarse throbbed like that of a randy farm lad witnessing his first breeding. Why did these thoughts plague him now, and why did his body decide to react so noticeably here? Was it being away from Tristan that had triggered it? Rhonwellt tried to put the image of Tristan from his mind, to calm his state of excitement. Until he did, he could not stand. In that moment, Rhonwellt knew he had crossed a line, one from which there was no stepping back. He could deny his feelings no longer and could not put off acting on them forever. And now that he was cognizant of it, he felt the anticipation creep in. Eventually, he and Tristan would be together in every way.

Another glance around the room and Rhonwellt quieted his mind. He continued to steady his breathing. Further work on the manuscript was useless. He would go for a walk in the cloister. He would resume what Prior Alwyn had bid him do, find out who had murdered William Fullecoppe. He put his pens and inks away, blew out his candle, bowed to Brother Gruffyd on his way out the door, and descended the stairs.

About to enter the cloister, Rhonwellt stopped short. He had heard Brother Remigius's account of that evening. Now he must hear Thomas's. He turned and headed for the gate. Something bothered him about the conversation he had shared with the Elder Fullecoppe on the journey here. The father had said his sons had been close as lads, but seemed to grow apart as they aged. Walter had also said that since his son's death, he now believed he knew why they had become distant. Rhonwellt felt sure it must have been to do with William's feelings for Jocelyn. He doubted William's inclination toward the affections of men had been unknown to Thomas, especially if the brothers had been close for a time. Even if Thomas had not known for certain, surely he must have suspected. Would his distaste at finding out such a revelation have been great enough to result in murder?

Rhonwellt quickened his pace. "Is it possible?" he muttered to himself, "Did Thomas Fullecoppe kill his own brother?"

TWENTY-NINE

A thin fog hung low to the water as Rhonwellt raced across the bridge. During his stay at the priory, it seemed he had spent far more time walking the three furlongs to town than he had in contemplation. He had intended spending his time in the scriptorium, pen in hand, dealing with his feelings about Merwenna's arrival and pondering any ramifications it might have on Tristan—and ultimately him. Instead, he found he put more effort into avoiding it than confronting it head-on. He did not want to think about it even now, and any fleeting thought of Tristan threatened to bring up the whole muddle.

Rhonwellt quickened his pace, staring at the road, pumping his arms to give him speed, pushing the unwanted conflict from his mind at least for now. The tally stick for the facts around the murder was not adding up. It had been much simpler when everyone thought Noah had done the deed. But Jocelyn fiercely believed in Noah's innocence, and Rhonwellt was having his own doubts. Especially since the issues between William and his brother Thomas had come to light. Fratricide was not uncommon, however it usually revolved around inheritance. Though there would be no title to pass on,

Walter Fullecoppe was a wealthy man and upon his death would leave a large estate as well as a thriving business. Is that what the murder had been about? Did Thomas want to inherit? And did he think William's secret, if found out, would not be enough to push him from their father's favor?

"Blessed evening, Brother," said one of the guards as Rhonwellt passed through the gatehouse.

Sketching the cross in the guard's direction, Rhonwellt replied, "To you as well." He was nearly through the second gate when he stopped. "The shops will soon close," he said. "Has Master Thomas Fullecoppe passed through?"

"No, brother, he stays late in his stall. You be finding him there at this hour."

"Which stall would that be?"

"What were the old parchmenter's shop, God rest him," said the guard, hastily signing the cross.

Rhonwellt nodded, said nothing and continued up the street.

As the day waned, darkness seemed to be in a hurry to descend over the land. Most of the stalls had already closed for the day's business, their awnings rolled back and their wooden counters folded up to cover the open fronts. Approaching the stall, Rhonwellt noticed a soft glow emanating from inside, turning the cracks between the boards the warm color of gold. It was true, Master Thomas had remained late to finish his closing tasks.

Rhonwellt was about to knock when he heard rustling inside. "Give me my penny," said a voice as the latch lifted. "I gots to go." Rhonwellt slipped around the corner in haste. Glyn Fowler emerged, depositing a coin in his pocket, glanced furtively around, and wasted no time in leaving. Though the lad claimed he had been with Thomas but once, it was clear he had lied. Beyond the obvious, why? Rhonwellt waited a discrete few moments and then knocked at the door. The door flew outward, slamming into Rhonwellt, nearly toppling him to the ground. Thomas Fullecoppe filled the doorway, in partial silhouette from the glow behind him. Thomas cast a glance over the street, growled and was about to say something when Rhonwellt stepped from behind the door and into the light filtering around from behind the merchant.

In an instant, the merchant erased his frown and hastily plastered a smile in its place. "Why, Brother, it is you," he said, his words oozing like thick syrup. "How may I be of assistance this fine evening?"

Thomas's insincerity was transparent and made Rhonwellt flinch. "I would pose a few questions to you about your brother's murder, if I may."

Thomas's face took on a wary look of a sudden, as he turned and re-entered the stall. "My brother is murdered, dead, and the one who killed him has paid with his life. What questions could you possibly have?"

"But, you see," replied Rhonwellt, "there is no actual proof that Noah killed William."

"I saw him run from the area! What more proof do you need?"

"That is only evidence he was there, not that he killed anyone. The lad said he only hit William and that your brother was alive when he left." Rhonwellt paused a moment. "Brother Remigius has given his account of the events. Now, I would have yours as you were the only other person present."

"I do not see what good retelling it can do. The outcome will not change, and the answer is obvious to me."

"After you present your account, Master Thomas, it may become clear that you are correct. However, if you would please, indulge this curious old monk and tell me what you saw—besides Noah fleeing."

Thomas went to the table and began the motions of smoothing the last few yards of fabric at the end of a bolt, all the while keeping his back to Rhonwellt. "As you can see, Brother, I have work to do. Ask your questions."

"How was it you happened upon your brother in the first place?" A sudden feeling of wariness, matching that which Thomas was emanating, overcame Rhonwellt, so he did not stray far from the door.

"It was about half-compline. Women must see everything you carry before making a decision. It can take a while to straighten it all out, so I remained late as I often do."

Having seen Glyn leaving moments ago, Rhonwellt was sure he knew the real reason Thomas stayed. "Were you alone?"

Thomas stopped for a moment and Rhonwellt watched as the merchant's shoulders grew tense. "As it happens, I was." There was a hesitancy in his answer. "I told William to go, that I could easily finish alone and would meet him at the tavern after."

"How long did you remain here?"

Thomas kept his back to Rhonwellt. "Nearly a whole ring. Wat's candles are inferior and tallow does not burn evenly, so I cannot be sure, but thereabouts. It took me longer than I expected to fold everything and put it away."

"And when you left?" asked Rhonwellt.

"I locked the shop and walked down the street to the tavern. I was nearly there when I saw something lying in the street."

"It was your brother?" Rhonwellt asked. Thomas turned slowly and nodded. He avoided Rhonwellt's gaze. "What did you do?"

"I rushed to him and knelt beside him. I lifted his head to see if he still breathed. My hand came away covered with blood. Someone had hit him on the head. I went into the tavern to get a pot-boy to fetch the *Infirmarian* from the priory. It took me a moment to negotiate with the taverner who did not want to let him go."

"You sent the pot-boy for Brother Remigius and returned to your brother?"

"I did, as quickly as I could. When I got there, I saw blood seeping from under his body. And, that is when I saw that Noah disappear around the corner into the alley to the stables."

"Then?" Rhonwellt could not believe his ears. "It was then you saw Noah? Not when you first arrived?"

"I did not see him clearly, only the flapping of a cloak fading into the night."

"Then how can you be sure it was Noah?" Rhonwellt rubbed the top of his head. Rhonwellt could not recall ever seeing Noah wear a cloak, did not know if the lad owned one. "Why would he come back?" He spoke more to himself than to Thomas. "You are saying he struck your brother, stabbed him, left and then came back? That makes no sense whatever."

"Maybe he hit him, saw me coming down the street, ran to hide, and when I went into the tavern for the pot-boy came back and stabbed him. I said I was in there for a fair bit."

Implausible as it sounded, Rhonwellt knew it could have happened just that way. "You did not notice blood under his body when first you came?"

"I did not. Only when I returned. It was seeping slowly from under him." Thomas's eyes filled with tears and a sob tore itself from his lips. "I sat down and cradled him in my arms. I told him help was on the way. He was quiet for a few long moments, then turned his face to me and said, 'Father...' I said, 'No, it is I, Thomas. I have you.' Then he closed his eyes and took his last breath." Thomas buried his face in his hands and openly wept, but made no sound.

Remembering Jesus's words as he spoke on the mountain top: 'Blessed are those that mourn for they shall be comforted,' Rhonwellt shoved his arms inside his sleeves and silently prayed for Thomas. The man's grief seemed genuine, yet he felt he must ask. "I have but one more question and then I will leave you to your sorrow. Your father mentioned that though you and William had been close as lads, you had recently grown distant. Why?"

Thomas raised his head and wiped his eyes with the back of his hand. "No particular reason. As lads we were much alike, but as we grew, our differences became more noticeable, nothing more. We developed different interests."

Was there more to it than that? Rhonwellt was not persuaded but decided not to pursue it. He placed a hand on Thomas's shoulder and signed the cross. "Thank you, Thomas. God's peace to you. I may wish to speak with you again."

Closing the door to the stall, Rhonwellt stepped out to find twilight had given full sway to darkness. The fog that slung low to the ground earlier had lifted to settle higher in the sky, obscuring all stars and covering the sliver of a moon like a veil. He was no closer to the truth, only more confused. Instead of uncovering answers, he found there were only more questions. Had William fallen victim to a knife at the same time he was struck? Or was he stabbed later, as Thomas suggested? It made no sense for Noah to come back to do it. The possibility of being seen was too great. Yet, the same would be true if someone else had committed the act. And who would that someone be? Or was Thomas's story no more than an elaborate ruse to throw Rhonwellt off the truth—that Thomas had murdered his brother?

Rhonwellt's head was spinning from all the possibilities. Perhaps a quiet pot of ale would soothe him. Hearing only hushed conversation coming from the *Thorn and Thistle*, rather than pass by as he had first intended, Rhonwellt went inside. The crowd was sparse, most of the customers long gone home to their families. He was on his way to a quiet table at the back when he stopped short. It could not be. Undoubtedly, his eyes deceived him for Jocelyn should be many furlongs from here by now. Rhonwellt paused to return a greeting and bestow a blessing and when he turned back, the person had vanished. He must have been mistaken. But Rhonwellt could not shake the feeling he had seen Jocelyn, dressed once again as a young woman. What was he doing here, and why had he vanished?

Rhonwellt went to a bench tucked in the small space under the stairs to the rooms above. It felt strange, as Rhonwellt had hardly ever come here while he resided at the priory. Yet, he had been to the *Saint George* in Ryd Lliw many times. The purpose of the cloister was to keep the religious separate from those they served. One thing he had learned since coming to Saint Tysilio's was for him to minister to a flock, it was essential he get to know them. The way to do that was to live among them.

He ordered a pot of ale from the serving girl, then leaned into the darkness, his back against the wall, and waited. She returned quickly with his pot and he immediately took a drink. It was cool, but bitter, as one could expect at the end of the evening after the best brew had already been consumed. Not at all the smooth quality of the alewife's brew that supplied the *Saint Goerge* in Ryd Lliw. Alone and quiet, he could feel the melancholia about to overtake him. He wanted to return home to his cottage and to Ciaran, to the hall and Tristan, that is if it was still his home.

Rhonwellt could not recall having ever thought of the priory as home, even after spending the majority of his life there. It was just the place where he lived. His fondness for Saint Cattwg's and his brothers was genuine. But, whenever he was away, he only considered the act of returning as just that—going back. It never felt to Rhonwellt like he was going home. Since taking on his duties at Ryd Lliw, he had come to feel a real sense of home. Somewhere he did more than live, a place he belonged. Some monks felt that same connection within the cloister, but it had always eluded Rhonwellt while there. Now that he had found it, he realized it was something he did not wish to lose.

Ernulf's arrival had brought a sense of family. It had blossomed in everyone, especially Hewrey and Ciaran. Merwenna's appearance and her surprising connection to Tristan, however, had caught him off guard and he had fled. Had he overreacted? Was he behaving like a petulant maid? Why was life outside the walls so complicated? While his head had been filled with religion, Rhonwellt realized that during his many long summers at Saint Cattwg's he had gained very little knowledge of village people or how the world worked. He suddenly understood that without that knowledge he could not lead a church.

Rhonwellt grabbed his head between his hands, shook it from side to side, forcing out a low groan. His head felt like it might burst from all the chaos. To make any progress, he must address things one at a time, first the murder, then what to do about Tristan. Though he felt he was no closer to finding the killer, he somehow felt it would be the easier of the two.

"More ale, brother?" The serving girl stood in front of Rhonwellt with a jug. Without thinking, he nodded and held out his pot. "A bit of eel stew left if you be hungry," she said. He felt his stomach lurch at the mention of eel and he shook his head. "Mistress pounded it so it be cooked through and tender. Used plenty of herbs, too."

"Though I praise God for his abundance of food," replied Rhonwellt, swallowing hard, "and though I know your mistress to be a fine cook, eel and I shall never have more than a passing acquaintance." He looked up at the girl. "I decline, with thanks." He took a long draft of his ale, suppressing a grimace. Slowly, his expression gave way to a smile as he recalled Ciaran and his look of sheer joy while eating an eel pie at market, the juice running down his chin and onto his robe. The memory tugged at his heart.

The girl turned as if to leave, when Rhonwellt saw a pair of grimy hands encircle her waist from behind. "What about me, girl?" Glyn stepped around her to look her in the face. "I has me a mighty thirst."

"And has you any coin, Glyn Fowler?" The girl wriggled out of his grasp and put her hand on her hip.

"As it happens, I gots me a shiny penny here," Glyn replied, holding up the coin.

"I needs to fetch a pot," said the girl with a wink. She sped off to the bar.

"They be a kiss for you when you gets back." Gly turned to Rhonwellt. "Good eve, Brother. You be out late."

Taking another long sip of his ale, Rhonwellt looked up at the lad over the rim of his pot.

"Master Glyn," replied Rhonwellt. "Just the lad I wish to see."

"You wants to see me? Whatever for?"

"You lied to me, Glyn Fowler."

THIRTY

Glyn's brows shot toward the ceiling and his wide eyes scanned nervously about the tap-room before looking directly at Rhonwellt. "Brother, you wounds me by such a accusation." Glyn pasted a smile on his face, albeit a nervous one.

"I would have expected you to get here sooner after leaving Master Fullecoppe's stall," said Rhonwellt, "what with a newly earned penny in your pocket and your infamous thirst."

"I had me things to do."

"Like earn another penny, perhaps?"

"Beg your pardon, brother." Glyn set his pot down. "I gots to go."

"You will talk to me now or later, lad, but you will talk to me and tell me all you know."

"Later be right fine," replied Glyn as he turned and bolted for the door.

Rhonwellt rose, gathered the front of his robe and hurried after him. Standing in the street, he looked up the road toward the castle and down toward the gatehouse. With but three or four people in the street, it was easy to see Glyn was nowhere in sight. The lad had vanished. He was deciding whether to bother looking for him or wait for another opportunity when he heard his answer.

"Let bloody go of me!"

The voice came from the alley that led to the stables. Rhonwellt was about to follow the sound when Glyn emerged, clawing at the rough hand firmly grasping a hank of his greasy hair. As he entered the soft glow of the lamplight at the front of the tavern, the inn's hostler materialized at the other end of the arm. Rhonwellt could only stare.

"Be you looking for this imp, Brother?" asked the stableman, holding the struggling fowler in front of him, a smirk skewing his mouth sideways. "I know if this imp be running the Devil be at his heels."

"I be running from no Devil and I says let me go!" Glyn's eyes flashed black as he continued to claw at the hand holding his hair.

Outweighing Glyn by a stone and two heads taller, the hostler held him fast. "Maybe not, but it be the Devil's hour and old Lucifer be prowling about looking for unruly lads like you to do his bidding. Better the monk catches you than him."

"Release him, please," said Rhonwellt.

The hostler let go of the lad's hair, keeping his wary eye on him. "I will if you says so, Brother. But, he are a slippery one. What he done this time?"

Glyn sulked and rubbed his head where the hostler had grabbed his hair, looking furtively around.

"Trying to escape be daft, lad," said the hostler. "If ye makes me hunt you down again, I not be so gentle next time. Just stay put and talk to the good brother."

"Though far from an innocent," said Rhonwellt, "Glyn has done nothing I am aware of that would interest me. I make inquiries into the murder of William Fullecoppe. Master Fowler's ability to keep abreast of the happenings in Cydweli are of some renown. I only wish to speak with him concerning that. If, however," said Rhonwellt, catching Glyn's eye and holding it for a brief moment, "the lad wishes to confess anything to me whilst conversing, it would be my duty to listen."

Glyn visibly tensed.

"Sunrise to sunset not be enough time for this lad to recount his sins," said the hostler.

"Perhaps so," Rhonwellt replied, "but his sins are between him and God, until he chooses to confess them to me." Rhonwellt turned to Glyn. "Come lad. Let us be about it."

"I be doing no confessing," said Glyn, attempting to puff himself up, but keeping his head down, avoiding Rhonwellt's eyes.

"Then we shall just talk, and you will tell me what you know. Let us walk down to the river. The sky portends no rain."

Their walk down the steep path to the Gwendraeth was quiet, neither Rhonwellt nor his young companion choosing to converse along the way. As the noise from the town faded away into the night, the only sound was the river as it covered the last few furlongs in its rush to meet its oldest friend, the sea. The great wooden wheel at the mill house stood motionless, tied off for the night, the usual scrape of the worn millstone silent.

"Could we sit here?" asked Glyn. "The miller be having his supper at the tavern, and the bench on his porch looks fair welcoming." Glyn spoke barely above a whisper. His shoulders hunched, likely from shame more than any chill to the night air. Slumping down onto the bench, Glyn leaned forward, his elbows on his knees, head in his hands. After many silent moments, Rhonwellt took in a breath, ready to speak.

"I hates geese," said Glyn, with no preamble. He turned his face to Rhonwellt, who only nodded, then looked back to the ground. Rhonwellt heard a thickness in the lad's throat. "I hates everything about them, the smell, the noise..."

Refraining from answering to just let the lad talk, Rhonwellt waited in silence for him to continue. "I think ma hates them too. The geese was pa's, him being sickly and not able to do a man's work. When he died, she were stuck with them." Moments passed. Glyn's fingers kneaded his hair. Rhonwellt sensed the struggle within him. "But, Elias," Glyn turned to Rhonwellt again, his face radiant with a smile at the mention of his brother, "he sure loves them birds. Calls them goosers like I did as a lad. Names every one of them and they knows their name. Elias can think like them. Knows where to find them when they runs away." He let out a chuckle. "And they sure likes him, too."

"They earn well for your mother," said Rhonwellt. "You have coin and meat to eat when others do not."

"Not so much coin," replied Glyn. "Only good thing ever come from them is eating them." He fell quiet, again. "I knows nothing else but geese, and I hates them."

Rhonwellt sensed where this was going. An uneasy silence lasted for several moments with each of them staring at the rushing water until Rhonwellt found his voice. "Tell me about Thomas Fullecoppe. How did he and his brother get on?"

Glyn thought for a moment. "About like most. There was ups and downs, but I think they held affection, sure."

"And, there were no issues between them? No arguments over money or possessions?"

"Master Thomas, he knowed his brother were the heir and would get the business and the estate. No doubts about that. But, Master Thomas always has plenty money. No telling where it come from, but he has it."

Rhonwellt hesitated before asking his next question. It was likely of little import but Rhonwellt was curious. "How did it start with you and Master Thomas?"

Glyn shifted on the bench and did not answer right away. "The lasses, they likes me," he said at last, scratching the lice at the back of his neck. "They likes my cock and laying with me." Glyn dug a booted toe into some loose dirt in front of the bench. "But, men like Thomas Fullcoppe have a keeness for that, too."

"Do you like it as well?" Rhonwellt wished he had not asked that quite so quickly.

"I likes cunts, but I finds buggering arses pleasurable, too." Glyn hissed in a breath. "I knows it be wrong, but they be no helping it." As what seemed like an afterthought, he added, "They be no pennies from the lasses, but men like Thomas gots plenty. It would take a sennight to earn what Thomas gives me for one time doing service to him. And buggering his arse be a damned sight cleaner than anything about geese."

Rhonwellt jerked in a breath. He was not sure whether Glyn intended him to be shocked or amused. But something niggled at him. "I sense there is more to it than what you have told me thus far."

Glyn pressed his lips into a hard, thin line until they turned white. His nostrils flared. "It were Elias he wanted," Glyn said, and immediately spit on the ground.

"Elias is so young," said Rhonwellt.

"He still be a babe," replied Glyn, "too young for any of that."

"So, you took his place," said Rhonwellt.

Glyn nodded.

"That just shows how much you care for him," said Rhonwellt, trying to instill sincerity into his voice.

"Not really," Glyn replied, his voice trailing off.

Rhonwellt was about to marvel at Glyn's candor and to wonder at the truth of what he was saying, when the lad looked directly into Rhonwellt's eyes and held his gaze. "You and me, we be the same. No point asking how I knows it, I just do. Folks says a lot of you religious kind be like that."

Rhonwellt's whole body tensed. He slipped his arms into his sleeves, wrapped them around his waist and held himself tightly. How could the lad know? The monk was about to deny it, but the lie would have stuck in his throat before it could pass his lips. Rhonwellt found he could not look away from Glyn, and the tiny glint growing in the lad's eye said he knew he was right. Rhonwellt felt the fowler peering into the deepest part of his soul, leering at all his most fetid secrets, felt the shame begin to rise, starting at the soles of his feet.

Glyn was wrong when he said the two were the same. Submitting to carnal lusts, acts devoid of emotion or connection, committed for profit, must differ from what he felt for Tristan. Yet, what did it matter? Rhonwellt felt sure somewhere in the Bible it said lust thought of in the mind or conceived of in the heart was a sin already committed with the body. To God, loving Tristan was the same as if he had lain with him. If he was to suffer the torments of Hell regardless, why should he go there without knowing the joy and comfort to be found wrapped in Tristan's arms? This was not proceeding at all as Rhonwellt had intended and he was beginning to think Glyn had no more useful information. All he had accomplished was to realize that it was not any form of morality that kept him from giving in to his feelings for Tristan, rather the real fear of possible earthly repercussions, something of which he already knew. Being beaten almost to death for it once left an indelible fear in him and he could not let it go.

"They be whispers about you, you know, about you and your knight, but I knowed before that. Since, you be a monk," Glyn went on, "and a man of God, a good man everyone says, and your knight was in the Crusade and brave and fought for God and the King, they pays little mind to the whispers." Glyn paused for several moments leaving Rhonwellt to deal with his own unease. "Is it true?" Glyn asked at last. "Are we bound for Hell, Brother Rhonwellt?"

It had never occurred to Rhonwellt there was talk about him behind his back, at the priory where gossip and secrets were rife, yes, but not among those in town. Had this always been so? Rhonwellt struggled to force out words in response. "According to the bishop, everyone is going to Hell. He believes we are all wicked and any real salvation is but an illusion."

Glyn's mouth fell slack. "How can a bishop believe that? They be holier than anybody. Right?"

"Some of them certainly think they are, our Bishop Maurontius, especially." Rhonwellt suppressed a smile as he thought of Maurontius's fall from grace two summers ago, and that little had been seen of him since.

"Well, if it are true and everybody be going there, Hell must be right big to fit so many folks in." Glyn turned to stare at the river. "It must be lonely for God, all alone in Heaven, with so many folks in Hell?"

Glyn's observation was as humorous as it was profound. Rhonwellt fought to keep his voice even and low. "Since the church says we are so evil, perhaps God is relieved at having little to do with us after we leave this world. Besides, He has his angels and saints to keep Him company."

"That would still leave plenty room." Glyn licked his lips and turned serious. "Are we that wicked, Brother?"

"What I think is of no consequence. It is what God thinks, and that...well, He is unfathomable."

The monk fell into a ponderous silence. Prior Alwyn had once accused him of having a crisis of faith which Rhonwellt had denied with vigor. Yet, here he was, again plagued by the same doubts he had carried with him his entire life, uncertainties that had never left him for long. They always arose at inopportune times to keep him on unsteady feet, often in a state of melancholia and preventing him from achieving any real peace.

Rhonwellt turned to look at Glyn and, startled, found himself alone, the sound of the river his only company, the bench beside him empty. Likely eager to escape further scrutiny, the fowler had quietly slipped away at some time during Rhonwellt's lapse into his inner misery. The monk had been so focused, he had not felt Glyn rise or heard him go. There was nothing to be done about it. The monk stood. As if he had awakened from a deep sleep, he stretched his arms high over his head to ease the weariness from his muscles.

Gazing up the path, Rhonwellt was grateful he did not have to climb all the way to the top, but could take the path to the bridge that intersected about half-way up. His conversation with Glyn had gone in a direction both uncomfortable and unexpected, and ultimately he had learned nothing of use as far as the murder of William Fullecoppe. He was right where he had been before running into Glyn.

The only things he knew for sure were that Noah had first attacked William, then Thomas had come upon his brother, had gone into the tavern to send a lad for Brother Remigius. When Thomas came back, his brother lay bleeding profusely from a wound to his back. Thomas swore the wound had not been there when he first came upon him. From the corner of his eye, he saw another figure flee into the night. Was it Noah fleeing on both occasions? Had he come back to make sure William was truly dead, or was the second person someone else and the one who thrust the knife into William's back? Or was Thomas lying, and it was he all along who had killed his brother? Rhonwellt's brain was swirling and his head hurt. So many unanswered questions, some having to do with life and others centered on death, but all weighing equally on him.

With a deep breath, Rhonwellt gathered his robe, putting one booted foot in front of the other, started to climb. Surface roots from a majestic oak growing on the hillside near the path had created steps that made the climb a little easier, especially when the path was muddy. About a quarter the way up he stopped to catch his breath. He could hear voices coming through the brush on Swyving Lane. It was too dark to see. Likely one of the tavern wenches earning a couple pennies with a lusty customer on the aptly named path. After a moment, Rhonwellt resumed his climb. Reaching the place where the bridge path intersected, his mind dwelling on Glyn, he tripped over a large root and fell to his knees.

"Christ's blood!" he muttered and was about to haul himself to his feet when he peered up through his eyebrows and saw a hand thrust in front of him. He grabbed it, stood, and found himself face to face with Jocelyn.

"Brother Rhonwellt," said Jocelyn. "Not exactly your territory, is it Brother?"

"Sadly, many monks are far more familiar with places like this than they have any right to be." Rhonwellt brushed the dirt from the front of his robe. "I see you are dressing as a lass again."

"It is how I am most comfortable and is how I earn my living."

Jocelyn's voice softened. "I know it distresses you, Brother Rhonwellt, but it is the way of it."

"I have learned much of the world and God's creatures in my two summers away from the priory, things I could never have dreamed. That I am finding them commonplace amazes me. And, yes, some things I find disturbing."

"Wicked things like me," said Jocelyn with a wink.

"Some would surely think you wicked." Rhonwellt gently laid a hand on Jocelyn's arm. "I do not think you are. I have seen into your heart. Beyond that, I cannot judge." Rhonwellt gave Jocelyn a furtive smile. "I thought you would have been far from here by now. What keeps you?"

"Do you believe Noah killed William Fullecoppe, Brother Rhonwellt?"

"Despite some scant evidence to support it, I do not."

"I know he did not. However, I am quite certain I know who did, Brother. I am here to catch a murderer."

THIRTY-ONE

Tristan had arrived with a hearty appetite that abandoned him with his first mouthful of wine. The knight pulled the jug of water to him and poured some into his pot before filling it with the strong red drink. A little wine always helped, too much never did. In his determination to stay sober, he vowed he would imbibe only diluted wine this evening but struggled to keep his commitment from wavering.

Upon arrival at Cydweli, Tristan had taken a room over the tavern, and asked to take his supper there so he could be alone. A once-steaming meat pie sat in front of him untouched and rapidly cooling, the gravy congealing to the point of growing stiff. He had broken the crust open with his spoon, picked at it and took a taste, then abandoned it. He knew from experience that Mistress Wen made delicious pies, still he could not eat.

Tristan had left Ryd Lliw full of enthusiasm and hope for a successful reunion with Rhonwellt. A bath and clean clothes, oiling his hair and a quick trim to his beard had given the knight confidence to go courting. Yet, nerves nagged at him, trying to dampen his ardor.

An incessantly chatty tinker, successful enough to possess his own horse and cart, had filled the hours on his ride to Cydweli. A stout man of about forty summers, the tinker looked as though he could hold his own in a fight. Traffic on the road had been sparse, leaving few travelers to band together for the journey. Though there had been no word of highwaymen roaming about since the attack on Merwenna's caravan, Tristan felt reassured by the tinker's company.

Now, safely tucked in his room, Tristan brooded into his pot, his confidence slowly bleeding away. Courting was not a thing at which he had experience. Amjhad and the other men in his life had simply been there, drawn by mutual want, available to pass the time when he needed them, no pursuit necessary. The same had been true with Rhonwellt when they were lads. Rhonwellt was to train to serve Tristan and as boys, the two together were a common sight. Rarely apart, they ate together, played the games boys played together. Rhonwellt sat in when Tristan spent time with his tutor. The change in their relationship had happened so gradually no one noticed, including the boys. When Rhonwellt eventually moved into the hall to assume his duties to Tristan, none knew that instead of sleeping on a mat on the floor at the foot of Tristan's bed, Rhonwellt snuggled next to him under a heavy brychan, their young bodies pressed tightly together, confident their world would never change.

But change it did, and here he was, a lifetime later, knowing things could never be as they were. Youth had abandoned them, middle age held them against their will and the rigors of life had come close to breaking them. Refuge in each other was their only hope. All his time in Outremer, his greatest wish had been for death and freedom from his misery. And if he could not persuade Rhonwellt to come home, he might find himself wishing for it again.

✟ ✟ ✟

RHONWELLT STARED AT JOCELYN IN DISBELIEF. "WHAT DO YOU mean you know who the murderer is?"

"Well, I am fairly certain I know. One thing I am sure of, it was not my brother."

"Then whom do you suspect?"

"Master Fullecoppe."

"Thomas?"

"No, his father, Walter."

Rhonwellt's disbelief was compounded. "Why the father? Everyone has said he was inside the tavern when William was killed, and none has said he left."

"Master Thomas said he saw someone fleeing as he returned to his brother after dispatching the lad for help."

"Yes, but what causes you to think it was the father?"

"Thomas said the person wore a cloak."

"Cloaks are common enough," replied Rhonwellt.

"For them that can afford them. It just proves it was not a local rough."

"Did Noah own a cloak?"

"Noah stole the cloak he wore," said Jocelyn, with a snort.

"Proving any rough could have a cloak," replied Rhonwellt. "Besides, what motive would Walter have to murder his son and heir?"

"Me," said Jocelyn. "William thought his father did not know the truth but I think he knew. William said he feared his father would rather him dead than with someone like me. Now he is dead. What else am I to think?"

Rhonwellt scratched at the stubble on his face, a faraway look in his eyes. "What you have said only confuses matters further. I had thought Thomas to be the most likely suspect. He had the most to gain much by his brother's death. And as for his account of seeing someone flee, we have only his word for that. And Thomas has secrets of his own."

"I must find out the truth, for Noah."

Rhonwellt ran his hand over the top of his head. "It is a dangerous business you are about, lad."

"Your words wound me, Brother," replied Jocelyn. "I may have a cock, but there is more lass about me than lad."

"Much about you is womanly, it is true."

"Before you saw the truth of me, you had no trouble calling me such."

"You are a creature like no other and I admit to being confused by you. But, as you are still a child of God, I am concerned for your safety, especially where this murder is concerned."

"You do not consider me a product of Satan?"

Rhonwellt shook his head.

A tiny smile lifted the corners of Jocelyn's mouth. "Then put your worries aside, Brother. I will do nothing foolhardy." Jocelyn grew quiet, turned her head and raised her face to the sky. "Folks never thought much of Noah and me, considered us downright low and sinful. They are probably right. I am what you see, and Noah was ruined from a boy. Da saw to that. But I will not have him forever remembered as a murderer, especially as he was innocent. Noah was my brother, and though largely worthless in that capacity, I loved him. We had only each other and I know he loved me too, in his own warped way. He proved that when he died. But one has to know love before they can give love properly."

A few moments passed before Rhonwellt spoke. "I must get back to the priory. While I reside there, I am bound by the same rules as the others. I have already missed Vespers. Brother Alwyn has been most indulgent with my absences, but I really should be there for Compline. Take care, child."

"Child?"

"Words from one old enough to be your father."

"I watched you with Ernulf. You would have made a good father." Jocelyn turned on her heel and climbed up the path. "Do not worry, Brother. I will be fine."

Rhonwellt stood staring after Jocelyn. Her words made him feel odd. He had never pictured himself as a father and he would likely never be one. Still, the idea made him feel warm and made him smile.

He climbed the few paces to where the path forked and took the path to the bridge.

He had just stepped onto the bridge when he thought he heard footsteps over the sound of the rushing river. He turned to see Glyn Fowler approaching, a walking stick in his hand.

"You disappeared quickly enough..." Before Rhonwellt could finish, Glyn swung the stick directly at Rhonwellt's head, hitting him just behind his ear. The monk saw a flash of light and felt his knees give way as he sank to the ground.

"I am sorry to do this to you, brother. I likes you."

Rhonwellt's head was spinning and he could not see Glyn clearly. His ear stung from the blow.

"Why you not just leave things be? Stop trying to say Master Thomas killed his brother. It were not him. Everyone knows it were that Noah what done it." As Rhonwellt's vision began to clear, he could see Glyn trembling, his voice shaky. Instead of anger on the lad's face as he expected, he saw fear. Glyn raised the stick over his head again. "Master Thomas and me got plans and I not be having you muck them up by hanging him for murder."

Rhonwellt put his arm up to shield his face as Glyn swung the stick in a wide arc. The blow glanced off his arm, his head missing the brunt of it.

"Why could you not just leave things be?" Glyn pleaded.

"Stop!" The voice came from the direction of the town. Rhonwellt heard Glyn's running footsteps recede into the night. As blackness overtook him, he heard the voice shout again—Tristan's voice.

✝ ✝ ✝

TRISTAN FOUND RHONWELLT LYING IN A HEAP IN THE MIDDLE of the bridge, not moving, the assailant's weapon abandoned on the ground next to him. Though it enraged him to let the would-be killer escape, Tristan could not give in to his fear that Rhonwellt was gravely injured or even dead, and was unwilling to leave him until he knew for certain. Peering through the darkness in the direction the man had fled, he could see nothing. The street lay deserted. He knelt down and put his ear to the monk's chest. The sound of a strong heartbeat eased the knight's apprehension but did nothing to quell his anger, not only at the attacker's escape but that he had once again failed to keep Rhonwellt safe.

Tristan lifted Rhonwellt by the shoulders, moved his knees under him and laid the tonsured head in his lap. Blood oozed from a wound behind the monk's ear and a knot was forming where the assailant had struck a second time. He gently pushed the sleeve back and felt Rhonwellt's arm which had taken the brunt of the second blow. Though beginning to swell and discolor, it was not broken. The thick wool cuff of Rhonwellt's sleeve had absorbed much of the force and prevented any serious damage.

"Rhonwellt," whispered Tristan, afraid that if he said it aloud and God heard him, The Almighty would play some diabolical trick on him and take Rhonwellt away. Trembling, Tristan cupped the side of Rhonwellt's face with his hand, caressing his cheek with his thumb. Only half realizing what he was doing, Tristan squeezed his eyes shut and offered up a quick prayer to the Blessed Virgin for Rhonwellt to awaken and for him to be unharmed. Lowering his head, Tristan pressed his lips to Rhonwellt's forehead and let them linger there a moment continuing to stroke his monk's cheek with his thumb. When he raised his head, he found Rhonwellt's eyes were open, staring at him. He released the breath he had not realized he was holding in. Rhonwellt raised his hand and wrapped his fingers around Tristan's wrist. They lingered for several moments looking at each other, Tristan trying to convey with his eyes what his mouth could not manage. Neither spoke.

The spell was broken when the priory bell tolled the hour of Compline.

Rhonwellt looked briefly toward the church and then back. "You smell of clove," he said. "It is how I knew it was you."

"Who attacked you?" Tristan asked.

"I have been so stupid," said Rhonwellt. "I should have realized his connection to Master Fullecoppe was more than he had let on."

"What are you talking about? Who?"

"Glyn, the fowler's lad," replied Rhonwellt.

"Is he the one who attacked you?"

The monk nodded. "Help me stand," he said.

"Are you certain you are able?" asked Tristan.

"Yes. I just need some assistance."

Positioning himself behind the monk, Tristan hoisted him to his feet then guided him to the bridge rail that he might lean and get his balance.

"Why would Glyn attack you?" asked Tristan.

"He thought I was accusing Master Thomas of killing William."

"Do you think he did? And, why would that matter to a keeper of geese?"

"Master Thomas is but one of many possibilities in Master William's murder." Rhonwell touched the wound behind his ear and winced. There was blood on his fingers when he pulled them away. "It matters to Glyn because he and Master Thomas are...involved."

Tristan did not even attempt to hide the amazement he felt. Apparently a lot had changed in the two summers since he had seen the lad last. "Exactly to what extent are they involved?"

"Glyn supplies favors," Rhonwellt paused, "of a carnal nature. The lad said it was only for the money, however it now appears he was not exactly forthcoming. Before he struck me the second time, he said he and Thomas had plans. He is desperate to change his station and I think Glyn saw an opportunity to improve his lot by aligning himself with Master Fullecoppe. When he saw that Thomas may be accused of murder, he saw the future he had envisioned for himself in jeopardy."

"I must get you to a bed at the priory," said Tristan, "then I shall see to our fowler."

"I do not need a bed. I will be fine."

"You are so bloody stubborn!"

"Then we are well-suited," replied Rhonwellt, a tiny smile on his face.

Tristan started to protest when Rhonwellt reached out and held two fingers to the knight's lips and shook his head. "Truly, I will be fine. We shall find Glyn together. In what direction did he run?"

Tristan pressed his lips together and snorted a silent breath. "He ran toward the church. Do you think that is where he went?"

"He will not be there," Rhonwellt replied. "He will have run to the safety of Master Thomas. Glyn will be at his market stall, I am certain."

"Then he would have to pass by here again."

"No, he could cross the fields beyond the churchyard and head for the river. He can cross the weir for the mill run and enter the town, unseen, by the rear postern gate near the guard tower at the castle. He would then be mere steps from the Fullecoppe's stall. Many of the villeins who live beyond the church use the weir instead of coming all the way in to cross. We, however, shall use the bridge."

With a nod, Tristan checked Rhonwellt's wound one more time for any fresh blood and found none. Satisfied, they headed toward the South gate, Tristan encouraging Rhonwellt to lean heavily on him. A hole opened up in the slow moving cloud cover to let a brief shaft of light from a half-moon shine through, casting an eerie pall over both their faces.

They found the gate tower deserted, no hails or greetings from above, no guards leaning over the edge to peer into the darkness at the two of them huddled together as they passed through. Neither had they encountered anyone in the road. It was as if the town was empty.

"Where is everyone?" said Tristan. Almost before he could finish speaking, the clamor of angry voices rang out in the darkness.

Veering to the right they entered Keep Street. In the distance, Tristan could see a score of men clustered under the torchlight in front of the tavern.

"Can you walk on your own?" asked Tristan.

"Yes, I am fine now."

Tristan took his arm from around Rhonwellt, put his other hand on the hilt of his sword. He could feel the hairs on the back of his neck stand out. What kind of trouble was this? He quickened his pace until he stood just outside the half-circle of men gathered. At the center, Walter Fullecoppe and Jocelyn stood toe-to-toe staring intently through angry eyes. Tristan pushed his way through the tangle of men, Rhonwellt right behind him.

"What is this about?" he shouted. "Jocelyn, what are you doing here?"

Walter Fullecoppe's head snapped to the side at the sound of Tristan's voice. "This ridiclous creature has just accused me of murdering my own son!"

THIRTY-TWO

R honwellt pushed his way past Tristan and into the midst of the crowd in front of the tavern. Fists clenched at his sides, he struggled to control his ire.

Striding forward, he confronted Jocelyn. "I can see," said Rhonwellt, "we have different ideas of what it is to be foolhardy, lass. Did you ever consider there may be consequences to leveling such an accusation?"

"This creature is no more a lass than you are, Brother," said Walter Fullecoppe, his face twisted into a grotesque sneer. "It is no wonder you were fooled. Apparently life away from the world where real men live has dulled your ability to discern such things."

"Jocelyn's sex has naught to do with this," replied Rhonwellt, pausing, fingers to his lips. "Although, as I think on it, perhaps it does. Are there merits to the accusation? You would have as much reason to kill William as any."

Master Fullecoppe took a menacing step toward Rhonwellt, jabbing his finger in front of the monk's face. "How dare you! Men like you should know their place when among their betters."

Before Rhonwellt could draw breath, Tristan thrust himself

between the two men, dagger in hand, pressing it up against Fulle-coppe's tunic where his heart would be. "Watch your tongue, sir. Do not let your next words be your last." With a slight flick of his wrist, the point of the knight's knife cut a small tear in the man's garment. "He is a man of God and there are few men better than Brother Rhonwellt."

Rhonwellt quickly took hold of Tristan's wrist and gently lowered the dagger, his eyes telling the knight to stay calm. "I may not know much about such things, Master Fullecoppe, but it appears your eldest son was all too familiar with the whole of it and was on the verge of creating a scandal that would blacken your good name."

"It is a lie!"

"It is not, Master Fullecoppe," said Jocelyn. "You know it to be true, and it is that has you so angry. You worry that perhaps your name is already in ruins."

Fullecoppe leaned in toward Jocelyn and shook his fist. "If he was so inclined, it is your doing!" Spittle flew in Jocelyn's face as Walter spoke. "You enchanted him with the cooing voice of an evil succubus, doing your vile satanic master's bidding."

"If I were a succubus, then I would have merely come to him in his sleep." Jocelyn waved her hands in front of Walter's face as though conjuring a spell. "However, I assure you he was fully awake when we lay together, and fully aware of his true nature long before I ever came here." Jocelyn gestured to the crowd gathered outside. "If they had the courage, I would wager there are those out there right now who would tell you it was but a badly kept secret."

Walter Fullecoppe roared and slapped Jocelyn across the face, hard enough to leave a mark. Before she could react, Tristan moved in and grabbed hold of Walter's tunic and slammed him against the wall. "Sir, your temper could be your undoing," said Tristan with a growl. "Proceed with care. I will not warn you again." Walter stared back for a long moment, then barely bobbed his head.

Jocelyn rubbed his cheek, his face impassive but unable to hide the hatred in his eyes.

Rhonwellt pushed Jocelyn behind him and, taking a small step forward, raised his clenched fists in front of Master Fullecoppe. "This display of rage is proof enough you would be capable of murder," said Rhonwellt, his voice booming in the small space. "And we now know there was more than enough reason for you to have killed William."

"You think I would kill my own son over such a thing?"

"Men have killed over less," said Rhonwellt, still shouting. "But you are not alone in that." Rhonwellt was again reminded of Tristan's family and the treachery of his brother Declan. He paused, mostly for dramatic effect. "Having thought it through for some time, I believe there to be at least five people who could have wanted your son dead." He scanned each of the faces before continuing. "The one everyone feels certain is to blame, Noah the smith, is already dead. Was that at your behest, Master Fullecoppe?"

Walter's mouth twitched as he regarded Rhonwellt. "I believe it was William's man that killed him, it is true. He had served William since a teen and was devoted to him as servants often are. But I did not order it and I have not seen him since. He knew I could not shelter him from the consequences of murder."

"Is it possible they were more to each other than master and servant?" asked Tristan.

Walter's eyes widened with surprise as though such a notion came from nowhere. However, he made no response, rather shrugged his shoulders and shook his head.

"That might explain the force of his anger as he attacked me," said Jocelyn. "At the time I never gave it a thought for the man made no such claim."

"It is not important," said Tristan. "What matters now is with Noah dead, four suspects remain." He turned to Rhonwellt. "Who are the others?"

"Four others!" The elder Fullecoppe's voice said he found the idea unfathomable. "You make an appalling claim. I am well regarded by all as are my sons. None should have the temerity to end his life let alone four."

"Well, someone did," replied Rhonwellt, "be that within the realm of belief or not. Perhaps if you will follow me to your place of business, we may find answers there."

"Why should I follow you anywhere?" Walter tried to maintain his air of superiority but Rhonwellt could tell the idea rattled him. "What could you hope to find? Only my son Thomas will be there at this late hour. You cannot think he is suspect."

Without a word, a tight-lipped Rhonwellt turned and headed up the street toward the castle. Tristan urged Walter and Jocelyn to follow. The chattering crowd of villeins followed at their heels, propelling them forward like an ocean wave pushes bits of debris just in front of its crest. No one carried a torch and the earlier hole in the clouds had closed, rendering the sky in roiling grays and black. Light seeped through the cracks of the Fullecoppe stall at the end of the street. Thomas was indeed toiling late.

As they approached, Walter surged forward and grabbed the handle to the stall door and yanked it open. Thomas stood bent over the table, carefully folding a bolt of cloth he had unrolled to show a customer earlier in the day.

"What do you want?" asked Thomas, without looking up. "Can you not see we are closed and I am busy here?"

"Thomas!" Walter's voice sounded like the crack of a whip. He burst into the stall.

The son turned his head casually toward the door. "Oh, it is you, father."

Rhonwellt wondered at the man's collected calm as he stepped in the door. Looking back, he could see the meager light from Thomas's candle as it bled out the door revealing the expectant faces of the crowd peering in. He motioned for Tristan and Jocelyn to come inside.

"What is the meaning of this?" asked Thomas, scanning the people standing before him. "Father, why have you brought these people here?"

"I have brought no one," said Walter, glaring at Rhonwellt and Tristan, then back to his son. "I am compelled here."

"I do not understand." Thomas's smile showed a small concern but remained congenial and he spoke smooth and evenly without the slightest sign of distress.

"Explain it, monk," said Walter.

"Where is Glyn the fowler?" asked Rhonwellt.

"What would the likes of him be doing here?" said Thomas.

Rhonwellt kept his face impassive as he stared at the merchant, impressed anew by his self-assurance.

"It is of no matter," said Thomas, "for as you can see, he is not here. So, I shall ask again. Why are you here?"

Rhonwellt took a careful glance about the room, letting his eyes linger for a moment in any dark corners. It was true, Glyn was nowhere in sight. Rhonwellt then let his gaze fall on each of the suspects. With so much at stake in the next few moments, Rhonwellt silently signed the cross and prayed that The Almighty would guide his lips and organize his thoughts.

"You try my patience, Brother," said Walter. "Get on with it." Walter turned toward the faces staring in from the outside. "Somebody close that bloody door!"

"You may shut them out, but these walls are thin and they will hear all regardless," said Jocelyn.

Walter stomped over and pulled the door closed. "I will not have my family business on display or have lowly villeins staring at me."

"They will not leave, but will hang on every word." Jocelyn's taunting only seemed to make Master Fullecoppe seethe more. "I'll wager this is the most entertaining thing to happen in this village since winter set in."

"The person responsible for William Fullecoppe's murder is in this room," Rhonwellt said at last. He let this sink in for a moment. Walter, Thomas and Jocelyn all looked at each other, eyes narrowed, accusatory looks passing back and forth between them. "Before anyone leaves, I mean to determine which of you it is."

"What you say is absurd," said Walter. "Everyone knows that wandering smith killed William. All that is left is to figure this one's role in it." He waved the back of his hand dismissively at Jocelyn who remained strangely quiet.

"Noah attacked William, it is true," said Rhonwellt. "We know that by Noah's own admission."

"And by the fact I recognized him as he fled the scene," said Thomas.

"So we need not look further for the initial attacker." Rhonwellt scanned the faces again. "Let us consider Jocelyn. What would be her motive for killing William?"

"There was plenty motive," said Thomas. "She...he...whatever it is, actually thought to have a future with William."

"And how do you know about that?" asked Rhonwellt.

Thomas's face went blank. He quickly cast his eyes to the floor.

"You know more than you are telling, Master Thomas," said Rhonwellt, his gaze boring into the merchant.

"He did promise to marry me," said Jocelyn, a rueful smile on her face.

"Absurd! He would never have done it!" yelled Walter.

"And if that promise were not kept?" said Rhonwellt, turning his eyes from Thomas to Walter. "Broken promises lead to broken hearts and often bring a desire for revenge."

"It was not worry over a broken heart," said Walter, "but anger at losing a fortune. Someone like this creature would have no prospects in this life or any other. Some innocent like William was his only hope. And I am telling you, it would not happen,"

"I know that better than anyone, Master Fullecoppe," Jocelyn replied. "William was no innocent. The only one who wanted to believe William's words more than I, was himself. I asked naught from him but his time and affection and received nothing more, so his fortune was safe." A look of sadness spread across her face. "I knew he did not have the courage or strength of character to see his promises through, but that does not mean I murdered him. If I had killed every man who made such promises, I would have left quite a trail of blood behind wherever I went." She spun to face to Walter. "His inability to keep his word was mostly due to his fear of you."

"Absurd! He would have no reason to fear me, I am..." Walter stopped, grew quiet. "I was his father."

"Anything you do not wish to hear, you declare absurd," said Thomas, suddenly busying himself with folding cloth again. He smoothed the fabric with his hands using slow and deliberate movements. Rhonwellt recognized this as a diversion so Thomas could carefully think on his next words. "It is the truth. Had he admitted his fear of you it would have been worse, so he hid it. We both did." Thomas stopped smoothing fabric, folded his arms and grabbed his elbows while looking toward the ceiling. "You are a hard and unforgiving man, sir." Suddenly, he lowered his face and glared at his father. "You rode William without mercy, never easing up on the rein to relax the bit. He could never please you no matter how hard he tried."

"I spent my life building my business and amassing my wealth," said Walter, pounding his fist on the counter, leaning in toward his son. "I needed to know it would be in good hands after I left this world."

"The business," said Thomas, the venom in his voice stinging like a poison, "always the business! All with an eye to leaving it to sons you knew nothing about or seemed to care for. William had no particular interest in cloth and little head for business, whereas, I am accomplished at both." Thomas turned away from his father and gestured towards the fabrics laying about the shop space. "It was I who kept all this alive and profitable. William was smart enough to realize that and we made an agreement. He would inherit as the law and custom dictates and I would run it as his partner. William would see a good living from it as would I, and he would be free to do as he pleased. But, of course, you would know nothing of that. Just as you claim to know nothing of his nature."

Walter sank down onto a stool, his shoulders slumped as he

buried his face in his hands. Gone was any pretense at superiority. His whole countenance exuded misery and defeat. Before him, Rhonwellt saw a man witness his well-built life crumbling before his eyes and found he could not help but feel some pity for him.

"I suspected," said Walter, the clarity of his words muffled by his hands. "As a lad, he was different. I hoped I was wrong, that it would pass, and he would come to his senses and marry."

Rhonwellt was struck by Walter's words, ones he had heard before. Tristan had told him they were the same his mother used. Glancing toward Tristan, he saw the knight visibly pale at hearing them again. Did all parents think this—hold out hope for it? Would his own family have done as much had they the chance? Rhonwellt shrugged off such thoughts.

"Thus we come to your motivation to kill him," Rhonwellt said to the father.

As Walter's misery became despair, Rhonwellt felt the man's pain.

"It is true, I might have thought him better off dead." Walter looked up briefly then let his shaking head fall back into his hands. After remaining that way for a few moments, he slowly raised his head. His eyes were red. "But I could not kill him, not my son, my firstborn."

Thomas picked up a bolt of cloth and threw it across the shop. "Firstborn! What of the second son? Does he matter so little?"

Walter raised his eyes to look at Thomas, but it seemed he could find no words.

"What of you, Thomas?" Tristan had kept to his own counsel until now. "I know much about firstborn and second sons. Knowing you were the lifeblood of the business that William was to inherit must have chafed at your sense of worth like a burr under a saddle." Tristan took a step toward Thomas, and the man flinched. "What better way to realize your own ambition than to have William out of the way."

"I have already told you," said Thomas through clenched teeth while rubbing the back of his neck. "William and I were to have a partnership."

"Being your own master," said Tristan, "with no one demanding any measure of it ends up being much more lucrative. Does it not? Why share when you could have it all?"

"You are correct," said Thomas, his words directed at his father. "I should have had the whole of it. I earned it!" He leaned against the counter, his head lowered. "William would not survive without an income from the business. He had no real skills. He could never have been a soldier." He looked over his shoulder at Rhonwellt. "A priest perhaps. Life secluded in a cloister with nothing but men would have suited him, I think." He stated his pronouncement matter-of-factly without a hint of sarcasm. Thomas paused a moment. "William was my brother. He could be kind to me where our father could not. In return, I vowed to myself I would see he never lacked."

"I would have cared for him," said Jocelyn, in a voice that seemed far away.

Thomas looked at Jocelyn for a moment. His face relaxed, became almost kind. "Yes, I think you would have. But you have already said you knew it could never be."

As Jocelyn and Thomas stared at each other, Rhonwellt felt an understanding pass between them, a brief acknowledgment that they both had loved William.

"With everyone professing abiding love for the victim," said Tristan, "we are no closer to determining who hated him, enough to want him dead."

"And that," said Rhonwellt, "brings us to our last suspect."

"More fantasy?" scoffed the elder Fullecoppe.

"The one person who appears to be missing from this little gathering."

"And who might that be?" asked Tristan.

"Why, Glyn the fowler."

Rhonwellt tucked his hands into his sleeves, gripped his arms, and offered up a prayer he was not wrong.

Walter Fullecoppe's eyes narrowed. "You cannot mean that greasy lad who herds geese and is drunk from cockcrow until well after the Devil's hour?"

"The same," Rhonwellt replied.

Jocelyn had confusion on her face.

Thomas went pale.

"Master Thomas, fare you well?" asked Rhonwellt.

"What has he to do with this?" asked Thomas, his delivery halting. "And why would that lad have any reason to hate William?"

"I do not think he hated William," replied Rhonwellt. "It would have been fear that drove him."

Thomas laughed out loud. "Fear? Ridiculous! No man had reason to fear William."

"It was not the man he feared, only in what he represented."

Thomas snorted. "You speak in riddles, Brother. What in the name of Heaven do you mean—represented?"

"Glyn said you and he had plans. He saw William as the one person who might get in the way."

It was Walter's turn to laugh. "What possible plans could a wealthy and prominent merchant have with a wretched herder of geese?"

Suddenly, Rhonwellt could bear it no longer. "Enough," he snapped, "both of you! I am finished with your denials and deceit. Now I will have the truth." He spun around. "Sir Tristan, if you were to thrust your sword into that pile of bolts, I am sure you would not miss your mark."

Rhonwellt could see doubt in the knight's eyes. The steel of Tristan's sword sang as it rubbed against the throat of its scabbard. Taking a firm grip with both hands, Tristan raised his blade high over his head. They all waited, the air tense, no one moving or making a sound.

Thomas inhaled audibly and put his hands to the sides of his head. "No, Please! Those cloths are silks imported from Lucca. They are worth a king's ransom."

Tristan hesitated only a trice before swinging the sword downward at the pile of bolts. At the last moment, he turned his wrists so the sword met its target with the flat of the blade.

A yelp pierced the cloths. "Please, do not kill me." The fabric rustled and Glyn slowly rose and emerged from behind the pile, no color in his face, hands palms-out in front of him. "Do not kill me."

"Come here, Glyn Fowler," said Rhonwellt. "The time has come to account."

Glyn stood, feet apart, licking his lips, wide eyes working furtively from side to side, finally landing on the closed door. Drawing in a breath, the lad bolted, pushing the door and thrusting himself outside and into the waiting crowd. Several men grabbed him and pushed Glyn back into the stall to within a hair's breadth of Tristan's waiting sword. The knight reached forward, clasped the front of the lad's grimy tunic and threw him into the middle of the room. Glyn began to turn like a caged animal.

"Master Thomas, tell them! Please."

"Yes, Thomas, tell us," said Walter as he moved quickly forward and delivered a fist to Thomas's face, then lost his balance and lurched sideways into a pile of bolts. "Abomination!" Looking overwrought, Walter at first attempted to right himself then fell back against the counter and slowly sank to the floor, his arms limp at his sides. "All my work for naught," he mumbled.

"What have you to say, lad?" said Tristan, keeping his sword aimed at Glyn's chest. "Is Brother Rhonwellt correct? Did you murder William Fullecoppe?"

Glyn's nose had started to run. He swiped it on his dirty sleeve. On the verge of sobbing, his chest heaved and his breaths came quick. His wide eyes darted from face to face, landing at last on Thomas.

"Did you murder William?" Thomas asked, his face exuding shock.

Glyn put the heels of his hands to his temples and squeezed his eyes shut. A sound escaped his throat that sounded much like he was keening his own death. "I done it for you." A sob escaped his lips. "I seen that Noah hit him, put him down right good. You come out to him, knelt down in a panic, then went back inside. I knowed he were still breathing. Took no more than a trice to do it. Used his own knife then wiped it on his tunic."

"Christ's blood, boy!" Thomas shouted. "William was no threat to you or me or anyone."

"You only ever complained about him, how he was taking what were yours."

"Oh, lad." Thomas calmed, sighed audibly as he hung his head. His chin trembled as he spoke. "It is what brothers do; they complain about each other, they argue. Poor William, I never wished him dead. How many times must I say? We had struck a deal."

Glyn began pulling at his hair, his eyes pleading with Thomas. "What do I do?"

"There is nothing to be done, lad. They will hang you."

"Hang?" Glyn's mouth hung slack.

"It was murder. Do you not see that?"

Glyn began to shake, his body out of control. "Hang?" he mumbled again. Looking down, his hose grew wet as he pissed himself, his fear running down his legs. He ran his eyes over the faces in the room then looked out the door.

"You cannot escape, lad," said Tristan. The crowd clustered near the door still blocked the way. "There is no use in trying."

After a quick glance toward the counter, Glyn reached out and grabbed a pair of large scissors, long as a man's forearm, laying on top of a bolt of fabric. His hand trembled when he pointed them at Tristan.

"Please, lad," said Tristan.

Rhonwellt could not take his eyes off the fowler as the lad continued to focus on Tristan. Glyn licked his lips again, his breathing became heavy, his hand continued to shake. Rhonwellt looked from Glyn to Tristan and back to Glyn.

"Do not do this." Tristan's expression turned into one of anguish. "Those are no match for a sword."

Do not do what? Rhonwellt was confused. Even he knew Glyn could not win a fight against a sword with a pair of scissors.

"I gots no choice," replied Glyn. The fowler and the knight stood rigid for several long moments, each one's gaze locked on the other.

Tristan spread his legs and assumed a battle stance, gripping his sword tightly with both hands.

"Brother Rhonwellt, pray for me and tell God I be sorry."

Eyes still locked on Tristan, arm still holding the scissors like a knife, Glyn thrust himself forward without hesitation, pushing hard against the point of Tristan's sword, leaning in to sink the blade deep into his chest. To Rhonwellt's horror, he saw Tristan push his sword slowly forward until it protruded out Glyn's back. The moisture in the knight's eyes spilled over and down his cheeks. Glyn took in a breath, held on to it, did not let it out, did not take another. The scissors dropped from his hand and his trembling fingers touched the sword where the blade pierced his tunic, caressing it like something beloved and precious. His knees buckled, and he began to sink slowly backward, the movement pulling his body off Tristan's blade. The air in his lungs made a gurgling sound when it came rushing out through the hole in his chest. As he continued to fall, Thomas waited with open arms to catch him before he hit the floor.

Walter stood, spun around and raced out the door, pushing his way through the crowd.

Mind swirling from what he had just witnessed, Rhonwellt quickly knelt down, crossed himself, then made the sign of the cross on Glyn's forehead, and began to pray.

More of the fowler's breath came rushing out. "I always acted brave. It were a lie. I never was. Not brave enough to hang, leastwise. But, I done it." Glyn lowered his head to stare at his wound. "I were not sure I could." Glyn struggled to breathe, grimaced with every attempt. "It be bad enough I done a murder, I not be wanting ma and Elias to know I were a coward too."

"Shush," whispered Thomas. "Dying is hard and you are proving yourself brave enough for that."

He forced his face into a smile. "You always treated me good, was kind to me. Why is it folks like me always loses and folks like you always wins?"

"No one has won here," replied Thomas. "Everyone here has lost, most especially me."

Glyn's voice grew raspy as he continued the struggle to breathe. "It were good with you and me," he said. Through his obvious pain, a mischievous look crept over his face. He crooked a finger, beckoning Thomas to lean forward for a private moment. Though Glyn whispered, Rhonwellt overheard him say, "Buggering you were good, too." Glyn started to laugh, but it quickly turned into a cough, droplets of blood flying out of his mouth, some gathering on his lips and running down his chin.

Thomas's face took on a painful smile. He nodded silently and pulled Glyn close.

THIRTY-THREE

Only Rhonwellt and Tristan remained in the stall. Thomas had accompanied Glyn's body to the priory and Jocelyn had melted into the crowd of villeins as they slowly drifted toward the tavern to drink and gossip about the fowler's death. Rhonwellt gripped himself inside his sleeves, rooted in place, unable to get his feet to move. He stared at the floor of the stall. Rhonwellt had felt compelled to accept Glyn's meager last words as his confession in order to shrive him, an act he knew he would eventually need to defend to Prior Alwyn as it did not fully comply with the church's position. But, though unorthodox, it was done.

The monk's mind resisted the full measure of what he had just witnessed—Glyn's gruesome act of self-murder. How could the lad commit such a sacrilege? At the priory, monks died in their beds or the infirmarium. The deaths of Brother Mark and Brother Jerome were the exceptions. Violent death was different and it left him feeling unnerved.

Worse was Tristan's part in it. Rhonwellt turned to face Tristan. The knight sat brooding on a pile of fabric bolts, leaning over his still bloody sword, forehead resting on his hands crossed over the pommel. The words were nearly on Rhonwellt's lips to ask Tristan why, but he stifled the question. Could there be any credible explanation for such an action? He was beginning to wonder, did he know Tristan as well as he thought?

The knight's voice sliced through the silence, raspy and thick with emotion. "Are you all right?"

Lost for a moment, Rhonwellt suddenly found Tristan gazing at him, the knight's pallor easily seen even in the dim light. Dark circles rimmed his eyes, drawing attention to the pain they showed like the frame around a portrait. What could Rhonwellt say? He was all right, and he was not.

"Murder," said Rhonwellt, "is a sin against your fellow man." The monk fought to steady the waver in his voice. "And self-murder is a sin against God. Glyn committed both. His punishment was up to God, not you. You aided him in his act of self-murder and now the wickedness has become yours as well."

"It is not my first sinful act, nor will it be my last," said Tristan, "and it is one for which I will happily give an account. God knows that of me."

"Tristan, this is no trifling matter, yet you act as if it were!"

"Death is no trifle to me. I have seen much of it in my life as a soldier, brought about slaughter with my sword daily. I am left quite immune to its effect. Yet, Glyn's death is different and hangs heavy on my heart."

"Glyn was not your enemy, and you were not acting as a soldier when you helped him die. Tristan, you are a party to murder. I am speaking about your soul."

The knight rose, wiped the blade of his sword on his cloak and returned it to its sheath. Tristan closed the few steps between them and gently took hold of Rhonwellt's shoulders. "I fear my soul was lost to God a very long time ago, and He has given up any real hope of reclaiming it. We have reached an understanding, God and me."

"Men do not reach understandings with God." Rhonwellt tried to wriggle from Tristan's grasp, but the knight held him fast. "I do not understand," said the monk, "and am sure God does not either! I cannot reason it, even after seeing it with my own eyes. You knew what Glyn was about to do and became collusive when you helped him to accomplish it. Why?"

"Are you truly unable to work it out?" asked Tristan, releasing Rhonwellt's shoulders, putting his hands in front of him as though presenting a gift. "It is as you said, Glyn took a man's life, an act of murder and one for which he would surely die on the gallows. He was terrified of hanging and he did not want his mother and brother to be forced to witness it. He saw self-murder as the only way to protect them from the humiliation of the ugly public spectacle of an execution. Times are changing. The world is not as sympathetic to our kind as it once was."

"Our kind?" replied Rhonwellt.

"Men like us, who love other men." Tristan let go of his shoulders. "The reasons and circumstances of Glyn's crime will spread quickly. He was one of us. The world is unforgiving, and men are cruel. Glyn knew that. If they had hanged him as a felon and gibbeted him, they would have allowed his corpse to suffer unspeakable indignities. His tarse would have likely been cut off and stuffed into his mouth or shoved up his arse."

With a gasp, Rhonwellt recoiled at Tristan's words.

"They would have taken his eyes," said Tristan, "before the birds could even get to them, and broken his limbs. I did not want that to happen to him. Glyn murdered a man and God will do with him what He will. That will be harsh enough. At least now he will suffer no dishonor at the hands of his fellow man."

"You cannot mean to compare the lust between Glyn Fowler and Thomas Fullecoppe to you and me." Rhonwellt did not try to hide the indignation he felt.

"It may not seem the same to you because of the feelings you carry. But, it is. Men who love men, whether it be simply lust or feelings that come from the heart..."

Tristan paused, strong emotion creeping into his voice.

"We are all sodomites, or so says the church. The church tries to tell us God cares not how we feel. But, I think the church has it wrong. If God is love, as scripture says, then He cares. Was it not obvious Glyn and Thomas shared feelings between them? It may have started out as lust, but eventually it became much more and not so very different from what we share."

"It is not the same at all!"

"But it is," replied Tristan. "Even Brother Jerome's passion for Brother Mark was the same in its way."

Rhonwellt snorted when he spoke. "That was lust born of confinement and nothing more."

"You cannot say that with any certainty unless you can see into their hearts. And though I find you a most remarkable man, I fear that beyond even your capability. You are misguided to consider our feelings more righteous than theirs."

"I know the brothers at the priory lusted after each other and often engaged in carnal acts to satisfy those desires, but I never thought of them as belonging to a group. Yet, you speak of this as though it were a common occurrence everywhere."

Tristan pried Rhonwellt's arms from the sleeves of his robes. He took the monk's hands in his and raised them to his lips. His hands were cold and Tristan's hot breath felt good on his skin. "My sweet and innocent Rhonwellt, you have lived nearly your whole life within one-hundred furlongs from where you were born and confined to a priory. There is a huge world out there where things you could never imagine happen with regularity. Everywhere I have ever traveled, I have found men like us. In some places, only a few, but in places where the people are many there are more, so many as to render it almost common."

"And they live openly?"

"Sometimes they do. Our acceptance varies from being an open secret and people looking the other way to being tolerated and even fully accepted. But, whatever the attitude, we are there and we find the places—the occasional taverns and hammams that are friendly to our kind, a dark alleyway or beside the curtain wall outside a postern gate, the reeds by the river, or a wood beyond the edge of town—places where men like us can steal a few moments of privacy to be together and be ourselves."

"You keep saying 'men like us' and 'our kind'," said Rhonwellt. "I have never considered you and me to be a kind of anything or that there were others like us. And yet, it was in front of me all the while. Am I really so blind?"

"It is because you keep separating you and me from everyone else," replied Tristan, "because what we have is not just lust but based in love. Is it not?"

Rhonwellt swallowed hard. He no longer could deny the way he felt yet the fear was still with him. Preceding events had done little to quell it, rather only proved that his reluctance had always come from the fear. His love for Tristan had never been in doubt, but the fear had kept him from fully admitting it. No more. Now he must face it lest he lose this second chance. He forced his head to bob in a nod.

"The stance of the church is changing and in order for it to change, the church must do two things," Tristan continued. "It must maintain we are corrupt and therefore concentrate not on what men like us feel, but what we do. It means the church cannot acknowledge any of the love, only the carnal nature of us. Second, it must convince the world we are a rare occurrence. It makes it easier to see us as an aberration and therefore, sinful. They cannot let us be seen as unremarkable."

"The time I have spent living a secluded religious life you, by your own admission, have spent at war with God. Now you propose to speak as an authority on the church. I have lived most of my life by the Rule of Saint Benedict and the Rule says nothing on this subject, only of lust in general and keeping ourselves chaste for the glory of God. Yet you speak as if the church has considered this a great deal."

"You could not know. In religious houses, one is removed from the world. Those who shelter there need not be concerned with earthly things and are left to contemplate God. It is why these houses exist."

"Religious houses exist for many reasons, contemplating God among them. But, I did not go there to contemplate God," said Rhonwellt, "I simply awakened there one day from out of a bad dream. And once there, I stayed on because I felt safe there, protected from your father and his wrath. Realizing a world without you would never be a place of comfort for me again, I buried my longing there with me."

"My father is dead, Declan is dead, they will trouble you no more. What if we did not have to hide away from the world in order to feel safe and free from shame or fear?"

"That is a miracle I cannot fathom," replied Rhonwellt. "It is not even something I contemplated until your return."

"Miracles do not just happen, sometimes they need help."

"Miracles come from God."

"Not always," Tristan replied. He planted a kiss on Rhonwellt's forehead. The monk resisted the urge to pull away. "The hour is late and I can see that you are chilled. Let us return to the priory."

"We will find no warmth there," said Rhonwellt. "The guest quarters are one of the few heated spaces there. And that is not where I am allowed to stay."

"Surely you can visit with me there," replied Tristan. "On our way, I will tell you about miracles. Then, after a night of rest, on the morrow we shall return home."

Tristan in the lead, they stepped from the Fullecoppe stall out into the night. With the clearing skies, a chill had settled over the town, and Rhonwellt could see a faint mist rise from the heat of his breath. He shivered inside his robe, only now realizing Tristan was right. Someplace warm would feel good. As they proceeded down the hill in silence, gazing at the ground, a small cluster of villeins came walking up the lane. The hairs raised on the back of Rhonwellt's neck as he sensed all eyes turn to look at them. It confirmed word had spread quickly of Glyn's demise as well as the knight's role in it. Rhonwellt glanced with side-eyes expecting to see anger or hatred. The people's expressions varied, but most looked simply bewildered. Glyn had been one of their own, a colorful character who dared to try for a better life only to pay the price. Now he was gone. In spite of the revelations about the lad, he would be missed and the townspeople would need time to get used to his absence.

"You and I have already received so many miracles," said Tristan as they walked, "including the fact we both survived, the fact that we found each other again after all this time and now have a second chance. Both of those things were never meant to happen, yet, by God's grace, we are here and I have you back. I am master over a prosperous estate and I was able to get you and Brother Ciaran assigned to serve at Saint Tysilio's so we could be near one another. And though I know this has been most difficult for you, I found I have a daughter and grandson, a wonder I would never have thought possible. Yet, they exist and await us when we go home. These are all miracles visited upon us by God."

"Do you really believe these things have all occurred because it was the will of the Almighty?"

Tristan stopped walking. "I do. What else could it be? Nothing occurs that is not according to His will. And, I am the first to admit being confounded by the mystery of it all." The knight resumed walking, talking of home.

Until two summers ago, Rhonwellt had always looked on Saint Cattwg's as home. However, since moving to Ryd Lliw he was beginning to realize home had to be a place where you wanted to be, surrounded by the people you love, not merely the place you happen to be. And he knew at last that place was Ryd Lliw with Sir Tristan and Brother Ciaran and Hewrey. All that mattered was that Tristan was there.

Though lost in his own thoughts, Rhonwellt realized Tristan had not stopped talking. "Ryd Lliw is a small, out-of-the-way place in the wilds of southern Wales. It is our home, our sanctuary, our place of refuge and safety. By the grace of God, it could be such a place for others as well."

"Suddenly, you speak much of God, more than I have known you to." Rhonwellt turned an inquisitive eye to Tristan. "Have you undergone a recent conversion?"

"Nothing has changed in my relationship with the Almighty. Like I said, we have an understanding. As long as He continues to bless me with miracles, I agree to remain stubbornly unworthy. He gets to use me as He sees fit and I get... well, it seems to work."

Tristan grew quiet as they passed through the gatehouse and turned toward the priory. The tide was in and slowed the water passing under the bridge, muting the sound of the river. Rhonwellt heard the knight take in a breath as though he might speak, then let it out. Tristan slowed his pace and eventually came to a stop in the middle of the bridge.

"Glyn's death," he began, "and the reason for it is not uncommon. Stories like his are ordinary yet told only as salacious gossip before they are forgotten. His circumstance was unusual in that he did not die alone and friendless as do most. He left this world in the arms of someone who loved him and in the presence of others who understood his nature. God willing, it should be so for any of us."

Rhonwellt reached out and put a hand on Tristan's arm. "Though we were not exactly friends, the boy's death has greatly affected both of us because he was one of us."

"His fate was to be ours all those summers ago. The circumstances are not identical, but they are the same nonetheless. But, destiny stepped in and changed the course of our lives. Have you never wondered why?"

"I have often wondered why I did not die," replied Rhonwellt, "but, beyond that, no. I only knew that I had escaped death and gave little thought to living."

"While I cursed God for keeping the freedom I sought in death just out of my reach," Tristan put his hand atop Rhonwellt's, "I know now it was because you awaited me here." Tristan looked down at the road. "It is on this very spot I feared I might lose you again when Glyn attacked you. I knew then, whatever time I had left I would not waste another moment of it without you by my side at Ryd Lliw." Tristan cupped Rhonwellt's cheek with his hand as he looked into his eyes. "Rhonwellt, please come home."

Rhonwellt's heart pounded in his ears. Tristan's hand felt warm on his face. This was the moment. He leaned in, rested his forehead on Tristan's chin for a moment.

Placing his fingers under Rhonwellt's chin, Tristan raised the monk's face to meet his. They came together, forehead to forehead. Rhonwellt breathed the words into Tristan's mouth, held so very close to his own. "I am ready. Take me home."

THIRTY-FOUR

Tristan rose before Prime and walked the three furlongs along the road bordering the stockade to visit Milisandia the fowler. He went to offer her son burial in the churchyard at Saint Tysilio's. As they had the last time he visited her, the geese raucously sounded a warning that someone approached her yard. He found the short, plump woman waiting in the doorway of her cottage, hands on her hips, her curly hair untamed, resembling a sheep's wool grown long past the time for shearing. Her younger son, Elias, was nowhere in sight. The look of sadness she carried made Tristan think she might never feel joy again. Her once-proud shoulders drooped, her eyes seemed hollow and held a vacant stare, her lips pressed in a thin line of resolve.

Tristan made his offer.

"I humbly thank ye, sir. My soul would rest much easier knowing my lad be resting in ground that been prayed-over. Glyn could not help how he was, and I knows his sin will keep him from being buried in the churchyard. But at least the potter's field be near enough I can walks down to visit him and say prayers whenever I likes." The woman squared her gaze on the knight. "Folks told me how he died."

Her chin began to quiver. "Glyn had a devil in him. I knowed my boy, and once he decided on a thing, there be naught for it until he done it. You may not think it, but you done him a kindness and I holds no ill-will on ye."

"Kind words to relieve a soul burdened by these events, mistress. I thank you." Tristan put his hand to his mouth and cleared his throat. "The loss of an able-bodied son will affect the prospects of a woman without a husband," he said. "Since I was a party to his death, I would gladly render an amercement directly to you."

The deep sadness in the woman's eyes nearly broke his resolve, and he wished to be away as quickly as he could.

"There was no crime, so amercement not be called for and not mine to take," replied the fowler. "But I be a poor woman with a second mouth to feed. I would thank God for any generosity and would offer up prayers in the church on your behalf. But I will not take charity."

"Prayers for me would likely go unheard, still I thank you just the same." Tristan hesitated a moment. "Will you consider this? Brother Simplicius delivers a tun of wine from the priory cellars monthly to the Saint George at Ryd Lliw. Perhaps he could bring two geese and a bundle of quills for Brother Rhonwellt on each trip as well. I would gladly send payment with the monk on his return."

"Now, that be proper business," replied Milisandia. "I accepts."

Tristan nodded, then looked down toward the ground. "Will you attend the burial, Mistress?"

With a deep sigh, Milisandia turned her gaze aside for a moment. She was a proud, strong woman and Tristan knew she would not let him see her tears. But, there would be nothing to hold them back once he had gone.

Milisandia straightened herself and turned back to regard Tristan. "No," she replied. A profound weariness had altered her usually strong voice. "I cannot bear to watch my lad thrown into a hole and disappear under the dirt never to lay eyes on him again. I shall go after. Elias are with him now. Hearing Glyn were dead nearly done him in. Glyn were a good brother and the lad fair worshipped him. Elias will not leave him until there be nothing left to see and Glyn be gone forever."

Her words reminded Tristan how all brothers were not the same.

He swallowed hard. "I bid you good day, mistress, and pray God watch over you."

The look on Milisandia's face staring after him as he turned away haunted his walk back to town. As he rounded the southern corner of the stockade, the church bell sounded the summons for Mass. At its conclusion, while Rhonwellt bid his brothers goodbye, Tristan waited for the hostler from the inn to deliver their mounts for the journey home.

Tristan was talking softly to Ambisagarus and stroking the horse's muzzle when Rhonwellt joined him.

"Have you a new sword made for you?" asked Rhonwellt, patting an oiledcloth-wrapped parcel tied to Tristan's saddle.

"It is for Hewrey. I think it high time he had a proper weapon, and I taught him how to fight." Tristan carefully opened the end of the bundle, slid the weapon out and held it for Rhonwellt to admire. "If this unrest between King Stephen and Empress Maude continues, Lord Robert may call me into service." A prospect Tristan did not savor. "In that event, I want Hewrey to be ready and at my side."

"It is truly handsome," replied Rhonwellt, running appreciative fingers over the hilt and down the flat of the blade.

"It is not showy, but looks a reliable weapon for his first." Tristan turned and swung the blade back and forth to test it. "It is balanced well and not too heavy," he said, returning the sword to its wrapping. "It should suit him."

"He will not fail you,"

"I know he will not," replied Tristan, gathering Sag's reins and putting foot to stirrup. "He is a good lad and serves me well. He has earned my respect. This sword will let him know I look on him with esteem." The knight swung into the saddle.

"It will hold great significance for him," said Rhonwellt as he mounted Epona. "His devotion already knows no bounds."

"I only hope I merit his regard."

"Masters do not usually worry whether their servants regard them well."

"For him to agree to serve a man like me makes him out of the ordinary." Tristan noticed Rhonwellt frown at his choice of phrase, but said nothing. "But ultimately, if Lord Robert calls us to war, I just want to increase his chances of living through it to die of old age. He deserves that at the very least."

Tristan was about to urge Sag forward when he noticed Rhonwellt looking back toward the town, a sorrowful look covering his face. Tristan felt a lump rise in his throat. "Have you reconsidered?" he said, forcing the words. "Do you now wish to stay in Cydweli?"

Rhonwellt continued to scan the road a moment before he turned to Tristan. He smiled. "No, do not fret. I have not reconsidered. I was hoping I might catch a glimpse of Jocelyn before we leave. Yesterday must have held as much trauma for her as any of us. I had hoped to see she was all right and ask if she might like to stay with us."

Tristan listened as he let his eyes roll over the road, pretending he too looked for Jocelyn. Should he tell Rhonwellt that he had seen her as he crossed the bridge on his return from the fowler's, dressed as a boy, aboard a small boat listing on the mud flats, awaiting the approaching tide? It appeared she had bargained passage on the larger ship anchored in deep water out in the bay. He too had hoped she might remain. But when he turned to descend the path to the water's edge and talk with her, they locked eyes and she slowly shook her head as if surmising his mission. She raised her hand and gave a small wave and Tristan knew she could not stay nor could she say good-bye. Seeing the forlorn look on her face, Tristan had a foreboding feeling that anything like real happiness would be elusive for her.

Finally, he turned to Rhonwellt. "With Noah dead, Jocelyn has lost her protector. As I have said, the world is not always a safe place for men like us. It is easier for you and me to blend in, to appear to be no different from those around us. Jocelyn carries another layer of difference that makes her more conspicuous. In a small village like Ryd Lliw, any local lad would risk much to associate with her. Though Cydweli is a port town, it is still small. She relies on strangers passing through to ply her trade. At least in a place like London there are strangers aplenty and she can find others like herself and disappear. She will be safer there. I pray God she can make it that far—alone. It is why I wish to make Ryd Lliw a sanctuary for those like us who need it."

"How will you accomplish that?"

"God will send them to us."

"You seem to think God looks on people..." Rhonwellt hesitated, "...like us with greater favor than the church sees us."

"It is because I want to believe God is kinder than the church believes Him to be."

Rhonwellt did not respond.

They joined a small band of about a dozen travelers heading toward Neath, lagging a little behind to talk without being overheard. After riding over one-hundred furlongs they stopped beside the road to water the horses from a sinkhole. After watching Rhonwellt grant blessings on those who asked, Tristan led them to a rock where they sat apart to eat some bread and cheese and drink watered wine, while the other travelers joked and talked amongst themselves. The day had progressed from gray to fair. A persistent sun, weakened slightly by wispy clouds rolling lazily by, did its best to warm those out and about. With no breeze to carry it away, smoke from hearth fires hung low over the landscape, the odors of peat and wood permeating the air.

"You have not mentioned Merwenna and Ernulf since I arrived," said Tristan, knowing Rhonwellt would not if he did not. "Her arrival changes nothing about you and me. It only means that I now have an heir should I choose to name Ernulf as such. You fret for nothing."

"Discovering you have a child and grandchild is not insignificant."

"No, it is not," replied Tristan. "It is quite unexpected and wonderful. Still, I have lived a very long time not knowing of their existence. I have known you all my life and loved you nearly as long. If you fear she may ask me to choose between the two of you, do not doubt I would choose you."

Rhonwellt opened his mouth as though he was about to make on objection.

Tristan looked squarely into Rhonwellt's eyes. "I would choose you," he repeated.

They held each other's gaze for several moments.

"Besides, she has lands of her own she must tend to. I think she will return north before too very long. She is still of Saxon descent in Norman territory. Her continued presence at home will do much to secure her rights in the minds of her neighbors."

"And what of Wulfric?" asked Rhonwellt.

"She will marry him. It was always her intention. Making him chase her the length of the kingdom while she looked for the father she had never met only served for him to prove how much he desired it and to put her in charge. From what I remember, she is very like her mother in that."

The rest of the ride to Ryd Lliw was uneventful. While Tristan told Rhonwellt what little he knew of Merwenna's mother, they rode, sometimes in front of but mostly behind a motley gathering of travelers, always remaining separate to chat idly and enjoy each other's company. Neither seemed inclined to talk further of Glyn's death.

Topping out on a low rise about a furlong from town, they reined in their mounts and sat looking out over the small valley below. Nones had passed and Vespers was still some time off. The work-a-day sounds of an industrious village drifted across the glen. Four lads, none over ten summers, strolled out of a pasture and onto the road nearby lugging bundles of firewood. At the sight of the riders, they ran in front of them, clumsily gripping their wood, shrieking, "They be coming! My lord and the priest be back!"

Tristan laughed out loud. "So much for returning unnoticed," he said.

They were back. They were home. Despite Tristan feeling a bit apprehensive as to the manner of their reception, Rhonwellt looked happy to be here. He sat gazing ahead, a soft smile on his face. After the declaration of their arrival, Tristan thought the monk appeared glad of these few moments to just sit and take it all in.

"Are you ready?" Tristan asked. At the sound of Tristan's voice, the monk turned. "We are announced," said Tristan, "and should not keep them waiting."

Tristan touched Ambisagarus's ribs with his heels and Rhonwellt clucked to Epona. They began their descent into the village. Passing the cottages and burrows, villeins raised a hand in greeting or simply stared as they rode by. More children swarmed the lane, running alongside the horses, laughing and talking excitedly.

Side-stepping the noise, Sag fidgeted and Tristan held the stallion steady with a firm hand on the reins.

"The unbridled excitement of the little ones has always unnerved him more than the tempest of any battle," said Tristan. "Has it not, old man?" He stroked the courser's neck.

Brother Ciaran opened the churchyard gate and stepped into the middle of the road, arms folded inside his sleeves, a broad smile on his face.

"Brother Rhonwellt, Sir Tristan!" said Ciaran as Rhonwellt reined Epona to a stop. "Praise be to God! You are home, well and unharmed."

The young monk reached out his hand to caress Epona's muzzle, his mouth quivering with emotion, his eyes damp as he gazed up at Rhonwellt. In the silence, neither spoke what they felt. Rhonwellt slid to the ground and folded Ciaran in a warm embrace.

"I leave you to your reunion," said Tristan as he gathered Epona's reins and headed for the stables. "We sup at the hall following Compline."

✝   ✝   ✝

RHONWELLT'S ARM ACROSS CIARAN'S SHOULDER, THE TWO monks walked to the church where each knelt briefly before the altar for a moment of prayer before retiring to their cottage. To Rhonwellt, the young monk was not his chattering self, but seemed unusually quiet. His joy at seeing them had appeared genuine. Now, Rhonwellt wondered what was going through his mind.

He pulled a bench up to the table and sat, while Ciaran went about preparing some bread and cheese and pouring them pots of ale. Rhonwellt did not push him, but knew that once the lad had collected his thoughts, he would tell Rhonwellt what was on his mind.

Ciaran stood with his back to Rhonwellt, busy with his work at the sideboard. His movements were slow, deliberate. Rhonwellt heard the knife saw through the hard-crusted bread, heard Ciaran drop the slices onto a wooden plate.

"I feared you would not come back," Ciaran said, his voice thick with emotion, "that you had abandoned us and returned to the safety of the priory." He stopped, seemed to study something on the wall in front of him. "I can never go back—to the priory. I do not think I am devout enough for that. Even if you returned, I would request I be allowed to remain here."

Rhonwellt was more than a little taken aback by Ciaran's announcement. He watched as the young monk raised himself onto the balls of his feet and leaned over the sideboard. He turned to the side, half-facing Rhonwellt as he pushed the knife down through the block of cheese.

"I like life on the outside, being part of the village, having friends in the world outside the church." Ciaran turned the rest of the way around with a quick movement. "Is that wicked, Brother Rhonwellt?"

Rhonwellt listened silently. He deemed it best to let Ciaran continue on until he had emptied himself of all he had to say.

Ciaran finished slicing the cheese, put it on the plate with the bread and brought it to the table. He took a seat opposite Rhonwellt.

"The world frightens as well as fascinates me. That such wickedness and such beauty exist side-by-side, at the same time, I find extraordinary. How does God allow that?" Back to his chattering self, Ciaran stuffed his mouth with stray bits of bread and cheese and struggled to talk around it. "Both seem to thrive. The wickedness does not overpower the goodness as the church would want us to believe. Instead, the world just goes on. It does not get worse nor does it get better."

"What you and Tristan share has given me a whole new way of seeing...well, men like you." Ciaran paused and lowered his eyes to the table for a moment, then looked up. "Brother Rhonwellt, you look distressed. Have I said something wrong?"

Rhonwellt was unaware his face had betrayed what was in his mind. "No, my friend, you have said nothing wrong. It is just that I have heard the phrase 'men like us' much mentioned lately. It is a concept to which I have yet to become accustomed. Like you, such a notion never occurred to me. I too am being forced to learn many things."

Ciaran gave a quick nod. "At the priory, it was so different," he said. "At first, I was unaware. It was only after Brother Mark's death that I recognized what was right in front of me. Actions I had not understood suddenly became clear. I never questioned anything that happened there. We were not to question, only obey. Being away from the priory, I feel as though I am more aware. And, now, I have nothing but questions—interesting questions, at least I think they are, like did God make Jocelyn the way she is?" Ciaran paused for a moment and the look on his face grew serious. "Is it wrong of me to still think of her as a lass?"

Listening to Ciaran talk was like hearing another voice speak the thoughts inside his own head. Recent events had repeatedly taught them both that people are not always who they appear to be. As is often the case, Ciaran's first experience with love and his first broken heart were with the same person. Rhonwellt was filled with wonder at how easily Ciaran seemed to accept it all. Not that the lad was without conflict, but that he worked through it so quickly.

"Jocelyn is one of God's more perplexing mysteries," replied Rhonwellt.

"I could never have imagined meeting someone like Jocelyn," replied Ciaran, "or even knowing that people like her could be found in the world. And yet, once overcoming my initial wonder, it did not seem so extraordinary. And that has me more confused than anything." Ciaran fidgeted with a piece of bread. "At the priory, so many of the brothers saw only wickedness in the world. They seemed surprised by any good they found. It felt like everyone spent their time trying to be more religious than anyone else. The villeins are too busy keeping warm and feeding their families to be looking for evil around every corner. Though they are poor, I think they are much happier. I know I like them better."

"Brother Rhonwellt, why do you smile?"

"Because, I have been so taken with my own troubles that I somehow missed seeing how wise you are becoming."

"I shall never be as wise as you, Brother Rhonwellt."

"I believe you always have been, my friend."

"I praise God you have come back, Brother Rhonwellt. Please, do not leave us again."

✝   ✝   ✝

RHONWELLT STOOD NAKED IN THE SILVERY LIGHT OF A RARE moon gazing out the window slit in the solar wall, steam rising as he relieved himself into the chamber pot. A low fog obscured the town and the buildings surrounding the manor demesne and reflected the moonlight, casting the silent world in a soft white glow. The household was quiet. He guessed the hour to be somewhere between

Matins and Lauds. The fire in the braziers had burned down, and the room had gradually grown cold. He hugged himself, but not against the chill. Despite the cold, Rhonwellt's body tingled and he felt warm.

Tonight they had joined. Tristan had been patient and gentle, told him nothing would unfold that he was not ready for. If all Rhonwellt could manage that first night was to lay in his arms, it would be enough. But to his surprise, once he lay next to Tristan, felt the knight's soft skin pressed to his, his heart pounding as if to escape his chest, Rhonwellt found he wanted it all: to press their bodies together, to feel him, to smell him, to abandon himself to Tristan's kisses, to take the knight into his mouth, and despite the few moments of initial pain that soon turned into waves of intense pleasure, to have Tristan wholly inside him, to give in to every sin he had feared, and every moment be caught in that precarious purgatorial place with Heaven on one hand and Hell on the other. He wept at the moment of release, for in those moments, he realized the root of his fear had not been for any retribution from the Almighty or any earthly authority, but rather fear that, true to the nature of sin, he would not be able to control himself, his own appetites could not be sated, that having everything he wanted would still not be enough.

And now, in the afterglow, Rhonwellt could hardly believe any of it had really happened. But it had, and there was no going back. If God felt a need to exact a price for it, he told himself he was more than willing to pay it.

The monk turned his face from the window, his eyes following the river of moonlight as it flowed across the floor finally to splash over the bed against the far wall—and Tristan's sleeping form. The dozen candles that had lighted the chamber earlier in the evening, that had illuminated them as they basked in each other's nakedness, had now gone out and left a lone taper sputtering in near darkness by the bed. The only movement was the thick fur coverlet as it slowly rose and fell with the knight's breath. How many nights had he stood just so watching his lover sleep? How many summers had passed since the last time? Rhonwellt looked quickly around the chamber to be sure of where he stood, to be certain he was not a lad of fourteen summers again, that this was not Tristan's room at Pont Lliw, that all the events that made up the most of his life had actually taken place.

"Come back to bed," said Tristan, his voice thick from sleep. "I am still here and your spot in the bed grows cold without you."

Rhonwellt smiled, waited just a few moments more before retracing his steps to the bed. He slid between the covers, settling into Tristan's waiting arms, the knight tucking his head under Rhonwellt's chin. He buried his nose in Tristan's hair and inhaled deeply. It was there as he expected, mixed with sweat and the scent of man—the savor of clove.

"After all this time, I still awaken to find you watching me sleep." Tristan's hand appeared from under the covers to rest on Rhonwellt's cheek.

"And you still stare at my nakedness as you once did."

"It was an image I carried with me for a long time to buoy my spirits through many a miserable night. Fortunately for these aging eyes, the passing time has made you no less wondrous to behold."

Rhonwellt's face grew hot with a surge of emotion. He traced a small scar on Tristan's bare shoulder with his finger, one of many he had noticed covering the warrior's body.

"Watching you sleep calmed me all those summers ago," replied Rhonwellt, "it gave me peace then, nearly the same peace I had to find through prayer in later years. You were my sanctuary, gentleness to counter an otherwise confusing and angry world." He pressed his lips gently into Tristan's hair. The knight snuggled closer, pressing his body tightly against him. Tristan's skin felt hot against Rhonwellt's, which had cooled while away from the warmth of the bed.

"I would be your sanctuary again if you let me."

"For a brief moment as I stood watching you," said Rhonwellt, "it felt as though I had passed back in time, that we were still young and our love was new."

"To me," Tristan said, smacking his lips, "our love was never new.

It had always been there, only its nature changed as we grew from lads into young men. I liked what it became far better than the mere childish affection it had been."

"As did I," replied Rhonwellt. "The memory of it kept me constantly swollen with lust for months after arriving at the priory."

"Say it," said Tristan, a small chuckle detectable in his voice.

"Say what?"

"That your cock swelled in its desire for me."

Rhonwellt grinned in the dark at Tristan's teasing. Nevertheless, he opened his mouth to say it, but the words would not come. He blew out his breath. "I find I still cannot say the things that come so easily to you." He felt himself blushing in the graying light. "But, yes, it did."

"And now?" said Tristan, pulling the monk closer and tracing his fingers lightly over Rhonwellt's abdomen, inching down to lace them through the hairs no one else had touched but himself for a lifetime. The monk shuddered as Tristan's fingers barely grazed his tarse. Rhonwellt chuckled inside himself. Would he always need to refer to his privates in polite terms? Would he ever be able to say the word cock as his lover had asked? To even think it was difficult. Would he even be able to call Tristan his lover out loud? What a difference a short passage of time had made. How could everything feel so strange and new, yet somehow familiar, so quickly?

Rhonwellt sucked in a sharp breath as Tristan continued his intimate explorations, felt his skin pimple-up like goose flesh. "I fear I shall never go limp again."

"Almost bold talk coming from an aging monk," teased Tristan. "As an aging knight, I shall do my best to see that you do not."

Rhonwellt grew quiet, closed his eyes, said nothing for several moments. Tristan was right, they were not the words of a man of God.

"I know what you are thinking," said Tristan. "Push those thoughts from your mind."

"It will take time."

"I know." Tristan stretched himself up and kissed Rhonwellt's neck.

"What if I cannot?"

"You will," said Tristan turning his face down and lightly blowing his warm breath on Rhonwellt's stomach. "It will come eventually."

Rhonwellt tried to steady his breathing, to relax and enjoy the feel of Tristan's touch. The last time had been so long ago, yet the memory of how it had felt was immediate. It was as if his skin had a memory of its own apart from his brain, that it had hung onto all this time in secret, and had only now decided to share it, waiting for his mind to catch up. He had done so many forbidden things in one night, and knew he would do them all again before cock-crow. Already he throbbed with anticipation.

FIN

AUTHOR'S NOTES

It bears repeating that though I write historical fiction, I am not a historian by any means. It is for that reason I stayed away from the political events of the period and simply told a story about people who might have lived then.

The conquest of Wales was never an all-out war with any major battle. After conquering Saxon England in 1066, the Normans wasted little time before venturing into Wales and, by 1094, most of the land was under Norman control. The initial incursion resulted in a series of Norman castles and fortifications being built mostly in southern Wales and establishing a solid Norman presence there. A mere six years later, much of the conquered territory in the north and west was back in Welsh hands. From that point on, maintaining a foothold in Wales was accomplished by a series of successful localized skirmishes that resulted in the taking of land and defeat of the Welsh princes ruling there.

Henry I was not the heir to the throne, but seized the crown from his brother Robert in 1100. King Henry I put considerable time and energy into legitimizing his claim. He married the same year and was therefore preoccupied enough to pay little attention to the happenings in Wales. Therefore, during the period my books take place, 1134-1135, things were relatively quiet in that area. And since the happenings were very local, something happening as little as fifty miles distant had little effect on those closer. At least that is how I interpreted it.

For authors who write historical fiction of any kind, an issue at the forefront of their minds is anachronism, i.e. something out of place for the time of the story. There is a book called Medieval Underpants and Other Blunders by Susanne Alleyn, Spyderwort Press, 2012, A great resource for historical fiction writers, its design is to keep us on the factual straight-and-narrow.

An easy example of anachronism would be a cell phone in a story that takes place in the 1940s or 50s. Unless, of course, there is time travel and I'm not even going there. A better example is from A Savor of Clove, Book I of the Sanctuary Series I published last year. In it, I wrote a scene that takes place in a garden and mentioned a camellia bush. This is in twelfth century Wales. Janis, one of the women from my writing group, gently pointed out that camellia did not come to the British Isles from China and Japan until the mid-1700s. Oops! I had to opt for something else. I really slipped up on my research on that one.

Another pitfall for anachronism besides objects and ways of living, is language. Also in A Savor of Clove, I was introducing the character Hewrey to the story. He was a runaway, petty thief who tried to steal Sir Tristan's stallion Ambisagarus. Hewrey was every bit the bad-boy, a scallawag, a scoundrel. A Jack Dawkins kind of character right out of Oliver Twist. When describing Hewrey, the term feral came to mind. I liked it. Hewrey was definitely feral. Gun shy from the camellia incident, I decided to look up the etymology of feral. Sure enough, not a twelfth century word, rather one that did not come into usage until the seventeenth century. But it was the best descriptor I could find. It just fit.

It was then (I'm pretty new at this) I realized every author must face the decision of when and where to avoid anachronism or conversely how to break the rules. I determined that Hewrey was feral and there was no other word I was willing to use. I went with it. However, even as a renegade, I refused to give him a cell phone.

Another area of language is swearing. In the twelfth century, swearing differed from the bad language we know today. In fact, many of the words that have become taboo today, were an acceptable part of the lexicon then. There were still instances when because of position, or level of piety, and often for women, a person might use innuendo instead of vulgarity. Bad language or vulgarity or obscenity were not the same as swearing. Swearing was most closely associated with an oath and had little to do with morality.

Christ's bones, By Satan's cock, Mary's teeth! When we think of swearing or curse words, most folks would not automatically think of phrases like these. They would likely have a very different idea of what swearing or cursing is. In the middle ages, folks would not have thought to demean someone by reducing them to the name of a body part. We consider it common obscenity today to call someone a prick or a cunt. In the twelfth century, words like cunt and prick or cock were in common usage and not considered obscene. It would not have had the same impact then that it has now. In fact, the word obscene did not come into common usage until the sixteenth century.

So, how did they swear? The answer is in the words themselves; swearing and cursing. Today, the most common curse and closest to the medieval practice might be *Damn you!* It could be expanded to *may you be damned,* or *may God damn you!* It is bringing down the wrath of the sacred.

Swearing was somewhat different. Swearing was to utter an oath. With Christianity being the dominant paradigm, yeah verily the only paradigm, in Britain at the time, swearing generally had religious connotations. It was still calling upon the sacred and kept religious connotation, just not always for something good and often with the addition of vulgar reference. *I swear by Mary's tits* or *Satan's cock* comes to mind. *I swear by the blood of Christ* might be shortened to *bloody Christ,* depending on your purpose for swearing. And, as it is today, whether or not your curses might contain the vulgar had to do with your degree of piety. Sir Tristan and Hewrey are both bad boys so naturally they go straight for the vulgar.

Confusing? Yeah. Somehow *fucking prick* seems so much easier.

ABOUT THE AUTHOR

tom r mcconnell had been running scared from a beast called writer for more years than he cared to count. Finally, it caught him by the throat and refused to let go until it had squeezed a book out of him.

He is recuperating slowly. That's the short story.

f facebook.com/Tom-r-mcconnell-2291191974480135

ALSO BY TOM R MCCONNELL

Book 1 in the Sanctuary Series

At the dawn of the twelfth century a lad on the verge of manhood, fell in love for the first time and it nearly got him killed. Thirty years later, can he find the courage to risk love a second time — with the same man?

Left for dead by a stream and found by a kindly monk, Rhonwellt ap Mwrheth has spent the intervening years as a brother at a small Benedictine priory in southern Wales. His days there are simple and predictable, ora et labora—prayer and work. His life takes a turn when Sir Tristan Cunniff, an embittered, war-weary knight rides back into his life. For the last thirty years, each thought the other dead, with only fading memories of the forbidden love they once shared and its tragic consequences. Reunited and faced with possibilities neither could have imagined, they must decide where to go from here.

The answer to that must wait.

One of the monks, savagely beaten in the village is brought to the priory, and dies on the floor of the church. Shortly after, the body of a youth is found outside the cloister.

With Sir Tristan's help, Brother Rhonwellt probes deeper, uncovering carefully held priory secrets as well as the truth surrounding the events of thirty years ago.

Available Now!